saffire_21

The game of life (and death) is best played by the unruly

by
Alexandra Lander

Cover art courtesy of Jack Denlinger

First published by Dog Ear Publishing
4010 W. 86th Street, Ste H
Indianapolis, IN 46268
www.dogearpublishing.net

ISBN: 978-159858-884-2

This book is printed on acid-free paper.
This book is a work of fiction. Places, events, and situations in this book are purely fictional and any resemblance to actual persons, living or dead, is coincidental.

Printed in the United States of America

Key of Online Terms

For the convenience of those who ~~aren't Internet addicts~~ aren't savvy to "Net-speak," here is a definition key:

* * *

avatar: the self-chosen, identifying image in the box next to a person's username on a message board or other online social utility

BFF: "best friends forever"

BTW: "by the way…"

effing: a phonetic version of "f-ing," when you want to be polite and avoid saying "fucking." (Example: It's effing *cold* in here!)

emoticons: tiny "smiley" graphics—either stationary or a moving gif image—that display various gestures or emotions in online conversations. They lend a visual picture of feelings that cannot otherwise be conveyed over the Internet

Facebook: a free social networking website

f*ck: a less offensive way of saying "fuck"

FWIW: "for what it's worth"

icon: a tiny image representing a specific operating program on a computer screen

instant messaging: text-based communication over an online network between two or more users; the lines typed appear in real-time

LOL: acronym showing that a user is "laughing out loud"

lurking: secretly watching all online conversations on message boards without posting or taking part in them

message board: an Internet forum in which registered members of a specific website publicly post and reply to messages on various discussion topics

MySpace: a free social networking website

OMG: "Oh my God!"

streaming: the technology for transferring musical or video data so that it can be continuously received and processed (Example: when someone listens to an online radio station, the streams are sent from the music website to a listener's computer and processed through a media player application)

Sys Admin: (short for System Administrator) person who manages a particular website

tagline: a creative message next to a user's avatar, proclaiming anything the user chooses (how the user is doing, a favorite quote, something witty, a song lyric, etc.)

thread: section of a message board with a specific topic or category (i.e. Film, Politics, Photography); there are often several threads that make up an entire online forum

username: a self-chosen name that a person uses in an online community; it can either be a real name, some kind of identifying nickname, or something completely made up to hide identity

WTF: "What the fuck?"

___ : in online conversations, things typed in between asterisks represent a gesture, action or movement (Example: *hands her a beer* or *gives her a big hug*)

For Heather,

and for all my friends at Radio Paradise

With deepest gratitude...for my family, from whom creativity has always flowed, and for their endless love and support of my endeavors; for the amazing talents of Elizabeth Chilbert (my Editor-in-Chief) and Jack Denlinger (my book designer); for all my encouraging friends who helped believe in and cheer on my dream of publication; for Suzanne and all of her expert "CSI" consulting; for Tracie and her perfect fundraising idea, for Mrs. Jeanne Duell, Mr. James Hemmert, and Professor Ann Cooper—who collectively helped foster my creative writing throughout my education; for the Santa Barbarians and the rest of my California "family" who helped me shape a wonderful life for myself in their beautiful city and state; for Krista and everyone at the Coffee Cat for providing the perfect haven in which to write this book; for the authors Christopher Moore, T.C. Boyle, and Elizabeth Gilbert—whose brilliant works helped inspire me through the writing of saffire_21; for Tim Tresslar, Bruce Hale, and especially Patricia Kambitsch, whose success and experience as published authors gave me the courage to finally do this; for Kyle, who always appears in my life at the right moment with all the right words—including my spot-on tagline; and for my generous Muses, who continue to provide everything I'll ever need as an author.

Living never wore one out so much as the effort not to live.

~ Anaïs Nin

Chapter 1

Moonflower: *I think Greg and I are breaking up.*

WhiteHeronMagic: *OMG!!*

smk02: *Seriously? WTF happened?*

Cara Shannon lifted her fingers from the keyboard and let out a long, rasping sigh. Was there a way to quickly articulate the nagging thoughts that had kept her awake for the last hour, pinballing around her head and finally driving her to an instant messaging window at 12:45 AM?

With cyber-friends, there was no such thing as "too late." Time zones, Internet addiction and insomnia provided a plethora of people who were *always* online, and two in particular answered Cara's SOS that night. WhiteHeronMagic was Caroline, a high school English teacher from Portland, Oregon who possessed extraordinary amounts of wisdom and compassion. Smk02 was Seth Kane, a thirty-something single dad from New York City who had turned late-night multiple chat sessions into an art form. Both knew her relationship history with Greg, which made things easier to explain.

Cara's hands flew back to the keyboard in a flurry of clicking and thwacking.

Moonflower: *He canceled an evening with me for the third time this month. We had plans to cook dinner and watch* The Office, *but he called from work and said that he'd rather get caught up on stuff around the house.*

WhiteHeronMagic: *Aw geez, how lame is that?*

Moonflower: *Normally I'd understand, but it seems like there's always a reason for not getting together these days. He has to do bills. He's installing a new flat screen TV. He's worn out from running too many errands. This is NOT the behavior I want to see from someone who I've been talking marriage with, you know?*

smk02: *HAVE you been talking marriage?*

Moonflower: *Yes. We both agreed last New Year's Eve that we'd talk seriously about engagement by autumn. Now it's October and every time I bring it up, he goes to Avoidanceville.*

WhiteHeronMagic: *Ah, the classic distancing act. I know it well. Did you two have a fight or disagreement recently?*

smk02: *Did anything happen at work that's bugging him?*

Cara shook her head, even though her friends couldn't see. There hadn't been any fights or problems with Greg. In their two years together, she could actually count the number of times they'd argued on one hand. She thought for a moment, then clacked out another reply.

Moonflower*: No, nothing like that, just a gradual withdrawal. I think it's this engagement deadline. It's totally freaking him out.*

WhiteHeronMagic: *Ah-ha! Cold feet. Maybe he just needs more time and is trying to figure out how to tell you? Hell, I don't know. Damn men! Why can't they just commit?*

smk02: *Uh, excuse me, but some of us committed just FINE until our wives bailed on us.*

WhiteHeronMagic: *I know. Sorry, Seth.*

smk02: *Cara, may I be brutally honest with you, or are things a little raw right now?*

Cara stared at his post and felt her stomach lurch. In-your-face honesty was never pleasant. She braced herself as she leaned forward and typed:

Moonflower*: No, go ahead.*

Immediately, words at the bottom of the chat window flashed on and off. *Smk02 is typing a message*. Cara held her breath until his post finally appeared.

smk02*: Well, the way I see it... after two years, a guy should know whether or not he wants to share his life with the woman he loves. Especially at our age. I suspect that your boy isn't keen on the marriage thing after all and doesn't quite know how to tell you. That's my guy's opinion, FWIW.*

Cara's breath caught in her throat. Even though she'd been suspecting the same thing all along, she still felt slapped upside the head. For a split second, sadness and anger jockeyed for first place inside her psyche. Anger won. With furious keystrokes, she pounded out:

Moonflower: *You know, I've sensed this for the last month. He TOTALLY changed his tune since the beginning of the year! I wish he'd have the balls to tell me the truth—that he's done!*

WhiteHeronMagic: *Yeah, right?*

smk02*: It's hard for guys, Cara. It absolutely kills us to have to deliver that kind of truth, and watch the look of pain on our woman's face.*

Moonflower: *Yeah, but do guys ever realize that it's much easier to get it over with in one big chop, rather than dragging it out for days and days with avoidance???*

After posting, Cara sat back and rubbed her weary eyes. Images of men from her past flashed through the slide projector of her mind. They always started out so charming and so absolutely *smitten* with her, writing cards and love poems and making convincing pledges to build a future together. Then, inevitably, things changed and they weren't as sure as they used to be. More often than not, Cara was left with the hollow feeling of being on the outside of their lives looking in.

"I can't believe it's happening *again*," Cara said out loud, then grimaced at the sting of imminent tears. *Why do I keep attracting men who change their minds? Why is there always some weird-ass complication?*

WhiteHeronMagic: *I'm so sorry this is happening, Cara. It must be really heartbreaking after being together as long as you two have.*

smk02: *Me too, Cara. You're a real sweetheart and I hate that you have to go through this.*

Cara put a hand to her chin and narrowed her eyes. One of her legs began to jiggle unconsciously until the flap of her bathrobe fell away from it. Something about this breakup felt different. This time around, she wasn't feeling a need for pity or condolences.

Moonflower: *Yeah, it pretty much bites. But I gotta say, my heart doesn't feel like it's breaking this time. It feels like it's slowly turning to stone.*

WhiteHeronMagic: *Ruh-roh. That's not good.*

Moonflower: *Well, this same drama has played out so many times in my life that I am BEYOND hurt or heartache. If Greg and I split up, I'm going to stay out of the dating pool until I regain my trust in men. Or perhaps trust in my ability to choose them.*

smk02: *Wow.* That's *some self awareness.*

A cool autumn breeze blew through the window, bringing with it the unmistakable smell of dry, crispy leaves and musky earth. Cara closed her eyes and inhaled, letting it be her solace for a few moments before dismal thoughts returned. She raised her hands to the keyboard once again.

Moonflower: *I need to just get all his crap together in a bag, take it to his house, and say goodbye.*

WhiteHeronMagic: *Wow, that's so…FINAL. Not even a discussion about the cold feet, first?*

Moonflower: *No, Seth is right. Greg's had two freakin' years of my life. That's enough.*

smk02: *Thank you for not taking that personally…I was really worried after I posted that.*

Moonflower: *I'm glad you spoke up. I needed the reality check.*

WhiteHeronMagic: *Well girl, I support you in doing whatever you need to do for yourself. Again, I'm sorry this is happening…* *keep me posted on what happens, okay?*

Moonflower: *I will.*

WhiteHeronMagic: *Hey, isn't it well after midnight in Cincinnati? You should try to get some sleep!*

Moonflower: *Yeah, I think I'll sign off now...thank you so much for listening, guys.*

smk02: *Any time, darlin'. Good luck with everything. If you need to talk on the phone I'll send you my digits.*

Cara smiled. It was good to have an additional group of friends that were just a click away on her computer. Oftentimes, they were more accessible than friends who lived in town.

Moonflower: *Ok, Seth. I'll see you two on the boards tomorrow.*

WhiteHeronMagic: *Same bat time, same bat website...ciao for niao!*

smk02: *Goodnight ladies...*

Moonflower: *Goodnight.*

When the chat window disappeared, Cara shut down her computer and sat in silence for a while. Nothing felt worse than staying in a relationship where a lover was half-hearted and uncertain. She was entirely ready to build a future with someone at this point in her life, and if Greg wasn't down with that, he would only keep her from finding the man who was.

"I'll end it tomorrow," Cara promised herself, standing up with resolve and heading back to her bedroom for another attempt at sleep.

As if in protest, a memory stole its way through the back door of her mind and gripped her by the heart: The evening of her birthday, one year prior. Greg had lit several candles in the living room and slow-danced with her to Van Morrison's *Tupelo Honey*. She remembered his scent—faded Aspen cologne on warm, clean skin—as he brushed his cheek against hers, nuzzled her neck, and whispered in her ear. He knew the mere sensation of breath on skin drove her crazy, and often used it as tantalizing foreplay. When the song ended, Greg held her more tightly than he ever had in their entire relationship. It was at that precise moment when a profound thought hit. *This man* loves *me, and the only thing that will ever take him away from me is death.*

Looking back, Cara was both shocked and dismayed to have been that dead wrong about someone.

She crawled into bed and curled up in a motionless ball under the covers. After lying numb for a while, a warm tear finally broke free of her eye, rolled across the bridge of her nose and fell to the pillow. She sniffed and blinked back the next one, then felt the light impact of Sophie jumping onto the bed. Lifting her head, Cara glimpsed silvery-gray fur in the widening patch of moonlight.

"Hi, baby," she whispered.

The cat padded closer to give her human companion's face a thorough sniffing. Bristly whiskers tickled Cara's nose, which twitched against them reflexively. Then Sophie collapsed against her and began to purr. Cara ran a hand through silken fur, soothed by the presence of the gentle little being. Gradually, her mind fell quiet and her eyelids grew heavy. Sleep was coming at long last to deliver her from the torment of what needed to be done.

Chapter 2

"Evening in Paris." Cara downed the last of her martini and set the glass on the lacquered wooden table with a thump. "What a great name for a lipstick." She focused on Frannie's mouth and noted how the newly-purchased, screaming red hue boosted her friend's black-cherry hair and sea green eyes into even higher realms of vivid than they already were. Cara zeroed in on the eyes, noticing a trace of worry in them, while the rest of the room blurred and swam. A server appeared out of nowhere and pointed to her empty glass. "Can I get you another one?"

Cara swung her head toward him. "Sure."

"No!" Frannie commanded, shooting him a solemn look. Then she gave Cara's arm a light whack. "You've already had two in the last half hour."

The server hesitated, looking back and forth uneasily between the women.

Frannie firmly instructed him, "Bring her a water with lemon."

He gave a quick nod and hurried off before there were any arguments.

Cara stared after him. "*Meow,* baby. How young do you think he is? Twenty-three?" She turned back to Frannie with devilish eyes. "Twenty-four? Is that too young for me?"

"Hon." Frannie reached across the table, bracelets jingling, and laid a hand over Cara's. "For one thing, I'm sure any woman who's drunk off her ass isn't very appealing to him, and for another...you're starting to scare me."

Cara tried to shake the fuzziness from her brain and concentrate on her friend's tone, which bore no trace of humor. "What? Why?"

"Because you *never* drink this much, and you've got that interview tomorrow morning! I'm afraid you're gonna blow it by feeling all hung over and terrible."

Cara grinned. She loved the way Frannie said *ta-ruh-bul* in her thick Queens accent. Why Francesca Angelina Bertollo ever transferred from her job at Doubleday to a small Midwestern textbook company was beyond Cara's comprehension, but she was glad it happened. After becoming cube neighbors, the two of them had struck up a fast friendship both in and outside of the office.

Frannie took a sip of her martini, keeping a close eye on Cara. "Are you gonna be okay? Cause I don't wanna have to haul your ass home."

Cara nodded. "Yeah." Her eyes dropped to the water rings on their table. Frannie was trying to make her come back down to earth, and she didn't want to.

"Lead Editor, Cara," Frannie said, reaching for her pack of cigarettes and shaking one out between two red fingernails. "How long have you been waiting for that position to come open?"

"I know."

Frannie put the cigarette between her lips, lit it, and inhaled until its tip glowed orange. After expertly blowing a puff of smoke up into the bar's fan-circulated air, she cocked her head to one side. "Look, I know you're still dealing with the whole Greg thing. But is it worth blowing a chance to move up in your job, and to make more money? No man is worth that, if you ask me."

Cara ran a hand through her hair and stared out the window at the Cincinnati skyline. Her eyes lingered on the pyramidal top of the PNC building, which was floodlit in red and green for the holidays. "It's not so much about Greg, Frannie. It's the fact that I keep getting it wrong. It's beginning to worry me."

Frannie took another drag on her cigarette. "Getting what wrong?"

"The *kind* of man I choose."

"You mean asshats who can't see that they've got a diamond in the rough? Who foolishly think they somehow don't deserve you and get all distant and weird until you finally prove them right and leave them?"

"Yeah, those guys." Cara didn't know whether to laugh or cry. The alcohol in her bloodstream suddenly felt heavy and toxic. She floated a hand over her head and twitched her fingers in a flashing gesture. "What's wrong with my little man-beacon, Fran? Whatever it is, I want it fixed. I'm tired of shopping around and I'm not getting any younger."

"Yeah, well, you're not even forty yet so don't worry."

"All my friends married and had their kids a decade ago."

"Not all of 'em."

"I don't even know if I want kids anymore."

Frannie leaned forward with intent. "What do you want, then?"

Slowed by her alcoholic fog, Cara had to stop and think for a while. Did she even know anymore? What was it about being in relationships that drew her focus so far away from her own personal goals? She opened her mouth and stammered, "I want…I want to be published."

"Much of your writing *has* been published."

"No, I don't mean in textbooks. I mean a *novel*. Not just any old novel, but a novel that sells millions of copies. One that stands out from the rest and gets talked about on Oprah! I've wanted that ever since I got my first A-plus in Mrs. Duell's creative writing class."

Frannie sat back in her chair, dangling her martini glass to one side. "*Really?* Why have you not told me this before?"

"Because *everyone* in our office wants to publish a novel. I'm just one more frustrated editor on the wannabe list. Where we work, the dream isn't very original."

"Doesn't mean you can't achieve it. What's your novel about?"

Cara slumped and lowered her head. "Um, I don't really have one yet. I've got a bunch of ideas and short stories, but nothing solid."

"That's a start. At least you've put pen to paper."

Cara shrugged. "I guess. I just don't seem to have much inspiration these days."

"Well, keep at it. And as for the man-beacon relationship stuff," Frannie pointed her cigarette for emphasis, "a man is either into you, or he's not. Just like the book says. From now on, if a guy isn't moving toward you with both arms open wide, I'm sure you'll be less likely to stick around as long as you did with Greg."

Cara leaned her head on one hand. "That's a comforting thought, but I sincerely hope I don't have to endure another waffler! *If* I decide to date again."

Frannie blew out another plume of smoke. "Oh, you'll date."

The server reappeared and set the water with lemon in front of Cara. She stared after him again as he left. "Maybe I'll date *him*. But it'll be purely physical. My little Cougar-toy!"

"Oh please," Frannie rolled her eyes. "Like *you'd* ever be that shallow…and what the hell? You aren't even old enough to be a Cougar!"

They both laughed, and Frannie gave her another once over. "How are you feeling? A little more clear-headed?"

Cara took a long drink of water. "I'll be fine."

Knowing better, Frannie crushed out her cigarette, summoned the poor server back to their table and ordered a sampler platter of munchies. After a half hour conversation about men, their coworkers, and the upcoming holidays, she checked in with her friend once more. "Are you fit to drive, now?"

Cara gave a firm nod. "I'm good."

"All right, then," Frannie replied, signaling for the check. "Cause I want you bright eyed and bushy-tailed for that interview tomorrow. It's gonna be long and involved, and you'll need to be one hundred percent."

Cara straightened in her chair, suddenly longing for the warm comfort of home. She brushed a strand of brown, baby-fine hair from her face. "Frannie…thanks."

"What for?"

“For going Christmas shopping with me, for drinking at Newport on the Levee on a weeknight, and for listening to me bitch.”

Frannie waved her off. “You can thank me by getting that damn job. No one in our department deserves it more than you.”

Chapter 3

Entering the Eclectic Café, a listener-supported Internet radio station, was something Cara did each morning with the same regularity as drinking coffee. She loved the ritual of watching the site's logo—a coffee cup with a wavy musical staff rising like steam out of its center—fade slowly into view in the upper right corner of the home page. Below it, a personalized greeting in small blue print welcomed: **Hi, Moonflower!**

"And a good morning to *you,* EC," Cara said under her breath, so as not to disturb coworkers. "What's the tune-age like today?" She clicked on the site's *Listen* link and watched her media player leap into action. As the quiet strains of Nada Surf's "Inside of Love" came through her tiny desk speakers, she scanned the list of active threads on the message boards. Like always, Cara chose the one called Planet Indigo. *Click-click.* An empty box opened in which to post a message.

Moonflower: *Hi, fellow Eclectics!*

An immediate flurry of posts went up from various listeners who were hanging out there, offering hellos, good mornings, and emoticon waves.

GreatScott: *Hey, Cara. Are you ready for the big interview today? What time is it going down?*

Cara giggled at the tiny photo in Scott's avatar—a close-up shot of a dog's wet snout. The tagline below it read: *Scotty's feeling snotty!*

Moonflower: *Ready as I'll ever be. Interview's at 9:00 sharp. Love the avatar, btw...*

One by one, good luck posts appeared from other forum members and brought a smile to Cara's face.

The Eclectic Café was like a home away from home where she first met Seth, Caroline, and a host of other cyber-friends. For the longest time, she'd only listened to the music and ignored the message boards. Then one day Cara wanted some opinions about an Audrey Tautou movie that she planned on renting. Unable to get them from anyone in her office, she posted a question in the film thread and waited. In the next minute, a reply from a random user appeared: *Welcome, Moonflower! Haven't seen you around before. I believe smk02 has seen this film—you can find him in Planet Indigo.*

Planet Indigo, always in the top five active threads throughout the day, was more or less a cyber-playground for grown-ups. Its regulars not only answered Cara's film question, but made her feel so warm and welcome that she couldn't resist going in the next day, and the next…until she was a regular herself. In the course of three weeks, she'd made friends across the entire country and beyond. It was always amazing to her that this radio station's particular blend of eclectic music attracted people of such like minds.

With the full support of her EC friends, she leaned forward to type one last reply.

Moonflower: *Thanks everyone, you're the greatest! See ya later.*

Cara shrunk the Internet window to an icon at the bottom of the screen and checked her watch. Just enough time to take a restroom break, gather her notes, and report to the interview. She met Frannie on the way out of the office, coming around the corner with a twenty-ounce cup of coffee in her hand. Frannie reached out and gave Cara's arm a squeeze. "Hey, good luck, you!"

Cara gave her a nervous smile. "Thanks, Fran."

Frannie's eyes pinned Cara to the wall. "No one else deserves this like you do. Make that clear to them, okay?"

Cara nodded and slipped out of Frannie's grasp. Despite her friend's encouragement, negative messages played in her head all the way to the restroom. *Doesn't matter how well this goes…they won't give it to me. I don't have as much seniority as Pete Webber. And maybe I don't even want the damn job. It's going to mean more work, more unpaid overtime, more…*

"Excuse me," said a coworker on her way out of the restroom, stepping aside for Cara.

"Me too," Cara told her, going in. She stopped and stared at her reflection in the mirror. *This is not me.* Her eyes scanned the black business jacket and skirt that looked a bit too short for her five-foot-ten frame. The crisp white blouse did nothing for her fair skin, and the black hose and pumps made her athletic-looking legs look even more muscular. Normally, employees of her company were allowed to wear jeans and casual attire. *Why do I have to play these dress-up games just to get promoted? How phony and stupid. And* uncomfortable. *I'm so sick of Corporate America.*

Cara had even tamed her wavy brown hair into a slick, professional bun. She touched her hand to it, smoothing it back for the tenth time that morning. Her golden-brown eyes widened at the dreadful thoughts picking up speed like a runaway train through her head. "Good God," she said aloud to her reflection. "With an attitude like this, you might as well kiss the job goodbye."

A toilet flushed, and Cara put a hand to her mouth in horror. She'd thought she was alone in the restroom. Before the unknown coworker could emerge from the stall and catch her muttering to herself, Cara turned and fled. Thankfully, she didn't have to pee.

* * *

Managers from all four departments were seated in the supervising editor's office when Cara walked in. They offered cordial good mornings and hellos as she sat down.

"Can we get you some water?" one of them asked.

"No, I'm fine," she told them, glancing around at each face. They were all people she'd worked beside for years, slaving away to meet deadlines, sitting in countless planning conferences, spending long hours of overtime...and now she sat before them, begging for a chance to move up. They already knew what she was capable of, how hard she worked, and how impressed clients were with her performance. The only things that would change were salary, title, and a bit more leadership. Why they couldn't dispense with the formality of an interview, she'd never understand. What more could they possibly want to know about her?

In another minute, the head of Editorial came in and sat down. "Okay, looks like we're all here," he said in a cheerful tone. "Patti, would you please close the door?"

Cara heard the door click shut to her left, cleared her throat, and waited for the first question.

* * *

"Pete doesn't do anything different than you do!" Frannie's eyes were ablaze as she walked to the parking lot with Cara. "This is just another example of sexism in the workplace."

Cara shook her head and waved a hand. "No way, Frannie, not as liberal as our company is." She rummaged in her purse for car keys. "I'm sure it was a hard decision for them, and I'm glad *I* wasn't in their shoes. It might've come down to who had more seniority, since both of us were perfectly qualified for the job. To be honest, I'm actually a little relieved."

Frannie's eyebrows rose. "*What?*"

Cara sighed and shook her head. "I'm not one hundred percent sure I wanted that job. My life is already so crazy-busy..." When she turned to look Frannie in the eye, the biting wind blew hair across her face. She swept it away. "Maybe I can just make due with my current salary a little longer and enjoy the time I'd probably be spending taking work home on weekends. I *like* my weekends, damn it. And I want to have time to write, so I can start that novel that I told you about."

Frannie shrugged. "Well, you do have a point there, but I don't know...it just doesn't make sense, this sudden change of heart. You're always griping about not making enough money."

Cara wrapped one end of her scarf more snugly around her neck. "I don't care anymore. I've made do up until now, so it won't kill me to continue with the peanut salary a little longer. See, I can't help but wonder if

I'm meant to do something else…some*where* else. My life here is getting a bit stagnant."

Frannie slowed as they approached their cars and gave her a long, hard stare. "Is this the breakup depression talking, or do you really mean that?"

Cara stared at her dark blue Rav-4, eager to get away from work, from Frannie's questions, and out of the biting cold. Turning to her friend one last time with a shrug and a smile, she answered, "I don't know. I just really need something in my life to change. I've been taking the same exit to work every day, looking out at the same boring interstate from my office window, taking care of the same empty house all by myself for over a decade, and showing up to all the same social events *alone*. I'm ready to try something else, now."

Frannie's eyes softened as she listened to Cara.

"There was a time when I wanted to be settled down with the husband, a couple of kids, and a minivan. But that didn't happen for me when I really wanted it to. Now, I'd be happy just to get the 'settled down with a husband' part before I'm forty." Frannie opened her mouth to speak, but Cara quickly added, "I know we just had this conversation last night, and I know you think marriage is overrated since your divorce. But I still believe in it, and I know it's out there for me. Just not here. Not in this town. And probably not any time soon."

Frannie sighed and put a hand on her hip. "Wow. I've never heard you talk this way before. All this time, I thought you were totally content with your life here."

Cara's teeth began to chatter. "Well I was, for a long time. But I swear, Frannie, there are times I feel like I'm just going through the motions. I accept whatever little things bring me fleeting glimpses of happiness, like the cheap consolation prizes by our place settings at birthday parties when we were little."

"Aw, *Cara*. Are you really that unhappy? 'Cause you seem so bubbly and enthusiastic all the time."

Cara straightened and mirrored Frannie's hand-on-hip stance. "Come on, now. When was the last time you saw me *bubbly?*"

Frannie's eyes darted upward to search the sky. "Well, I guess it was…" her eyes met Cara's. "Aw crap. You're right. You *haven't* been yourself lately. I thought it was just the Greg stuff and the interview stress."

"That was only part of it."

Frannie hugged her arms to her chest and began to shiver. "Listen, I don't wanna keep us both out here in the cold." She reached out and put a gloved hand on Cara's shoulder. "I'm real sorry about today. And about your life not being what you want it to be. Normally, I'd get all 'tough love' on your ass and tell you to go back in there and at least demand a raise. But

I'm seein' a look in your eyes I've never seen before, and quite frankly, it's freakin' me out. So I'll just say…take care of yourself this weekend, girl. Call if you need anything, or if you'd like to see a movie or grab a bite to eat. Capisce?"

Cara nodded, hesitated, then put both her arms around Frannie and gave her a squeeze. "Thanks."

Frannie's hand gave a light swish on Cara's back as they hugged, then she pulled away. "Awright…ciao, Caralina."

Cara grinned at Frannie's endearing Italianization of her name. She backed closer to her car door and waved. "Ciao, Francesca." As she turned and crunched the car key into the near-frozen lock, her feet anticipated the warm, plushy goodness of leopard-print slippers waiting at home, just inside her front door.

Chapter 4

The disc of instrumental Christmas music played for all of thirty seconds before Cara stomped across the living room, hit the eject button, and snatched it from the holder. For some reason, the old festive carols weren't resonating with her that evening. Browsing the rest of her Christmas collection, she chose a classic rock-themed CD instead. In seconds, the bouncy intro to Brenda Lee's "Rockin' Around the Christmas Tree" filled the living room.

Cara bent to collect the first green boughs of the artificial tree from their dusty box. After fastening them in their color-coded holes, she straightened and winced at the music that was far too happy for her morose mood—which perhaps had something to do with the fact that she and Greg had been listening to this very disc the Christmas before, while decorating the tree *together*.

Once again, the CD was ejected and Cara stood staring at its Christmassy cover. She thought putting up the tree would help her feel the magic of the season, maybe bring a little light back into her life, but no. It was only making things worse. To try and conjure cheer on the first holiday after a breakup was futile. Shaking her head, Cara tossed the CD on her coffee table next to a cup of cocoa that she hadn't touched. Her heart was too bitter for sweet chocolate that day.

"There's gotta be something," she told herself, shuffling into the kitchen. A sweeping glance ended at the cabinet door above the stove. In two steps she was there and swinging it wide to reveal a bottle of Absolut and some white vermouth. "Oh, *hell* yes."

Cara nearly salivated into her martini shaker as she poured ample amounts of liquor into it, then loaded it with ice. She shook vigorously while retrieving her one and only martini glass (a birthday present from Frannie), and in the next minute it was filled to the brim with the clear, icy beverage and two skewered olives.

Back in the living room, Cara stared dispassionately at the partially assembled Christmas tree, the strings of lights—which Sophie had begun to bite and paw—and the gaping box of ornaments. She took a huge gulp of her martini and muttered, "I don't think I can do it this year. I am *so* not into it." Just as she was setting her drink down to begin the disassembly, a particular CD caught her eye from the multitudes on the storage rack. She slipped the Red Hot Chili Peppers' *Californication* from its spot and held it up with a gleam in her eye.

As the first grinding bass notes of the opening track exploded through the speakers, Cara saw poor Sophie's ears lay back in alarm. Then, during the steady build up of bass and thrashing drums, they twitched in all directions, trying to make sense of the drastic change of atmosphere in the once peaceful room. When the opening riff hit its peak and blended with Anthony Kiedis's angry howl, a slow smile spread across Cara's glum expression like a new coat of paint. She caught the groove of the plucky guitar solo and jived her way across the room toward the tree. Inserting branch after branch, she chanted along with the music. *"Born in the north, and sworn to entertain ya...cause I'm down for the state of Pennsylvania..."* Before she knew it, the tree was assembled and she was circling around and around its branches, hanging glowing white strands of lights.

Cara felt like a woman possessed. Her head was teeming with thoughts darker than any she'd ever had, *especially* at Christmas time. Fuck Christmas, she thought as her inner rant railed on. Life had screwed her over one too many times and she was pissed. All she'd ever done was shower love, compassion, thoughtfulness, and joy on the world like a goddamn fountain in Rome, and to repay the kindness, the cosmic universe had simply dropped her on her unsuspecting ass time and time again. As far as Cara was concerned, she owed no peace on earth or goodwill to *anyone* this year.

"Christmas is experiencing a little technical difficulty," she said aloud as she hung a crystal angel on one of the highest boughs with the rest of her angel collection. "We will return you to your originally scheduled Merry Christmas *next* year." Then she cackled at herself, partially from the pleasant martini buzz and partially because it seemed utterly insane to be hanging beautiful, sacred ornaments with a scowl on her face and the Chili Peppers blaring.

When the trimming was done, Cara stepped back to survey her work. It looked lovely, as always, but there was no magic emanating from it. She switched off the overhead light in the room and let the tiny white bulbs, shiny gold ornaments, and sparkling crystal illuminate the room. Still nothing. With a long sigh, she looked down at Sophie. "Oh well, at least it's done."

Cara threw all the boxes back into their storage closet, washed the dust from her hands, and settled onto the couch. The CD had ended, leaving a deathly silence in the room. Before she could stop them, gloomy thoughts returned and circled like wolves outside her door. *Last year, Greg helped decorate the tree. Last year, the two of us woke up Christmas morning and opened presents and made love right in the middle of all the wrapping paper.*

"Son of a bitch," Cara sobbed. "You foolish son of a bitch! I had so much love for you! You said I was the best woman you'd ever found, then you changed your mind! Why…*why* did you lead me on for so long?" The sobs grew more violent. "It makes no sense!" She leaned back into the couch cushions, drew her knees up to her chest, and buried her face behind folded arms. *I'm alone at Christmas, when I was supposed to be getting an engagement ring…and looking at bigger homes with Greg…and planning a future with him. Now, it's all over. Just like that. Bzzzzz! Wrong answer. Game OVER.*

After a long, gut-wrenching cry, Cara fumbled for the portable phone on the coffee table, knocking off the TV remote control and a magazine in the process. She speed-dialed number one.

"Hello?" said a smooth, confident voice on the other end.

"Jenn?"

There was a short pause. "Cara? Is that you? What's wrong?"

"I'm in a really bad space right now. Do you have time to—"

"You betcha. Let me switch phones and go into the bedroom."

Cara plucked a tissue from a nearby box and wiped her nose and face during the short silence that ensued. She heard the sound of a TV in the background, a few clicks, then Jenn's reassuring voice again. "Go ahead, baby girl. I'm listening."

"Oh Jenn, it's been two months and I'm still having waves of grief over this damn breakup as if it were yesterday!"

"Two months isn't all that long, Cara."

"You know what it feels like?" Cara tossed the sodden tissue away and wiped her nose with the back of her hand. "Life after a breakup feels like when you're watching a movie in color, and then your TV blips and goes black and white. Remember how it used to do that when we were little? There is a sudden loss of all that was bright and pleasing…and even though you know certain features have color—the grass should be green and the sky blue—it all blends into a gray murkiness that just isn't the same. That's how it feels right now…even at Christmas."

"Hmm."

"All the joy, all the appeal of everything in my world is running down the drain. Gurgling loudly to make sure I know it's gone and past the point of no return. And the pain inside…it feels like a cannon's been shot through me, leaving a gaping hole."

Jenn's voice was low and soothing. "In a way, you *have* lost a part of yourself, Cara. I really do believe a piece of us dies with the severing of a relationship."

Cara nodded, even though her sister couldn't see it. "But you know, it's not always this bad. Most days, I'm focused on work and writing and friends. Then, in an unguarded moment of free thought, the feelings come back again worse than ever. Tonight was one of those nights. I put up my Christmas tree, thinking it would make me happy, but I felt *nothing*, Jenn! Absolutely nothing!"

"Well, then, give yourself permission to just *skip* the whole holiday cheer thing this year. You can always have it next year."

Cara told her sister about the martini and Red Hot Chili Peppers incident. They both had a good laugh, followed by a long silence.

"What are you thinking, Cara?"

Cara sighed heavily. "I'm thinking that I really miss my best friend. I keep having all these flashbacks…the nature walks, hanging out in coffee houses, listening to new CDs together in the car, and even the damn putt-putt golf game last summer!"

"Putt-putt golf game?"

"On a spur of the moment, we went to play putt-putt and Greg was extra affectionate. He kept kissing me right in front of other people, and he was *so* not a big public-display-of-affection guy!"

"Those are precious memories you made with Greg. I hope one day you can remember them with a sweetness that has no pain attached to it."

"That'll be a good day, whenever it comes," Cara murmured dismally. "It doesn't feel like it'll be anytime soon, though." She reclined sideways and wedged the phone in between her ear and the couch cushion. "I miss the smell of him. He had such a pleasant natural scent. I miss the feel of his strong arms around me, and being his lover. To think that we will never have that again makes my heart hurt so bad I can barely breathe."

"Wow."

"That's how I feel sometimes, Jenn, and it's such a hollow, empty place. When I'm in that place, I start thinking of Arianna."

Jenn's voice lost its airy, calming tone and grew sharp with alarm. "What do you mean?"

"Well, I imagine that kind of 'hollow' is what she was feeling just before she…anyway, I feel like I should call on her for strength when I feel that way."

"Cara?" Jenn's voice was low and cautious. "Are *you* feeling suicidal?"

"I would never ever act on it, Jenn. I'm just sometimes overcome by desolate feelings…to the point where I wish I could just go to sleep and not wake up. At least, not until the intense pain is gone. But don't worry, it always passes."

There was a long silence. "Honey, if you're ever feeling that way again, promise me you'll call."

"Well, that's exactly what I did tonight." Cara closed her eyes, overwhelmed with sudden sleepiness.

"How about you come over and spend the night with me and Liam?"

"Oh crap, I've worried you now, haven't I?" Cara ran a hand through her hair. "Look, I'm not as bad off as you think. I'm not going to off myself, okay? If I were, I certainly wouldn't have called you."

"Yeah, well, Arianna called a few times and I didn't see the warning signs. Maybe if I had, she—"

"Jenn," Cara gently interrupted. "No one could've stopped Arianna. No one had that much power."

Jenn's voice dropped to just above a whisper. "It still haunts me, though. Even after all this time. The things I would've said to that girl if I'd only known our last conversation was going to be our *last conversation*."

"I know. I really miss her, sometimes. I miss her Christmas visits and the rare 'hey, I'm in town can I drop by?' surprises."

"Yeah, those *were* special, weren't they? She was always more like our little sister than our niece."

"She would've been thirty-four this year."

"Wow, are you serious?" Jenn's voice raised several pitches. "*Thirty-four?*" There was a sigh of exasperation. "That's depressing as hell. Ari could've done so much with her life by now. She had so much going for her...what a complete and total waste."

Another silence followed. Cara turned to look at the Christmas tree once again. The lights blurred through leftover tears hiding in the corners of her eyes. She fought the urge to yawn and lost.

"Aw, listen to you. Sounds like it's beddy-bye time."

Cara laughed softly at the term she hadn't heard since toddlerhood. "Sorry, I didn't know you could hear that."

"Gosh, Cara, I hope I haven't depressed you even more with all this talk of Arianna."

"You haven't, Jenn. It actually felt good to get that out. No one's talked about her in a long, long time...as if she never even existed."

"Yeah, we really should try to keep her memory alive a little more. Go ahead and *call* on Arianna if you want, and be where you need to be with the holidays. People will understand. And if they don't, fuck 'em."

Cara burst into incredulous laughter at the rare occasion of hearing her sister swear.

"I knew I could make you laugh, if I tried hard enough. Are you okay now?"

"I am. Thank you so much for being on the other end of this phone. I really needed to connect with someone tonight."

"Any time, Cara. Night or day. You know that."

"I do, and I appreciate it. What a sister. You know you rock, right?"

Jenn's voice still registered unease. "Do you really feel better?"

"Mostly."

"Are you sure you don't want to come over? I'll get the thermal blanket out that you love."

"I doubt I'd make it over before falling asleep."

"Want me to come over there?"

"Naw, that's okay."

"Then sleep well, and sweet dreams to you, darlin' sister."

"You too, Jenn."

"Goodnight."

"Night-night."

The call ended with a beep, and Cara dragged herself to her feet. She trudged into the bathroom and stared at her withered reflection in the mirror. *I want to tell him about things going on in my life. I want to hear him laugh and see the twinkle in his eyes. I want to know that I can look forward to his warm arms on a Friday night after a long week.* She took the toothbrush from its holder, wet it, and squeezed blue and white gel onto its bristles.

As Cara did a brisk sawing motion across molars, she wished she could turn off the incessant voice of grief playing like a radio station in her head. For just one precious minute. But it droned on, with a life of its own. *I hate that I have to let go and feel layer after layer of feelings. I hate that it's ruining Christmas. I hate that it's going to take time. A long, long time before I can feel this kind of love for someone else.*

Chapter 5

Cali4nyapix: *I woke up to a freezing cold house this morning, and realized that the temps got down in the forties overnight! Brrrrr!! Had to turn on the heater.*

Bellybutton: *Yeah, same here in Austin! And it hasn't stopped raining for three days.*

GreatScott: *Aw you poor, poor babies. Waaaaa. The thermometer outside MY window reads -10°. Yeah, you heard me...NEGATIVE ten. Welcome to Wyoming. Still whining? I didn't think so.*

Cara laughed out loud as she scrolled down the page of posts. Planet Indigo was hopping when she'd logged on to The Eclectic Café that morning. There were so many pages of posts that she didn't bother to back scroll all the way to the first one of the morning.

Moonflower: *Well WE have a heavy snowfall here in Cincinnati! I was late getting into work because of it. I've been inside for a half hour, now, and I'm still shivering.*

Cara refreshed her screen to see the newest posts, and a smile lit up her face. Caroline had appeared in rare comic form.

WhiteHeronMagic: *Are we really having a pissing contest about who's colder than who??? Get a life, people! Oh, and FYI...it's supposed to be sunny and beautiful in Portland today. I gotta wake up the Doofuses and get going...have a great day everyone!*

Cara giggled at Caroline's pet name for her sons and scrambled to get a post in before it was too late.

Moonflower: *Goodbye WHM! You have a great day too!*

Caroline found time for one last reply.

WhiteHeronMagic: *Hey, sweetie! I saw your journal post over the weekend about your winter blahs. I hope this week's much better than last. I'll catch ya later, okay?*

Others in the forum had also posted their hellos and good mornings to Cara. She responded to them hastily before putting the radio screen in the background so she could get busy on her latest manuscript edits. Normally, she could master the art of alternately posting and working without losing any time at all, but today she was swamped and had to put her full nose to the grindstone.

Around noon, when her eyes were bleary from staring at copy, Cara peeked into the Café and saw an unusual flurry of activity in Planet Indigo.

An entire page of animated lovey-dovey emoticons jumped out at her when she brought the radio station window to the foreground. They were a flood of greetings for a female listener called saffire_21, who appeared to be very much loved by the community. Her appearance brought members out of the woodwork whom Cara had never even met. They all wanted to know the same thing: How *was* saffire, and where had she been?

saffire_21: *I'm doing okay. I just needed a little break from the EC for a while...had some business to take care of. You won't hold it against me, will you?*

Another wave of posts assured saffire that all was forgiven, but people reiterated how much they missed her. Not_Morrissey, the resident jokester and pervert, chimed in.

Not_Morrissey: *No, but there's something else I'd like to hold against you...heh heh...*

Cara shook her head and continued to watch as saffire_21 finished her replies, then quickly disappeared. Having no recollection of ever seeing this EC member before, Cara was intrigued by the woman's subtle ability to call everyone to attention faster than General Patton himself. With mounting curiosity, Cara clicked on saffire's boldfaced username that linked to her profile. Most of the data was left blank with no email, birth date, occupation or interests listed. Her location simply read: *In a constant state of flux*.

"Damn overly-private people," she muttered, backing out of the profile with a loud click. She spotted Seth, who'd just come online, and quickly entered the private message function of the site. She asked him who saffire_21 was, and why her little drive-by appearance had been such a big deal. In another minute, a reply came back.

smk02: *OMG! You don't know who saffire_21 is???? If you go back to the very first post in Planet Indigo, you'll see that she is the one who started the thread. She used to be a regular for the longest time, then just disappeared. We were all pretty worried about her, because she has a history of depression and other mental issues, but she finally came back. She only does drive-by posts, now, so people say hi while they have that two-minute window of opportunity. Saffire's a pretty elusive chick, but we love her anyway. Her hilarity and charm totally make up for it. And she's the one who gave me the nickname "smokin' hot"...kind of a play on my initials.*

The reply was good enough for Cara. She sent him a quick thank you, then called over the cubicle wall, "Hey Frannie?"

The steady clicking of computer keys stopped. "Yeah?"

"Did you bring your lunch?"

Cara heard the squeak of Frannie's chair, imagining her friend turning toward their shared wall. "No, I gotta go run some errands at lunch. I'll probably just grab something while I'm out."

"Oh," Cara told her, not bothering to hide the disappointment in her voice. "Bummer."

"Sorry, hon. Want a rain check?"

"Naw, don't worry about it," Cara said, rising from her chair and stretching. "I just thought I'd be more sociable today and go to the break room instead of eating at my desk."

"Wanna come with me?" Frannie invited, standing up and peering over the top of the cubicle wall. "I'll swing by Skyline, if you want."

The thought of Cincinnati's signature Skyline Chili was tempting, but Cara shook her head. "Not today. I've got leftover Chinese food, so I think I'll just stay in and maybe surf the Net."

"Ya gonna talk to those online friends of yours?" Frannie asked with a snide tone. "In that Pink Palace or whatever it's called?"

"Planet Indigo," Cara corrected, with a laugh. "As a matter of fact, I am. You say that like it's a *bad* thing."

"It is if you spend every waking hour there, instead of having a life in the 3-D world."

"I don't do that!" Cara protested, throwing a wad of scrap paper over the wall and missing Frannie's cheek by an inch. "And you really should listen to The Eclectic Café, Fran. It's so much better than lame-ass corporate radio."

"Oh, anything's better than corporate radio," Frannie replied sourly, rolling her eyes. Her head disappeared behind the wall once more. There was a jingling of car keys. "Last chance, Cara. Want anything?"

The frosty image of a chocolate malt popped into Cara's head. A malt from the United Dairy Farmers convenience store. She slid the cap of her editing pen off and on, deciding whether or not to have Frannie bring her one, until a memory flashed through her head of the last time she'd tried on her favorite pair of jeans. Buttoning them took a little more effort than she cared to admit.

"No thanks, Fran."

"Okay, then. I'm out."

After Frannie left, quiet settled over Cara's corner of the office. She picked up a new pile of social studies manuscripts to review before lunch, but her concentration was shot and her eyes kept stalling out over the same sentences until she finally threw her pen down in frustration. "I should probably just eat," she muttered to herself, feeling a wave of hunger clutch at her stomach.

Turning toward her computer screen, Cara was struck with a sudden impulse to see who might've joined the denizens of Planet Indigo. Noon was peak time for forum participation, since many of the East Coast listeners were on lunch break. Reflexively, her hand went to the mouse and brought the window to the foreground. The massage therapist from North Carolina, appropriately called TheRub, was making a rare appearance. He was the newest member of the fold, and still getting to know everyone.

TheRub: *So why is your username Not_Morrissey, anyway?*

In a flash, BloominElle, a florist from Philadelphia who always appeared out of nowhere to help at the most opportune moments, posted an image of Morrissey, the British alt-rock legend. Cara compared it with the photo in Not_Morrissey's avatar. The resemblance was uncanny, down to the signature *woe is me* pout, but Not_Morrissey had a mischievous gleam in his eye that Morrissey did not.

TheRub: Wow, Elle! That's amazing! They could be brothers, at the very least.

Not_Morrissey: *In college, people were always mistaking me for him. My girlfriend at the time made me a t-shirt that said, I'M NOT MORRISSEY on it, so I could be left in peace. And so gay guys would quit hitting on me. Not that there's anything wrong with that, right Bellybutton?*

Cara grinned, waiting for their resident lesbian's response. Bellybutton was a sassy and hilarious middle-aged woman who worked for the city of Austin, Texas. She also played bass guitar in an alt-country band. Bellybutton didn't appear to be on the boards, but her name was on the list of members who were currently logged in and listening. After a bit, her post appeared.

Bellybutton: Damn right, y'all!  Um, what are we talking about?

Then, out of nowhere:

GreatScott: *Wait a minute! Why would people think you were Morrissey, out in the middle of Po-dunk, Kansas?*

Not_Morrissey: *Didn't go to college here, Buttmunch! It was in California.*

This brought cali4nyapix out of the woodwork:

cali4nyapix: *No way, dude! You never told us you went to school out here! What city?*

Cara smiled to herself. Although she'd only seen a few random posts from cali4nyapix, something about him intrigued her. Perhaps it was his playful, animated cat avatars. Or the way his facetious, Eddie Haskell-polite remarks made her laugh out loud. After perusing some of his entries in the Journal section, which were mostly travelogues laden with vivid and stunning photography, Cara decided that—more than anything—she was drawn to the way he viewed nature, people, and the world.

Not_Morrissey: *It was Berkeley. Not that it matters...I was a lazy slacker and never finished.*

Cara's fingers flew across the keyboard, interjecting a post of her own.

Moonflower: *That's okay, NM. There's no law that says you gotta have a sheepskin to be successful. What is it you do for a living these days?*

Before Not_Morrissey could reply, a post appeared in response to hers from cali4nyapix, with a waving emoticon.

cali4nyapix: *Moonflower, good to see you! How's life in the Queen City today?*

A warm waterfall of delight trickled down through Cara's core. It was always nice to be noticed, let alone greeted in such a personable way by one of the EC's most respected members. Hardly anyone outside of Ohio knew that Cincinnati's nickname was the Queen City, so she was doubly impressed. She returned his waving emoticon and raised him a hugging one.

Moonflower: *Life is good, thanks. Just working on some editing and thinking about grabbing lunch. How are you?*

Cara refreshed the screen and saw Not_Morrissey's response to her.

Not_Morrissey: *I run a local Irish pub with an old high school buddy. And when I'm not doing that, I'm Superdad Extraordinaire.*

Cara said out loud, "Aw, what a cool guy."

GreatScott wasn't quite ready to give up the jabfest with Not_Morrissey.

GreatScott: *Message board perv by day, family guy by night!*

She let out a chuckle just as a little red message appeared at the top of the window:

1 New Private Message [click to read]

Getting a PM from another user was one of the perks of being on message boards. PM's were a cut above emails because they could be livened up with emoticons to drive home a point. She went into her inbox and saw that it was from cali4nyapix.

Hey Moonflower!

This place can get downright addictive, can't it? Like cyber-crack. Run while you still can! (Just kidding... don't you go anywhere!)

So I was looking through your profile and saw that you are a writer and editor. I've really been enjoying your journals. You seem to find just the right words to capture the ups and downs of life that we all go through. What else do you write?

My name is Kevin, by the way. Feel free to use it on the boards. You have been such a refreshing new "voice" in Planet Indigo, and I'm honored to make your acquaintance.

Sincerely,

Kevin Tierney

Cara grinned at the "good vibes" emoticon next to his signature, with its eyes closed in Buddha-like bliss. Another warm feeling swept through her, along with school-girl curiosity. She clicked on Kevin's highlighted username in his post, which brought up a profile page.

cali4nyapix

Location: Santa Barbara, California, USA

Occupation: Digital Design/Drawing Instructor/Photographer/Prankster

Interests: Photography/Live Music/Hiking/Surfing /Travel/Film

Birthday: October 26

Zodiac Sign: Scorpio

Age: 46

Cara picked up her editing pen and tapped it thoughtfully on the desk. The last thing she'd expected at that point in her life was a bunch of fascinating people reaching out to her from all over the country. Finding this new community was like stumbling upon a spilled trunk of gold left behind by pirates in the middle of an island. Eclectic Café listeners were some of the nicest, funniest, and most interesting people she'd ever met—right there at her fingertips every day.

Kevin Tierney seemed even more intriguing now, with his artistic career and similar interests as her. And what a healthy dose of accolades he'd just served up to her out of the blue! *Eight years older than me. Hmmm…wonder what he looks like?* After re-reading his message a few times, she thought of an appropriate reply.

Hello Kevin Tierney!

Thanks so much for your kind words. They were a nice surprise in the middle of a dull workday.

What do I write? Well, at work I edit and write excerpts for educational books. In my personal time, I write fiction, short stories, poetry, and other dablings.

Don't worry, I am definitely here to stay in Plant Indigo and the EC. You people are far too interesting and fun for me to leave any time soon! My friend and coworker makes fun of me for spending so much time talking to you all, but I tell her that these are how many friendships are made in the

Age of Information. Just because we don't all physically sit in a room together doesn't make it any less real, you know?

This year has been an especially challenging one for me, so I'm glad I have an additional bunch of friends to help me through. I consider you one of them.

Cara Shannon, a.k.a. "Moonflower"

With a click, the PM went flying off through cyberspace to Santa Barbara. She scanned Kevin's profile once more and noticed a link to his professional website. Cara was about to investigate when a long rumble from her belly interrupted; a not-so-subtle reminder to get her Moo Goo Gai Pan to the microwave posthaste. On the way out of her cubicle, she made a mental note to look at Kevin's website that evening in the luxury of her own home, with plenty of time to explore. She had a feeling it was going to be good.

Chapter 6

At six o'clock, a welcome stillness settled over the office. The day had been riddled with ringing phones, people stopping by with last-minute demands, and mad scrambles to make Fed-Ex deadlines. Only the soft hum of the heating system could be heard as Cara sat poised over her manuscript. When words began to jumble and blur on the page, she buried her face in her hands and rubbed for a few moments, then looked out the window across the aisle.

The setting sun still cast long, wintry rays across the snow mounds in the parking lot, but she could tell that daylight was lengthening again, a couple of minutes each day. *Thank God, because I can't take much more of this endless cold and gray.* With a heavy sigh, she threw down her editing pen and muttered, "All right, I'm done."

Rising from her chair with creaking joints, she yawned and lifted her arms into an overhead stretch. A quick scan across the cube farm told her she was the only one left in the office, which was surprising considering all the overtime being worked on the latest project. Cara's coworkers often took work home and finished it in front of the TV or at their dining room table. How they could concentrate through blaring commercials or children running amok through the house, she couldn't fathom. There would definitely *not* be any homework on her evening agenda, thank you very much. Her five remaining pages of manuscript, due to ship the next day before noon, were going to have to wait until early next morning.

Cara bent to check her Internet screen and saw Planet Indigo going strong with members posting what they were making for dinner, who they wanted to win on the next *American Idol*, or how long they spent on their basement treadmills working off winter "storage." In one click, they all disappeared and in another few seconds Cara relished the satisfying decrescendo of the computer's fan as it shut down. She buttoned her coat all the way up and wrapped her hand knit Italian scarf twice around her neck.

Trudging out of the office, Cara noticed the dulling eggshell walls and the worn carpet beneath her feet. The company hadn't sunk a lot of money into aesthetic improvements, and the whole place emanated a rather prison-like sterility. Or perhaps it was just her psychological outlook on her job these days. *Stagnant* was the word that kept popping into her head. Walking through the same aisle ways, riding down the same elevator, strolling across the same parking lot next to the loud, busy interstate day after day after day…there was nothing new or exciting taking shape in her life. No lover to go home to and cuddle up with as the snow fell outside. Impulsively, Cara pulled her cell phone from its compartment in her purse and speed-dialed Frannie.

Two rings, then a breathless, “Hello?”

“Winter absolutely sucks ass when there’s no man in your life.”

A pause, then, “Cara? Where are you?”

“Just leaving work.”

“Good lord, woman! You stayed late again.”

“Yeah, well, you know how those damn deadlines are.”

“Well I got ‘em too, hon, but I took my stuff home—oh, that’s right. You don’t take work home, do you?”

“Fran, are you at the gym?”

“Yeah, just got done with my workout.”

Cara stomped her foot and heard salt crunch beneath her boots. “Crap! I was going to come meet you there.”

“Well, if you hurry, we could meet in the hot tub. I’m soaking and steaming for a bit before leaving.”

“Okay. See you soon.”

“Is everything okay, Cara?”

“Yeah, why?”

“I dunno. Just checking, since you called out of the blue about winter sucking ass.”

“I wanted to make sure you were still at the gym.”

Frannie’s voice turned chipper and staccato again. “That’s cool. Okay, then, see you in a bit.”

“Bye.”

Cara signed off with a beep, put the phone back in her purse, and ducked out of the cold into her car. As the engine turned over, the soft crooning of Chris Isaak started up on the radio.

No I don’t wanna fall in love...(this world is only gonna break your heart)...with you.

“*Nice,*” Cara snarled, turning out of the parking lot and cruising down the access road to a stoplight. “Just mock me by playing one of the ultimate make out songs of all time, when there’s no one to share it with.” Through another heavy sigh, she tried to remember the reckless abandon of making out, falling onto a bed with a lover, pulling off clothes and nuzzling each other’s necks...

Honk-honk!

Snapped violently out of her erotic reverie, Cara saw that the light had turned green and the man behind her was scowling as if he had hemorrhoids the size of golf balls. She accelerated and eased into the thick flow of traffic moving steadily down Columbia Parkway, looking forward to the coming of spring more than ever before in her life.

* * *

The gym was awash with sweaty, straining bodies, clanking weights, pulsating electronica music, and the over-amplified voice of an aerobics instructor shouting commands to her energized class. The place was always impossibly crowded in wintertime, glutted with new members and their New Year's resolutions to lose holiday poundage.

Cara lugged her gym bag down the main aisle past the treadmills and elliptical machines, stealing surreptitious glances at some of the more toned and delectable male biceps flexed over handlebars, or quadriceps moving up and down on pedals. Her eyes lingered on one man in particular, with curly dark hair and a Celtic tattoo encircling his left arm. *Oh meow, meow, MEOW, baby!* His skin glistened as he breathed heavily, and she imagined him in a candle-lit bedroom, lying atop her. Cara's breath caught as she squeezed her eyes shut and shook off the second bout of eroticism that had struck in the last hour.

"There you are!" Frannie called from her locker when Cara entered the women's dressing room. "I stayed in the hot tub as long as I could, chick. But I started getting pruny."

Cara shook her head in frustration. "Traffic absolutely *sucked* on the Parkway. I was hoping it would thin out after rush hour, but something must be going on downtown."

"*Mamma Mia!* opened tonight at the Aronoff Center," Frannie confirmed, wrapping her wet swimsuit inside a towel and stuffing it into her gym bag. "And why is your face so red?"

Cara put a hand to her face. "Is it? Must be the cold."

Frannie grinned over at her. "That's not a cold kinda red…that's a *blush.* Can't you feel it?"

Cara glanced around to make sure no one was within earshot and leaned in closer to her friend. "It's probably these horny daydreams I keep having. I swear, Frannie, it's only been about five months but I'm about to explode."

Frannie cocked an eyebrow and gave her a long, hard stare. "Have you looked into those, uh, *toys* we talked about yet?"

Cara sighed and rolled her eyes. "I get along just fine without batteries, thank you…and nothing, I mean *nothing* can take the place of warm, strong muscles wrapped around you or the earthy scent of male pheromones."

"Well, you can always do what Ian and I do." Frannie held up a hand. "And I know you said it wasn't your trip, but you never know till you try, right?" She bent to zip up her bag then slammed the locker shut.

Cara's mouth twisted as if she'd just put a lemon drop in her mouth. "Yeah, I just can't do the 'fuckbuddy' thing, Fran. Wherever my libido goes, my heart follows. Besides, I don't even have any guy friends who are available to do that with. How did you find one, anyway? Seems like everyone our age is married with three kids."

"Ian is divorced and living in my apartment complex. There are plenty of divorced guys or newly broken up guys. You just gotta look harder."

Cara removed layer after layer of her clothes. "That's been my whole problem. Until now, I haven't even had the will to look. It was too soon to move on. I think this is the first time since the breakup that I've actually felt ready and willing to meet someone new." She was thoughtful for a moment, dangling a sports bra in one hand. "Actually, I feel like I've reached a place where I'm totally comfortable with *myself* again. Man or no man."

Frannie flashed a glowing look of approval. "*That's* what counts the most. Hell, many women never get to that level of self acceptance."

Cara beamed as she pulled on her workout clothes. "It's a good feeling, let me tell you, especially after all that grieving for Greg. I am so over that man." She turned to Frannie, who was now bundled in her winter coat. "I have totally let him go."

Frannie put a tender hand to Cara's cheek. "Aw, girl, that's really good to know."

Cara giggled and mirrored Frannie's smile, which morphed into a devilish look.

"Now that you've said all this, you know some guy's gonna come sneakin' into your life from out of left field, don't you?"

Cara's mouth fell open. "*What?*"

Frannie's eyes widened. "Oh yeah, it never fails. Bjork even wrote a song about it. Just when you get comfortable with yourself and your single status, in comes another guy to shake up your world. And always when you least expect it." She pointed a finger at Cara. "Just watch."

Kevin Tierney flashed through Cara's mind, and a shiver rushed up her spine. In the next instant, she dismissed the notion completely. "Well, we'll see. In the meantime, you have a great evening, Fran."

"I will do just that, and you have a great workout."

They walked out of the locker room together, and as Cara climbed aboard one of the elliptical machines, she called to Frannie, "See you tomorrow."

Frannie wiggled her fingers in the air as she turned and headed for the gym's exit.

Cara punched in her startup information on the machine's keypad and made another mental note to look at Kevin's website when she got home. She couldn't wait to see what those "California pix" were all about.

* * *

"What? What do you *want* from me?"

For the third time since parking herself at the computer, Cara heard Sophie's annoying little whimper that sounded like *brrr?* In cat language, this meant *could you please get off the frickin' computer and give me some attention right NOW?* Cara stared down at her gray cat's lovely golden owl-eyes. Sophie stared back with two rigid forelegs, paws pressed stubbornly into the carpet.

"You need some play time, don't you?" Cara cooed, reaching out a hand to pet her.

Sophie ducked away and opened her mouth in a half-hearted attempt to bite.

"Yeah, I know you're pissed at me," Cara laughed. "I leave you alone all damn day, then I come home, eat, and promptly ignore you while I play on the computer. Life's a bitch, isn't it?"

Sophie's tail began to swish back and forth.

Like a cheetah, Cara sprung out of the chair and slapped her thighs. The cat bolted from the room with a scratching of claws on carpet, initiating her favorite game of chase. Cara ran after Sophie and indulged her pet in a few minutes of chasing, sparring, and playing catch-the-mouse-on-the-bungee. Afterward, Cara dropped a few kitty snacks on the kitchen floor and headed for the den once again, hearing contented crunching in her wake.

Before the *felinus interruptus,* Cara had made it as far as the index page of Kevin Tierney's website. She looked it over once again, admiring the simple yet stylish display of links to his various categories: Web Design, Drawings, Cartoons, Photography and Classic Cars. Her eyes stopped and lingered on the last button. *Classic cars?* With a click on the tab, she was transported to a page of photographs displaying old cars from the late 1950's to 1960's. Most appeared to be small British or Italian convertibles. From the little blurb he'd written at the top of the page, it seemed that her new acquaintance once enjoyed doing restorative paint jobs on vintage vehicles in addition to his other work.

"Huh," Cara uttered with a budding smile of amusement, then clicked on his biographical page. When it loaded, a headshot of Kevin appeared at the top left. "Ooh, *hello*."

Looking much younger than his forty-six years, his sandy-blonde hair was stylishly unkempt in a sort of jagged shag, framing his face like drooping palm fronds. She liked the way one of his eyebrows arched up slightly higher than the other, creating an old-Hollywood charm about him. But it was the eyes that captivated her the most, with their clear shimmer matching that of the sea behind him. Cara leaned in for a better look, but no matter how close she put her face to the screen, she was unable to tell if they were blue, green or gray.

"Nice lips, too," Cara remarked, yearning to kiss their fullness as they curved upward in a slight grin. Until that moment, she'd never seen a picture of Kevin. His avatar was usually one of the little feline cartoon characters from his collection, or a beautiful nature image. It was nice to finally see who she was talking to. A definite *meow* for this guy.

From his mini-biography, Cara learned that Kevin Tierney was born and raised in Monterey, California. He had lived briefly in Colorado and San Francisco before settling in Santa Barbara. Kevin did freelance work in both digital design and illustration, and also taught a human figure drawing class one evening a week.

"You are one busy guy," Cara murmured to his image on the screen, then moved the mouse to explore his body of work.

His web design page had links to all the sites he'd created, for all walks of business: restaurants, galleries, spas, and even public libraries. His photography collection covered a multitude of California landscapes from Death Valley to Lake Tahoe.

Kevin's images were so vivid that she could smell the sage and feel the waves of heat radiating from the dry, rocky ground. Some scenes were drenched in sun, while others showed minimal dappled beams falling onto a forest floor through overhead redwood limbs. One of the photos was so perfectly captured she could almost see the shadows dancing and wavering.

This man is brilliant, she thought, sitting back in her chair and letting out a sigh of awe. *He must have a lot of beauty inside of him to recognize and capture it so perfectly.* Eager for more, she clicked the Illustrations link. The pictures ranged from children's book renderings to sophisticated posters for social events. One was a close-up of a handsome Latino man holding a beautiful, dark-skinned woman in a dance embrace, nose to nose, breathing each other's breath. The title *Tango!* was emblazoned in red above their heads. It was an ad for a cultural showcase of Argentinian tango dancers that happened in Santa Barbara some months before. Cara slowly shook her head. She hardly knew this man, yet something about him stirred a wordless fascination within her.

Finally, she took a quick browse through the cartoons. There were jaunty cats in zoot suits driving old MG convertibles down palm tree-lined boulevards. Beatnik-looking cats with berets and sunglasses sat atop a wall by a moonlit sea, jamming on guitars and bongos. Cara giggled at such a playful and whacked imagination. "I like this guy," she declared out loud, nodding several times. "This guy definitely rules."

She found the contact page, clicked on Kevin's email address, and carefully composed:

Hello again, Kevin!

I finally had a chance to browse your website. Excellent work! Actually, "excellent" is way too vanilla of an adjective for it, but I've been editing all day and I'm tired of finding the most appropriate words! :) Have a great weekend.

~ Cara Shannon

After hitting the SEND button, Cara burst into a reflexive yawn and heaviness tugged at her eyelids. The computer's digital clock told her it was just about bedtime. She cast a fond glance across the room at Sophie, who lay curled up on a window seat with one paw draped over her face. "You got the right idea, girl," she cooed to the cat.

As she logged off, shut down the computer, and rose from her chair, Cara anticipated the comfort of flannel sheets and her electric blanket—the next best thing to sleeping with a warm man.

Chapter 7

"Ah, so I see there's another fool in here at the butt-crack of dawn."

With eyes that wouldn't quite open all the way, Cara turned and faced the owner of the low, Eeyore-like voice. She'd been waiting for coffee to brew in their break room's industrial-sized machine that was entirely too loud for six o'clock in the morning. The voice belonged to Mel, one of the senior editors who could be a highly qualified poster child for Workaholics Anonymous. She yawned and asked him, "Mel, do you ever go home?"

He stared at the black stream shooting steadily into the glass carafe and chuckled. "Of course not! Why do you think I had that shower installed in the second floor restroom?"

Cara gave him a faint grin and quietly willed the coffee to brew faster. The five manuscript pages from the night before were laying in wait on her desk, and she was in desperate need of a caffeine infusion to jump-start her motivation to work at this godforsaken hour. When she eventually returned to her desk, steaming cup in hand, she brushed the pages aside and logged into The Eclectic Café.

The Europeans, well into their afternoon, were exchanging hellos with the east coasters of America. Eire_Forever ran a bed and breakfast in the west of Ireland, and NoShite was a seventeen-year-old student and rock musician who lived with his family in Edinburgh.

Eire_Forever: *It makes perfect sense to me, Foxie...I think the average person gets more done when they're in the comfort of their own home with no coworkers to distract them. Best of luck to you!*

Foxie was 20thCenturyFox, an architect from the gulf coast of Florida. Her avatar was a pair of sexy legs clad in white go-go boots, and her posts were always a unique blend of witty, flirtatious, fun-loving, and wholesome. Before Christmas, she'd announced that she might be able to work from home in order to spend more time with her five year-old daughter. Back scrolling a bit, Cara realized that Foxie had finally sealed the deal.

Moonflower: *Foxie! This is GREAT news. Are you working at home right now?*

20thCenturyFox: *Noop, not until next week. But I'm pretty excited about it. And good morning, btw!*

NoShite: *Morning Moonflower! How's things?*

Eire_Forever: *Well if it isn't Herself! A bright good morning, Cara!*

The Europeans wanted to know why Cara and Foxie were up so early. Speaking for herself, Cara explained about the five pages of editing.

20thCenturyFox: *If you want to get that work done, girly, you'd best back slowly out of Planet Indigo! You know what a black hole it becomes when everyone starts checking in for the day! I also came to work early to wrap up some final projects, and look at me! Slacking away in the EC!*

Cara laughed silently to herself, knowing all too well about the black hole. When favorite cyber-friends dropped in every few seconds, saying hello or posting something hilarious, it was impossible to leave without responding. Sure enough, the morning onslaught began with Seth checking in just before his commute to the city. BloominElle, who always spent some time in the EC before her shop opened, posted an image of a delectable morning breakfast buffet. Beneath it, she'd typed: *Breakfast is on me, everyone!* This of course brought several others out of the woodwork, including TheRub.

TheRub: *Yum! Don't mind if I do, Ellie! I have two deep tissues and one 90-minute Swedish massage this morning. I need the energy!*

Cara stretched her head to one side, then the other, and responded to his post.

Moonflower: *Man, I could use your magic fingers right now. I must've slept on my neck wrong or something, because it's all stiff!*

After hitting the enter key, she stole a sidelong glance at the five pages waiting patiently for the strokes of her purple editing pen, then hurriedly refreshed the screen to see his reply.

TheRub: **administers cyber-massage to Moonflower's neck* There. Better?*

Cara put one hand to her neck and rubbed, wishing his gesture were real. Then she leaned forward and made one last post before getting busy.

Moonflower: *Thanks*—Cara paused, trying to remember his real name. Charles? Edward? It was one of those English monarchs, but which one? And wasn't it also the name of an alt-rock band? It came to her in the next second—*James. I think it's all winter's fault...I tense against the cold whenever I walk outside. I cannot WAIT for spring.* She considered adding a "grumpy" emoticon to her message, but didn't want to spread the negativity. After hitting SEND, she quickly shrunk her Internet window to an icon. This laid bare a second window containing her webmail, which she'd opened first thing but hadn't yet read. At the top of the list was a brand new email from Kevin Tierney, sent the night before after she'd logged off and gone to bed.

Hey, Cara Shannon (I see that we are both descended from good Irish stock!)

I just wanted you to know that your email made my day. Most of it had gone pretty crappily...you know, one of those days where you choose a traffic route that's the most congested, things get misplaced, deadlines are shortened, your grocery store line is the longest with ten million price checks...and to top it all off, I was told that I might not have a high enough enrollment for my upcoming spring class in Adult Ed. Anyway, your email put a smile on my face for the first time all day. So thank you.

Isn't The Eclectic Café the greatest? Not only its incredible blend of music, but this welcoming community of unique personalities! I was never an "online" person before this, and now all these EC friends are a huge part of my life. I've even met several of them in person. Seems crazy, sometimes, but then I completely agree about the Age of Information bringing people closer in a different sort of way.

I look forward to having you around and getting to know you better in the coming days.

Thank you for taking the time to browse my site...and for your flattering words. I consider myself very fortunate to be making a living at something I love to do, and to be working from home. I have never been a corporate 8 to 5 guy!

Well, you have a great day, Ms. Moon. See you on the boards!

~KST

Cara sat back in her chair and felt the glacier that encased her heart slowly begin to melt. Little drops at first, then steady streams and finally big chunks of ice breaking off and plunging into the sea of healing within. She read the email a second time, then a third. Not only was it sweet, but very straightforward and real. Just as she began to formulate a reply to Kevin's message, the clock in the corner of her computer screen reminded her that she'd already blown an entire half hour of her morning. *Shit.* Playtime was over.

Cara turned to the opposite side of her cubicle and spread the five pages out across her countertop. I have a new online friend, she thought absently to herself with a tiny grin. My very own grown-up pen pal.

* * *

"Damn, woman! How many pots of coffee have you had?"

Cara looked up from violently cramming pages into a stubborn FedEx envelope. Frannie had just blown in from the arctic, sunny morning.

"I've lost count," Cara chirped, finally fitting the dog-eared pages into the package. "Got started at six this morning."

"*Six?* Sweet Jesus in a jumpsuit!" Frannie shook her head and started for her desk, then stopped.

Cara hastily scrawled the address on the outside label with a felt-tip pen, then glanced up again. "Yes?"

Frannie eyed her friend closely and sprouted a slow, crooked grin. "Cara Shannon, what is that big-ass smile about?"

"What big-ass smile?"

"Aw c'mon!" Frannie dipped her chin and raised an eyebrow. "No one in their right mind smiles like that when they've been here since six. You met someone, didn't you?"

"Shh!"

"Aha! You *did*. What's his name?"

With a slight blush, Cara put up her hands and shook her head. "I didn't meet anyone, Fran, now keep it down. That's how rumors—"

"Cara's got a new guy?" came the eager voice of a coworker across the aisle, who prairie-dogged her head over the wall. "Tell, tell, tell!"

Cara rolled her eyes, still smiling. "I *don't* have a new guy. Honest! Can't a woman just be happy once in a while?"

The lingering look on Frannie's face clearly stated that she didn't believe Cara, but she shrugged and proceeded to her cube, setting her things down with a clatter. "You're not fooling anyone, you know," she said through the partition. "I know that look."

* * *

The stack of three finished work packets in two hours was justification enough for Cara to check back into Planet Indigo, where she found Kevin posting morning greetings from the west coast.

cali4nyapix: *I just got back from the gym...and am now re-thinking this personal trainer bullshit. Do we really need sadistic young punkass jocks standing smugly by while we torture ourselves? I can do that to myself, on my own time, and without paying the extra twenty-five dollars a month! I am so effing sore...where's James?*

Cara leapt to the keyboard, wanting to be the first to respond.

Moonflower: *He was here earlier, but had to go to work. Can I fill in for him?*

Before she could stop herself, she added a winking emoticon and hit SEND. Good God, I'm *flirting,* Cara cried internally, putting a hand over her mouth. It was too late to delete the post.

cali4nyapix: *Hey there!* *Be my guest! *hands Cara the massage oil**

Cara giggled. *And what was that...a* butterfly *in my stomach? What the hell!?*

"What's so funny over there?" Frannie demanded.

"Just a funny email someone passed to me," Cara lied.

After bantering back and forth with Kevin down the page, Cara switched to the PM screen. She sent him a quick note stating that she'd gotten his email and would respond at lunch time. Then she shrunk all her screens to icons, rose from her chair, and called, "Ready for the department meeting?"

Frannie was already in the aisle. "Come with me to get some coffee first. I haven't had a *drop* this morning and I'm ready to hurt someone."

Cara grabbed her empty cup and as they walked side-by-side to the break room, she noticed her friend's sharp new outfit with low-rider pants and a black lycra top. "*Mee-ow,* Frannie, what's with the hot bod all of a sudden? Have you lost more weight?"

Frannie beamed but stared straight ahead unobtrusively. "I've been doing Pilates."

"Really?"

"Yeah, I have an instructional DVD at home and I also go to the Saturday morning class at our gym. I'd much rather sleep in, but hey…if it gets me this…" she held her arms out on either side of her hips.

Cara thought about all her friends—both online and locally—that had been getting back into fitness lately. Kevin Tierney even had a personal trainer. Having seen just his face on the website, she wondered what the rest of him looked like. Did he have a middle-aged paunch like her brother-in-law, or a sinewy surfer's bod? She glanced down at her own body and regarded herself through the eyes of someone who might possibly want to date her. The pitfalls of the winter season—comfort food and cozying in on the couch at night—had taken their toll and left her a little thicker around the middle than she cared for. Her legs didn't look as toned as they used to, either. *This damned sedentary desk job!*

She turned to Frannie. "I think I might join you this weekend. I've wanted to get into a fitness regimen since before Christmas, and Pilates is so state of the art. I keep seeing pictures of all the hot-bodied celebrities who do it."

Frannie nodded. "It also helps posture and breathing, and just makes me *feel* good in general."

Cara paused at the door to the conference room, letting Frannie enter first. "What time is the class?"

"Ten-thirty."

"That's cool. I'll have plenty of time to get ready. Sophie never lets me sleep past seven-thirty anyway."

Frannie gave Cara a dark look as she walked by. "I don't know how you put up with that insanity, Cara. If I had a cat that stepped all over me in the morning when I was trying to sleep, I'd boot him out the window."

Cara laughed. "Well, I guess that's what happens when you don't have kids. Suddenly, you're referring to yourself as 'mommy' to your cat and letting her get away with murder."

Frannie glanced over her shoulder with another look of disdain.

Silent, bleary-eyed people filled the chairs of the conference room. Some sipped cautiously on hot coffee and stared into space. Others talked in hushed tones. Cara and Frannie took their places among them at the long meeting table.

The department manager began with a weekly update on the status of the company, the most recent projects, and everyone's alleged five percent pay raise that was still up in the air. It only took two minutes for Cara's mind to tune him out. He'd been saying the same things month after month, yet situations never seemed to improve. The company certainly wasn't paying Cara or anyone else their worth, yet they all seemed to be working harder and harder with each project.

Rather than listen to the redundant drivel, her brain decided to take a little mini vacation to a beach—warm and sun-drenched—with the sound of screaming gulls overhead and the crash of waves on the shore. She could almost feel the heat rising up off the sand as she sat on a beach blanket…enjoying a luxurious morning with no deadlines, highway commutes, or late winter temperatures that couldn't seem to make up their mind when to let spring return.

Cara began to illustrate the daydream on her memo pad. She drew a grove of palm trees, a shining sun, and a sailboat riding c-shaped waves. Just as the next pen stroke began a rendering of herself, a sharp nudge in her arm forced a blue streak across the page. She glanced over at Frannie, who pointed at the drawings with a quizzical look. Cara hurriedly wrote the words *Escapism…before I die of boredom* and tapped them with her pen.

Frannie nodded and rolled her eyes.

Cara resumed the cartoon with a figure of herself standing on the shore, her long sundress blowing in the breeze. Instinctively, she began to draw a male figure standing beside her. When it was time to add facial features, she paused. Who *was* this mystery guy? Then, like a soundtrack to her little cartoon, the opening lines of the Bobby Darin classic "Beyond the Sea" began to play in her mind. She stopped drawing as photographs of "cali4nyapix" flashed through her mind. California was such beautiful country…desert, ocean, lakes, mountains, and forests all residing within the same border. People of the Golden State had it all.

The Shannon family had vacationed to Southern California when Cara was a teenager, and her most prominent memory was how the landscape often appeared bathed in golden light. She recalled swimming for hours in the San Diego surf with Arianna, then crawling wearily onto the beach for an ice cold Coke from the family cooler. It was one of Cara's favorite memories from a happier era of her niece's life. Before the depression crept in, locked Arianna in a stranglehold, and never let go.

"So if no one has any questions, that's all I've got for today." The department manager finished his mind-numbing oration with a loud clearing of the throat.

Jarred back to reality, Cara glanced around the table, hoping no hands would go up. Mercifully, none did.

Chapter 8

"I don't know what's going on with me, Fran," Cara said on their way back to the office. "I've been daydreaming way more than I usually do. My mind keeps drifting to warm, oceanic settings and it's been extremely hard to focus. What the hell's that all about?"

"Yeah, come to think of it," Frannie flapped her notebook in the air, "I've been having daydreams and focus problems too. Only my fantasy place is the desert. A Native American spiritual retreat center with wind chimes and chanting and crap."

"It's Seasonal Affective Disorder," said a voice from behind them. They turned to discover Mel walking behind them with his low, monotone voice and ambiguous expression. "Very common in wintertime. Serotonin levels are at an all time low, so people begin to daydream about warm, bright places. They either lose their focus or worse yet, sink into heavy depression."

"Is that why I'm getting a sudden urge to go buy a tanning package at Totally Sun down the street from my house?" Cara said to no one in particular.

"No!" Frannie chided. "Don't you dare! Those tanning beds are cancer coffins."

"What about the cancer sticks that you smoke?" Cara retorted with a wink. "Relax, chick, it's just an urge. And now I know why. We're all craving frackin' *sunlight!* Damn, I wish it were the beginning of May instead of early March."

"Aw, it'll come soon enough," Frannie assured her. "In the meantime, we should take advantage and go over to Snowshoe for the weekend. I'm in the mood to ski, aren't you?"

Cara considered the offer. Flying through pine-scented woods on blankets of frosty whiteness was *very* tempting. "I like the way you're thinking, Fran. Make hay while the sun shines…or *doesn't* shine as the case may be."

Frannie gave a nod. "Precisely."

"Let me look over my finances and think about it."

"Don't think too long. The ski season will be over before you know it."

Back at her desk, Cara brought up the Internet window to check her bank statement. Planet Indigo was flying by at ninety miles per hour. And no wonder…saffire_21 was back. There was a full page and a half of people saying hello to her again. Saffire replied to each and every one of them with her own special nicknames, and something about them sounded vaguely familiar to Cara.

BloominElle: *saffire!*

saffire_21: *Lots of lovely, fragrant flower-nummies to you, Ellie Mae!*

smk02: *Hello gorgeous! Why don't you ever answer your phone?!*

saffire_21: *Aw... long-time-no-see nummies for you, smokin'-hot!*

Bellybutton: *saffire you beotch, why don't you fucking stick around for more than two minutes this time?*

saffire_21: *BB! Well, since you asked so NICELY ...maybe I will. Ha!*

Not_Morrissey: *Hey sexy! You ready to meet for that Nooner today?*

saffire_21: *Darlin, you couldn't handle me! They don't call me saf-FIRE for nothing! But Nooner-nummies to you anyway!*

WhiteHeronMagic: *Hey, dear one! I'm glad I caught you on my morning break between classes!*

saffire_21: *WHM! I hope you're whippin' those kids into shape! They're our future, ya know!*

Cara poised her fingers over the keyboard and tried to think of an eloquent way to introduce herself. Giving up, she simply typed:

Moonflower: *Hi there, saffire. I don't believe we've met before. My name's Cara. *shakes hands**

There was a slight pause in posts, then:

saffire_21: *Greetings, Cara-Moonflower! *shakes hands back* Welcome to Planet Indigo! Newcomer-nummies for you!*

There it was again. *Nummies*. The expression took her back to a family gathering on a cold winter day in the seventies. Melanie, Cara's older sister, had just arrived with her husband and four-year-old Arianna. When she was free of her puffy pink coat and snow boots, Arianna ran around the room with rosy little cheeks and flaming red pigtails giving everyone a kiss on the cheek. "Nummies for Nanna!" she cried, standing on tiptoe to kiss Cara's mother. Grandma leaned down from her chair to receive it with fluttering eyelashes and a big smile.

"I want nummies, Arianna!" Jenn had said, waving a hand in the air.

Arianna giggled and ran across the room to where Jenn sat on the edge of the couch. She dove into her aunt's lap and planted a big one on Jenn's cheek. Around and around she went, doling out "nummies" until she finally got to Cara, who waited patiently on the floor with her Barbies.

Arianna looked her over, smile fading, then plopped down and helped herself to Cara's favorite doll—Malibu Barbie.

"*Arianna,*" Melanie chided. "Don't you have nummies for Auntie Cara?"

Arianna pretended not to hear and began to undress Malibu Barbie.

"Arianna?" her dad repeated. "Say hello to Cara."

Not wanting to belabor the rejection from her impertinent little niece, Cara had rolled her eyes and let out a huff. "Never mind! I didn't want her nummies *anyway.*"

Despite the initial power struggle, the two girls were playing happily together in a matter of minutes. That had always been Arianna's way: moody, saucy, and hard to impress…but lovable.

Snapping back to the present, Cara glanced over the copious amounts of "nummies" saffire had given everyone. Thinking of one more question, she typed:

Moonflower: *What inspired your username, saffire?*

After a few moments, the reply came back.

saffire_21: *The sapphire is my birthstone, but I spelled it wrong on purpose, because I like to appear fiery!*

"Okay, this is just freakin' *weird,*" Cara muttered to herself, putting a hand to her chin. Sapphires were the birthstone for September, and Arianna's birthday had been September 16th. *Oh, you and your overactive imagination…is it any wonder you're a writer? Get back to work, already.*

With a resolute sigh, she shrunk the EC window from view—completely forgetting about her bank statement—and picked up the next two chapters of a social studies book that someone had left on her desk before the meeting.

* * *

By five o'clock Cara had sat through three meetings, FedEx'ed four packages to clients, and met every impossible deadline that had been laid on her at the last minute. Her final challenge was to call the art department to rectify an image in her latest chapter that was too dark. She dialed the extension, then idly wiggled her mouse and brought The Eclectic Café to the foreground. It was the first time she'd looked at Planet Indigo since the morning and three PMs were waiting in her inbox. *Three.*

Waiting through the voicemail message, Cara clicked on the PM from cali4nyapix, a smile lighting up her face. "Hi, this is Cara from Editorial. I need to get with you on the Grade Four project as soon as possible, to finalize the enlarged visual on page 70. You've probably left for the day, so if you could return this call first thing Monday morning that would be great." Cara practically threw the phone into its cradle and leaned forward, eager to read what Kevin had to say.

Dear Cara,

Just wanted to send you a quick good morning PM and give you the courtesy of seeing who you're talking to. Sometime, if you're down with it, I'd love to see one of yours.

Well, that's all for now. I've got another grueling appointment with my trainer at the gym, in which he will surely kick my ass and make me hurt.

Have a fantabulous day,
Kevin

And there, embedded in his PM, was a digital image of Kevin standing in a park with a line of palm trees behind him. His hair was longer in this photo, and he was gazing off to the right with a laugh frozen on his face.

"What a great smile," she said out loud, without thinking.

"Ah ha!" came Frannie's voice from the doorway, making Cara jump five inches off her chair. She whirled around and put a hand to her heart.

"Geez, Frannie!"

Frannie moved closer to Cara's computer screen, bent and peered at the picture of Kevin with a gleam in her eyes. "*There* he is. I knew you were hiding a Mystery Internet Man."

Cara leaned back in her chair, still recovering from the adrenaline burst. She let out a long breath and explained, "He's no mystery, he's just a new acquaintance named Kevin."

Frannie straightened again, still staring. "Not bad looking, either. Oh hey, there's another one. Scroll down."

Cara reached for the mouse and paged down, then perked up as another photo of Kevin was revealed. "Hey! I didn't see this one."

The second photo showed Kevin with half-lens, rimless, barely-there glasses. He was gripping a pool cue and looking intently at a potential shot on a billiards table.

"Ooh, that one's very professor-like," Frannie remarked.

"Well, he *is* a teacher. In addition to his digital design job, he teaches Figure Drawing at Adult Ed."

Frannie hung her head in exaggerated drama. "Aw, geez! Not an *artist!* How many times I gotta tell ya to stay away from those damn moody artists?"

"But he's not really an—"

"Designers, writers, painters, actors…all of 'em! They're passionate, they're sexy, they're funny, and they're nothin' but trouble in the end." She shook a finger at Cara. "I'm tellin' ya. Trouble with a capital T."

Cara giggled. "One moody writer for an ex-husband and you're going to put all artists in a pigeonhole?"

Frannie put a hand on her hip. "Can you name me one artist who *isn't* moody?"

"Yes, as a matter of fact." Cara blinked in self-righteous slow motion. "Jenni, one of my dear friends from high school, is a painter. She's very down to earth, sweet and doe-like."

Frannie narrowed her eyes. "Well, she's an exception." She studied Kevin's picture once more. "Where does he live?"

Cara turned and took another fond look before logging off. "California."

Frannie opened her mouth in a wide smile and gave Cara's shoulder a little nudge. "No *wonder* you've been daydreamin' about the beach."

Cara looked away.

"Well, all power to ya, chick. You gettin' outta here?"

"Yeah, I'll walk out with you," Cara replied, slapping a post-it to her desktop and scrawling quickly: *left mssg with Art…call first thing in the AM on Monday.*

As they gathered their coats and purses, Frannie asked, "So I'll see you at Pilates tomorrow?"

Cara nodded. "Absolutely! Thanks for reminding me."

Walking out of the office, Cara contemplated the awesome power of the "new man" in a woman's life. He was the reason for the perpetual smile on her face, the cause of forgetting what she was going to say, and bumping into things she swore hadn't been there a second ago. The new man could be such a huge impetus for *change.* Although Kevin was thousands of miles away and might not ever lay eyes on her, she was more driven than ever to jump on the fitness bandwagon and reclaim that body she had back in college.

Chapter 9

Since the addition of Sophie to her household, there was no more sleeping in for Cara on weekends. The cat's internal clock remembered that most mornings the two of them got up at six and that she was always fed five minutes later. Saturday was just another day.

Sophie usually began her wakeup call with a soft *brrr*. Half asleep, Cara would turn the other way and ignore it. The little beast's next strategy was to lean on her human companion—as close to the bladder as possible—with both paws. That one usually did the trick, but if Cara still refused to get up, the troublemaking ensued. After a mattress-jarring launch, little cat paws could be heard thudding to the ground. Then the floor lamp next to the bed would begin to wobble, or something would get knocked over in the next room. This was Sophie's ace in the hole. It always got her food source stumbling out of bed with an angry, "So-*phie!* What are you doing? "

On the day of her first Pilates class, Cara took advantage of the early rising and had a leisurely morning. With her cat safely grazing in the kitchen and the coffee brewing, Cara logged onto the Internet to see who was awake in Planet Indigo.

As usual, Eire_Forever and NoShite were having afternoon chats from across the Atlantic. Seth had popped in a page earlier, accompanied by a yawning emoticon, claiming that "the rats" had gotten him up *way* too early. Rats—short for rugrats—was the nickname for his two children that stayed with him every other weekend. When Cara realized that the sporadic conversation was idle chatter, moving at the speed of glacial ice (Eire was most likely cleaning house in between posts, and NoShite playing a video game), she decided to go write in bed with her coffee.

Writing in bed on a Saturday morning was a luxury in which Cara loved to indulge, especially during winter. Most times, she'd write a long entry in her journal. Other times she'd scribble out verses of poetry or play around with short stories. That morning, she chose to work on ideas for her "someday" novel. She hadn't been under the covers for five minutes when Sophie, who'd finished her breakfast, stood staring at Cara from the doorway as if to say, *What the hell? I thought you were getting up!*

"Go play with your mouse!" Cara snapped, pointing toward the hallway. "You're a *cat,* damn it! You're supposed to be independent!"

Sophie took a few running steps and leapt onto the bed. When Cara ignored her, the cat settled—in graceful accord—for a grooming session in close proximity to her owner.

Cara sighed and stared down at the notes once more. They seemed promising. There were a few believable characters with the potential to make people laugh, and the Cincinnati setting—a downtown office overlooking Fountain Square—would be extremely unique, compared to all the glamorous "Chick Lit" settings in New York, London or Los Angeles. She'd jotted down some pages of witty dialogue that took place by the office water cooler of said characters, and even contemplated some racy after-hours sex scenes in the copy room…it was all there in pieces and parts, but she could never seem to pull them together into a main storyline.

Cara continued staring at the pages, sipping coffee and stroking Sophie's head as the sunrise transformed the sky from pale pink to blue. Before she knew it, the leisurely morning was over and it was time to head for the gym. She couldn't resist taking one last peek into Planet Indigo, where a conversation was taking place between two early risers on the West Coast—WhiteHeronMagic and StarAngel.

StarAngel was Astrea, a hippie-chick from California's central coast who worked on an herb farm. Her avatar was usually some celestial body or a beautiful fairy, and her online demeanor was very earthy and laid back—to a contagious extent. Whenever Astrea came onto the boards, it was as if a magic dusting of serenity had settled over everyone.

That morning, StarAngel displayed her actual photo; long hair the color of burgundy, porcelain skin and the most gorgeous gray-blue eyes Cara had ever seen. Her natural beauty was so stunning, Cara couldn't help but stare as one would stare at a Renoir in an art museum.

StarAngel: *As a matter of fact, we do sell a lot of Echinacea. Even if people don't have colds, they take it as preventive medicine.*

WhiteHeronMagic: *That makes sense. Just like Vitamin C. Are you working today?*

StarAngel: *Yes, I work every Saturday. But not until ten, so I still have time to enjoy the sunrise with Earl Grey!*

WhiteHeronMagic: *Ooh, sounds wonderful. I do love to cuddle up with Earl in the morning!*

Cara was about to interject a quick hello to the women, when a new post appeared from saffire_21.

saffire_21: *Hello, lovelies! I'm having some fresh brewed coffee in my little moka!*

WhiteHeronMagic: *Your what?*

saffire_21: *My espresso moka pot! A little stainless steel container that perks enough for maybe one or two cups, right on the stove. It's the only way I brew my coffee these days!*

As an afterthought, saffire edited her post with an embedded image of a moka.

Cara's lips twitched with a faint smile of nostalgia. Her first introduction to a moka was through Arianna, who'd brought one back from Italy after her post-college European tour. And, come to think of it, Arianna had declared the same opinion about not liking coffee brewed any other way. Cara seized the opportunity to jump into the conversation.

Moonflower: *I've had coffee from a moka pot before—delicious! Good morning, chicas! You western peeps are up WAY too early for a Saturday!*

Caroline responded in her usual nanosecond.

WhiteHeronMagic: *Hey gorgeous!* *What are you up to this morning?*

Moonflower: *I thought I'd try a Pilates class with my friend. Wish me luck. I am SO out of shape!*

saffire_21: *Oh honey, I don't think anyone could be more out of shape than me right now. So don't worry!*

Cara raised her eyebrows at the sudden display of affection.

StarAngel: *I've tried Pilates, Moon. It's a lot of fun. Hard on the abs, but fun. And great toning to be had! I felt two inches taller after doing the class for a few months.*

Cara started to type a response, but her eyes were instantly drawn to saffire's avatar, which had been updated in the last few seconds. There was finally an image in place, and it was the kindly face of Snuffleupagus—the elephant-like muppet from Sesame Street. The tagline below it read: *Oh, bird...*

A faint smile hung on her face as another teen-aged memory surfaced. She and Arianna had been sitting in the kitchen one summer night, slurping homemade milkshakes and listening to the cricket chorus outside the window.

"You know who my favorite character was on Sesame Street?" Arianna asked out of the blue, her face oozing fondness.

Because she shared the adulation, Cara instantly guessed, "Snuffy?"

"Yes!" Arianna cried, pointing her long-handled soda spoon. "He was so cute with his long, blinky eyelashes and that deep voice...and always sighing, 'Oh, bird...' just like Eeyore used to say, 'Oh, Pooh...'"

"This is unbelievable," Cara said out loud, snapping back to the moment. "This saffire chick and Arianna must've been separated at birth!" She continued her dialogue with saffire.

Moonflower: *saffire, I've been meaning to ask...did you name Planet Indigo after that place on the kiddie show called Mr. McAfee's Universe?*

There was a slight delay as saffire answered recent posts from both Caroline and Astrea. Then came the one Cara awaited.

saffire_21: *You got it, chick! You must've been a MMU fan too!*  *Did you know it was the longest-running kiddie show in the history of American television next to Sesame Street? Remember the panda named Ultraviolette??? She RAWKED! I always wished they would've made a stuffed animal of Ultraviolette. I would've bought one for me and all my friends.*

Cara laughed. She'd forgotten all about Ultraviolette, who had certainly been one of the more endearing characters on the show. Ultraviolette was a person in a panda suit, rather than one of the creepy puppets that neither Cara nor Arianna could stand.

Moonflower: *The stuffed animal idea is a good one. In fact, now that Mr. McAfee has passed on, perhaps they could make a whole "retro" series of stuffed animal likenesses from the show—puppets and all.*

As Cara waited for saffire's response, she checked the time and gasped. Only ten minutes left to get to the gym.

Moonflower: *Where did saffire go?*

StarAngel: *No idea.*

Moonflower: *Well, if she comes back, tell her goodbye. I hope you both have a wonderful Saturday!*

StarAngel: *Will do, dear one! You have a great day too!*

Cara was just about to log out when a last minute post appeared.

saffire_21: *I'm back! Did ya miss me? I went to make more coffee.*

Cara stood over the keyboard tentatively. She didn't want to be late for class. Hoping someone else would pop in and talk with saffire, she turned and left the Eclectic Café behind for the morning.

On the short drive, Cara pondered all the bizarre coincidences between saffire_21 and Arianna. She laid them out in her mind like solitaire cards: the birthstone, the *nummies,* the moka pot, Snuffleupagus and the number twenty-one. Twenty-one had been Arianna's favorite number.

"Why twenty-one?" Jenn asked Arianna the day she declared it to her aunts.

"Because it's Paul O'Neill's jersey number!"

Paul O'Neill had been right fielder for the Cincinnati Reds at the time. The teen-aged Arianna had developed a crush on the tall and lanky athlete with blue eyes and a dazzling smile. Her Christmas present that year had been season tickets in the box seats over right field.

"But *thousands* of people have the number twenty-one in their username," Cara reasoned to herself.

Still, with all the other coincidences, she couldn't help wondering. Who *was* saffire_21 and why was she so secretive about her real identity? As Cara drove along, her musings began to dissolve into those of another subject. What had Kevin been up to? He hadn't left her an overnight email or PM as he'd done for the last couple of days. Perhaps he'd been busy with a project. Or maybe he went on a date with some local Santa Barbara hottie. The idea of this sent an unexpected wave of disappointment through her.

"What?" Cara shook her head and came back to her senses. "No way can I have a crush on someone across the country. That's not an available man, and I need someone who's available."

With a resolute sigh, she flipped on her turn signal and entered the gym's crowded parking lot that was stained white by several winter saltings. Cara sincerely hoped all her muscles were ready for the punishment she was about to inflict on them.

* * *

"Fifty more?" Cara hissed, turning her head toward Frannie who lay on a mat beside her. "That's a lot of sit-ups! And didn't we already do these?"

"They're not actual sit-ups, hon," Frannie told her, flexing her abs expertly and launching into the set with intense concentration. "Focus on the core."

Cara set her jaw and squeezed her abdominal muscles as best she could. "I don't think I can feel my abs anymore, Frannie. They've gone numb."

Contemporary jazz music played as all the people in class flexed and strained and breathed deeply. The Pilates instructor, Chad, walked around the room with a watchful eye, offering assistance where needed. Cara saw a pair of Nike cross-trainers stop short next to her mat, and then two athletic-looking knees sank to the floor. "Okay, do you feel how much you're using your neck and upper body right now?"

"Uh..."

"Is it hurting right in here?" Chad briskly cupped one of her shoulders with one hand and gave a little indicative rub on the muscles behind it.

"Well—"

"Because you should only feel it in the abs and the obliques, right around here." This time both strong hands ran quickly and lightly up and down her sides. "It's all about flexing, not lifting. The flexing should bring your lower back to the floor. Try it."

Cara could scarcely move after feeling the warmth and strength of male hands on her body. She made a willful attempt at the sort of flex that would satisfy Chad.

"There you go, feel that?" he asked, an excited smile flashing across his face. "Now do that again, and feel your lower back hit my hand."

Cara gave a slight gasp as the young, toned, and very hot instructor slipped a hand under her lumbar region and waited. Cara flexed her core muscles and made contact with that wonderful hand once again.

Chad winked and removed the hand to give her a clap on the shoulder. "You got it. Good job."

Then he was up and on to the next person. Cara felt the flush in her cheeks and instinctively turned her head toward Frannie, who was already cocking an eyebrow.

"You need a cigarette now?"

Cara laughed, staring at the ceiling. "I'm a mess, Fran. A mess!"

When class came to a merciful finish, the two of them crossed the gym's running track and joined the long line at the water fountain.

Frannie turned to her friend. "You're not a mess, Cara. I think you're just a normal, healthy woman who's ready to get back in the dating pool. And that's a good thing, considering it's only been about five months."

"Do you think it's too soon?"

"Didn't we have this conversation last time we were here?"

They both moved a step forward in line.

Cara shrugged. "Yeah, we did, but I keep going back and forth about it."

"Why don't you try something completely different, like speed-dating?" Frannie suggested.

"Would you do it with me?"

Frannie noticed she was next in line and conveniently escaped the question by dipping her head toward the stream of water. When they'd both had a turn at the fountain, Cara cornered her by the exercise bikes.

"Well, would you?"

"I already tried it once."

"Was it a worthwhile experience?"

"Not really."

"So why are you recommending it to *me?*" Cara gave her a playful whap on the arm.

"You're way more outgoing than me, and something tells me you'd have more fun with it."

Cara walked with Frannie back to the locker room, giving Chad one last glance as they passed by the aerobic area. His firm little butt was pointed right at them as he bent over the sound system to shut everything off. She gave one shake of her head and growled, "Rrrrff!"

Frannie followed Cara's gaze. "Man, you and those younger men. He's probably not even out of college yet and what are you, thirty-nine?"

"Thirty-eight!"

"Well, you see my point."

"Speaking of age, I'm making it my mission to look as good as you when *I'm* over forty."

Frannie hung her head. "Aw, stop."

"I mean it. You're one of the hottest forty-something women I know."

Her friend waved off the compliment once more as they entered the locker room. In minutes, the two were neck deep in the steaming whirlpool, enjoying the rumbling force of water jets on their backs. Again, thoughts of Kevin Tierney slipped silently into Cara's mind like a cat padding into a carpeted room.

"Frannie, have you ever fallen for an older guy?"

"Yeah, once."

"When? And how did it go?"

"In college. He was the divorced father of a friend of mine, and it was purely physical." Frannie shook her head. "Man, talk about wrecking a friendship! Barb couldn't get past the fact that I was fucking her dad."

"Ugh, that *would* be weird."

"Maybe, but I couldn't help it. That guy could go at it like a stallion! He'd honed his skills down to a smooth polish in *every* way. And Viagra wasn't even around back then, it was all *him,* baby!"

Cara chuckled and rolled her eyes. "How much older was he?"

"About twenty years."

"Holy crap!"

"Rock stars do it all the time, and no one thinks anything of it."

"True."

For a moment, there was only the din of bubbling water between them. Then the inevitable, "Why do you ask?"

Even in the hot tub, Cara felt a blush coming on. "Kevin, the online guy, is eight years older than me. Guess it's not really that much older, compared to *your* sex machine."

Frannie, who'd been lying back with her eyes closed, opened them and turned her head to get a read on Cara's face. "You're really into this guy, aren't you?"

Cara's eyes widened but she said nothing.

"You *are.* Look at you. 'Just an acquaintance' my ass."

An involuntary giggle betrayed Cara's attempt to be secretive. "He fascinates me, Frannie. You should see his website and the work he does. And the way he talks to me! So *real.* So different than any guy I've ever met around here."

Frannie waited for more, her lips parted in a grin of amusement. "Has he seen *your* picture yet?"

"Actually, he asked for one the last time he wrote. I'm still deciding which one to send him."

"What about the one on our company website? It's a good close-up of you."

Cara wrinkled her nose. "I look too pale in that one, and I was having a bad hair day when it was taken."

"Well, there's the one of you at the Austin City Music Festival last summer—the one Greg took."

Cara raised her eyebrows and nodded. "That is a good one. I have my little tank top on and I'm nice and tan."

"I think that's one of the hottest pictures of you *ever*. Use that one."

"Okay. Soon as I get home, that'll be the one."

They settled back and lost themselves in the comfort of the water again until Frannie muttered, "*California*. What the hell?"

"Yeah, right? Who'd have thought I'd meet someone online?"

"Who would have guessed you'd be an 'online' person in the first place?"

Cara's thoughts shifted abruptly to saffire_21. She was tempted to tell Frannie about the strange parallels between the mystery user and her niece, but it was all too weird…and probably just coincidental. After a minute or two of internal deliberation, Cara decided to keep it to herself for the time being. It would be too hard to explain.

Frannie's eyes opened again. "Hey Cara, you hungry?"

"Starving."

"Feel like grabbing some Thai? Or maybe a chicken teriyaki bento box from Sukara's?"

"Oh, meow!" Cara felt her mouth water just thinking about their favorite sushi bar. "That is *exactly* what I want. Then maybe we can hit a matinee later."

"Ah, Saturdays," Frannie sighed, letting her legs float out in front of her luxuriously. Her burgundy toenails broke the surface of the water, along with a glistening gold toe ring. "What would we do without 'em?"

"It seems like we live for the weekends in this eight to five grind, you know?"

"Well, doesn't everyone?"

"No," Cara told her firmly. "Not everyone. I'd love to become one of those people who sets her own hours and works from home. God, if only I could be a full-time writer. I would love to squirrel away in some cottage by the sea and do nothing but write novels for a living."

"Or if you want to be more practical until then, you could do your own freelance writing and editing. Remember, the cat's gotta eat."

Cara laughed at their inside joke. It was Frannie's humorous way of pointing out her financial responsibilities. But inwardly, the little voice that kept urging her to make a change in her life was getting louder by the day and harder to ignore.

Chapter 10

"Choices, choices," Cara said to Sophie as her eyes darted between one digital image of herself and another. The first was a picture of her standing on a street corner in Austin, Texas wearing a Lilith Fair tank top. Her sunglasses were shoved back on her head, sweeping windblown hair with them, and her smile was radiant. That was a great day, Cara thought to herself with only a sprinkling of wistfulness instead of a flood. Austin was the best trip she and Greg had ever taken together.

The second image was a close-up of her sitting in a bar with Frannie, raising a martini glass toward the camera. Its resolution was poor, but Cara thought the picture accurately conveyed her fun-loving spirit. She glanced down at the cat, laying in an evening sunbeam, eyes half closed. "I know! I'll send them both!"

Sophie lifted a sleepy gaze to her human companion, politely acknowledging the sound of her voice.

With a flutter in her stomach, Cara attached the images to an email and sent them off to ktierney@pacificlink.net. There was still no PM from him in the Eclectic Cafe, but to her utter surprise, there was one from saffire_21.

Hi there, sweetness!

So nice chatting with you and the girls this morning. I hope you had a great Pilates class. How very cool that you know about Snuffy and Planet Indigo and all those rockin' shows from when we were little! I miss those days, sometimes, don't you? When we were little and innocent and carefree? Oh well, how I blather on...have a good Saturday.

Ciao ciao ciao,

saffire

"Why doesn't she share her first name, like the rest of us?" Cara cried, pounding a fist on the desktop. Sophie's eyes opened wide at the sudden noise and her ears laid back. Cara looked down at the cat and laughed. "So sorry, kitty. Didn't mean to scare you. It's just...all this mysterious shit is really starting to annoy me."

A sharp ding of incoming mail turned Cara's head back to the computer screen. "Kevin Tierney! *There* you finally are." With a lightning-fast click, the message was opened.

Good afternoon, Ms. Cara

Thanks so much for the pictures! You seem to radiate a lot of joy.

Color me the guy who's never satisfied...but now that I've seen what you look like, I would absolutely LOVE to hear your voice! Would you like to talk on the phone sometime? Are you down with that? I have tons of anytime minutes, so I could call you. *Just let me know. :)*

Okay, back to the drawing board to finish up a project. You have yourself a wonderful Saturday. Hugs and more hugs,

~Kevin

Cara felt her heartbeat quicken. *He wants to call. Wow. Frannie was right—I wasn't even looking for anyone and here comes this California dude from out of nowhere!*

In the span of twenty seconds Cara hit reply, told Kevin that of *course* he could call, typed her phone number, then gave the SEND button a mighty thwack. She had no idea when he'd get the email, since he'd just gone "back to the drawing board," wherever that was. When her breath began to slow again, she rose from the computer, bent to give Sophie a stroke on the head, then walked into the living room.

"Oy!" she cried, realizing that the entire house needed a massive cleaning. But Cara didn't feel like housework after such a wonderful day of leisure. Glancing into the kitchen, she saw a mound of dishes staring ominously at her from the sink. Three days' worth, she calculated with horror. Deciding that dishes were the lesser of two evils, Cara donned yellow rubber gloves, found the soap wand, and turned on the hot water. Just as she reached for the first plate, the phone's ring pierced the silence of the house. Her head turned sharply. *No way! Could that really be Kevin, calling so soon?*

The phone rang again.

Cara slammed one hand on the faucet and hurriedly peeled the gloves from her hands. She made it to the phone on its fourth ring and, in the sexiest voice she could muster, answered, "Hello?"

"Is this Moonflower?" asked an affable male voice.

Cara's heart melted at the sound of its youthful, "boy next door" quality. There was also a familiarity about it, like that of an old friend calling after years of separation. "It *is,*" she replied, unable to hide the smile in her voice. "And this must be cali4nyapix!"

"The one and only."

Cara just stood there holding the phone and grinning like a fool.

"How are you doing on this fine Saturday? Or… *is* it fine?" he asked with a sheepish laugh. "It's probably cold and snowy, right?"

Cara found her voice at last. "Well, it's cold but the snow's mostly melted. It feels like spring might come a little early this year. I actually heard a robin this morning."

"Wow, those birds are a sure sign of spring where you live, right?"

"They used to be, but the weather patterns are so unpredictable these days…spring might come and go several times before May, and it's only early March. Why don't you tell me about *your* weather, so I can at least pretend to feel warm."

"Santa Barbara, believe it or not, is cloudy and chilly right now."

"Get out!"

"Yeah, I mean, this isn't the tropics. Our winters have a lot of rainy, cloudy days. I love it."

"You wouldn't love it if you had it for four straight months!" Cara chided. "And oh my God, are we actually talking about the *weather?* How cliché is that?"

She heard an impish chuckle on his end. Something about the way Kevin spoke—a calm, unhurried and caring tone—reminded her of some celebrity's voice she couldn't quite put her finger on. There was a slight pause as both of them thought of what to say next.

"So," Kevin continued, "your voice is very endearing. It sounds exactly how I imagined it would."

Cara's smile brightened by a few hundred kilowatts. "Does it?"

"Totally. And it's funny, because I've talked to other EC peeps on the phone and some of their voices don't match their online personas at all! The guys you'd expect to have deep, gruff voices have high-tenor, nasally voices and some that you'd expect to be all flowery and feminine are actually tough and tomboy-like."

Cara padded toward her couch. "I have to say, this is a first for me, talking with an Internet friend on the phone."

"It's so much nicer than typing, isn't it? It's one thing to see all the words someone uses to express themselves, but once you hear inflection and tone…it changes everything."

"It really does," she agreed. "So…which EC members have you talked with?"

Cara sank deep into the couch cushions as Kevin talked about some of their online friends and how many years they'd been hanging around the message boards. They discussed which ones they liked best, who made them laugh the hardest, and members they didn't trust. Somewhere in the middle of the conversation, she decided that Kevin Tierney's voice had such soothing qualities that she would be content to sit and listen to him read the dictionary. But who the hell did it remind her of?

"So I saw your post about going to a Pilates class today," he said, changing the subject. "Am I pronouncing that right? It's puh-lah-teez, not pie-luhts?"

Cara breathed a soft laugh. “Yeah, that’s it.”

“How was it?”

“Oh man, Kevin. You think you get punished by your *trainer.* Have you ever done Pilates?”

“No, no I haven’t. Pretty harsh, huh?”

“It was *incredibly* harsh, especially on my abs, but it made my entire body feel so strong and healthy afterward. Just like yoga does.”

“You do yoga too?”

“Sometimes.”

“It sounds like you’re a health and fitness kind of woman.”

“I am,” Cara confirmed, tugging at a strand of her hair and twirling it around and around her finger. “Part of that was inspired by you, Mr. Go To The Gym Every Morning At The Frickin’ Crack of Dawn. Although, there’s no way I could exert myself like that first thing in the morning.”

“Yeah, well, I tend to be a morning person. I’d rather get it over with early, so I have the rest of my day to get things done.”

“I’m a morning person against my will,” Cara grumped, “because I have a cat who steps all over me long before my alarm even goes off.”

“Oh, *tell* me about it. I’ve got two that start yowling for food at five o’clock sharp.”

“Oy!” Cara cried. “If Sophie ever tried anything earlier than six, I’d lock her out of my bedroom.”

Kevin laughed a quiet but engaging laugh that made Cara melt a little more. “See now, I couldn’t do that even if I wanted to. I *have* no bedroom door.”

Cara imagined a little bachelor pad by the ocean with palm trees swaying out front. “No bedroom door? Can’t you install one? I mean, you own the place, don’t you?”

Exaggerated laughter was his response.

“No?”

“Not only is the answer no, but *hell* no! These days, even the smallest cracker box of a house is half a million bucks. I feel a little hopeless about ever owning in this town.”

Cara put a hand to her heart, wide-eyed. “Half a million! Good lord, my cracker box was only fifty-two thousand when I bought it. Now it’s worth, oh, maybe seventy-seven.”

“Ha! Wow. I hate to tell you, but I don’t think a person could buy a garage for that amount in Santa Barbara.”

“Hm,” she mused, drawing one knee to her chest and wrapping an arm around it. “Amazing what warm, sunny weather and an ocean can do to real estate.”

"No shit."

Then it hit Cara like a lightning bolt. "Matt Damon!"

"Excuse me?"

"You sound like Matt Damon," Cara explained. "It's been driving me nuts trying to figure out who your voice reminds me of, and it just now came to me."

"Who even remembers what *Matt Damon* sounds like?" Kevin teased. "Jack Nicholson, yes. Al Pacino—*hoo-ah!* An extremely memorable voice. But Matt? Hell, he's so generic."

"I happen to like Matt Damon's voice!" she protested. "It's a nice blend of confident, caring, and sexy."

"Oh, well, if you put it that way…then I'll take it as a compliment."

Another long pause, but Cara could tell they were both smiling.

"So you have *two* cats?" she asked, recalling his comment from before.

"Yup. Renoir and Monet, named for two of my favorite Impressionist painters. But I call them Rennie and Mo for short."

"They're both male?"

Kevin snickered. "Actually, they're *female*."

"Female?!" she cried. "Named for male artists?"

"They're just cats. They don't know the difference."

"True."

"How about yours? Female?"

As if on cue, Sophie came stalking around the corner like a panther, shoulder blades moving up and down gracefully. She stopped in front of the couch and peered upward, negotiating the leap.

"Yes, and here she is now," Cara told him, patting the couch beside her.

Sophie's eyes continued to scan all available space above. Only after Cara ignored her and resumed talking again did the cat finally jump up, settle in, and begin a thorough grooming.

Kevin and Cara chatted on about their mutual appreciation of cats, the funny things their cats did, and what low maintenance pets they were.

"But there's a huge challenge in being a single cat person," Cara told him with an exasperated sigh.

Kevin sounded intrigued. "Do tell."

"It seems like everywhere I go, all the single guys are walking these big-ass dogs. I need to find a *cat* man. But cat men are hard to come by."

"I'm definitely a cat man. And man enough to admit it."

"Yes you are," she told him, her voice softening. "Too bad you're all the way across the country."

There was a brief silence. Cara heard Kevin let out a long breath. "Yeah, that blows, doesn't it? If you were here, I'd ask you out in a New York minute. I'd take you up to Lobo's for the best margarita you've ever tasted."

Cara's heart skipped two beats then came back with a thud like a cannon going off in her chest. Her first instinct was to react with sarcasm. "Are you sure about that? How do you know I'm not some high-maintenance princess or a creepy stalker, or…or a man posing as a woman?"

They shared a duet of laughter, then Kevin admitted in a serious tone, "I realize there is a great deal we don't actually know about each other, but what you say online rings genuine to me. I felt an affinity for you before I even got to know you, just from reading your compelling journals."

"*Aww…*" Cara uttered, unable to find an adequate response.

"Then when you sent your pictures, I thought, '*Oh my God!* She's even got looks to match that personality.'"

Cara dropped her head back against the couch cushion. Why was she feeling such resistance to all of Kevin's flattery? A tinge of sadness struck as she became acutely aware of the steel wall around her heart. Not enough time had passed since the Greg heartbreak. Her trust in men had not been fully restored.

"Well, thank you for the kind words, Mr. Tierney. You're a pretty fascinating man yourself. So now that we've established our little mutual admiration club, can we talk about something else? This is getting embarrassing."

"Absolutely," he quickly replied. "And hey, I didn't mean to make you uncomfortable. Sometimes stuff just flies out of my brain unedited. That's not always a good thing."

"Yeah, no, it's okay. I guess I'm just…" Cara ran a nervous hand through her hair. *Guarded? Are you actually going to admit that to him?* She cleared her throat. "Anyway…"

"Okay, we're talking about something else now, I swear. Anything you want. Hell, I'm just enjoying finally *talking* to you."

"I know what we can talk about," Cara brightened, lifting up her head again. "You said you were finishing up a project today. What are you working on?"

"I'm touching up photos of Big Sur for a layout."

"*Nice*. I've seen pictures of that place in a friend's slide show. It's stunning."

"I think everyone should travel up the Pacific Coast Highway at least once in their life."

"Santa Barbara's on that highway, right?"

"Yeah, it's on the 101, where the PCH merges with it for a stretch," he affirmed.

"What's Santa Barbara like?"

With a swell of pride in his voice, he replied, "It's a magical place. America's Riviera."

"That's a lovely name for it."

"It's one of the city's nicknames."

Cara cocked her head in curiosity. "Is it really that posh?"

"Have you ever seen pictures, my dear?"

"Hm…I'm not sure."

"You'd remember if you have. It's a gorgeous, Mediterranean-like town situated between the mountains and the ocean."

As he continued an enthusiastic description of his coastal town, Cara closed her eyes and tried to go there in her imagination. "Wow, that sounds so incredible, Kevin. I'll have to Google some Santa Barbara images later. And how perfect, having both the ocean *and* the mountains in one place."

"Both of which are completely novel to the Midwesterner, right?"

"Exactly." She scooted over an inch to make more room for Sophie, who had finished grooming and closed her eyes for a nap. Cara ran a hand down the silky fur and soon felt the familiar rumble of purring.

"So what are you up to this evening? Got any big plans?"

"No, I spent the entire day running around with my friend Frannie. I think I may just stay in tonight. It's not real motivating to venture out into the cold and dark."

"I'll bet."

"What about you? Any hot dates?" Cara's eyes squeezed shut. *What in the HELL ever possessed me to ask that? Please don't say yes.*

Kevin gave a cynical snort. "Who, me? All I do these days is putter around the house and mutter to myself."

"And to the cats?"

"And mutter to the cats—exactly."

Cara breathed a quiet sigh of relief as her smile returned. "Well, at least we both get a phone date tonight. I am having so much fun talking to you, Kevin."

"Me too, but I still wish we could hang out."

Cara imagined sitting across from Kevin in some outdoor café by the ocean. Waves pounded the shore in the background and seagulls shrieked overhead. It was a wonderful daydream, warming her all over as the chilly winter evening fell. She turned her head to look out the picture window and saw a bright star in the sky—or perhaps it was a planet. "Wow, Kevin, how long have we been talking? It's dark here."

"Let's see what my clock radio says..." there was a brief scuffling noise. "Holy crap, it's been nearly two hours!"

"Are you serious?" she cried, squinting to see her kitchen wall clock from where she sat.

He let loose another of his boyish laughs. "Marathon conversation, huh?"

"Especially for our first one!"

The two debated whether to wrap it up and sign off, but one farewell comment led to another and before they knew it they were knee-deep in discussion about their families.

"I have two sisters who are a lot older than me," Cara told him. "I'm the youngest, and what they call a menopause baby."

"What exactly does that mean?"

"Well, I was conceived when my mom was forty-seven and entering menopause. She was less cautious about birth control because she assumed that the 'baby factory' was closed for the season. But surprise! Along came baby Cara when she already had two teen-aged daughters."

"Yikes!"

"I *know!* It worked out great for me, though, because I pretty much had three moms who loved and doted over me. How about you, Kevin? Got any siblings?"

"I have a brother in San Francisco and a sister in L.A., neither of which I see very often. We all lead very different lives. My brother's a high-powered corporate attorney, and my sister is a former hippie who's into all kinds of New Agey, money-making schemes these days. We're a motley bunch."

"I guess so," Cara agreed. "Hippie chick, designer and suit."

"We sound like some reality show, don't we?"

After laughing over more family dynamics, they moved to the subject of careers.

Kevin admitted that he was getting burnt out from teaching Adult Ed, having done it for the last ten years. "I think this will be my last year. I'll miss the extra money, but I can always put that energy into doing more illustration work."

"At least you have an exit plan," Cara sighed. She proceeded to tell Kevin all about her editing job and how she too was reaching a point of stagnation, but didn't know what changes to make.

"What about your writing?" he asked her. "Maybe there are other things you can do with that outside of your job."

"I sometimes write features for the local free paper. And Frannie thinks I should do freelance work from home. But neither of those would be steady enough to pay the bills. I need something a little more lucrative."

"Well," he said with a voice full of encouragement, "it sounds like an attainable dream to me. If anyone can make it happen, you can."

Cara sat a little taller on the couch and smiled. "*Thank* you for that vote of confidence."

The next lull in conversation induced a long sigh from Kevin. "Well, Moonflower, it's time for me to run some errands downtown before things close. But I have *really* enjoyed talking with you. Can we do this again soon?"

"Absolutely we can!" Cara felt her heart rate quicken once more. "This is so cool, Kevin, I feel like I've been gifted with a wonderful new friend that I wasn't even looking for."

"Aww…well, so do I."

"Have a good rest of your weekend."

"You do the same."

They said goodbye simultaneously, laughed, and hung up.

Cara sat holding the portable phone and staring into space. Her mind did a few rewinds back to the best parts of their conversation. The ones that made her heart feel alive again. Finally, she let out a long exhale and absently stroked her cat's head. Sophie, who'd entered a deep sleep, jumped at the sudden contact and uttered a *brr* of sleepy acknowledgement.

"Sorry," she told the cat with another ruffling of the fur on her head. "Didn't mean to wake you."

Sophie lay her head back down on daintily crossed paws.

"I've got a new guy in my life," Cara informed her with a wondrous grin.

Tolerating yet another interruption, the cat raised her head.

"He's just a friend," Cara quickly added, but even after saying the words out loud she still could not shake the nagging suspicion that Kevin Tierney would play a much more significant role in her life.

Chapter 11

"What are you up to this afternoon?" asked the cheery voice of Seth Kane.

Cara surveyed the fallen timber in her suburban backyard—a few branches here, a smattering of sticks there—nothing unmanageable. She replied into her cell phone, "I'm about to launch into some minor yard work."

"Oh crap, should I let you go?" he asked quickly.

"I can talk for a little while."

"Good, because I haven't seen you on the boards in awhile and wondered how you were."

"That's really sweet of you," Cara said with a smile. "I guess I haven't been online as much now that spring is here…" she broke off with a deep inhale. "Oh my *God* I love that smell!"

"What smell?"

"The smell of thawed earth in springtime, waking up from its long winter nap. There's nothing in the world like it."

"That is definitely a good smell," he agreed. "I should take the kids out to a park and let them romp. They could use the fresh air."

Cara stepped into the sunlight. "I'm looking at the new patches of green dotting the soggy brown grass, and they remind me of the uneven spots on a giraffe's fur."

"Heh. *That's* imaginative. Spoken like a true writer."

Cara stooped to examine a few tender blades. "I should enjoy these 'giraffe patches' now, because in about two weeks this grass will be out of control."

"And the season of never-ending lawn mowing will commence," Seth grumbled. "You know, that's one thing I don't miss about being in our old house. Now I just watch the condo maintenance guys cut my grass and go, '*Ha*-ha!'"

Cara turned and cast a reflective gaze on the pale blue ranch that had been home for over a decade. "I hear ya, Seth. For years I've been muddling through the love-hate relationship of home owning. I guess the love part—feeling extremely proud of an investment I've managed since age twenty-five—is what makes it all worth it."

"Wow, you've owned that long?"

"I know, right? It feels like eons since I sat at the closing with a trembling hand, signing all that paperwork and thinking, 'My God, what am I doing?'"

Seth laughed. "Ah yes, I remember that day as well. So what's the hate part?"

Cara's smile slowly faded. Talking about it caused more than a little shame, even with Seth. "Well, it's having done everything by myself for twelve damn years. I fully expected there to be a husband and kid in the picture by now. So sure, in fact, that I bought a four-door Toyota with easy access for car seats. Things haven't gone according to plan at *all*."

She took another long look at the house, which seemed to stand as a symbol of failure. Three lovers had come and gone within its walls. Each one transformed the place into a cozy love nest when they arrived, then left it a little colder and emptier when they went away. The ghosts lurking in every corner were suddenly outweighing the reasons to stay, so Cara thought seriously of renting the place out and starting over in a condo.

"Believe me, I know all about things not going according to plan," was Seth's somber reply. "I don't know which is worse; having a house without a mate, or having both and then losing them."

Cara sighed. "Wow, now there's a thought provoker. How long has it been since your divorce?"

"About a year and a half. But it's all good. With hindsight, I know it was probably the best move we could've made before things got really ugly."

"That bad, huh?"

"A word of advice, Cara. When you choose someone for life, make sure you fall in love with and accept who they truly are. Not some projection of who you *think* they are, or who they might potentially be if you just love them enough."

"I wish someone would've told Greg that," she muttered. "Sometimes I wonder if he really knew me at all. Anyway, I'm giving the 'for life' thing a rest right now. I'd be happy just to find someone who's single and available around here. At our age, they're a little harder to find."

"I have one word for you. *MySpace*."

Cara thought of Kevin and all the wonderful conversations they'd been having on the phone every night. Was it any wonder she wasn't out looking for a date these days? "Naw, that's not how I want to meet someone."

"Why not? It's a great way to screen people without joining some bogus dating site. I've met lots of nice women on MySpace. And Facebook, too."

"Thank you, no. I spend way too much time online as it is."

"Well, suit yourself then. Hey, listen, I should probably get the rats out of bed and let you start your yard work. It was great talking with you, Cara-love! Don't be a stranger."

"Okay, Seth. Thanks for calling."

After shoving her cell phone into a pocket, Cara tilted her face toward the sun and closed her eyes. It felt warm and soothing again after all those winter months. She sang the first verse of The Beatles' "Here Comes the Sun" softly to herself.

Bird choruses accompanied her at full volume from the treetops. Two yards down, a dog barked. From the block behind her, little boys in the midst of a raucous game of ball cried, "Throw it here! THROW IT HERE, Riley!"

Cara smiled, opened her eyes, and studied the house once more. Before sticking a For Rent sign out front, there was lots of work to be done. The first task on the list was clearing the yard of winter storm debris.

She worked diligently, gathering up sticks of all sizes and scowling at the odd pile of poop that a marauding dog had deposited while she was gone. Just as she was throwing the last armful of branches on her brush pile, the cell phone rang in her pocket. She wiped one hand on her jeans before digging it out and flipping it open. "Hello?"

"How is the fair Moonflower today?"

Cara felt an automatic smile light up her face. "Good morning, Kevin. Moonflower is *very* well, thank you. I'm standing in the spring sunshine and finishing up some yard work. What are *you* up to?"

There was a tinge of weariness in his voice as he replied, "Oh, being driven insane by an illustration project that's kicking my ass. So I figured it was a good time for a Cara break."

"Awww," she cooed, tilting her head to one side. "I'm so glad you thought of me. But why are you working on a Saturday morning?"

"I know, right? I had so many deadlines this week that it was a necessary evil."

"I guess it's good you're that busy, eh?"

"Yes it is. And that's what I keep telling myself every time I'm tempted to go out for a beach walk."

"Oh hell, go on the beach walk! That's what I'd do if I were there."

"Would you?"

Cara reached down and massaged one of her legs. "Yes I would. I'm in need of a break, myself. This business of bending over and picking up sticks has worn out the old knees and hamstrings."

"I'll bet it's a rewarding sort of pain, though."

"What do you mean?"

"Well, I'm thinking it must be the most satisfying feeling to take care of a piece of property. To sculpt a yard into whatever design you want, and all the while knowing it's *yours*. I really wish I had a yard."

"So you've told me," she said, shaking a stray piece of dried mud from her arm. She walked toward her side door, scowling up at a section of gutter that was coming loose from the house. "If it's any consolation to you, Kevin, home owning isn't a cakewalk. It's hard work! Especially if you're doing it all by yourself. I'm seriously thinking of moving out of mine soon."

"What?" he cried. "And give up that investment?"

Cara let herself into the house and immediately removed her muddy gym shoes in the service porch. Sophie came trotting over to sniff them. "I'm not exactly giving it up, Kevin. I'm going to rent the place out and move into something smaller and more manageable, like a townhouse. I'm tired of the upkeep and…" she hesitated, debating whether or not to share her sob story again. Was there a way to explain without sounding like a total failure at relationships? "Well, let's just say that there are too many Ghosts of Relationships Past hanging around here. I want to go someplace where I can start over again, with fresh memories."

There was a thoughtful silence on Kevin's end as he mulled over her response. Then she heard a small chuckle. "Man, you're trying to shake up your whole world, aren't you? You want a new job and now a new place to live! Sounds like you're in the market for a radical reinvention of the self."

Cara jutted an emphatic hand in the air. "That is *exactly* what I need. Man, I know I've been whining about this for the last month, but stagnation is seriously choking the life out of me. The time has come to do something about it—either find a new place to live or a new place to work. Or both."

"Last time I felt that way, I found myself in Colorado."

Cara held the phone with one hand and attempted to wash the other in her kitchen sink. "No kidding?"

"Yeah, I just hitchhiked over there one winter and got a job at a ski resort. Thought it might be a nice change of pace."

"When did you do that?"

"Oh, back when I was about twenty years old."

"Wow, that young?" Cara made an awkward attempt at drying her wet hand on a dishtowel without using her cell phone hand. "That's pretty adventurous to just set out with nothing…not even a car!"

"I've done some crazy shit," Kevin admitted. "If you knew the half of it, I wonder if you'd even be associating with me."

Cara cocked an eyebrow. "Oh, *really?*"

"Yeah, but I was young and stupid. And those are stories for another time."

"Well," Cara switched the phone to her clean hand and stuck the other under the faucet, "just as long as you don't have any bodies buried in your backyard."

"Ha-ha! My backyard is a public beach, and the only dead bodies down there are the occasional washed up dolphin or seal."

"You live on the beach?" she cried, realizing that her premonition had been correct.

"It's nothing fancy…but yes."

"You lucky bastard!"

Copious laughter came from Kevin's end of the line.

Cara grinned as she dried her other hand, then knelt and stroked Sophie's head. "So what is this illustration project that's kicking your ass?"

Kevin let out a long, vocal sigh. "It's a website for a local radio station, and they keep changing their minds about what they want. I spend all this time doing one thing, then they decide to do something else….and of course the deadline is Monday. Good thing I'm charging for time spent on the project, that's all I can say."

"Yeah, that'll teach 'em."

"But damn it, what I really wanted to do this morning was finish a charcoal figure drawing I started so I can get it into a gallery show in May."

"Do you show your pieces in galleries very often?" Cara stood up again and leaned against the kitchen counter.

"I've had a few shows here and there," he told her, nonchalantly. "Nothing groundbreaking."

Cara began to see the jigsaw pieces of Kevin's life form a picture. He seemed to have several irons in the fire when it came to his work, but what about a social life? Did he spend most of his time online instead of in the "3-D world" as Frannie called it? This prompted her next question. "So, have you been in Planet Indigo today? Did anything big happen?"

"I went in this morning, briefly," he replied. "All the usual suspects were there, and—" Kevin gave a snort, "—*Not_Morrissey* was actually in there! On a Saturday!"

"Oh my God, he's never in there on Saturdays!"

"I know! And he was giving saffire a bunch of shit. They were cracking me up. I love it when those two go at it, because saffire can really dish it back to him. Feisty redheads are good for that."

Cara's smile faded. "Kevin, how do you know she has red hair? Has she ever posted an avatar of herself?"

"No, but she's often referred to herself as a feisty redhead."

Cara was motionless, phone pressed to her ear. An image of Arianna's fiery red hair filled her mind's eye, adding to the list of freaky coincidences between her niece and saffire_21.

"Cara? Hello?"

Cara shook her head and responded quickly, "I'm here. Sorry."

"I thought maybe our call dropped."

"No, I was just…I'm really mystified by saffire, Kevin. I've talked with Seth, and he affirmed that she's an extremely private person who people don't know much about. What do *you* know about her?"

"Well, I've talked with her on the phone a couple of times."

Cara's eyes widened. "You have?"

"She called me once when I was having a rough week. We both have similar funks, sometimes, although I think hers are more clinical."

"Yeah, Seth told me she had some mental issues going on." Cara absently pointed a toe and moved her foot around in ballet-like swishes on the floor. "So, what does she sound like?"

"She's got a very unique and memorable voice. It's sort of husky like Demi Moore's."

Cara's foot froze in the middle of her rond de jambe. Arianna had that same type of voice from the time she was a little girl. "Has she ever told you where she lives?"

"Are you kidding? Saffire never gives that up to *anyone*. She even uses a blocked cell number. We just respect her anonymity, and we don't ask. But Astrea—you know, StarAngel—she thinks saffire might actually be working out here in California."

Cara put a hand over her chest, subconsciously trying to stop the arrhythmic heartbeats that were beginning to hurt. "Wh—what makes Astrea think that?"

"Well, saffire apparently mentioned working in the tasting room of a winery. She kind of let that slip, once."

"But there are wineries all over the country, you know? What makes her think it was California, specifically."

"I think there was something else saffire said that sort of pointed to California, but I forget what. You'll have to ask Astrea."

Cara's head was reeling with questions. Could Arianna actually be alive and living in California? Ever since vacationing there as teens, her niece had always vowed to move to the Golden State when she grew up. But Arianna had moved to England instead. She'd died in England, and come back in a small black urn. Had news of her death been some sort of mistake? A mix-up in the coroner's records? Or even—staged?

Chapter 12

Cara hurried to the den, Sophie following closely at her heels, and tucked one foot beneath her as she plopped into the computer chair and logged on to the Eclectic Café. She'd felt slightly guilty for rushing Kevin off the phone, but he had to get back to his project anyway, so there was no harm done. Upon entering Planet Indigo, she found that the forum had been inactive for the last two hours. This was typical of Saturdays, when everyone was out enjoying their weekends. "Okay then," she said out loud. "Time for a little cyber-stalking."

Cara went into the Members section of the Eclectic Café and did a search on saffire_21. When saffire's profile came up, she hit the *Show Forum Posts* option, which listed a history of posts made by the user. Cara saw the battle of wits between saffire and Not_Morrissey that Kevin spoke of, and giggled. She scrolled back even further and skimmed down the page.

saffire_21: *I was telling Kevin earlier, I slept a full ten hours for the first time in ages and boy do I feel good!*

saffire_21: *Good to see you too, Astreababy! Have fun at the herb farm!*

saffire_21: *OMG! I love, love LOVE Ottmar Liebert! It's about time they play some of him in the Cafe!*

Cara's eyes fixed on the post. "Good God, there's another one."

Arianna was the one who'd turned Cara on to the flamenco guitarist years ago, sending several compilation CDs of his music. They'd even played one of his pieces at Ari's funeral. Shaking her head, she read the first few posts saffire had made that morning.

saffire_21: *Man, Kevin, you got up at the butt-crack of dawn! How do you DO it? This Princess Hineybutt slept from eleven until nine! But I really needed it, believe me. It's been a rough week.*

"Oh, wow," Cara whispered. She sprung from the chair, ran to the storage closet and flung open its door. On the top shelf was a large plastic bin of old letters and keepsakes. Standing on tiptoe, she gripped the container and pulled it out inch by inch until it toppled over the edge and into her arms. Then she eased it to the floor, peeled off the lid, and rifled through its contents until she unearthed the bound pile of letters marked *Arianna – 1999*.

Sitting cross-legged on the floor, Cara opened and skimmed through each one until she found what she was looking for.

Cara,

Sorry it's been so long since I've written. When I got back from Brazil, my sleep schedule was all screwed up, which caused me to get sick. So I laid in bed a lot for the last few weeks. I felt like Princess Hineybutt again! But today I got up at the butt-crack of dawn and decided to catch up on things. Correspondence was one of them....

Cara sat with the letter dangling from her hand, trying to reason her way out of this newest bizarre coincidence. Princess Hineybutt was the name Melanie had given teen-aged Arianna when she used to sleep too late on Saturday mornings and skip out on chores. Although Cara had heard people use the term "butt-crack of dawn," no one had ever used the inside nickname of Princess Hineybutt. Who else in the world could possibly know about Princess Hineybutt?

Scrambling to her feet, Cara ran for the phone and speed-dialed Jenn. After three rings, Liam's deep voice answered, "Hello?"

"Liam! Is Jenn there?"

"Well hi there, Miss Cara. How goes your Saturday?"

Cara's voice grew more urgent. "Okay so far. Is she there?"

"Yeah, yeah, I'll get her...everything okay?"

"I don't know," Cara breathed.

In a few seconds, Jenn's voice came on. "Cara, what's wrong?"

"Jenn, I've got something huge to talk to you about. Huge with a capital H. Can I come over?"

After an apprehensive pause, her sister replied, "Well sure, Cara, come on over. Are you okay?"

"Yeah, I'm all right, but brace yourself for something very, very weird."

* * *

"What's this place again? A chat room?"

Cara sat at the opposite end of the couch trying to will away the trembling in her body that hadn't stopped since she'd left home. Telling her sister the whole unbelievable story of saffire_21 had been more difficult than she thought, especially with Jenn's unyielding and wary expression that seemed to say, *Girl, have you gone off the deep end?*

"No, not a chat room. It's the message boards of an online radio station."

Jenn studied the couch cushions for a speechless moment, then looked up at Cara. "You're right. Those things the girl said are too specific to be coincidences...but yet, how could it *possibly* be Arianna?"

"Maybe she didn't die after all, Jenn."

"What? That's absolutely crazy. There was a signed death certificate. Her body was found at the lake house."

"Or so her husband told us," Cara said, leaning forward and placing a hand on her sister's knee. "Those remains could've been someone else's."

Jenn frowned. "Why would Arianna's own husband lie about her *death,* Cara?"

"Well, how much did we really know about that guy or his sense of ethics? We always did suspect that their marriage was a sham for green card purposes. If they were merely friends and Arianna decided she wanted to disappear—which was not unusual for her—it's possible he could've helped out. It was a strange-ass situation from the get go."

"You mean the coroner's report?"

The two stared at each other in grim silence. No one in their family ever liked to recount the details of how Arianna's unrecognizable remains were found by a lake, weeks after her death. Although many clues pointed to her identity—a wedding ring, clothing, empty prescription bottles inside the cabin, and her car parked in the drive—the one piece of evidence that British authorities needed had been destroyed years ago when their family dentist's office had burned to the ground. No dental matches could be made for a positive identification, but they ruled the case a suicide based on Arianna's history of depression and her friends' eyewitness accounts of recent erratic mental behavior.

Jenn covered her mouth with a clenched fist and tried to make the memories dissipate by squeezing her eyes closed. "Whose body was it, then?"

"Believe me, Jenn, I've gone over it a million times, borrowing ideas from all the weird movies and forensic TV shows I've ever seen about stuff like this. Maybe someone she knew overdosed, enabling her to trade identities. Or perhaps it was some unidentifiable homeless person who OD'd by the lake and they planted all the evidence with the body."

Jenn shook her head. "This is just so insane that I can't even begin to wrap my brain around the possibility of it."

"I know. But things like this *can* happen. If we spoke with Arianna's husband, he might have some answers."

"What the hell was that guy's name? I can't even remember! Is Melanie still in touch with him?"

"I don't know," Cara sighed, sitting back in her seat. "That's why I'm here. Before I even think about bringing this up to Melanie, which I'm terrified of doing, I wanted to process it with you first. Find out how to handle things appropriately, without causing any sort of relapse." She cringed as she remembered the many months their sister had withdrawn from everyone, gaunt and thin, trying to cope with the death of her only child.

Jenn thrust out a hand in the *stop* gesture. "No, for God's sake don't say a word to Melanie!"

"What about Tom?"

Jenn curled an index finger and put it to her mouth in consideration. Tom was Melanie's ex-husband and father of Arianna who lived in the nearby college town of Oxford, Ohio. He hadn't kept up much contact with the family since the funeral. She shook her head and answered, "I don't know about Tom. He'd really think we were nuts."

"Yeah, you're probably right," Cara agreed. "If we only knew where that so-called husband is living, we could have him questioned by the authorities."

Jenn gave an incredulous snort. "On what grounds? Just from some posts in a chat room? Did you even keep copies of them?"

"Message boards," corrected Cara, with slight irritation in her voice. "And no, but the posts are still there. I'd just have to do lots of back scrolling to get to them. Then we could contact the London coroner's office and have them re-check Arianna's file."

A pained expression spread slowly over Jenn's face. "Why would she do it, Cara? Why would Ari fake her own death?"

Cara shrugged. "Arianna wasn't a happy woman. She was extremely reclusive toward the end. So it isn't all that crazy to think she might've wanted to just disappear."

Jenn absently traced a finger around a sunny spot on the green velvet between them. Then she looked up at Cara with narrowed eyes. "How could she do something so cruel to Melanie and Tom? I mean, leading your poor parents to believe you're dead? Even Arianna wouldn't have been that heartless. She could've just as easily run away, broken contact and disappeared. It's a pretty elaborate thing to fake your own death."

"But if there's a death, then no one comes looking." Cara felt more ridiculous by the minute. She let out a long breath. "You know, you're right. This is all too impossible. It's probably just the world's longest string of bizarre coincidences. Maybe I should just forget all about it and get on with life."

Jenn put an emphatic hand on Cara's knee. "But...Princess Hineybutt."

The two sisters stared at each other for a long while.

"I still have Tom's number," Jenn said, finally. "I'll call him tonight and see if he has any info about Arianna's husband. In the meantime, see if you can get this saffire chick to give up her name or picture or something."

"Well," Cara said doubtfully, "it's never been achieved by anyone else in the Eclectic Café, but I'll certainly give it a try. Or maybe I could just ask her."

"Ask her what?"

"Ask her if she's Arianna."

Chapter 13

saffire_21: *Moon, darling, everyone knows I don't do pictures!*  *Besides, I haven't seen YOURS in here, yet! Have you ever posted it?*

Cara glanced at her cubicle door to see if anyone was watching. The office had been crazy-busy with deadlines from the minute she'd walked in that morning, and the last thing she needed was to get caught playing on the Internet. She hurriedly typed a reply to saffire, whose rare presence in Planet Indigo was too important to miss.

Moonflower: *I did post a long shot of myself once, taken in a garden at a local arboretum. Maybe you weren't around that day.*

While Cara waited for a reply, the sudden and piercing ring of her desk phone made her jump. She reached out and picked it up. "Cara Shannon speaking."

"How's the final pass going?" the abrupt voice of her team leader asked.

"Almost done," Cara lied, glancing over at the partially completed pages that had been placed on her desk a half hour earlier.

"It needs to ship by one o'clock."

"No problem," Cara replied, refreshing the computer screen and looking for saffire's post. "I'll bring it over as soon as it's done."

With her team leader appeased, she hung up and found what she was looking for.

saffire_21: *Hm, I guess I didn't see the picture. You should post it again. Maybe one of these days I'll show ya something, but only because I like you.*

Cara's mouth fell open. "Damn. That was easy." She typed one more post.

Moonflower: *Well good, because I want to see why everyone calls you a feisty redhead! But now I must enter lurk mode. I have a 1:00 deadline!*

After hitting SEND, Cara logged completely out of the Eclectic Café, lest she be tempted to linger or peek in again. Then she turned once more to the pending publication on her desk—a pictorial book about Appalachia—that was part of a social studies series on the regions of the United States. She leaned over it in utter concentration, chin resting on hand, admiring page after page of rich photography taken along sections of the Blue Ridge Parkway.

In the midst of her editing, a flash of inspiration hit. *What a perfect idea for my book! A pictorial travelogue on the Blue Ridge Parkway or some other scenic place. Just travel along, record everything I see in a journal, recommend places to eat and sleep, take some high quality photos, and voila! A marketable, "coffee table" book. Although, it's probably been done before...but maybe I could put some new twist on it.* Cara stored the idea somewhere in the recesses of her mind and kept reading. Even when her stomach began to grumble, she pressed on and worked through lunch until the last page was complete.

After ridding herself of one deadline, Cara went back to her desk to face the next looming project. It was a "hair on fire" kind of day, as Frannie liked to call it, so Planet Indigo and any responses from saffire_21 had to wait until Cara got home that evening.

* * *

With a plate of crab alfredo linguine balanced in her lap, Cara nibbled on dinner while searching for saffire's posts in the Eclectic Café. The last entry she'd made, as expected, was saffire's final comment to Cara that afternoon.

"Of course she didn't come back online," Cara huffed, backing out of the profile and entering the forums. "And we probably won't see her again until next frickin' *month!*"

Her scowl quickly melted away when she saw Kevin in Planet Indigo.

Moonflower: *Hey you! How was your day? Did you get the illustration project done?*

In another minute, his reply appeared.

cali4nyapix: *Well hello there, Cara mia! Yes! All done, and finally back to the drawing again. Thanks for asking. How was YOUR day?*

The ding of an incoming email prompted her to put the Eclectic Café in the background and click over to her inbox. It was from Jenn.

Subject: **Talked to Tom**

The words sent a chill down Cara's spine as she opened the message.

Cara,

I called Tom and he still has the contact information for Arianna's husband. The guy's name is Colin Huxby, and his address and phone number are in this forwarded email from Tom. Of course Tom wondered why we wanted to get in touch with Huxby, so I lied, saying that we just wanted to know how he was doing these days. If you decide to contact Colin, let me know what you find out.

Your partner in this insanity,

Jenn

As Cara skimmed through Tom's email, her mind launched an internal debate. If she called this Huxby guy, would the number still be a current one? And was there any sense in contacting him, if he did indeed help Arianna fake her own death? It would be grounds for arrest, after all, so he'd never admit to anything. Perhaps it was smarter to simply contact British authorities and deal with Huxby later.

Absently, Cara refreshed her Planet Indigo screen and saw that saffire had entered the forum with a brand new avatar. "What the hell *is* it?" She leaned closer to the monitor, squinting. After a few seconds, she realized it was an extreme close-up of an ear with a dainty earring dangling from it. A strand of red hair was tucked behind. "Is that your idea of posting a picture of yourself? Come *on!*"

Cara put her plate on the floor and typed a quick hello to everyone.

saffire_21: *Oh good, you're here! How do you like my av? It's really me!*

Cara rolled her eyes, shook her head with a long suffering sigh, and peered again at the picture. Zeroing in on the tiny earring, her eyes widened. "Wait a second…"

She typed her next post so furiously that she kept making mistakes and having to backspace.

Moonflower: *saffire, is that a pewter hummingbird earring?*

Amidst the others' posts—saying how cute saffire's ear looked and how they were glad to at least see *part* of her—was her reply to Cara.

saffire_21: *Yes it is! It was a gift from someone very special to me.*

"Oh, Ari!" Cara wailed. "It's you! I *know* it's you!"

Chapter 14

The earring in saffire's avatar was an identical match to one of a pair that Cara had sent Arianna for what would be her last birthday on earth. The hummingbird was in the very same position, with wings spread upward. Tears brimmed in Cara's eyes as she opened her file of digital images and selected a close-up of herself. She hurriedly sized it to the correct dimensions for an avatar, then uploaded it into her Eclectic Café profile. Once it was showing on the boards, she wiped tears from her face and typed a private message to saffire_21. This time, Cara was going for broke.

Arianna, is that YOU? This is Cara! Look at my avatar! Please let me know that you're okay!

After hitting SEND, she went back to the boards and waited. She waited through all the posts from other users telling her that she looked beautiful, and why hadn't she posted a close-up of her face sooner? Sniffing, Cara crossed her arms and kept her eye on the red bolded print that would appear with a new PM, but nothing happened. Five minutes passed, then ten. She watched dismally as post after post went by, and not a one of them from saffire.

Not_Morrissey: *Did saffire leave already? I was just getting ready to serve her up a new can of whoopass tonight! Dammit!*

GreatScott: *Dude, it's* saffire! *Did you actually think she'd stay for more than five minutes?*

smk02: *Those hummingbird earrings were SO apropos for her…always flitting in and out of here like she does.*

BloominElle: *I didn't even get to say hello this time!*

Bellybutton: *Yeah, not even one nummie! WTF? Is she PM-ing anyone right now?*

Cara buried her face in her hands. The fact that saffire hadn't fired back a *what the hell are you talking about?* PM said everything. Saffire was Arianna. She had no doubt in her mind, now. There was no need to call Colin Huxby or the British authorities. And "saffire" would probably never come back again, unless it was under a different identity. Her worst nightmare had finally happened. She'd been exposed.

The phone rang in the living room, raising Cara's head. *Dear God. Would Arianna actually call? Does she even have my current number?* She sprung from her seat and got to it on the fourth ring, just before her answering machine kicked in, and answered breathlessly, "Hello?"

"Where did you go?" asked Kevin. "Did you see my two posts to you?"

Cara sniffed, cleared her throat and tried to make her voice normal again as she padded back to the den. "Hey, Kevin. I'm really sorry. Something…something really funky is going on."

"What's up?" he asked, his voice softening with concern.

Cara sat down at the computer and did one more scan for any sign of saffire on the boards. "This is really unbelievable, okay? Be forewarned. I mean, it sounds like something straight out of a movie."

Curiosity crept into Kevin's voice. "Wow…okay."

"I had a niece who allegedly died about seven years ago, and her name was Arianna. She was almost twenty-seven years old."

"Oh Cara, I'm so sorry to hear…wait a minute, did you say *allegedly* died?"

"Yes, and it's because I have reason to believe …" Cara hesitated, then let out a nervous breath. "…that Arianna is saffire_21."

There was a long silence. Cara heard Kevin's stereo playing in the background—an older REM song, from the garbled Rickenbacker chords that she could make out. "Are you *serious?*"

"I'm dead serious."

"But how…what…?"

With a sudden sense of calm, Cara told him about all the parallels, right down to Princess Hineybutt. It felt good to finally tell someone from the EC.

"Man," was all Kevin could say when she finished. "That's pretty wild."

"My sister Jenn and I have run through the logic of everything several times. How could Arianna possibly fake her own death, right? We're checking into it and contacting all the people who were involved with her back then. Trying to fit the pieces together and solve the mystery. But Kevin, there isn't a doubt in my mind that it's her. She hasn't made one post since I put my face in my avatar and confronted her!"

"Yeah, everyone was noticing her abrupt disappearance."

"I would really like to talk with Astrea about the whole saffire-working-in-a-winery thing. I wonder if she'd be willing to give me her phone number."

"I've got her phone number," Kevin said.

"Do you think she'd mind if you gave it to me?"

"Oh no, I don't think she'd mind at all," he replied. "Astrea is the nicest, most laid back woman I've ever met."

Cara felt an unexpected sting of envy, then immediately judged herself for it. *He's not yours, Cara. You only talk on the phone. Even if he does seem to fawn over you a lot, he still has every right to compliment other women.* Shaking it off, she replied, "Well, thanks. I have a feeling she could really be of help, living so close to the wineries."

"We both live close to them, Cara. Wine country stretches from here all the way to Napa Valley."

"Have you been to many tasting rooms in your area?"

"I've been to some."

"Are the owners pretty cooperative? I mean, do you think if I sent Arianna's photograph to some of them, they'd be able to tell me if she's an employee? Or would they not give out such information?"

"Well, if you had the authorities assist you, the wineries would definitely cooperate. But Cara, what if your niece doesn't want to be found?"

"What?"

"If she went to such lengths to disappear, then maybe it's for a good reason. I'm just saying..."

"Kevin, how could we *not* look for her? If it were your niece, wouldn't you?"

He let out a slow, thoughtful breath, "I would most definitely look. I was just playing the devil's advocate for her, I guess. I didn't mean to offend."

"You didn't. It's okay."

"I'm still trying to grasp the concept of saffire being your niece, let alone such an enigma in the EC."

"Yeah, and you've actually *spoken* with her. If only I could tap into your brain and hear your memory of her voice on the phone. Then I'd know for sure if she was Arianna, because her voice was one of a kind."

"Well, after talking with her, I know she's definitely a one-of-a-kind woman."

"Did she sound like she was doing okay? I mean, I know you said you were both in a funk, but the other times you talked with her...?"

"She was fine, Cara. Pretty irreverently funny, as I recall, talking about the weird things people do that she can't understand. She's got lots of resistance to authority and her family and *stupid, fucking unaware people*, as she always put it." Kevin chuckled at his recollections. "She was, in every sense, a feisty redhead."

"So was Arianna," Cara marveled. "And then some."

A long pause followed.

"Well, so what will you do now? Come out here and start a search for her? California's a big state."

She let out the heaviest of sighs. "I really want to, just to put my mind at rest. But I need some time to plan it out and research the wineries first. God, just hearing myself say all this feels really crazy!"

"I'm sure it does," he agreed. "It's a lot to wrap your brain around, so if there's anything I can do to help…"

"Aw, Kevin," Cara told him, putting a hand to her heart, "you're the *best*. I'll start by calling Astrea, and then take it from there."

After Kevin retrieved the phone number for her, Cara said goodbye to him for the night and hung up. Then she thought about alerting Jenn to the latest discovery. *Once she finds out about the hummingbird earring, all bets are off. Hell, she might even go to California with me!*

Before making the call, she went back into the EC and brought up saffire_21's profile. It was time to dig up all the "evidence" over the last few months and print it out. But something was wrong…things didn't look right. With more than a little trepidation, Cara brought up the oldest post in saffire's entire history and gasped. "You have got to be fucking *kidding* me."

Chapter 15

"They're gone!"

Jenn's face filled with alarm at the sight of her distraught sister standing in the pouring rain. "What's gone?"

Drops splattered on the top of Cara's raincoat hood—which made her face appear recessed in a shadowy cave—and dripped over the edge. Her voice cracked as she replied, "Saffire's posts on the message boards! We don't have a leg to stand on, Jenn."

"Well get in here out of the rain," Jenn commanded, holding the door open so Cara could enter.

With her wet coat removed and a comfy seat secured on the green velvet couch, Cara unloaded the story she'd been obsessing about the entire workday.

"I *thought* all the old posts were still buried in the cumulative pages of Planet Indigo," Cara explained, "but when I did a search last night, I found that a good-sized chunk of them had disappeared. I asked Seth, one of my online friends, what was going on and he told me there was some sort of server crash the other night. When the system administrator brought it back up again, he only reinstated half of the site content. I don't know if it was lost or purposely deleted." Cara's eyes filled with tears. "The only evidence we ever had is gone, and we can't really enlist the help of the authorities without it."

Jenn's brow creased. "Every single conversation is gone? What about Princess Hineybutt? That was fairly recent."

"Princess Hineybutt is there, but that's about it. I doubt police would believe our story based on one isolated post."

"No?"

Cara shook her head. "As weird as that nickname is, they wouldn't rule out someone else using it too. And remember that picture of the hummingbird earring? *Gone.* Saffire removed it after I sent her the PM. We got nothin', Jenn."

Jenn stared across the room for a thoughtful moment, then turned to her sister with hopeful eyes. "Do they back that stuff up, or is it gone forever?"

Dejected, Cara shook her head and murmured, "I don't know."

"Is there someone on the site you could ask? Is the system administrator's contact info listed anywhere?"

Cara raised her eyes slowly. "I could find out."

Jenn gave an emphatic nod. “Do it. Ask that Seth guy, if you have to. We can at least *try* to get the info we need, you know? Before giving up?”

“Yeah,” Cara agreed. “I’ll work on that tonight and I’ll try calling Astrea again.”

Jenn fluttered her eyelids and shook her head. “Astrea? Remind me who Astrea is.”

“Astrea is a woman in the EC who used to talk on the phone with saffire. Remember how saffire let it slip that she was working in the tasting room of a winery? Astrea is the person she told, who might have more information about where to find her.”

“Ah-ha. And you’ve already tried calling?”

Cara gave a low growl of exasperation. “She never answers her phone. All I get is voicemail. Maybe I’ll send her a text or a PM and ask when a good time to call would be.”

Jenn sat back against a fluffy couch cushion. “What about Colin Huxby?”

“Psh…forget *him*. The more I thought about it the more I realized how utterly futile it would be to contact the guy. If he did help Arianna fake her own death, he could be arrested! Why on earth would he admit that to us?”

“You’re right.” Jenn gave a *duh, why didn’t I think of that?* toss of the head. “Well, at least we know where he lives. Just in case. And I’m still not going to rule out the police. I could call them and find out what it would take to start an investigation. Who knows? At the very least, they could suggest a good private investigator.”

Cara combed fingers through her damp hair, sunk deeper into the couch and closed her eyes. “I’m so tired, Jenn. I hardly slept last night after finding out about the missing posts. My ass was dragging at work today and it was all I could do to focus. In my business, that’s not good. One slight mistake could be costly.”

Jenn donned the “worried big sister” face. “Oh Cara, don’t let this consume you. It might be a false alarm, yet. Just take one thing at a time. Call Astrea tonight, then contact the radio station guy. That’s all you can do for now.”

“I know.”

“And take some melatonin, so you can get a good night’s sleep.”

Cara opened her eyes and turned to her sister with a smile. “Okay, Mom.”

Jenn shrugged. “Hey, I don’t want you getting sick or losing your job over this.”

Cara stared into space and once again pondered the abysmal limbo that was her editorial job. "You know, I'm starting to think that wouldn't be such a bad thing."

* * *

The bright red text caught Cara's eye as she poured over her manuscript with a purple editing pen. Looking up, she saw: ***2 New Private Messages.***

"Not now," Cara whispered to herself, eyeing the huge stack of pages she had to edit before two o'clock. She shrunk her Internet window into a tiny icon at the bottom of the screen.

The messages were most likely from Astrea and the system administrator of the Ecletic Café, respectively. They probably held answers to the entire saffire mystery, but Cara promised herself she'd get work done first.

"Hey Cara," came Frannie's voice from across the cubicle wall.

Cara tore her gaze from the sentence she'd read five times. "Yeah?"

"Guess what I finally did?"

"Cleaned your filthy apartment?"

"No, smartass. It's something I said I wouldn't do, but I've changed my mind."

Cara rolled her eyes. "I have an idea, Frannie…why don't you just *tell* me?"

"I signed up for speed dating."

"Get out! I thought you didn't like it the first time you tried it. I thought Ian was enough for you right now."

"Well, I figured it wouldn't hurt to check it out one more time, you know? I'm kind of amused by the whole thing…and besides, I'm doing it for you."

"For me?"

"Yeah, I signed you up too."

Cara was about to revisit the manuscript when she heard this and snapped her head back up. "You *what?*"

"Speed dating was supposed to be for you, remember? I'm just along as your wing man—or woman, as the case may be."

"Aw Fran, you should've consulted me first," Cara whined. "I'm really not interested in that right now. I have other issues to deal with."

"Like what?"

Cara felt a spark of irritation. Her shoulders tensed. She wanted so much to blurt, "None of your goddamn business!" but restrained herself. There was no way she was going to sacrifice the story of saffire_21 on the altar of Frannie's cynicism.

"It's that California guy isn't it?" Frannie persisted. "I'm sure he's great and all, but you can't go on dates with him, can you?"

Cara set her jaw, and felt her face grow hot. "Let's talk about this later. I have a shitload of pages to get through today."

"All right, all right," Frannie conceded. Cara heard the rustle of papers as Frannie dove back into her own stack.

With a huff, Cara leaned her head on her hand and picked up the purple pen for the sixth time. She watched its fine tip hover over words that no longer registered in her brain. All the while, the PMs called to her like voluptuous sirens to a sailor.

Click-click.

In a microsecond, the private message window was open. One from Astrea and one from…Seth Kane? Seth hadn't written to her in ages!

Cara read the first one:

Hey Cara,

I am SO sorry about missing all your calls! I've been out of town for the last couple of days. Please try again this evening, okay? I promise I'll be waiting by the phone. How about nine o'clock your time? I'll be home from work then.

Kevin said you needed my help…I would love to help in any way possible!

Talk to you soon,

Astrea

Cara tore a yellow post-it from the stack on her desk and scrawled onto its surface: *call Astrea at 9:00PM TONIGHT!* Then she stuck it on her black leather planner. Next, she opened Seth's brief message.

Cara, I heard you were looking for some information about saffire_21. Here are my new cell phone digits. Call me tonight, anytime after 6.

~Seth (212) 555-8463

"How does he *know* these things?" Cara whispered to herself with a shake of the head. She scrawled the number onto the bottom half of her post-it, and turned back to the manuscript pages with a heavy sigh. With her mounting anticipation of these phone calls and the revelations they would bring, the rest of the workday was sure to move at the speed of glacial ice.

* * *

"Hey, slow down!" Frannie commanded, speeding her pace from a saunter to a trot. "Where's the fire?"

Cara took huge strides past the ellipticals, stair climbers, and weight machines, heading for the women's locker room. "I have important stuff to do at home."

"Aren't you going in the hot tub?"

"Sorry, Frannie. It's *way* important." She stripped off her black work-out top as she passed the treadmills, and noticed a few of the men's heads turn reflexively. Once they saw her black sports bra underneath, they turned forward again.

"Man, it must be. You never skip the hot tub!"

The two carefully maneuvered around other women coming out of the locker room.

"Everything's okay, right?" Frannie asked with a sideways glance.

Cara came to an abrupt stop at her locker. "For now, it is. I hate to be so mysterious, Fran, but there is some really weird shit going on in the family sector of my life. One day, hopefully, it'll all be clear enough to tell you about it."

"Your *family?* Oh, God..."

Cara put a hand on her friend's shoulder. "Really, don't worry your little head about a thing. Everyone's okay."

They both opened their lockers in silence. Frannie grabbed her swimsuit and Cara pulled out sweats.

"How's your California dude?"

Cara smiled. "He's just fine. I talked to him for three hours Sunday night. Funny how you don't even realize the time passing, then you look at the clock and it's one-thirty AM."

"Wow!" Frannie snapped a swimsuit strap over her shoulder and turned to Cara. "I'm amazed that you don't run out of things to say, after awhile. Is this a bona fide long-distance relationship, now, or what?"

Cara hesitated as a gleam lit her golden-brown eyes. "I'm not sure, Frannie. All I know is that I feel very at home with Kevin. His voice soothes me. I love hearing all about his California life...the view outside his studio, the design work that he does, the art show where he sold two pieces to a drunken millionaire!"

"Seriously?"

Cara's smile widened. "And he's so damn funny! We spend at least half of the time laughing our asses off. He talks about his favorite episodes of *The Office,* or the strange things his cats do, or the weird people at his favorite bar. Sometimes my stomach literally *aches* after I hang up with him."

Frannie nodded. "It's a real good thing to have someone you can laugh with."

"So, I guess we're just friends and mutual admirers. Even though he tells me all the time how beautiful he thinks I am and how much he loves my voice."

A dark look erased Frannie's smile. "Oh, I see. A *flatterer.* Online guys can do and say anything from their safe distance."

"I dunno, Fran. He seems pretty sincere." Cara grabbed the last of her belongings and slammed the door. She was in no mood for Frannie's pessimism that evening.

Frannie flapped a hand in the air. "Well, whatever. Just don't forget about our little engagement this Saturday evening. Seven o'clock at the Queen City Brewing Station."

Cara, who'd started to walk away, looked over her shoulder quizzically. "Engagement?"

"Speed dating."

Cara grimaced. "Oh God, Frannie…"

"Don't you bail on me." Frannie shook a finger. "I've already paid the fee for both of us."

"Isn't there anyone else you can take?"

"Are you kidding? Everyone's married!"

"What about those friends from your New Age women's group?"

"The ones that aren't married are lesbians, hon. You've met them."

Cara rolled her eyes and tossed her head. "Fine. But you're driving, because I'm going to need a whole lot of alcohol to get me through it."

Chapter 16

When Seth's voicemail kicked in, Cara stomped her foot.

Sophie, who'd been grooming her nether regions with intensity, snapped her head up in alarm, hind leg jutting into the air.

"You tell me to call, then you don't answer your *frickin' phone*," Cara grumped.

"...please leave a message at the tone." *Beep.*

"Seth, hi, this is Cara. Call me when you get this message."

After clicking the phone off, Cara stepped over the cat and into her kitchen. She was ravenous, but nothing in the refrigerator looked appealing to her and everything in the cupboards required too much cooking time. Flinging open the freezer, she braced herself against the cold air and spotted a bag of frozen edamame. "That'll work," she said, reaching for it.

Minutes later, Cara stood over the stove watching the green pods boil in her little pot. She sung along with Sting's "Fields of Gold" playing on the radio, trying to soothe herself out of the angst that had been slowly building throughout the day.

Sophie finished grooming and repositioned herself atop the refrigerator, keeping an eye on her caregiver's every move. Cara locked eyes with the feline. "Am I crazy, Sophie? Am I just hitting some sort of pre-midlife crisis as a result of my dead end life? Am I looking for some sort of high drama deliverance?"

Sophie lowered her lids halfway.

Cara shook her head. "Maybe I just need to go find someone and have a torrid fling. Maybe that speed dating thing isn't such a bad idea after all." As she tapped the wooden spoon against the side of the pan and switched off the burner, the phone—sitting on the counter beside the stove—rang sharply. Cara grabbed it. "Hello?"

"Cara?"

"Hey, Seth. How ya doin'?"

"Ohhh...a little worn out from working late. That's why I missed your call. Sorry."

"Damn, you sound just like John Cusack when you're tired," she marveled.

"Really?"

"Yeah, what is it with all the EC guys sounding like celebrities?" Cara laughed. "You sound like Cusack and Kevin sounds like Matt Damon!"

"Or maybe Moonflower has a vivid imagination," Seth teased. "And hey, what are you doing talking to *Kevin?* Is something goin' on there?"

Cara ignored the question and cut to the chase. "So what's this information you have about saffire_21? And how did you know I was looking?"

"I'm the Master of Lurk, haven't you heard?"

"Yeah, but I never posted—"

"I'm messin' with ya, sweets. I talked to Astrea the other night, and she said that *Kevin* said you were wondering about saffire living nearby in wine country."

"Geez, word gets around fast in this community." Cara frowned and secretly wondered about the Kevin and Astrea connection. Apparently, they talked often. Was there more to their relationship than Kevin was letting on?

"So I have to ask, why the sudden interest in saffire? You're the only one who refuses to let her stay a mystery!"

Cara's heart skipped a beat. Her brain scrambled to formulate a reply. "I just…oh hell, it's a long and crazy story. Can I just leave it at that for now?"

"Sure, sure…didn't mean to pry. It just sounds a little more urgent than everyone else's passing curiosity."

"Hey, *you've* talked with her," Cara pointed out. "What sort of things did she talk about, if not her work or where she lives?"

"Oh, we'd talk about the Café, other members, our local friends. Most of the time, she'd complain about *not* being employed and her dwindling bank account. So even if she did work at a winery, she may not anymore."

Cara's heart sank. Of *course*. Saffire could've moved on. She could be anywhere, really. The idea of pursuing her started to feel pointless again. "Has she made any more appearances on the boards?"

"No, not for a long time."

Since I confronted her, Cara thought to herself. "And have you gotten any PMs from her recently?"

"No, I don't think anyone has. But I do know how you can find out where saffire's posting from."

Cara gripped the phone more tightly. "How?"

"Talk to Vincent Gold and ask if he can reveal her IP address."

"Who's Vincent Gold, and what's an IP address?"

"He's the owner and system administrator for the Eclectic Café—whose voice you always hear announcing the songs and promotions. I thought everyone knew that."

"Everyone but me, apparently."

"Vincent has access to everyone's IP address; the geographical locations of their computers provided by their Internet service. And if saffire's are coming from one of the major wine country towns of California, you may have something."

Cara's eyes widened. "You mean it's that easy? Why hasn't anyone else tried this?"

"Weeeeell," Seth's voice began to spell out doubt, "it *isn't* that easy, actually. Sys Admins aren't allowed to give out the private information of users. But with a little social engineering, it just might work."

"I hate to ask again, but what's *that?*"

"You could contact him, say that you're getting harassing messages from the user saffire, and ask where she's located for your own safety. Or maybe send him an email, claiming you're an employer who suspects that one of her employees is doing a little too much cyber-slacking at work, and saffire_21 seems to be the guilty party."

Cara considered this with a "Hmph." *I wonder if Vincent Gold would be helpful if I simply told the truth...that saffire might be a niece who allegedly died years ago and we're hoping she's still alive.*

"Anyway, you could try."

Cara nodded. "I'll do that, Seth. Thanks for the suggestion. I had no idea about these things."

"Oh yeah, IP addresses can always be traced."

"So how are the rats?" Cara changed the subject, forcing cheer into her voice. More than anything, she wanted to dash to the computer and send Vincent Gold a PM right that second, but proper social etiquette had to be followed.

"Well, one of them lost another tooth today..."

Cara tried to take in the sweet and tender details of his children, but her mind was off and running again with all things saffire. When Seth finally said goodnight, she hung up and glanced at the kitchen clock. Seven-thirty. Plenty of time to snarf down her edamame and compose a convincing email to Vincent Gold.

* * *

Cara was so intent on her editing that she didn't hear the phone. Her weary eyes squinted against the glare of the monitor as she read aloud, "Our California employee, Ms. Arianna Watts, is currently on probation for excessive personal use of the Internet during work hours and..."

An insistent second ring pierced her concentration. Then a third.

"...and we believe most of her activity is conducted on your site, The Eclectic Café, as the user saffire_21."

The machine finally kicked in. "Hi, this is Cara. Sorry I missed your call. Please leave me a message and let me know when I can get back with you. Have a great day." *Beep.*

"In order to take disciplinary action against Ms. Watts, we are requesting verification of saffire_21's IP address..."

Kevin's disappointed voice filled the living room. "Aw, Cara, where are you? I have a surprise for you and you're not even home! When you hear this message, call my cell phone. Or maybe I'll call yours. I hope you have—"

Cara sprung from the computer and bounded to the phone, cutting him off in mid-sentence. "Kevin, I'm here! I just couldn't pick up in time. How are you?"

"Hey, there you are!" he cried. "I'm pretty good, thanks, and I have a little surprise for you tonight."

Cara grinned at the anticipatory delight in his voice. "Oh, *really?*"

"Are you ready?"

"Yes! What?"

There was an airy laugh on the other end of the line. Then a high, breezy voice greeted, "Hello, Moonflower."

It took a few seconds for Cara's brain to register. "Uh…hello. Who—?"

"It's StarAngel!"

Surprise, confusion, and a tiny sliver of envy did a do-si-do inside her. When she finally found her voice, she stammered, "Oh, *Astrea*. Are you—"

"Astrea came down to Santa Barbara for the day and we're about to grab some dinner," Kevin announced, sounding way too happy.

"So I figured we better call you first," Astrea explained, "in case we don't make it back in time for the nine o'clock phone call I promised you."

"Oh, okay." Cara put a hand to her forehead, picturing the scene. Kevin only had one phone in the house. This meant that their heads were probably extremely close together so they could both listen and talk to her…like George Bailey and Mary Hatch on the phone with Sam Wainright in the movie *It's a Wonderful Life*. Just before they started making out! *Arghhh!*

"I'll sign off and let you women talk," Kevin offered. "And Cara, I'll try to give you a call later if it's not too late."

There was a soft rustling as the phone was handed off, then Astrea's voice. "So how are you, Cara?"

Cara sunk onto the couch and slumped forward. "I'm all right. How 'bout you?"

"Just splendid, thank you. The drive down was clear and gorgeous, and I got all my herbs delivered in time to have a little fun before heading back."

"What's on the agenda?" Cara asked, sounding polite but feeling nosy.

"We're going to Kevin's favorite sushi bar on the Mesa. Mmmm, my mouth is already watering."

Cara scrunched up her face in bewilderment. Were the two of them just friends or were they hooking up? Despite his affectionate contact and non-stop attention in the last couple of months, was Kevin just a player?

As if reading Cara's mind, Astrea added, "We get together every once in awhile when I have deliveries in Santa Barbara. It's so nice to meet a fellow EC-er in person. I wish I could meet *all* the beautiful people of the EC, including you."

Cara sat back with a sigh. It was hard to resent Astrea when she was so damn *nice* all the time. But this didn't stop another taunting voice from rising up in the back of her mind. *They probably get together every once in awhile for the same reason Frannie and Ian do.* Shaking it off and sweeping pettiness aside, Cara got down to business. "So Astrea, how long ago was the conversation you had with Ari—I mean with saffire?"

"Which one?" Astrea asked. "We talked a few times."

"The one where she alluded to working at a winery."

"Ah, yes. That one." There was a soft laugh as Astrea recounted the conversation. "Saffire was in an *exceptionally* pissy mood that day."

They both giggled at this.

"She was on a rant about how she hadn't had a day off in over a week because her workplace was horribly understaffed during a busy event. She told me she couldn't stand the 'prententious bullshit' that went on there, and on top of that the owner really took advantage of all the employees. She was thinking about switching to a smaller, less-commercial, family-owned winery.

"So I told her, 'Wow, saffire. You work at a winery? I never would've guessed.' And then, after a very pregnant pause, I hear a quiet, 'Oh *shit*.'"

Cara pressed the phone more tightly to her ear, not wanting to miss a word.

"I laughed and told her it was no big deal if I knew where she worked, but saffire was noticeably upset that she'd given up such a personal detail. She's always been a real stickler about her privacy, as I'm sure you've heard."

"Yeah," Cara replied. *Especially when you're supposed to be dead.* "But has anyone ever asked her *why* she's so private? I mean, is she running from the law? Is she in Witness Protection? What?"

Astrea breathed her airy laugh again. "Whenever people used to ask that question, her answer was always, 'can't you just accept me as saffire_21—the beautiful and fabulous chick who launched Planet Indigo? Is that not good enough for you? What more do you need to know?' So we all eventually gave up and respected her wishes."

"I suppose she never indicated whether or not the winery was in California? Kevin said you had reason to believe that it was."

"Saffire never indicated, but since she always seemed to be awake and posting on west coast time I figured it had to be California."

"What about a number in your caller ID?"

"My caller ID said private cell, and when my phone statement came there was a *Blocked Number* on the incoming list. Not even an area code to clue us in."

"Yeah, that's what Kevin told me." Cara turned this new information around in her mind for a brief moment. "When was that phone call, anyway?"

"Oh, let's see…about a year and a half ago."

"Did you ever check any of the local wineries, out of curiosity?"

"Wow, you sound like a real Nancy Drew," Astrea teased. "Actually, I did ask my housemate who works at a nearby winery if he or his associates had ever seen a young redhead working anywhere in the area. They hadn't, but that didn't prove anything. People come and go all the time, and there are a few hundred wineries in the Central Coast."

Okay then, Cara thought. The only remaining lead will come from Vincent Gold, if he chooses to reveal saffire's location.

"Listen, Cara, Kevin told me a little about why you needed help with this."

Cara winced. *Oh damn, Kevin, you didn't!*

"He told me you have reason to believe that saffire has some vital information about a family matter. So of course I am mystified, but eager to help. I really hope whatever it is gets resolved soon."

Cara's shoulders relaxed a little. "Well, thanks. I do too."

"Is there anything else you need to know?"

"Yes." Cara took a deep breath and tried to keep her voice steady as she asked, "When you spoke with her, did she seem happy?"

"Oh, well…" Astrea slipped into a contemplative pause. "…for the most part. Saffire never got very in depth with her conversations. She mostly kept things light and asked what was going on with *me*. Or she vented about a boring social life and the lack of decent men in her town."

"So she's not married," Cara said, answering the question of whether Colin Huxby had joined Arianna in the States. Just the idea of her niece being alive, *period,* made her stomach do back flips.

"No, she's not married," Astrea's musical voice responded, "but she did mention a couple of guys she'd dated once or twice. Neither of which sounded very promising, poor girl."

Cara thumped her fist on the couch. "Man, I wish I would've discovered the Café a few months earlier than I did. Maybe I would've been one of the people she called. Then I would've known if her voice—" she quickly realized that she was treading into dangerous territory with details. "—er, I mean, I could've asked her things in person. But now I'm afraid I've scared her off with too many questions. You haven't seen her on the boards, have you? I keep doing a check on her posting history, and so far she hasn't been back since my deadly PM."

"Deadly PM? What on earth did you say? Or is that too private?"

Cara stood up, too nervous to sit any longer. "I just asked her a very honest and direct question about the 'family issue,' and she hasn't been back since. I scared her off, Astrea. I feel really bad."

"Oh no," Astrea's voice grew tender. "It's not about you, Cara. She does this all the time."

Ah, but how many people asked saffire if she was their dead niece? Trust me, she won't be back. "Well, anyway, thanks for all your help."

"No problem, babe. It was great talking with you. You have a lovely voice, by the way."

Cara felt a slight blush in her cheeks. "Wow, thanks. Yours is exactly how I imagined it…it fits your serene nature on the boards."

"Ooh, *serene nature,*" Astrea cooed. "I like the sound of that."

There was a scuffling noise on the line as Astrea covered the receiver. Her muffled voice asked, "Kevin, any last minute words?"

Cara heard his muted voice in the background.

"Okay, Kevin says 'goodbye Cara mia' and he'll talk with you later. And I say have a wonderful evening too. Good luck with all this saffire stuff."

Cara thanked her again, then added begrudgingly, "Have fun at the sushi bar."

"Mmmm, we will," Astrea purred.

"Take care."

"You too. Bye."

Cara clicked the phone off, threw it onto the couch and stalked back to her study. When she brought the Eclectic Café to the foreground, there was a new private message waiting from Vincent Gold, finally answering her question about the archives.

Dear Moonflower,

Thanks for your inquiry about the deleted posts. I'm sorry to report that we didn't back them up this last time. The site has been experiencing a host of other issues that prevented this. However, we've increased our server space tenfold and will (hopefully) never have to delete any posts again.

Sincerely,
Vincent G.

"Oh, that's just fucking *great,*" Cara snapped. She sat and fumed for awhile, accepting the fact that the "evidence" was gone forever. She also tried hard not to imagine Astrea and Kevin sucking suggestively on edamame and Rainbow Rolls, while playing footsie under the table. After taking a cleansing breath, she opened the "fake employer" email again. "Well, let's see if Mr. Gold can come through for us on this one last shred of hope."

She labored over it a few minutes more, adding just the right finishing touches and reading it out loud. Then, just before hitting the SEND button, she lowered her arm and frowned. "*Crap!*"

The email needed to come from a corporate address rather than an address associated with Moonflower's account, or it wouldn't appear legitimate. Just when she was about to despair, an idea hit. She would forward the message to her work account. The next morning, she would copy it into a new email which bore her company's title and signature. Problem solved.

Cara leaned back, swept her hair atop her head with interlaced fingers and held it for a moment. What next? Was there nothing left to do but wait? Her brain felt like it was about to explode. She stared comatose at the Eclectic Café screen until her eyes zeroed in on the private message inbox. The majority of them were from Kevin, which brought an easy smile to her face. She'd saved them all to re-read on days when she needed uplifting. But as she sat forward again, hair falling down around her shoulders, her smile quickly disintegrated. "If you like me so damn much, why are you having sushi with Astrea tonight?" In a full-on huff, Cara closed all the windows and sent her computer into sleep mode.

"This day has been seriously fucked up," Cara informed Sophie, who had slipped silently into the doorway of the den. "And there's only one way I want it to end."

In seconds, Cara was headed for the bathtub armed with a candle, a glass of Chardonnay, and a bottle of Jasmine bath oil. The ringer on her phone was set to silent.

Chapter 17

"I'm sorry to be such a quitter, Jenn."

The line was so quiet for a moment Cara thought they'd lost their connection.

"It's not really quitting, Cara, considering this was all a wild turkey shoot to begin with. Whatever you decide to do, I'll support your decision."

Keeping an eye on the driveway outside her front picture window, Cara switched the phone from one ear to the other. "It's just that Vincent Gold hasn't answered my email all week. If I don't have any evidence whatsoever that saffire is posting from California, where would I even begin to look?"

"A very good point."

"So that's why I've decided to let this whole thing go. I'm chalking it up to a bizarre coincidence combined with an overactive imagination." With dusk settling outside, Cara noticed her faint reflection in the glass. She turned this way and that, noticing with a smile that the Pilates classes had finally paid off.

"Yeah, and when you think of the practical aspects of trying to find Arianna, could you really afford to take all that time off from work? I mean, the search could take awhile. We'd be better off hiring a private investigator, like the police suggested."

"Truthfully, Jenn, I could use a long sabbatical. I'm a little burnt out these days."

"So you've told me, again and again," Jenn replied with an air of impertinence. "Have you started looking for a different job yet?"

"No," Cara admitted, secretly thinking of her desire to leave town altogether. It wasn't time to share that part with Jenn. Not just yet. "But I did put my house up for rent."

"Really? You finally took the plunge?"

Cara heard a car engine and peered through the organza sheers. Frannie's green Volkswagen Beetle rolled neatly into her driveway. "I did, and I've shown it to about five prospective tenants already. I'll tell you more about that later, but right now I gotta go. Frannie's here."

"What are you two doing tonight?"

Cara's face soured. "You don't wanna know."

"What's that supposed to mean? I do *so* want to know!"

"I'll tell you later. Byeee."

After hanging up on a highly annoyed sister, Cara grabbed her purse and gave Sophie a goodbye pet. She locked the door, closed it behind her and trudged to Frannie's car like a junior high student to a bus stop on a Monday morning.

* * *

"Three minutes, people!"

The overly zealous moderator's voice was worse than nails dragging down a chalkboard. This was partly because of its natural shrillness, but also because of a hyper-amplified microphone into which she barked directions at the speed daters sitting in the Queen City Brewing Station.

"Ladies go first for one minute, then gentlemen take their turn for the second. You may both ask each other questions if you've got time left over, until a third bell rings, and then the men—I repeat, the *men*—"

Cara cringed as the woman raised her voice.

"—will move on to the next table. Ladies, you have the luxury of staying put. So! Any questions? Is everyone ready?"

I am *so* not into this, thought Cara as she glanced around the trendy microbrewery. The gaggle of men hovered on one side of the room all spiffed up and freshly shaven, swimming in a sea of various colognes. The women were smoothing their lipstick, straightening their skirts, and trying to discreetly boost their push-up bras. Both sides looked equally uncertain. Cara took her tent card with the number seventeen on it, set it on a table under a softly lit Tiffany lamp, and sat down. Frannie sat three tables over with a huge shit-eating grin on her face. She winked at Cara. Cara crossed her eyes and stuck out her tongue.

"Okay, gentlemen, the ladies are situated. Go find your first table!"

The men shuffled around the room, planting themselves in the empty chairs across from the women until every seat was filled.

A tall, lanky man who looked a lot like Ben Stiller sat down and gave her a warm smile. "How ya doing?"

Cara smiled back. "Just fine, thanks."

"I'm Marc."

"Cara."

There was nothing left to say, so Cara glanced awkwardly away.

"Okay, let the speed dating begin!"

Ding.

Cara's gaze returned to her prospective "date." With raised eyebrows, she took a deep breath and said, "Okay, well, I work in the editorial department of a small publishing company here in town..."

"Really? How cool is that?" he interrupted, entirely too chirpy and eager.

Cara blinked, gathered her thoughts again, and continued, "Uh, I like it pretty well. I own a house in Mt. Washington, but I'm getting it ready to rent so I can live somewhere that's less of a responsibility…"

"Oh hey, if we hook up," he shot her another chipper grin, "I could help you with all that. I'm a pretty good handyman."

Okay, Mr. Dudus Interruptus, that's about enough active listening! You'll get your minute, so just chill. Cara tried not to let her irritation show as she finished talking. And since he'd been so forward and familiar, she intentionally kept the conversation shallow—about her cat, her car, and her gym. Then she patiently listened through Marc's uninteresting spiel about working in a bookstore until he finished up his radiology program at school.

The welcome sound of the bell brought a smile of relief to Cara's face. After shaking her hand, Marc stood up and moved to the next table. Then a stocky, athletic looking man with sandy hair, a neatly-kept goatee and an affable smile took his place.

Ding.

He offered her a hand to shake. "Hi there. Joe."

"Cara."

Cara went through her intro once again, changing it up here and there. She decided once again to leave out the finer details, such as moving or needing a change in her life. It felt like too much information. Finally, it was Joe's turn.

"Soooo…my name's Joe. I'm thirty-one. I work at K. R. Steel. Live in Hamilton. Got one roommate…"

And do you ever talk in sentences longer than four words? Guh!

"…he's the one who dragged me out here to do this, but it's cool. I'm having fun. Good times, you know?"

Cara tried to smile, but only one corner of her mouth raised in a sort of sneer.

"I don't date much. I'm kind of shy." He looked down.

Cara felt a brief moment of compassion for Joe. God love him, he certainly was trying. When he couldn't think of what to say next, she prompted, "What are your hobbies, Joe?"

"I like sports. Football, mostly. Baseball in the summer. You like sports?"

"I'm a big Reds fan."

"Awesome."

Ding.

Two down…eighteen to go. Holy shit.

Cara met Tony, the stereotypically-macho son of a local Italian restaurant owner who kept feeling her up with his gaze. *Ew!* Then there was Todd, the martial arts instructor with a bod like Apollo, but an ego bigger than the Hoover Dam. The next five were really nice guys, but they all blended together because of their vanilla personalities. Where was the man who stood out? Where was the man who offered unique qualities that she'd never even considered before? Where was the man who made her laugh until her tummy hurt? *In California, that's where. And you know it. Why the hell are you even sitting here?*

Ding.

"Hey," greeted a low, overly suave voice.

Oh holy hell, you've gotta be fucking kidding me.

The man who sat down at Cara's table was sporting a thick, wavy, bona-fide Billy Ray Cyrus mullet. Right down the middle of his back. "I'm Caleb, nice to meet you."

"Hi," Cara choked, fighting both a cackle and a look of underlying horror. "Um…" She felt as though her brain were short circuiting. Erratic thoughts shot off in every direction, like a defective Tommy gun spinning around on the ground as it discharged. *That's it. This guy is the last straw. If this is a cross-sampling of what this town has to offer in the way of single men…then I can't stay. I gotta leave…gotta get the fuck out… sayonara… adios…and arrivederci!*

Cara stood up, chair screeching on the floor as it flew back behind her. Caleb winced and a few heads turned from the other tables. "I'm so sorry. I'm not feeling well, and I have to go." Putting a hand to her stomach and leaving the bewildered man behind with his mullet, Cara stalked across the restaurant, shoved open its glass door, and let herself out into the balmy spring night.

* * *

In the comfort and safety of home, Cara kicked off her dress sandals and flopped onto the couch. She flung one forearm across her eyes and waited until stress levels fell and normal breathing returned.

Not only had Frannie shown great disdain for her sudden and dramatic departure from the restaurant, but was doubly ticked off when Cara wouldn't go somewhere else for a drink.

"I just need to get home," Cara had pleaded. "I think I'm having some kind of anxiety attack."

All she wanted was to be alone and think about her next step. A step she felt certain would be a giant one. *Check your work email,* a voice from some higher realm seemed to whisper. In seconds, Cara was up and scurrying down the short hallway to her den. Thankfully, the tech guys at the office made it possible for her to transfer work emails to her personal account, for those rare days when she worked from home. After going through the necessary steps, she watched the black, bolded subject lines load into her inbox one by one.

Frannie Bertollo **Fwd: Next Two Chapters**
Kyle Reynolds **Monday Meeting**
Martha Meikle **Art Specs for Chapter 12**
Vincent Gold **Re: IP Address**

"Oh my God," gasped Cara, clicking open the last one. "Oh...my...*God.*"

Greetings,

As I'm sure you're aware, the personal contact information of our members is confidential. However, I can certainly understand your dilemma as an employer. My compromise is to let you know that the IP address for the user saffire_21 is indeed located in the state of California. I hope this is enough information for you to work with.

Sincerely,

V. Gold, Station Owner

"So she *is* at a California winery," Cara whispered to herself. This revelation certainly narrowed the search, but it would still be a needle-in-a-haystack situation. California was a huge state. She stared at Gold's email for a long while, her mind churning. She could make a list of all the California wineries on the Internet, sort out the ones with tasting rooms, then send pictures of Arianna to inquire about her employment—past or present. Of course, not all of them were likely to respond. Inevitably, there would be a list of wineries she would have to investigate in person.

Cara picked up the phone, which sat on her computer table, and speed-dialed Kevin Tierney.

Chapter 18

Cara threw her luggage into the back seat, then opened the passenger door to climb in beside her sister who reached out to give her arm a little squeeze. "Are you ready for this?"

Cara let out a nervous breath. "I think so."

Jenn's eyes darted quickly about her sister's face. "I meant to tell you last night, I really *love* the new hairstyle! It makes you look ten years younger."

"Yeah?" Cara gave her head a shake, enjoying the flippy feeling of her shorter, more contemporary hairstyle. "In the hair catalog, the style was described as 'carefree layers in a disarray of curls.' I like it because I don't have to mess with it as much, and my neck stays cooler being half bare. It was time for a change."

"Oh, like you haven't made plenty of *those* in the last couple of weeks."

They laughed together while Jenn put the car in reverse, turned her head, and backed slowly down the driveway. Cara spotted Sophie in Jenn's front picture window, a forlorn little face watching them drive away. "Aw, look at my poor baby. I'm going to miss her."

"Sophie will be in good hands."

"Yeah, but cats don't like 'different'."

"She'll survive. I'll keep her so buzzed on catnip she won't even remember you've gone."

Cara giggled. "Well, thanks for watching her…and for putting me up the last two weeks. I guess with my house rented and all my stuff in storage, I'm officially homeless."

"Does it feel strange?"

"No, it feels *liberating*."

They drove out of the suburban neighborhood in Northern Kentucky and headed for the interstate. Cara lowered her sun visor and peered up into its mirror to apply a coat of lipstick. Jenn took a sip of coffee from her travel mug. "How long do you think you'll be gone?"

"I'm not sure." Cara smacked her lips together and threw the black tube back into her purse. "That's why I only bought a one-way ticket to Los Angeles."

"We've both been so busy in the last month that I've hardly had time to ask about this whole trip. Tell me again what became of your job. Did you actually quit?"

"I took an unpaid leave of absence." Cara looked over at her sister with one eyebrow cocked. "They weren't very happy with me, but they also didn't want to lose such an experienced employee for good. So they complied."

"Did you have to give a reason?"

"I told them it was some family business that I wasn't at liberty to discuss. That's no lie."

Jenn shook her head. "Nope." Then she accelerated down an on-ramp to merge with the long lines of traffic on I-75. After another thoughtful pause, she sniffed and asked, "And who is it you're staying with, once you get out there? One of your cyber-friends?"

Cara turned away, a slight blush in her cheeks. If she told any of her family members that she was flying across the country to stay at the studio of some 'Internet guy,' there would be endless worry. So she'd been referring to Kevin in plural form. *Some friends.* It was only a white lie, considering that Astrea would most likely enter the picture at some point.

"Yeah, just some of the people who live out in Santa Barbara. They're going to drive up the coast with me when I look for Arianna."

"Wow, you know, that's going to be a really beautiful trip along the Pacific Coast Highway. I wish you were going there under different circumstances."

"Yeah, no kidding. Like a romantic getaway or a honeymoon."

Cara stared out the window in a pensive silence. The night before, she had lain awake with millions of thoughts pinballing around her head. *Was* she just friends with Kevin, or would they end up getting sexual? There had been a lot of flirtation back and forth in the few months they'd known each other. But what if she found there was no chemistry after meeting him in person? And what if he was already Astrea's lover? How awkward would that be?

And what about this crazy search? Could she realistically go through a hundred wineries and ever hope to find the saffire-Arianna mystery girl? Or would it all be a wild turkey shoot, as Jenn had dubbed it?

"You're awfully quiet, Cara."

She turned back to Jenn with a faint smile. "Got a lot on my mind, I guess. But you know what? As crazy as this whole thing is, I'm really excited to be getting the hell out of Dodge for awhile."

"Yes!" Jenn reached over and put a firm hand on her sister's arm. "Those stagnation blues can suck the life out of you, so this will be a good thing no matter what."

There was a long silence as they merged onto I-275, with morning traffic buzzing around them in all three lanes.

"Jenn, do you think I'll find her?"

When she didn't answer right away, Cara looked over and studied her sister's face but it gave nothing away. Finally, Jenn shrugged.

"I honestly don't know. Arianna has been dead for so long, it's hard to imagine things any other way. On one hand, I would love to know that she is still alive. But on the other, can you fathom the upset it would cause?"

"Yeah, I've thought about that several times over…how hurt and angry Melanie and Tom would feel, and everyone else."

"And I'm wondering how Arianna would feel about being discovered. After going to such lengths to disappear, she may not like it one bit."

"That's exactly what Kevin said."

"Who's Kevin?"

Cara hesitated. Jenn didn't know any specifics about Kevin, and Cara wanted to keep it that way for now. Only Frannie knew, and even she had been slightly uneasy about him. Not being privy to the whole Arianna drama, this looked to her like a whimsical visit to meet an Internet crush and she'd told Cara as much.

"Kevin's one of the friends in Santa Barbara."

"Oh," Jenn said, and thankfully asked no more about him.

"The way I see it, we have every right to know if she's still out there, living and breathing."

"And you know, if it *is* Arianna, she probably changed her name."

"Yeah, I kept that in mind when I contacted the wineries. I only used her picture."

"What did you tell Mom about this trip?"

"I told her I was going to California on business."

Jenn gave an incredulous laugh. "You *lied* to her?"

Cara hung her head. "I did, and I'm not proud of it, but I wasn't about to tell her I was staying with Internet friends. That still spells danger for some people. *Especially* people Mom's age."

Jenn just shook her head. "What if she finds out?"

"How would she find out?"

"Damn it, Cara! Now I'm going to have to perpetuate your lie if she asks me any questions!"

"Oh, it won't be as bad as all that. I'll call her from time to time."

"Well you better call me too!"

"*Jenn,*" Cara said in a low tone.

"Okay, okay…I'm just sayin'."

Their discussion continued as they neared the airport. At the terminal, Jenn pulled up to the curb and put the car in park. She turned to face Cara. "Be safe. I mean it. If anything goes wrong or if you need anything at all, please call me."

"I will."

Jenn grabbed Cara and squeezed her tightly for a good minute. "I love you, girl."

"Love you too."

"Good luck."

They separated and gave each other one last meaningful look before Cara stepped out of the car, removed her bag from the back, and trudged into the front entrance of the Cincinnati/Northern Kentucky International Airport. As she walked up to the ticket counter, her stomach did a few somersaults, finally hit with the reality of what she was about to do.

* * *

The low, crackly voice of the pilot radiated confidence as he announced the final approach into Los Angeles, where the sunny afternoon temperature was a balmy eighty degrees. Cara's stomach began another round of its lurching gymnastics that had begun in Ohio and continued intermittently throughout the flight. In minutes, she would lay eyes on Kevin Tierney for the first time. He would no longer be just a photograph or a series of affectionate words on the computer screen. He would not have to use an emoticon to hug her. Cara would behold, incarnate, the endearing Matt Damon voice on the other end of the phone. Animated and smiling at her. The anticipation was so intense that she let out a small gasp when the plane's wheels thudded against the runway.

After exiting the jet bridge, Cara darted into the nearest women's room to check her appearance. Amazingly, her makeup was still fresh after eight hours of flying and layovers. Her hair was a bit tousled, but the new style made it look intentional. She fluffed it up with her fingers, took a deep breath, and gave a nod of approval to the outfit in which she'd chosen to make her first impression. Capri jeans and a floral-patterned peasant blouse with shirring around the bust. Casual, yet sexy and feminine. *Okay, cali4nyapix...ready or not, here I come.*

Cara followed signs to a long escalator leading down to the baggage claim on ground level, which was teeming with human traffic. People of all shapes, sizes, races and nationalities churned and circulated around her. Limousine drivers held up placards with the black-lettered names of their passengers. *Where is he?* She waded through, glancing in all directions and nearly getting jostled off balance. Kevin was nowhere to be found in the vast sea of faces.

A loud buzz and a flashing red light brought her carousel to life. It rotated slowly as pieces of luggage began to slide down the chute in its center. Cara felt like a spectator at a tennis match, ricocheting between scanning the crowd and watching for her bag. At last, her gaze rested on a tanned face that brightened when their eyes met. The sandy-brown hair looked shorter than all the pictures she'd seen—slightly spiky with a messy texture on top—but it was definitely Kevin, making his way toward her with a radiant smile. Cara's own grin widened as the space between them grew shorter.

"Cara mia!" he cried as he closed in, grabbing her up in a bear's embrace and slowly rocking back and forth. Then he set her down and gave her a kiss square on the lips. It could have been a scene in a movie with the camera somewhere above their heads: two people embracing for the first time with a sea of people swirling around them. As he pulled away, Kevin studied her face and hair. "Oh, *look* at you, lovely Moonflower!"

Cara giggled, unable to take her eyes off his. They were indisputably *blue*. The most rare and oceanic hue of blue she'd ever seen. Just the idea of finally being close enough to see them was thrilling in and of itself.

On the same wavelength, Kevin cradled her face in his hands and marveled, "Your eyes! They've got such a wonderful *light* in them…and your smile is even better than your pictures."

"Funny, I was thinking the same things about you," Cara told him, raising a flirtatious brow. Then her eyelids fluttered as Kevin moved in for another kiss that lasted a bit longer than his first. *My, what soft, full lips you have, Mr. Tierney.* She watched his eyes linger on her breasts, scout out the long legs below, then dart quickly back up to her face again looking as if they'd thoroughly enjoyed their tour. *Oh Kevin, you rule. You just made every grueling Pilates class I struggled through well worth it.*

A longer look at Kevin confirmed everything that she'd gathered from his pictures. He was a different flavor of handsome than most. Not the pretty-boy sort found on the cover of a magazine, or that turned coeds' heads on the street, but charming in his own unique way…with one of the most contagious smiles she'd ever seen.

Echoing her thoughts from the plane ride, Cara told him, "It's so cool to see you *animated,* instead of frozen in a picture."

He laughed and released her slowly, sliding warm hands down the lengths of her arms. "Shall I get your bag?"

Together they turned to watch the luggage travel round and round the carousel until Cara's compact blue suitcase approached. "There it is," she pointed.

Kevin reached out with a strong arm, grabbed the bag effortlessly, and led the way toward an exit. As he walked just ahead of her, Cara studied his easygoing gait and physique…ideally tall, maybe six foot one, toned, and solid. A body that validated the faithful gym workouts he used to mention online. *Meow.*

Exhaust fumes hung in the air outside the terminal as they rushed across the access road into a parking garage. Overhead, a warm wind fluttered the graceful palms.

"Wow," Cara said, looking up at them. "I'm in California."

Kevin slowed his quick pace to walk beside her. He switched the suitcase's pull handle to his other hand so he could throw a warm, protective arm around her. "Welcome to the Golden State, Cara mia."

Cara looked over at him, still in awe that she was finally *with* him, and even more in awe that they took so instantly to each other, without any initial awkwardness. Had she let anyone else be so physically demonstrative upon their first meeting? It was hard to recall, but she didn't think so. Perhaps it was their frequent emails and phone conversations during the past few months that put them at ease, allowing them to know each other on a deeper level.

"Are you hungry?" he asked, giving her shoulder a squeeze.

"Not really," she told him. *Like the dancing butterflies in my stomach would allow any room for* food *right now!*

"The reason I ask is that we have a bit of a drive up to Santa Barbara from here. It's about an hour and a half—*if* traffic isn't bad. It's a Thursday afternoon, which usually isn't too hateful, so we may be in luck."

"Yeah, no, I'm good."

Kevin stopped behind a dark green vintage MG convertible with historic California plates. Cara's eyes widened and she instinctively ran a finger across its flawless, shiny paint job. Beaming, he pulled a ring of keys from his pocket that was so full it sounded like wind chimes. "I don't know if you saw the restored vintage cars on my website, but this is one of my babies that I actually got to keep. Her name's Molly—a 1969 MGC soft top. Got a great deal on her a year ago, since she was nearly totaled in a wreck."

"Why Molly?" Cara asked with a curious grin.

"Well, for awhile there were two of them. I sold Desmond to some woman in Santa Monica and kept Molly. So they were named after—"

"Desmond and Molly Jones!" she cried. "*Ob-La-Di, Ob-La-da!* What a great inspiration! I'm a huge Beatles fan, born and raised on their music."

Kevin high-fived her. "Yet *another* reason to like you."

Once Cara's suitcase was safely stowed, they climbed into the cozy two-seater and she listened with delight as the exotic engine started up with a metallic whir. "Oh wow," she breathed, looking over at Kevin.

"Yeah, huh?" he replied with a wink.

As they pulled away from the terminal, Cara glanced upward at the famous LAX landmark—a huge white tower structure with two crossing arches over it. Kevin followed her gaze. "There's a restaurant up in the top of that. It was built in the sixties when everything was all space-age."

"That explains why it looks like George Jetson's house," she told him, watching it as they passed by.

Kevin chuckled, threw the car into high gear, and merged onto the interstate. His newly acquired speed was immediately thwarted, however, as the 405 became a sea of congested cars, trucks, and lane-splitting motorcycles.

"Good God, is it always like this?" Cara asked loudly over the noise. "How can anybody stand to live in this parking lot?"

Kevin pulled a pair of black Ray Bans from the dashboard, slid them on and shot her a quick glance. "It's the price you pay for living in La-La Land, where it's all *happenin'*. I lived in Venice for a few years, back in my twenties, and that was enough for me. Give me the Central Coast over Southern California any day."

"Why?"

"Oh, just wait till we get north of Ventura. Then you'll know *exactly* what I'm talking about."

Chapter 19

Cara studied the passing tapestry of golden-green hills, dry desert foliage, and Spanish-titled canyons. When they passed through Ventura, she put a hand on Kevin's shoulder and said loudly over the wind, "Ventura is the ultimate California-sounding name! It conjures images of old woody station wagons, surfboards, palm trees and sunsets."

Kevin glanced over at her. "When did you say you were here last?"

"I vacationed in San Diego in the mid-eighties. It was one of the best summers of my entire…" Cara trailed off as something to the left of the highway caught her eye. Something blue and glittering. Her eyes lit up as she pointed and cried, "The ocean! *Finally!*"

Kevin watched her with the face of a parent watching his child tear open presents on Christmas morning.

"I *love* the Pacific, Kevin."

"Well good, because there's a lot more of it where we're headed."

They exchanged affectionate looks, then he reached down to turn up the Zero 7 CD that was playing—a perfect choice for the coastal drive.

Cara leaned back in her seat, eyes glued to the vast water stretching over the horizon. She delighted in every wave that crested, crashed and frothed against the rocks and sand below. To their right, layers of eroding cliffs sloped dramatically toward the highway's edge like sandcastles diminishing in high tide. With every mile, the hills began to shed their dry desert brown and grow a thick coat of green chaparral. It's like we're entering an oasis, she observed inwardly. After awhile, she broke her reverent silence and turned to Kevin. "Do you have any idea how novel it is for me to experience sea *and* mountains, side by side like this?"

"I can just imagine. I think it suits you much better than Cincinnati."

"I think you're right."

Cara squinted against the sun as she studied Kevin's profile, strong and handsome against the backdrop of the sea. His short hair blew stiffly in the wind and his youthful demeanor made him seem ten years younger. Compared to the other men who had passed through her life, Kevin Tierney was a breath of fresh air. Something about him was different from the rest, but she couldn't quite figure out what that something was. Maybe after spending some time with him, she'd know for sure.

Feeling the weight of her stare, Kevin looked over and flashed another smile that rivaled the sun's brightness. She couldn't help but reflect it back to him. Impulsively, he threw his right arm around her shoulders, pulled her close, and planted a tender kiss on her cheek.

With mounting elation, she threw both arms into the wind above her head and cried, "Woo-hoooo! I'm riding up the California coast in a sa-*weet* vintage MG with cali4nyapix! I have *arrived!*"

Kevin shook his head, laughing.

"I'm tellin' ya, it doesn't get any better than this!"

"Oh, I beg to differ," he told her, dipping his chin and peering over the tops of his sunglasses with a pointed look. "Just you wait, Miss Moonflower. This is only the tip of the iceberg."

Cara let out another whoop as Kevin cruised into the high-speed lane and picked up the pace. The empty coastline eventually gave way to civilization again, in the form of little beachside towns. Then the first sign for Santa Barbara appeared when the highway's median filled with aesthetic shrubs, flowers and brightly colored bougainvillea. "Ah, home sweet home," Kevin said with a proud grin. "All these coastal towns are scenic, but nothing holds a candle to Santa Barbara."

Around the next bend came a full view of the city in all its splendor. Misty clouds hovered over blue-green mountaintops. Glowing white homes and buildings dotted the foothills below. Throughout the town, orange Spanish-tiled rooftops shone brightly in the afternoon sun, and palms of all shapes and sizes lined the streets and beaches. The vision of the city was so breathtaking it nearly stopped Cara's heart.

"My God," she marveled in a hushed tone. "You never told me you lived in Heaven."

"Indeed."

Cara turned an envious gaze to Kevin. "You lucky bastard!"

Kevin opened his mouth in silent laughter and geared down as cars in front of them slowed to a sudden rush hour crawl. "Oh well, at least this'll give you a chance to look around a bit."

For the next ten minutes, Cara did just that. She watched as Kevin pointed out various peaks, structures, and city landmarks that were visible from the highway. She also observed people in the cars around them who either yakked on cell phones, talked and laughed with friends, or bobbed their heads to thumping music. Every driver—whether they were in a brand new BMW or an old beater with surfboard racks—sported fashionable sunglasses as they drove into the late afternoon sun. It was so *California*.

Exit after exit moved slowly past until Kevin took the one called Las Positas.

In a matter of minutes, they were across the highway and cruising through a grassy canyon. When the road dead-ended at the coast, Kevin made a right turn and passed the parking lot of a small public beach. "This is Arroyo Burro—also known as Hendry's Beach. We can walk to it later, if you like."

"Walk?"

"Yeah, we're really close to home." He downshifted as the lane pitched into a winding uphill climb edged with green shrubs and wildflowers. Near the top of the bluff, Kevin turned left into a hidden drive that disappeared over a steep incline. At its summit, they were met by a clearing of blue sky over an ocean view. Cara smelled the salty sea wind as it hit her face. The pavement then spilled down into a circular brick drive next to a coral-colored house perched on the side of a cliff.

"Welcome to my humble abode," he told her as he pulled up next to it and killed the engine.

"Studio? This is no studio!" Cara whipped off her sunglasses for a closer look at the breezy and elaborate home.

With an impish look, Kevin admitted, "Okay, *part* of it is my humble abode. The bigger part belongs to my landlords, Mr. and Mrs. Winters. I'm in the guest cottage right next to it."

Cara stepped out of the car, her mouth falling open. "Oh, *meow!* What a place! You lucky, lucky man!"

"Meh." He waved off her envy as he grabbed the bag from the trunk. "Wait till you see how small it is on the inside."

She gave him a playful shove. "I was talking about the *view*."

"Oh, right, can't complain there." He beckoned her to follow him. "Come on back, it gets even better."

Kevin led her down a stone walkway lined with various cacti, succulents and exotic shrubs. Some had leaves so thick and shiny they seemed plastic. Others looked Dr. Seuss-like with long shoots sprouting clusters of spherical flowers. Birds of Paradise stood poised like Vegas showgirls, and Cara couldn't help reaching out to see what one felt like. Kevin turned when he became aware that she was ten paces behind him.

"Sorry," she laughed, stopping to sniff the heavenly fragrance of an orange tree laden with fruit. "None of this stuff grows back home, and it's way cool."

He gave a bemused shake of the head and waited for her to catch up before moving on. The path ended just outside the guest cottage where small bonsai plants twisted and stretched their tiny limbs from marble pots. Cara stooped to give one a delicate caress. "Kevin, do the Winters' make these themselves?"

"I make them."

She looked up at him in wonder. "Seriously? My God, Kevin…design, illustration, vintage cars…and bonsai plants. What *don't* you do?"

Kevin hung a humble head as he pulled out the jingling keychain, unlocked his hand-crafted wooden door and held it open for her.

Cara walked inside and took a sweeping glance around the hexagonal studio. A kitchenette was tucked into an alcove just to the left of the door, separated from the rest of the room by a bar and two Art Deco stools. To the right was a small fireplace with a thickly woven Oriental rug lying in front of it. On the rug stood a Japanese-style coffee table, surrounded by throw pillows. In the center of the room, shiny hardwood floors reflected the light from the huge bay window overlooking the ocean.

Kevin's work area filled the corner to the left of the window. It consisted of a small drafting table and a computer desk. Amazing, Cara thought, how neat and orderly all his things looked within such a small space. She inhaled deeply, trying to identify the pleasing scent that permeated the entire dwelling, and wondered if it was the very wood used in its construction. Cara turned to him, thoroughly enchanted. "This has to be one of the coolest places I've ever seen!"

"Seriously? You must not get out much."

Cara grinned and followed him into the middle of the room.

"Okay, Cara. If you stand right here, you can get the grand tour without even moving. It'll take all of two seconds." Kevin threw a sarcastic wink over his shoulder, then gestured from one area to the next. "Living room, work studio, bedroom and bath. Four for the price of one!"

From this new vantage point, Cara had a full view of the bedroom nook. Her gaze drifted through the wide doorway and rested on his double bed. It was draped in a satiny, blue-gray, bachelor-looking duvet. For a split second, she imagined what the slippery fabric might feel like beneath her naked body. Squeezing her eyes shut, she shooed the brazen thought from her mind and turned back to the ocean view.

"Go look, if you want," he invited.

Cara moved to the window and studied the calm ocean, sparkling in the early evening sun. A pocket of white fog out on the horizon had begun to dull the blue of the sky. "Does this view ever lose its novelty for you?"

"Never," was Kevin's immediate reply as he quietly appeared by her side. "I feel so lucky to have landed such a sweet deal on rent here, and Mr. Winters is one of the coolest landlords I've ever known. He's pretty conservative, politically, and we often get into some heated debates…but other than that, he's like a father to me. He's got all kinds of interesting stories from his past, about the California of his day."

"And you mentioned a Mrs. Winters?"

"Yes! She's pretty amazing too. The Winters are one of those rare couples who stayed in love all their lives and still hold hands even in their seventies."

Cara felt half jaded and half envious as she caught herself thinking, yeah, that *is* pretty damn rare.

Kevin turned to glance at the clock on the mantel, then put a hand on her shoulder. "How does Happy Hour at a beachside café sound?"

Cara's face brightened. "It sounds *perfect*."

"You might want to grab a jacket or some long-sleeved shirt to throw over later. It cools down quite a bit in the evenings."

When Cara knelt by her bag and began to sift through her belongings, something pink and fuzzy caught her eye. A toy mouse lay staring up at her from the floor. She turned quizzical eyes toward Kevin. "Hey, where are the cats?"

Kevin reached for a black, long-sleeved shirt draped over his desk chair. "They're outside. See that open window over the kitchen sink? That's where they come in and out."

Cara glanced at the window. "Is it safe for them out there, on this cliff?"

"Yeah, my girls never wander very far. Rennie likes to sun herself on the patio and Mo is such a little chicken shit, she'd never get within ten feet of the cliff. If anything, it's the skunks and coyotes that worry me."

Cara finally unearthed a black, macramé, button-down sweater and stood up. "Well, I can't wait to meet them."

"Be warned," Kevin told her with a grin. "You'll fall in love."

As they headed for the door, Cara felt the words on her lips, but held them back. *My dear Kevin, as far as falling in love, it's not the cats I'm worried about.*

Chapter 20

"Oh my *God* do I miss the ocean!"

Cara scrambled for the water's edge, hopping on one foot to remove a sandal and then the other. Kevin followed behind, smiling as she leapt over half-submerged rocks and rubbery pieces of kelp. She stopped when the first gentle rush of water lapped over her feet and glanced back at him wide-eyed. "It's cold!'

"Yeah, the Pacific isn't as warm as the Atlantic." He caught up with her and pointed to her feet with concern. "Also, there's a slight issue with tar. Check the bottoms of your feet."

Cara lifted each one up and found them spotless. "Are you serious? Is it from those?" She gestured to a row of oil derricks sprouting out of the ocean a few miles off shore.

"No, believe it or not, it's a natural substance called asphaltum that seeps out of the ocean floor. The Native Americans in this area used to patch their canoes with it, once upon a time. Every so often it washes up on the beach."

"Oh, no!" Cara looked down, horrified. "Should I put my sandals back on?"

Kevin smiled and gave her shoulder a little squeeze. "I think it's pretty clear today."

They turned and strolled down the long beach, sneaking little sidelong glances and relishing the novelty of seeing each other in the flesh. Ten minutes later, they reached Hendry's and the Blue Dolphin Cafe.

"Oh, crap." Kevin observed the crowded patio tables with a frown. "Maybe we should've come here *before* going home. I hope you don't mind waiting a bit."

Cara shook her head. "I'm fine. And waiting's fun when you're in good company."

He turned and threw her a look of gratitude, then did another elevator stare. "Man, you're a vision this evening!"

Cara felt her cheeks go warm. It had been quite awhile since she'd been looked at that way by someone who meant a lot to her, and it felt damn good. "You are *such* a charmer, Kevin."

"No, a charmer usually says things for effect and not because he means them."

Before Cara could respond, Kevin turned and approached the hostess about the wait. To their pleasant surprise, there was no wait at all. A table for two had opened up in the middle of the patio with the best view in the house. Once they were seated, a server appeared to take drink orders.

"Let's have their Iguana margaritas," Kevin told her, leaning forward emphatically. "They're made with Midori and taste pleasantly different."

Cara nodded. "Sounds really good."

When the server walked off, the two were left staring across the table at each other. Cara became transfixed by Kevin's blue eyes again, her writer's brain carefully constructing their perfect description. *Closed doors with a wreath of warmth and friendliness hanging on their exterior, and a hint of seductive mystery as to what lay behind them.*

"So…here you are."

Cara sighed. "Here I am."

"Are you feeling a little crazy?"

A burst of nervous laughter escaped from deep in her gut. "Yeah, you could say that." She put a hand to her heart. "Kevin, seriously, I can't thank you enough for being my tour guide on such a ludicrous mission."

Kevin's face softened as he waved her off. "Hey, I'm happy to do it. I just hope you'll be okay. I mean, I can't even imagine the emotional roller-coaster you've been on in the last few months, and I worry about the outcome. How you'll feel if you find her, the devastation if you don't…"

Cara's smile faded. "Yeah, I know."

Trying not to spoil the mood, he leaned forward with reassurance. "The upside of this is that you get a tour of some of California's finest landscapes. That, and we're finally getting to spend some time together. This is *so* much nicer than talking on the phone or 'reading' your voice in a PM."

Unexpected, embarrassing tears welled up in Cara's eyes and she felt like a baseball had lodged in her throat. She looked away and shook her head, "I'm so sorry…"

"No, no," Kevin soothed, reaching across the table and putting a warm hand over hers. "You've gone through a lot of drastic change in the last month, Cara. Be where you need to be."

His touch was like the coziest campfire she could remember, its heat radiating up her arm. The contact only increased her tears until they spilled down her cheeks. With her free hand, she hurriedly wiped them away.

Instinctively, Kevin grabbed his napkin, shook out the silverware, and handed it over to her.

"Thanks," she choked, then dabbed at her eyes and attempted to collect herself.

When the server returned and set their margaritas on the table, he took a quick look at Cara and asked, "Do you need a few minutes?"

Kevin nodded in appreciation before turning back to Cara who sniffled, let out a long breath, and managed a weary smile. He mirrored the smile, a tinge of concern in his eyes. "Everything's going to be okay."

She nodded, eyed their drinks, and gave a little laugh. "Talk about perfect timing."

"Yes!" Kevin seized his glass and lifted it to hers. "To Cara's California adventure."

"And in honor of our Irish heritage…*sláinte*."

"Sláinte."

A sharp clink and the two cyber-friends downed healthy swallows of their icy, neon-lime elixirs.

"So," Cara said, watching people stroll past on their evening beach walks, "is this insanely beautiful place where you plan on spending the rest of your life?"

"I don't know, Cara," he answered, settling back in his chair. "I've never looked that far into the future."

"Not even a little? As in, where you plan to retire?"

"Yeah, I realize other guys my age are dumping money into 401Ks and planning for retirement already, which is great, but I've lived a very unconventional life if you haven't noticed." He swished his drink around and around in the glass. "I have no wife, no kids, no regular corporate paycheck…so who knows where I'll be in ten years? I guess you could say I'm an *in the moment* kind of guy, breaking all the rules."

Cara considered his answer while uncrossing her legs and crossing them the opposite way. In doing so, her foot accidentally brushed against Kevin's. When he didn't move it, a tingle flew up her leg and she felt the delicious crackle of ripe chemistry between them. All those months of wondering, and now there was no doubt. Even better was the fact that there hadn't been one awkward moment since meeting at the airport. They were both totally at ease with each other, sitting there sipping margaritas as if they'd been friends for years.

"Well," she finally replied, "according to the Zen Buddhists, nothing else exists outside the moment."

"Yeah?"

"So I've read."

"What about you? Do you see yourself living out your days in Cincinnati?"

"I used to," she said with a far away stare, "but now I'm not sure of anything anymore. I sometimes feel like I'm having an early midlife crisis, Kevin."

He raised one eyebrow. "At your age?"

"I know I've mentioned more than once about my growing need to get away. To go someplace else and start completely over. But it seems a little late in my life to be doing something like that, you know? I'm almost forty, for godsake. By all rights, I should be picking up my kids from soccer in a minivan right now."

Kevin tilted his head back and puffed out a laugh. "There's an image. Somehow, I can't picture you in the soccer mom role."

Cara's eyes flashed with equal amounts of indignation and jest. "What, you don't think I would've been a great mom?"

"Oh, I'm sure you would have. It's just not the Cara I know. The independent writer on her illustrious career path."

"Well, those certainly weren't my only goals." A heavy sadness settled into her chest, so she took another dose of the margarita and drained it. "I really *did* want the family life, Kevin. It just…never happened for me. So I kept adapting and moving on to things I actually had control over."

With a grave stare, Kevin slowly shook his head. "Man, *I* didn't want it. I never felt like my life was stable enough to take on fatherhood, let alone marriage. Then after I started my business and began to feel slightly comfortable with the idea, I couldn't seem to find the right woman. Now I feel too old to be a dad."

"Then I guess we've had the same problem, haven't we?" Cara laughed. "All these years of looking, and I haven't found the right person either. I hope men don't find it suspect that I'm nearly forty and have never been married."

"They won't think that around here," Kevin told her. "There are a lot more people in California who put off marriage and kids until their forties or even fifties."

"Wow, that's refreshing. People back home have such a *mindset* about marital statuses…and they're always asking about it. Every damn time they see you. Then when you tell them no, you're not married and you have no kids, and you're not actually seeing anyone right now…they sometimes look at you like you've just told them you have cancer."

"Well that sucks."

"It really does." Cara leaned her chin on her hand and felt the pleasant buzz of tequila setting in, warming her face and loosening the tension in her shoulders. "Maybe this is the place for me, then. Where other people my age are still single and where I won't feel like such a fish out of water like I do in Midwestern suburbia."

Kevin shrugged and held up his glass in a toasting fashion. "Hey, we've always got room for one more."

Spotting their dwindling drinks, the server immediately appeared at the table. "Can I get you two more?"

"Yeah, let's do another round," Kevin said, glancing up at him, then at Cara. "Sound good?"

She lowered her eyelids halfway. "Mmmm…*meow*."

The server nodded. "Perfect. And are you two ready to order now?"

Kevin clenched his teeth in a slight wince. "I'm sorry. We haven't even been looking at the menus. Cara, are you hungry yet?"

Cara looked down at her closed menu, then up at Kevin. "If I'm going to keep drinking, then I'd better eat. I'm a major lightweight."

He grinned and looked back at the server. "Five more minutes?"

"Oh, absolutely. Take your time. I'll get those margaritas while you decide."

Cara's eyes widened as she dutifully picked up her menu and opened it. "Oops."

"No worries," Kevin laughed. "We have every right to enjoy ourselves and take our time."

"Just like in Europe," she told him, studying the list of entrees. "You can complete an entire conversation about the rise and fall of the Roman Empire before the waiter even shows up at your table. Then when he does, it's all very unhurried and leisurely. I *love* that."

"You certainly are well traveled." Kevin regarded her over his menu in admiration. "Do you know I've never even been to Europe? Home to some of the most famous artists and art museums throughout history, yet I've never even set foot there!"

"Well, what are you waiting for?" Cara shook a finger at him. "Get your tanned little California butt over there." *Oh God, the tequila is taking over. Stop talking. Stop talking until you've eaten something!* "And pick an entree before our server gets back."

He snapped a salute. "Aye-aye, Captain."

Cara giggled, then resumed her study of the menu.

Kevin closed his and set it on the table. The he cleared his throat and sniffed a few times. "So Cara, tell me something."

"Yes?"

"Why do you always *meow?*"

"What?"

"Several times, now, I've heard you say 'meow' or 'meow, baby' and wondered what was up with that. Is one of your idols Catwoman or something?"

Cara burst into full-on laughter and rolled her eyes. "It's a weird thing of mine, ever since I was a teenager. You know how back in the roaring twenties, if women thought something was cool, they'd say it was the cat's meow?"

"Yeah, yeah," he replied with a few quick nods.

"I always thought that particular idiom was hilarious…and kind of cool. So my modern version of it, when I highly admire something, is just *meow.* See?"

Kevin broke into yet another grin, shook his head and looked away, then stared at her. "You're whacked, girl. But in a *good* way."

Cara batted her eyes innocently over the top of her menu, then snapped it shut when she saw the server returning.

After their meal was ordered, Kevin raised his drink to the pinks, salmons and lavenders swirling in the sky over the cafe. "Isn't that fantastic?"

"Beautiful."

"I brought you here on your first night to give you a taste of the beach, but just so you know…this isn't even *close* to being the best place for margaritas in Santa Barbara."

"I know, I know," she nodded. "Lobo's."

"You remembered!"

"Well, you mentioned it more than once in our phone conversations."

"I've gotta take you up there, Cara. It's not fancy, but it's got character…and a vintage jukebox!"

"Whoa, you never told me *that* before. How utterly cool!"

"Oh, you're gonna love it. Their chef is outstanding, too. It's hard for me to go anywhere else for Mexican after sampling *his* cooking. Best Mexican food in Santa Barbara, best margaritas in California. Hands down."

"Oh, you've sampled all the margaritas in California, have you?"

He gave a tiny roll of the eyes. "Well, you know what I—"

"Because it's a pretty big state, and every time I talked to you on the phone you were all, 'yeah, I'm off to *Lobo's…*' so I'm wondering how you can make this claim never having set foot anywhere else…"

Kevin nudged her foot with his. "Oh *stop,* would ya?"

Cara tittered and drummed her hands lightly on the table. "Sorry. I forgot to tell you that tequila totally annihilates my inhibition…and makes me stupid. I know it's only been one drink, but I haven't eaten in awhile and I'm the world's biggest lightweight."

"You already said that."

"Yeah, well, I guess tequila makes me stupid *and* forgetful, then." Cara let out a raucous laugh.

Kevin folded his arms on the table and watched her with the wide-eyed fascination of a kid watching animal tricks in a circus.

"Man, I *love* your eyes," Cara gushed, realizing that alcohol had rendered the speech-monitoring function of her brain completely inoperable.

He blinked and retracted his head in mock surprise.

"No, really," she leaned forward for emphasis. "All those hours we spent on the phone, I kept wondering what your eyes looked like. What they were saying when you weren't talking. Now here they are…and I can't stop staring at them."

He blushed and studied his silverware. "Wow, you're not kidding about that tequila thing."

Cara swallowed hard, regretting yet *not* regretting what she'd just uttered. Before she could say anything else, Kevin looked up with a gleam in his eye.

"So, what are they saying?"

Cara dropped her head to one side, quizzically.

"My eyes. You said you wondered what they were saying when I'm not talking."

Cara's mouth opened in a tentative smile. *Well, they're telling me that you're very amused and excited to be with me right now…and every once in awhile they let on how you'd probably like to touch what you keep staring at…but they're not revealing everything just yet. No, there's probably far more to you than meets the eye, Kevin Tierney.*

"Well?"

Cara did a mental arm-wrestle with the tequila in her bloodstream. Must. Not. Speak.

The server wove his way through the tables and set a basket of bread between them.

"Ah, just in time, before I make an even bigger fool of myself." Cara reached for a slice of sourdough and took a quick nibble.

Kevin offered her a pat of butter from a little porcelain dish, then selected one for himself.

As they buttered, she glanced around the other tables. "So…how do you like living in a city of Barbie dolls?"

Kevin looked at her, knife poised in mid-swipe. "Barbie dolls?"

"I've been noticing a lot of women who look like Barbie. Perfect figures, tight-fitting clothes, identical straightened hair with chunky highlights…" She leaned in closer and whispered "… and many with artificial pieces and parts."

Kevin glanced around. "Yeah, that is totally the influence of L.A. It finds its way up here a lot. But you'll also see a good deal of no-makeup-wearing hippie chicks, too. The faction of 'earthy' people is just as strong."

"Hm." Cara popped another bite of bread into her mouth and did one more glance around the patio. Then she leaned in and lowered her voice. "I think I'd rather be average looking than blend in with a bunch of Stepford Barbies."

"Average? I don't know about average, Cara. I think you're exceptionally beautiful in a wood nymph sort of way…tall, voluptuous and solid."

Cara laughed. "Gee, thanks...I've never been called a wood nymph before. But a former boyfriend of mine used to call me Zena the Warrior Princess. Large frames run in my family."

Kevin gave her a slow shake of the head, his eyes savoring every inch of her. "Nothing wrong with that."

Cara placed a hand over her stomach to quiet the butterfly dance, while resisting the urge to crawl across the table and plant a juicy one on those delectable lips. Thankfully, their food arrived and blocked her path. After sampling the first few bites of her Thai spring rolls with peanut sauce, she waved a fork toward Kevin. "So, when did you get the new do?"

Kevin looked up from his mahi-mahi. "What, my hair?"

"Yeah, it's shorter…but all rock star-like."

He swallowed his bite of food and nodded. "As long as I was getting it cut, I thought I'd let Kristi do something inventive with it."

Cara chewed thoughtfully. "It's a good look for you…makes you look younger."

Kevin ran a hand through his hair and winked. "Well damn, I should've done this sooner, then." He reached for his glass of water, paused, and pointed a finger at her. "*Your* hair's different too!"

She watched him study her head like a painting.

"It's shorter, right?"

Cara shook her hair, making it swing from side to side. "Yes, and I love it! I love the feel of flippy hair with healthy ends. When it gets long, the ends get thin and crispy."

Kevin nearly spewed his sip of water. "You make them sound like pizza crust!"

Her shoulders shook with silent laughter. "Or Kentucky Fried Chicken?"

He pointed an *exactly* finger at her, then resumed eating.

The two chattered on as dusk faded into night. When the check arrived, Kevin grabbed it before Cara could even look at it. "Are you exhausted yet? It's about one A.M. in Ohio right now."

Cara checked the time on her cell phone, and admitted with a half-lidded smile, "I wondered why my head was starting to feel a bit swimmy. I thought it was the tequila!"

"Well let's get you home so you can go to sleep."

On their way back up the beach, Kevin and Cara walked silently so they could enjoy the serenade of waves in the darkness. When they were far enough away from the lights of the parking lot, he pointed upward. "Look, Cara."

Cara tilted her head toward the heavens and saw millions of bright stars like diamonds on the black velvet of a jeweler's case. She opened her mouth in a wide smile. "*Beautiful*."

"Isn't it?"

As a gust of bone-chilling wind hit, she hugged her arms close to her body and added through chattering teeth, "And the air smells so *fresh* here on the coast…what a perfect first night! Thank you, sweet man."

Kevin put a warm arm around her, and when she leaned in close to him she caught a whiff of something woodsy and pleasant. "Mmm, you smell good. What cologne are you wearing?"

There was a faint chuckle in her ear. "I'm not wearing anything."

"It's a fresh, clean smell…like woods after a rain. That's the best way I know how to describe it. Your house smells like it, too."

"I think you're smelling my fabric softener!"

She laughed. "Are you serious? That would make an excellent commercial for the fabric softener, wouldn't it? A girl sniffing a guy's shirt going 'Oh wow, your cologne is so intoxicating!' and he just winks at the camera as a voiceover goes, 'Fools her *every* time!'."

Kevin laughed with her, then snuffled in Cara's hair. "Hey, what are *you* wearing? I feel like I'm in a botanical garden in Hawaii!"

"Ooh, you're good!" she cried, peering through the dark at him. "It's pikake flower oil. Which is Japanese, actually, but they have them all over Hawaii. I take it you've been there?"

"I went surfing on Oahu one winter, when I was still in my twenties."

Cara shook her head. "You've been everywhere and done *everything*."

"Not everything," he argued. "And look who's talking, Ms. Europe."

"We should go to Europe, Kevin," Cara suggested playfully. "I'd love to sail with you down the Grand Canal of Venice."

"That would be sweet," he told her, playing along with the fantasy. "Thinking of all the photo opportunities in that city makes me drool."

Talking about future plans with Kevin felt more than a little premature to Cara, having only just met him in person that day, but one never knew. At their age, *carpe diem* held more significance than ever before.

"Here are the steps," he said, guiding her to the right. "Thank goodness the railing's painted a bright glow-in-the-dark white, eh?"

Cara stared until the railing came into focus. "I'll say. I never would have found that otherwise."

Kevin held tightly to her hand until they were both safely at the top, where a motion-detector light flashed on. It illuminated their path to the front door, which he held open for her, and where Rennie and Mo were waiting with a hungry duet of frantic meows.

"Okay, okay," Kevin appeased, stooping down to give them both pats on the head and long strokes down their backs. While he attended to filling up their food dishes, Cara knelt down to meet the kitties.

Mo was a fluffy, petite tabby with lovely green eyes and a silky coat. Rennie was the short-haired, older and less spry version of Mo. Cara took turns petting them as they blissfully elevated their hindquarters and grazed her hand with the sides of their faces. "Hi sweeties," she cooed. "Look how beautiful you both are! *Yesh.*" She looked up at Kevin in delight. "You were right, I'm in love! They're so *friendly,* compared to my little stuck-up princess. She always takes awhile to warm up to new people."

Once the cats were fed, Kevin straightened and leaned on a bar stool. "You know, Cara, you came to Santa Barbara during some uncharacteristically good weather."

"Did I?"

"Yeah, that's the clearest night sky I've seen in awhile. We usually have what's called the June Gloom. It's a marine layer of clouds and fog that hovers over the coast most of the day. This year it came a little early and seems to be over with…which is perfect for driving up the coast! You *never* want to miss those spectacular views."

Cara rose up from her kneeling position and stood tall. "I must be a good luck charm, huh?"

Kevin stared at her with a fleeting look of fondness, then took a deep breath and studied the floor. "Okay, about the sleeping arrangements. I don't have a guest room, as you can see, and no couch. So if you want, I can—"

She crept up to him as he talked, looped her arm through one of his and looked at him with conviction. "Kevin, I don't mind sharing your bed if you don't. I mean, we've talked about how nice it would be to cuddle up together before, and…we're just going to be sleeping, right?"

He hesitated, then quietly assured her, "Of course."

"That's not an unreasonable request, is it?"

"Not at all." Kevin took both her hands in his. "Actually, I think it's a very sweet request and one that doesn't happen every day, you know?"

Cara squeezed her eyes shut in relief. “I’m so glad you’re down with that. I felt really silly hearing the words leave my mouth…but all this is still pretty strange, you know?”

“I know, and it’s not silly at all. Cuddling is actually pretty nice.” He lifted a hand to caress her cheek. “You’re very special to me, Cara. I don’t want anything to ruin that.”

“Me either.”

Kevin’s shoulders seemed to relax as he let out a long sigh. “It’s so nice having you here.”

Cara collapsed forward into his arms and gave him a long, exhausted hug.

Minutes later they lay beneath the silky duvet on Kevin’s bed, which provided just the right buffer against the cool breeze floating through his partially-open window. Snuggling next to a warm, strong, body again was incredibly comforting to Cara, especially when it belonged to a new and trusted friend.

“Oh, listen…” she told him softly, “…you can hear the waves.”

“It’s nice, isn’t it?”

“You’re so fortunate to live here.”

“Yeah.”

After soaking up their newfound closeness for a few moments, Cara’s lids grew unbearably heavy. She leaned over and kissed him on the cheek. “Goodnight, Kevin. Thank you for such a warm welcome today.”

“It was my pleasure, Cara mia. Sweet dreams.”

Cara remained on her side with one hand draped lightly over his shoulder. She listened to his breath move in and out while thoughts meandered through her contented mind. *My God, I’m in California sleeping next to Kevin Tierney. Just sleeping. What a fantastic man! I love his house, I love the feel of his warm, strong energy. Six months ago I didn’t even know who he was and now...now I feel so at home.*

Just before drifting off, she noticed with a sleepy smile that the rhythm of their breathing was in perfect synch.

Chapter 21

The first thing Cara saw when she opened her eyes was a ball of striped fur, curled snugly into a letter C. She thought it might be Rennie. On the other side of the cat, Kevin's back expanded and contracted in the slow rhythm of sleep. Gingerly, she lifted her head to gaze out at the morning ocean, silvery-gray beneath a brightening sky. The sweet, woodsy aroma from the day before hung thick in the air, and she breathed it in deeply. *I'm in heaven. I've died and gone to heaven. And Kevin gets to wake up in heaven every damn day!*

As if hearing his name in her thoughts, Kevin roused and turned to face her with a groggy smile. The sudden movement drove Rennie up and off the foot of the bed with a thud. Then, without a word, Kevin reached out and pulled Cara gently into his arms. "Mmm, this is so nice."

"Isn't it?" Cara wrapped her free arm around his waist and snuggled against his chest. Then she felt his hand in her hair, gently stroking it back from her face and sifting the strands through his fingers.

"Your hair is so baby-fine and soft," he murmured above her head.

"I know," Cara replied in a drab tone. "It's really hard to deal with, sometimes."

"No, no…I mean that in a good way. I like it."

Cara smiled and planted a tender kiss at the base of Kevin's throat. He sighed and moved his hand from her hair down her cheekbone till it cradled her chin. Then he slowly turned her face toward his and reciprocated with a longer kiss. Enjoying the feel of silky, moist lips against her own, she extended the kiss for a moment more, then said goodbye with the tip of her tongue before pulling away. *You're it.*

Not wasting a second, Kevin's mouth began to explore. He nuzzled his way to Cara's neck and left a languid trail of nibble-kisses down its length, sending a shiver across her skin. *Oh, bravo! BRAVO! How will I top that?* Cara paused for only a moment, then began to trace feather-light circles on his back with her fingertips.

"Oh, oh, I *love* that!" he exclaimed, his deep morning-voice rising a few pitches. "Not to creep you out or anything, but my mom used to do that when I was little, to calm me down and get me to go to sleep. I've loved it ever since."

"Well then," Cara whispered against his cheek, "I'll just have to keep doing it."

As she continued, Kevin also began caressing, working his way down to the small of her back. He traced the curve of her hip, lingered there hesitantly and let out an even deeper sigh. Cara froze, feeling a surge of electricity as she anticipated his next move. Ever so lightly, he slid the satin nightie away from her creamy skin and mesh panties. She could hear blood pulsing in her ears. *Oh God, if he goes any further, I won't have the willpower to stop him.* Slowly, reluctantly, the hand returned to her back and they both exhaled. He encircled her in his arms and hugged her warmly to him. Cara slid one bent leg in between both of his and they lay there for what felt like an eternity, enjoying the feeling of being intertwined.

"Kevin?"

"Yeah?"

"Thank you."

"For what?"

"For being okay with all this…all this yummy touching, and not needing to go further."

Cara felt Kevin's warm breath in her ear. "Hey, it's completely enough for me, just being close to you."

She lay in his arms, marveling at the beauty of the moment. A bond was steadily forming between them, and history was being made in her life. Kevin was the first man she'd ever become close to before meeting him in person. He was also the first man she'd ever spent the night with at first meeting without it leading to sex. Not that sex wouldn't have been fantastic after the dry spell she'd endured over the past few months, but sometimes…timing was *everything*.

"How would you like some nice, hot, dark-roast coffee, Moonflower?"

Cara sighed, lying back against her pillow. "I would like that *very* much."

"All right." Kevin raised his arms over his head, stretched luxuriously and opened his mouth in a wide yawn. "Two coffees, coming up."

When he turned toward her again, she smiled at his disheveled bedhead and crinkly morning eyes. Their blueness lit up with a twinkle of adoration.

"I *love* the way you're always smiling, Cara. It's infectious."

Cara's grin widened even more and she felt the color rise in her cheeks. *Oh Kevin, if you only knew how many months I* haven't *been smiling…and how, ever since getting here, I haven't been able to stop.*

With a couple of grunts, groans, and mutterings about being old, Kevin was out of bed and on his feet. He pulled a fleecy, forest-green robe from a nearby closet and padded away into the kitchen. Cara also arose and slipped into a satin-lined, terry robe purchased from Victoria's Secret days before her trip. It felt deliciously warm in the chilly morning air as she made her way to the picture window and its ocean view. Half way across the room, Cara's mouth fell open. "What the—?"

Out on the horizon were the pointed blue-gray peaks of two long mountain ranges.

"Kevin, am I losing my mind? Are those *islands* out there? I don't remember seeing those yesterday!"

Kevin turned, spilling a few coffee grounds from the scoop he dangled over the filter basket, and laughed heartily.

Cara put one hand on her hip and glanced back and forth between the view and Kevin, completely befuddled.

Shaking his head, Kevin explained, "I'm so used to it, I forget how confusing that must be to outsiders."

"Used to *what?*"

"Those are the Channel Islands, often hidden behind a layer of sea mist at this time of year. It all depends how the weather conditions are off shore."

"Weird!"

"Now you see 'em, now you don't! Our magical islands do their own disappearing act."

Cara silently laughed at herself, then pulled her robe more tightly around her body, which did not go unnoticed by Kevin.

"Are you cold? Would you like a nice hot bath, Mademoiselle?"

"In that vintage claw-foot tub you've got in your bathroom?" she replied, clasping her hands together. "Would I ever!"

"Isn't it cool? The Winters gave it up when they remodeled their bathroom in the main house. It's so nice and deep." Kevin dumped another scoop of coffee into the basket. "Or would you rather use the outdoor shower that Mr. Winters and I built? It's like a mini-Stonehenge with a shower head inside!"

"Wow, I'd love to see that!"

"I can take you out there as soon as this coffee's underway."

"Tell you what," Cara said quickly, "I'll take the bath this morning and the shower another time. I'm a little stiff from my long day of flying yesterday, so I could use a good soak."

Kevin slid the coffee filter in with a click, snapped the button to "on" and brushed his hands together in the air. "One bubble bath, coming right up."

"Bubbles?" she repeated, eyes widening. "You've got bubble bath?"

"Well, technically it's a 'foaming milk bath.' A really great aromatherapy elixir my sister gave me, with ylang ylang, jasmine and lord knows what other great-smelling oils in it."

"Oh, *nice,*" she told him, closing her eyes in bliss. Then she turned and watched the ocean as it calmly undulated and reflected a glowing streak of gold from the rising sun. The coffeemaker began to gurgle and hiss, permeating the air with its nutty, mouthwatering aroma. From the tiny bathroom came the inviting thunder of water against porcelain. Cara leaned her head against the window, took a deep breath and savored every cozy detail of her first morning in California.

Minutes later she was lying in the finest, most sweet-smelling bath she'd had since childhood. "Oh *meow*, Kevin!" Cara shouted out. "This is so luxurious being able to sink all the way under without any body parts sticking out!"

Cara heard a chuckle from the studio, where Kevin was busy at the computer. "I'm so honored that it earned a meow!"

"I love it! You're the *best!*"

"I'll tell everyone in Planet Indigo that you said so."

Cara stiffened. "What? You're telling them I'm here?"

"Didn't *you?*" he asked with a touch of alarm.

"No!" she replied, sitting up and clutching the edge of the tub. "I didn't say a word, because if Ari—I mean, if *saffire* is still lurking, she'll see your post and maybe assume that I'm coming to find her. Then she might run somewhere else and I'll be completely screwed!"

"Hm, sounds a little far-fetched, but okay. I was just going to let them assume that you're taking a vacation."

"Did you post anything yet?" Cara was one frazzled nerve short of frantic.

"No, no, don't worry," Kevin soothed. "I'm just saying hi to a few folks and checking my email. Sorry to cause any alarm."

"It's okay." She sank back heavily, a clump of white foam flying out from behind her, and eased into relaxation once again.

In another few moments, after some scuffling noises in the kitchen, the bathroom door opened a few inches. "I have your coffee, Principessa. Are you submerged enough for me to bring it in to you?"

"Principessa? You certainly know how to make a girl feel—" she stopped as Kevin appeared around the edge of the door. Boxers with M&M candies printed on them were hanging from his head like a puffy Rastafarian hat. A thick blue towel was wrapped around his waist and a mug of coffee steamed in his hand. Cara broke into a fit of laughter, putting one foamy hand to her mouth.

In a completely normal tone, he asked, "Where would you like this?"

Still giggling, Cara pointed to the edge of the nearby sink. The movement of her arm caused the bubbles around her chest to shift, and she glanced down nervously. Sure enough, a clear spot opened just above her right breast. "Oops!" She wriggled around until the foam once again provided ample coverage.

"Oh! Did we have a wardrobe malfunction there?" He placed the coffee on the sink. "Right when I was looking the other way, too. Damn!"

"I think I like this 'class clown' side of you," she said, catching her breath after the laughter subsided. "I always had a weakness for the guys who made me laugh, in high school."

Kevin rolled his eyes and pulled the shorts from his head with a grin. "I'll be outside in the shower for the next five minutes. Enjoy your coffee and your bath, Cara mia."

Cara glanced at the coffee, then turned to him with eyes aglow. He'd remembered, from their phone conversations, that she took hers with cream. "Thanks for all the pampering, Kevin. Seriously. It means the world to me, after the year I've had."

Kevin, who had listened to countless stories about the breakup and job woes and home-owning ordeals, gave her a meaningful stare. "I know. And believe me, it is my utmost pleasure to make your stay here as enjoyable as possible. You deserve it."

Cara's gaze lingered on his for a long moment. *Go away. Go away* now, *before I start falling in love with you, damn it.*

As if reading her mind, Kevin broke out of the trance, turned and said over his shoulder, "See ya in a few."

Cara sat up and stared after him, admiring his form beneath the towel. For the first time she noticed what a shapely and muscular ass he had. His well-sculpted torso moved oh so nicely as he walked, too. *Meow.* She reached for the mug and took a long, delicious sip of the coffee. "Mm, ten more points for Tierney! The man definitely knows how to brew!"

After setting the cup on the sink again, she sunk deep into the water and closed her eyes. The jasmine and ylang ylang hanging in the steamy air made her feel as though she was lying in a hot springs on some exotic island. *I could get real used to this place. Good thing we're only staying for a couple of days.*

During their last phone call before her flight, Kevin had asked Cara if she'd like to hang out in Santa Barbara before starting the search. His dual motive was to show off his town and give her a chance to rest a bit before traveling on. She had immediately consented, thinking to herself that she also needed time to gear up emotionally for the possible meeting of a relative who'd been dead for the last seven years.

As much as she tried to empty her mind and stay in her "aromatherapy moment," Cara's thoughts kept spiraling back to Arianna and the business at hand. She'd spent weeks contacting hundreds of major wineries from Napa to Santa Barbara. Her ruse was always the same: an email that would throw off all suspicion of her being a nosy stranger trying to gain personal information about an employee.

Dear (Winery),

My husband and I took the most delightful wine tour last summer, and had the privilege of working with a steward who was of great help to us in creating a collection to take home. We're doing a return trip this June, and hoping very much to connect with her again, but cannot remember her name or vineyard to save our lives! Can you please help us? We've attached a photo taken of her on our last tour.

Sincerely,

Catherine Carroll

The name, attached to a non-descript hotmail account, was borrowed from one of Cara's sophisticated college professors who had always seemed like a wine snob. The attached image was a close-up of Arianna holding a glass of wine, taken at a sunny cookout the year before she died. Many of the wineries had been surprisingly helpful, although their apologetic responses turned up nothing. The rest had never sent a reply and therefore ended up on Cara's search list. She worried about facing these people, and whether or not they would cooperate.

Astrea had volunteered to help with the Central Coast locations, inviting Cara and Kevin to make a base camp of her communal household in Cambria—a tiny seaside town near San Simeon and Hearst Castle. Since one of Astrea's housemates was an employee at a local winery, she was definitely a vital resource on the search. Yet Cara was apprehensive about meeting her, still wondering if she and Kevin had something going on. If so, it would be a little too Bohemian sharing beds with him when he already had a lover. Or a former lover, or whatever the hell she was. Jealousy was an emotion Cara tried to avoid at all costs, but this little something between Astrea and Kevin bugged the crap out of her. Perhaps she'd just ask him, point blank, at the next opportune moment. Get it out of her system once and for all.

The sound of the outside door opening brought Cara back to the moment.

"Doing okay, Cara?" Kevin called to her. "Need a refill?"

Cara took another sip from her mug, finding it half full. "Not yet, thank you."

"Well, take your time. I'm going to throw on some clothes."

Just then, the door opened another inch as Mo nosed her way into the bathroom and stared up at Cara.

"Well hello there," Cara said in a high-pitched tone. Then she called out, "Hey Kevin! I've got a little visitor."

"Oh, you do? Is it Mo? Yeah, it's gotta be…Rennie's having a second helping of breakfast, the little pig!"

As he spoke, Cara noticed that the curious feline had widened the door's opening on her way in, leaving a partial view of the bedroom. Unable to stop herself, she peeked through just in time to see Kevin pulling the M&M boxers on. *Wow…a wonderful ass indeed! Mm-mm-mm!* It was all she saw as he stepped out of view, but it was enough. *Good kitty, Mo, good kitty!*

She relaxed into the bath once again, but it wasn't long before her thoughts were penetrated by wonderful cooking aromas wafting from the kitchen. *Oh, that sweetie, he's making breakfast!* Cara's stomach, which had begun to grumble in protest of its emptiness, was motivation enough to wrap up bath time and get dressed. She chose an emerald-green rayon sundress—a favorite that she'd bought from a vendor at an outdoor music festival—for her day of sightseeing. With a short skirt that flared out when she turned this way or that, it was the perfect outfit in which to be both sexy *and* comfortable.

When she sauntered into the kitchen, Kevin turned from the stove looking very pleased with things. "These are my famous California omelets, and they're almost..." His eyes widened mid-sentence as he looked her up and down. "Whoa! Look at you all dolled up!"

"It's just an old hippie-chick dress," she poo-pooed. "I got it ages ago from one of those Indian clothing vendors."

"Ah, but it's the *way* you wear it," he assured her, bringing fingertips together and kissing them in a gesture of approval.

Cara sidled up to the bar and perched on one of the chrome stools. "Ever the flatterer, aren't you cali4nyapix?"

Kevin slid the omelets expertly onto two plates, then turned to her, pan and spatula still in hand. "Only when I really mean it…*Moonflower*."

Cara blinked a couple of times and stared down at the counter. Her mind flashed back to the early stages of Greg's courtship and how freely his compliments flowed. The professions of her beauty, the declarations of how wonderful she was…then once he'd won her over and claimed her heart, they tapered off one by one. It happened with most of the men in her past. Thankfully, this was a different situation. She and Kevin were operating strictly in the moment, so whatever flattery he chose to throw her way, she would simply accept and enjoy. Meeting Kevin's gaze again, she told him, "Well, you sure know how to make a woman feel special. Thank you."

Kevin sat down on the stool next to Cara and pushed her plate closer. "You're welcome, now take a bite!"

Cara looked down with a grin and felt her mouth begin to water. An omelet oozing mushrooms, tomatoes, cheese, and olives sat in a perfect fold on her plate. Avocado slices adorned the top of it, and a tiny ceramic dish of salsa sat on the side. "This is too pretty to eat, Kevin."

"Oh, go on!" he commanded, then checked her place setting attentively. "Where's your coffee?"

Cara put a hand over her mouth. "Oops. Left it in the bathroom."

"I'll go get it, you eat!"

As she tasted her first forkful of the lovingly constructed feast, Kevin fetched the coffee, replenished it from the steaming decanter, and set it down by her plate. Then he watched her face expectantly.

Cara's eyes were closed in delight. "Mmmmm."

Again, Kevin looked pleased. "Meow?"

"Definitely meow," she told him, nodding. "I'm going to eat this super-slow and savor every bite."

Kevin stabbed at his own omelet, gathering huge and ravenous forkfuls. "Well, excuse me while I wolf mine down. I am *so* hungry this morning."

Cara stared down at the immensity of her omelet, which covered the whole plate and drooped over the side like a Salvador Dali clock. "You can have some of mine, because this is way too much."

"Oh, don't be so dainty, girl. You're going to need all that fuel for the long day I've got planned for you."

She grinned and took another bite.

Kevin looked over and mumbled through a mouthful of food, "You think I'm kidding, don't you? I'm taking you downtown, and we'll be doing a lot of walking. All morning, I'll get to watch how your hips move in that flouncy little skirt."

Cara shook her head, blushing.

There was a playful spark in his eyes. "Am I being overly flattering again? 'Cause I can stop..."

"No, no!" Cara held up a hand and waved it lightly in the air. "You go right ahead. Flatter away. I think I'm starting to like it."

Chapter 22

After her first cruise down State Street, Cara immediately understood why Santa Barbara was called “America’s Riviera.” There wasn’t a single spot downtown—not even a back alley—that was without a beautiful view; colorful Spanish tile, ivy-covered buildings, trickling fountains in shaded courtyards, and stucco walls reflecting sunlight in dazzling hues of white. Primary streets were lined with tall, thin palms while others were canopied by tunnels of eucalyptus and Italian stone pine. And no matter where they walked or drove, the blue-brown Santa Ynez Mountains loomed majestically in the background.

“This is the time of year when people-watching is the most fun,” Kevin told her as they strolled into Paseo Nuevo, a sprawling city center of stores, galleries and cafes. “It’s tourist season, and they come from all corners of the world. Want to sit down for a bit?”

“Sure,” Cara answered, surveying a cluster of iron patio tables teeming with the lunchtime crowd. Behind them, a blue-tiled fountain splashed invitingly. After walking around town for most of the morning, it seemed like the perfect place to put her feet up. Kevin snagged a table that had just been vacated by a group of businessmen, and pulled out a chair for her.

They sat for a long while, taking in all the sights. A stylish, forty-something mother with Jackie-O sunglasses talked on her cell phone nearby, keeping a watchful eye on her toddler who gleefully swished his hands in the fountain. Groups of chattering teen-aged girls—younger versions of the “Stepford Barbies”—strolled past, laden with shopping bags. They alternately checked their text messages and complained about some *playah* most of them had dated. Young professionals in dress clothes and sunglasses shared a quick power lunch of sushi and smoothies, laughing and talking and checking their cell phones. People of all ethnicities circulated around Kevin and Cara, some with a hurried purpose and others meandering and taking pictures.

“Can you see the difference between tourists and locals?” asked Kevin, nudging her with his elbow.

“Yes,” Cara nodded, tracking a long-bearded homeless man who schlepped a large backpack while leading a black dog on a leash. “I’ve only been here a day, but I think I actually can.” She locked eyes with Kevin across the table and smiled. “What a beautiful and cultural town. I love it here!”

"I *thought* you'd like buzzing around for a bit before hitting the road."

"It was a great idea."

They were quiet again, scanning the crowd. Cara wondered if Arianna had been to Santa Barbara—if she was indeed living in California—and if she'd fallen completely in love with it too. She imagined what it might be like to sit here with Ari, catching up on seven years of lost time.

"Aw, geez!" They'll let *anyone* in here!" Kevin barked out, interrupting her thoughts.

Cara turned to see a young couple walking toward them with wide grins on their faces. The man wore a backwards ball cap over his sun-washed hair and a casual t-shirt. The woman had on Capri jeans and a light blue peasant blouse that greatly enhanced her dark, Hispanic features and killer body.

Kevin stood up and introduced them. "Cara, these are some fellow Santa Barbarians, Matt and Marisol."

"Do you know that guy?" Matt asked his girl, thrusting a thumb toward Kevin with a mock sneer.

"Yeah, yeah, smartass..." Kevin waved him off. "You guys, this is my friend Cara from Ohio."

The friends shook hands and welcomed her.

"Matt and I took some photography classes together back in the day," Kevin explained. "He's much better than me, though... he's got his own studio and everything."

Matt rolled his eyes and gave a humble half-smile.

"So are you two just bumming around, or are you on a mission?"

"We're on a mission from God," Matt replied, doing a solemn imitation of The Blues Brothers.

Marisol offered a shy smile revealing perfect white teeth and held up a Nordstrom bag. "I'm exchanging some shoes."

Kevin was suddenly distracted by a mother struggling to get a cumbersome stroller through the door of a café. He jumped from his chair, darted through the crowd, and held the door open for her. The woman's face brightened as she thanked him and moved through with ease.

"Wow, that was so nice," Cara remarked, staring after him.

"Yeah, that damn Kevin..." Matt gave a mock sigh of exasperation, "...always trying to make the rest of us look bad."

"He is a sweet man," Marisol told Cara in her lovely accent. "A real smartass, sometimes, but sweet."

Cara laughed, eyeing Kevin as he returned to them.

"What?" he demanded, looking from one face to another. "Were you talking about me?" He turned to Cara. "Whatever they told you, it's not true!"

Cara and Marisol exchanged a conspiratorial laugh.

Kevin nudged Matt in the shoulder. "Hey, do you still need help with those panels for the show in July?"

"Yeah, man, if you've got the time to spare."

"Just name the day and I'll be there."

"Awesome. Thanks." Then he glanced at Marisol. "We should probably go if we want to make the movie in time."

Marisol smiled at Cara. "It was nice meeting you."

"You too," Cara replied, nodding to both of them. As they wandered off into the crowd, she thought about the compliment Marisol had paid Kevin, and the evidence he'd shown in two obvious displays of selflessness and generosity. The entire interaction was impressive. A good sign.

Kevin gave her shoulder a light squeeze. "So do you feel like shopping or anything?"

Since they'd stopped to rest, Cara's eyes were repeatedly drawn to the mountains peeking over the rooftops of the mall. She pointed to them and said, "What I'd really like to do is hike. I'm thinking there must be some killer trails here, with fantastic views." Her face turned sheepish. "I gotta confess, I'm not a big fan of shopping."

Kevin fell back in his chair. "Are you for real?" He removed his sunglasses so she could witness his look of awe. "Sitting in the middle of all these stores and she doesn't want to *shop*? I think I love you, Cara Shannon."

Cara gave a little chuckle and shrugged.

"And hiking trails! Do we have hiking trails! What do you like—strenuous, medium or easy?"

Cara shrugged. "Medium, I guess."

"Well, be warned," he told her with a smug look. "No matter what the level, all trails in Santa Barbara go *up*."

"I don't care, as long as there are waterfalls. I like playing in waterfalls."

"Oh, there are *tons* of waterfalls. Ask and you shall receive, my dear."

Cara sat forward, elation lighting up her face. "What an absolutely *perfect* day this is!"

Kevin winked and put his shades back on. "And it's not even half over."

Chapter 23

"A lot of celebrities live around here," Kevin informed Cara as they trudged up the rocky ascent of Cold Springs Trail. It was a popular hike that wound through the mountains above Montecito, Santa Barbara's neighboring town where gated mansions lay nestled in hillside woods and canyons.

"Cool," was her brief reply as she attempted to conserve the dwindling air capacity in her lungs. As promised, the hike was an endless uphill climb, but after awhile its many rewards began to show themselves. Sonorous waterfalls greeted them around every bend, and a rushing stream kept intersecting with the trail on its way down the mountain. The smell of earth, eucalyptus and other forest fragrances hung deliciously in the air.

"The woods are so different here," Cara observed as they plodded along, stopping every now and then to catch their breath. "Back home, leaves and shrubs are a brighter, more Ireland-green, and everything around you feels lush and moist. In this place, everything is a pleasant *dry*." She turned to look at Kevin, who was warily eyeing tree roots and treacherous drop-offs. "I sure don't miss the humidity back home. It makes me feel sluggish and out of shape."

Kevin nodded. "Yeah, the one summer I spent in Savannah about killed me. I don't think I could ever live in a humid climate."

"Savannah, Georgia?"

"Yup."

"When was that?"

Kevin squinted, thinking back. "Oh, it must've been…what, early nineties? Yeah, around then."

"What took you to Georgia of all places?"

"A crazy affair."

Cara didn't want to know, but couldn't help asking, "A love affair?"

His sigh was heavy with regret. "Yes."

The lone sound of feet clomping on dirt filled the air as Cara tried to make sense of it. "How in the world did you meet, living on opposite sides of the country? That was a little before online dating, right?"

"Right. I was in Florida doing art direction for a major cruise line's magazine ad. She was one of the models at the shoot. I sort of followed her home afterward."

One of Cara's eyebrows lifted. "Wow. Quite the adventurous chick magnet, weren't you?" She cast a grin and a wink over her shoulder, but Kevin just hung his head and shook it a few times.

"That had to have been the most irrational skirt-chasing I've ever done in my life. I suppose it's far enough in my past where I can laugh about it now."

"So what, did you just tell her the humidity wasn't going to work for you, then hop the next flight to L.A.?"

"Heh, well, after about two months, we realized things weren't going to progress past a summer fling. Her family was so wonderful to me, though. You can't beat that southern hospitality."

"It's great, isn't it?" Cara agreed, trying to ignore the intimidating fact that Kevin had once hooked up with a model. "I've taken several trips to various places in the South and I could almost live there. Like maybe in the mountains of North Carolina."

"Why there?"

"Well, it's a more temperate climate than Ohio. There are lots of pine-filled woods. The Blue Ridge Mountains are sprawling and gorgeous, and the ocean is just a few hours away."

"All good points. I can see the attraction."

"And did you know that the Appalachian Trail runs through that state?"

"Does it?"

Cara remembered the Appalachian social studies book that she'd edited and told Kevin about it. "When I saw the landscape photos in your studio, it made me think of pictures in that book. I'd almost be tempted to say you missed your calling, Kevin, but your design work is just as exceptional. I suppose you are the quintessential well-rounded artist."

One step behind, Kevin put a hand on her arm and squeezed. "That means a lot to me. Thank you."

She slowed until they were walking side by side, then smiled over at him. "Have you ever considered doing a photo book?"

"Never."

The abruptness with which he replied, along with the exaggerated look of seriousness on his face made her laugh. "Well, you should."

"Whatevah."

Cara whapped him in the arm.

Kevin gave a sidelong smirk as they hiked on in silence, listening to the bird calls overhead, and turning their heads at little rustlings in the brush along the trail.

"Was that a lizard?" Cara asked, stopping and peering into the weeds.

"Probably."

She turned with the same look of delight as a kindergartener on a field trip. "We don't have those in Ohio, either!"

"What? No lizards? The horror!"

Cara giggled, then looked upward. "And the sky. It's such a clear and vibrant shade of blue. Bluer than it gets on the clearest day of an Ohio summer."

"Really?"

"It's because of all the haze from vegetation and trees."

"Wow."

"Yeah, getting off the plane anywhere in the West makes me feel a little like Dorothy when she steps out of the black and white house into the colorful Land of Oz."

"Ha! Great analogy."

"Not to say that my state doesn't have its charms." Cara held up an emphatic finger and kept walking. "There are many beautiful woodlands, foothills and lakes. And it's not always humid. Some days in the spring and fall feel just like this." She made a sweeping gesture in the air around her.

"I don't doubt it," Kevin told her. "I've been to all corners of this country and every state has its own beautiful…" he trailed off when he saw Cara stop in her tracks. He followed her gaze to a small creature ambling toward them on the trail ahead.

"Oh my gosh," she whispered, clutching his arm. "I've always wanted to see a wildcat."

"That one's a bobcat," he informed her in a low, hushed tone. "See its short, bobbed tail?"

As if on cue, the grayish-tan, spotted feline turned gracefully to one side, showing off a curled tail. It regarded them calmly before slinking down into a ravine.

Cara looked with wonder at Kevin. "Did you see how unafraid it was?"

He nodded. "That, my dear, was a rare thing to see up here. The cats are usually pretty elusive with people. It must be that magic charm you brought with you."

"It *was* magical. I feel like frickin' Snow White!"

Kevin's face broke into a grin of adulation. "I just love your enthusiasm for everything, Cara. It was nice on the boards, but it's ten times better in person."

Cara was about to make a nonchalant comment when something in his eyes caught and held her, and they shared yet another moment of wordless chemistry. In the next second he moved in close and kissed her…deep, lingering, and ultra-exhilarating because they were in the middle of nature with no one around. She felt her heart rate quicken as she pulled away to catch her breath. Then she looped her arms around the back of his neck and returned the kiss with even more fervor. She pressed against him, full body, and slid her fingers through his hair.

Kevin tightened his embrace like a boa constrictor, picked her up off the trail and swung her around. Cara squealed in surprise and giggled like when she was seven and her sisters used to swing her around by the arms. Finally he set her down and ruffled her hair. "I'm so glad you came out here."

She tilted her head slightly and nodded. "Me too."

He turned and pointed beyond where the bobcat had made its appearance. "Over there's your waterfall. Its pool is one of the deepest on this trail."

Cara clasped her hands together. "So I can go *in*?"

Kevin swept a Vanna White arm toward the water. "Knock yourself out. It's fucking *freezing* in there, but whatever turns you on."

With cautious steps they climbed across a few boulders to where a wide, bowl-shaped stone pool shimmered with sunlit water. The rock slabs around it were hot from baking in the afternoon sun, so Kevin removed his shirt and lay down to bask. Cara sat next to him on the pool's edge, lazily swishing her legs around in the water. From behind the safety of her dark sunglasses, she stole a glance or two at his tan chest, moving up and down with relaxed breaths. She studied the curve and shape of his long leg muscles, quietly admiring the solid way he was put together. The fantasy thoughts that followed, sitting alone with him in the middle of the woods, brought Cara to the conclusion that perhaps cold water was just the thing she needed.

"Kevin?"

"Mmm?" he said without opening his eyes.

"I have to go in."

"What's stopping you?"

"Um…clothing?"

He opened one eye and fixed it on her. "So take them off. At least down to your undies. I won't watch."

She gave him a playful shove. "I'm thinking of other hikers, silly."

"Bah," he waved. "Go for it. You're in California, remember?"

"Good point," Cara said, crossing her arms in front of her to grab the hem of her tank top and lift.

Kevin opened both eyes and shielded them against the sun.

With a wicked grin, she told him, "I thought you said you wouldn't watch."

"Yeah, well…you've got breasts that refuse to be ignored."

She glanced down, inwardly thankful that she'd worn her black *Angels* bra, from Victoria's Secret. It was a great shape enhancer and created the illusion that gravity was *not* taking over just yet.

He shook his head. "I'm so sorry. Was that inappropriate?"

Cara threw the tank top on his face. "Of course not."

"They really are lovely," came his muffled voice through the fabric, before he reached up and removed it.

She pushed them out and purred in her best Mae West voice, "Why thank you, Mr. Tierney. Unlike the other dames around this joint, mine are one hundred percent *real*."

Enjoying the sound of his highly amused cackle, she stood up and unzipped her low-rise denim shorts. *Black satin panties. Another good choice.* It would've been more romantic had she left her sundress on. Then she could've pulled it all off in one sensual swoop. But Kevin had insisted she change into something more suitable for climbing rocks and getting dusty.

"Behold, the beautiful wood nymph," he announced, taking in the view with obvious delight.

Turning toward the pool, Cara dipped one foot in then retracted it quickly.

"Told you it was cold."

"Yeah, this is going to have to be all or nothing." She took a deep breath, closed her eyes, and slid gracefully under the water's surface. An electric jolt zinged every nerve fiber in her body and gave her an instant ice cream headache. In the next second, she vaulted back up with a splash like a dolphin in an aquatic circus, letting out a low, growling moan.

"I don't know how you can stand it," Kevin said, shaking his head and reaching for his camera bag.

"Oh, it's great!" she panted, running her fingers through the wet strands of her hair and wringing them out. "An invigorating rush!"

"Do that again," he urged, pointing the camera at her.

Tentatively, she held her hands near her head. "Now I feel silly."

"Just pretend you're a model." Kevin switched to a thick, non-descript European accent. "Work it, darling, work it."

She laughed and leaned back with eyes closed, running slow and seductive fingers through her hair.

"There ya go."

Click.

Cara opened her eyes, turned away from the camera, and looked back over her shoulder with her best come hither expression.

"Beautiful." *Click. Click.*

"Okay, look out!" She climbed from the pool, dripping water everywhere, and sat down beside him once again. Then, thinking better of it, she laid all the way back on the warm stone to dry. After lying there for a minute or two, Cara heard another click of the camera. Her eyes flew open in time to see Kevin lowering it from his face with a grin.

"What did you just take a picture of?" she demanded.

He turned the camera's monitor toward her. On the screen was an image of her bellybutton surrounded by a few shiny drops of water. "It looked so cute, I couldn't help it."

"My *bellybutton?*"

"It's no ordinary bellybutton…it's damn sexy. And I used the macro option, so it's all artsy-fartsy with the water drops around it."

Cara burst out laughing.

"You could use it for your next avatar!"

"But then people would think I was Bellybutton."

"Hey, she was on the boards this morning," Kevin said, putting his camera back in its bag. "She told everyone she was taking the day off and going fishing with the wifey."

"Oh yeah?" Cara shaded her eyes and looked up at him. "I love her. She's so funny."

"There were some new users in there too, whose names I didn't recognize."

She sighed. "Gosh, it's seems like forever since I was the newbie."

"When *did* you join the Cafe?"

"Well, I started listening about two years ago. But I didn't post until this past autumn. Just before the…"

Kevin set his camera bag on the rock. "The what?"

"The breakup."

"Oy."

"But you know," Cara sat up to better emphasize her words, "the Eclectic Café really helped me through that whole yucky phase of life. It was a place I could go where no one knew about me and Greg. Where I could meet new people and distract myself from the pain and heal."

"Who knew that you could get all that from a radio station in cyberspace? Kind of cool, isn't it?"

"I'll bet I'm not the only one who's had that experience there, either."

"I'll bet you're right. Just read people's journals. It's amazing how we all gravitated toward one another and felt safe enough to share our lives so openly. All those personalities…different, yet similar in so many ways. It's like it all happened for a reason."

"Yeah, and just think…I wouldn't even be *sitting* here if it weren't for the Café."

They pondered this thought for a moment, then Kevin slipped an arm around her. Gradually, Cara let her head rest on his shoulder. Time stood still as they lost themselves in the sounds of trickling water, birdsongs and a light breeze through the treetops. The sun beat down on their skin forming a hot cocoon against the cool air wafting from the woods. After a long while, they both turned to each other and smiled. Kevin asked, "You ready to move on?"

"Soon as I'm clothed again," she replied with a wink.

Before Cara had a chance to get up, he quickly grabbed her bra strap and snapped it.

"Hey!"

With a victorious clapping of hands, he cried out, "HA-ha!"

She pointed a threatening finger at him, then grabbed her clothes and slipped them back on.

Refreshed and fueled with water, the two found the trail again and continued all the way to its breathtaking vista. The late afternoon sun was dazzling as it reflected off the bay, and the Channel Islands floated—fully visible—on the horizon.

"What a view," Cara exclaimed after staring for a full minute and catching her breath. "It made every step of this long and arduous hike worth taking." Her thoughts turned to her niece once again, and she wondered if Arianna was also staring out at the Pacific that very minute…maybe from some steep hill overlooking the San Francisco Bay.

Kevin stood with hands on hips, breathing hard. He pointed out various places in the city below where they'd gone that morning: the courthouse, the long line of palms along Cabrillo Boulevard, Stearns Wharf, and the spot by the Mesa where his house was. Then he turned to her with eager eyes. "Well, are you up for some more fun tonight? Maybe I can finally get you that margarita from Lobo's!"

"Ah, the infamous Lobo's," she laughed. "Hell yes, I'm up for it!"

"Okay, then. It's on."

As they trekked back down the mountain, Cara couldn't help thinking about their next night together. The growing attraction between them was starting to spark like downed telephone wires after a storm, and she wondered if she could trust herself through another platonic sleep.

Chapter 24

"Oh, you've gotta be fucking *kidding* me."

Cara turned to Kevin in alarm as they coasted down his sloping driveway. "What's wrong?"

He directed his scowl toward a silver BMW SUV parked in the circular drive. "Why the hell didn't she call first?"

"Who does that belong to?"

Kevin parked his MG and killed the motor with an exasperated sigh. "My sister, Gillian, from L.A. Looks like she dropped by for one of her little surprise visits."

Cara didn't know what to say. Apparently, a visit from his sister was not a good thing, but she asked anyway, "Don't you like her?"

A crease formed in Kevin's brow just above the bridge of his sunglasses. "Oh, it's not entirely that. Just wait. You'll find out in a matter of minutes."

Cara grinned. "I'm actually looking forward to meeting her. I mean, it's your *sister.*"

"I know, it's just…I need to prepare myself for Gillian's visits. She's got one of those overwhelming personalities. And I'm a firm believer in calling before dropping in, no matter who you are."

Cara conceded, "Yeah, I have to agree there. It's only common courtesy. But let's just make the most of it."

He gave her an apologetic smile. "Okay, you're right. I've done enough bitching."

Cara scanned the house and sidewalk. "Where is she? Does she have a key?"

"She's probably down on the beach or on the Winters' bench swing. Hell, I don't know…" He grabbed his camera bag and both their water bottles, then opened the car door. Cara met him on the sidewalk and together they walked to the studio, peeking around every corner for the elusive sister.

"What the hell?" Kevin muttered, seeing the front door wide open. A hint of garlic and olive oil wafted out at them.

As they walked in from the bright sunlight, their eyes slowly adjusting, they found Gillian hunched over a messy culinary project like a mad scientist in a lab. She spun around when she heard her brother's voice. "Kevin, love!"

Cara smiled timidly as the woman came around from behind the bar. She wore a black beaded tank top and a black crepe skirt with silver sequins. Her graying brown hair was thrown haphazardly into a clip atop her head with frizzy strands escaping down her neck. A faint tinkling could be heard as she hurried to greet them, coming from a necklace of tiny chimes around her neck. She smiled with eyes as blue as her brother's, peeking over Ben Franklin specs. "And who is this lovely woman?"

"This is my friend Cara Shannon, from Cincinnati."

"*Cincinnati?* Well *you've* certainly come a long way!" She gave a loud cackle and reached out for Cara, who submitted to a giant bear-hug and nearly got the life squeezed out of her. "Welcome to California!"

"Hello," Cara managed to say through fish lips, her cheek pressed tightly to Gillian's—which smelled of Nag Champa oil. When she was released, she offered a crooked smile.

"How the hell did you get in?" Kevin asked, scratching his head.

"Nice to see you too, little brother," his sister said dryly, hand on hip. "For your information, you left it open. Now gimme a damn hug."

Kevin gave his sister a quick squeeze, managed a tolerant smile, and asked, "What brings you to town?"

"I had to deliver some jewelry to my friend Rosa, who works at Bacara Spa. So I figured as long as I was up, I'd stop by and make you dinner. It's a new recipe I learned last week in cooking class."

Kevin set the water bottles down and followed her back to the counter, surveying the bowls of diced tomatoes, cheese, avocado, mushrooms, and olives. "What do you call this concoction?"

"Mediterranean-Califusion Wraps," she said, giving a pan of spiced couscous a proud stir.

"Mm, smells good," Cara said, sniffing the air.

"Yeah, but I'm so sick of that *word,*" Kevin complained, rolling his eyes.

"What word?" Gillian asked, lifting a lid and checking a pile of steaming rice tortillas.

"*Fusion*. It's so overused. If anything has avocadoes or olives in it, it's automatically California *fusion*. If there is barbecue sauce and chili peppers in the dish, it's Tex-Mex Fusion. Avocado and peanut sauce? *Thai-Cali* Fusion! Hell, I even saw an ad on a bulletin board for Tennis-Golf Fusion. What the hell is *that?* Do you play on a court or a course? Pretty soon, the world will be one big amalgamated bundle of everything fused together. And they'll call it Con-Fusion."

Gillian stared at Kevin, a wooden spoon poised in her hand. Then she threw a long-suffering look Cara's way. Finally, she turned back to the stove and muttered, "You need to get laid, man. It's been far too long."

Cara's eyes widened and her mouth fell open in an incredulous smile. She'd never dream of saying something like that to Jenn or Melanie in front of a complete stranger! Kevin's sister definitely had her moxy on.

Kevin rolled his eyes and parried, "Gillian, that is your blanket response to everything. Get an original line, would ya?"

"Shut up and have some wine!" she commanded. "It's there on the bar…gift from Rosa."

Behind his sister's back, Kevin gave Cara a *didn't I tell you?* gesture and walked back out of the kitchen.

"So did Cara get a tour of the city?" Gillian asked over her shoulder.

"Yes!" Cara answered, leaning on one of the bar stools. "And I'm thoroughly enchanted. We even had time for a hike in the mountains, where a bobcat came right up to us!"

Gillian whirled around, looking from Cara to Kevin. "Get the fuck out! It actually came up to you?"

"Well, he was a few yards away," Kevin corrected. "But the golden eagle I saw last week at Lake Cachuma flew right over my head!"

Gillian's face soured with envy. "Man, you guys see all the *exotic* wildlife! Whenever I go outside, all I see is someone's goddamn yap-dog! Taking a shit in my front yard!"

Cara lost all ability to stay civilized. She doubled over, clutched her stomach and shook with laughter.

"Oh stop, you'll only encourage her!" Kevin admonished. "And hey, didn't you want to use that outdoor shower?"

"Oh!" Cara took her hand off the stool. "I almost forgot."

"Look at him, trying to get rid of you!" Gillian barked, followed by another loud cackle. "See how he is? Man, I hope you're not planning on falling in love with him, Cara. He's in the California Peter Pan Club, you know!"

Cara's brow wrinkled. "The what?"

"Have him tell you about Maya sometime."

"Gillian, don't make me get the duct tape," Kevin said in a low tone, grabbing a fluffy, sage-colored towel from a shelf. There was a hint of irritation in his voice and he wasn't smiling, so Cara refrained from asking any more questions. He beckoned for her to follow him out back, where he gave her a brief tour of the shower. Then he left her to enjoy the rare luxury of the aquatic Stonehenge.

The shower's base was made of black slate, while blocks of stone with wooden bracing in between encircled her. From its fragrant smell, Cara guessed that the wood was cedar. What a unique sensation, she thought, to look up through the steam at a clear blue sky instead of a ceiling. She inched the left faucet handle a little higher and when the hot water hit her tired muscles, she felt them unwind like a taut rubber band snapping back on itself.

"Mmm," Cara purred, closing her eyes and stretching her neck to the left and right. She drew in a deep breath and felt an unexpected sob catch in her throat. *Good God, not another meltdown?!* It felt rather insane, having just been laughing uncontrollably five minutes earlier. But as tears mixed with water on her face, she began to realize that they were *joyful* ones…born of the monumentally wonderful day that Kevin had shown her. She couldn't even remember the last time she'd felt so happy.

* * *

"How was it?" Kevin asked cheerfully when Cara crept back into the house. He caught sight of her bloodshot eyes and asked under his breath, "Hey, are you okay?"

With a deliberate smile, she put a hand on his arm. "I am more than okay. That thing is *fantastic* and I never want to take another shower inside again."

Just then, Gillian came out of the bathroom rubbing lotion on her hands. "Ah, you say that now…but I don't think you'd wanna be standing buck naked in the middle of one of those Ohio blizzards this winter! You'd freeze your hoo-ha off. And life without a hoo-ha is no fun at all!"

"Sweet Jesus, Gillian!" Kevin looked as though his sister had force-fed him a lemon.

Gillian ignored him and clapped her hands. "Throw some clothes on, girl. It's bon appetit time! Shall we dine outside?"

Cara ran for the bedroom, calling over her shoulder, "Yes, outside! I definitely vote for outside!"

Minutes later, they were all seated at the wooden umbrella table on the long deck that ran between Kevin's place and the Winters'. The breeze and the view of the beach below created the perfect dining experience that Cara had envisioned. After the first bites of Califusion were taken, Gillian turned to her with a smile. "So, how did you meet my baby brother?"

Cara glanced at Kevin for permission, wondering how much he wanted to reveal to his sister. Reading her mind, he took the reigns and explained the whole story of the Eclectic Café and their online community.

Gillian listened with mounting interest. "Wow, you guys met online! Hm. I guess that's the shit these days." She raised her glass of wine, declaring loudly, "Well then, here's to the Internet! I swear, it's done wonders for my business."

"What is it you do?" Cara asked.

"Oh, all things metaphysical," she said, taking a huge gulp of wine. Then she smacked her lips and grabbed the bottle, peering at its label. "Chardonnay…from the Santa Barbara Winery. This is *fabulous!* And I'm not even a Chardonnay fan, either. Mm-mm-mm! Thank you, *Rosa*." Gillian set the bottle back on the table as she turned back to Cara. "Anyway, yeah. I make and sell gemstone necklaces…according to each client's spiritual and energetic needs. I also make and bottle blends of essential oils…little bit of this, little bit of that."

Cara swallowed a bite of wrap and reached for her wine. "That sounds really fun, Gillian. Do you have a shop?"

"No, I operate from home. But I got some punk-ass high school kid to design a website for me, so I could start an online catalogue. Gotta stay with the times, you know?"

"Absolutely. And these wraps are delicious, by the way."

"Why thank you!" Gillian beamed. She leaned forward and set her glass on the table. "So are you in California just to—"

"Are you still doing massage?" Kevin interjected, trying to prevent a grand inquisition of Cara by his nosy sister. He reached for a second wrap, having wolfed down the first.

Gillian shook her head. "Not at the chiropractor's. But I still work on friends and family."

"You do massage too?" Cara's eyebrows lifted. "Wow!"

"What *hasn't* she done?" Kevin joked, giving his sister a look. "She changes careers more often than her underwear."

"I don't *wear* underwear, you little mook!" she cried, reaching across the table and swatting at him.

Kevin glanced around nervously. "Yo, keep it down, Gil, I don't think the whole city wants to know about your intimate attire. Or lack thereof."

Gillian pursed her lips and did a "sistah neck" of attitude. "I don't care *what* the hell the city thinks! If anyone has a problem with me going commando, they can bite me!"

Cara hung her head and tried not to laugh too loudly that time.

Kevin lifted the bottle of Chardonnay and swished it around, noting its meager contents. "You were into this long before dinner, weren't you?"

Gillian raised her glass, shameless. "I was indeed. And I could seriously go for another…*damn* this stuff is good!"

"So when did you quit the chiropractor's?" Kevin persisted. "Was everything okay there?"

"Oh, sure." Gillian flipped a hand. "I just got tired of doing so many massages and only getting half of the profit…but that sweet man, he still gives me adjustments for free!" She gave Cara a pointed look. "Do you have a chiropractor?"

Cara looked up from her plate, realized she was the one being addressed, and shook her head. "My spine's been pretty solid, knock on wood." She reached out and knocked on the table beside her.

"Well, let me tell you, chick. Every time I wake up with my neck feeling like it got screwed on wrong, I just go to Dr. Powell and let him wring it. I swear that's what it feels like, the way those guys grab on and twist. And when those vertebrae go off like a pack of firecrackers…aaaah, sweet relief!"

Cara nearly sprayed a sip of wine all over the table. Gillian had her laughing so hard that she gave up trying to eat and set her wrap on the plate. Kevin, who'd begun to lighten up a little, seemed highly entertained but tried not to let it show as he shook his head and sighed into his wine.

Gillian shrugged with a mischievous gleam in her eye. "I'm just sayin'…"

The three of them fell into a temporary silence, munching the last of their dinner and draining their glasses. Then Gillian asked the dreaded question before Kevin could stop her.

"So Cara, did you come out to see Kevin exclusively, or is Santa Barbara a stop on a larger tour?"

Kevin lowered his wine glass from his lips and shot Cara a worried look.

"It's okay, I don't mind telling her." She gave his shoulder a light squeeze, and looked over at Gillian. "Something tells me she's whacked enough to understand."

Gillian wrinkled her nose and raised an eyebrow. "Ooh, I sense something very intriguing, here. Do tell."

Cara put it as succinctly as possible. "I have reason to believe that my niece, who's been dead for the past seven years, is actually alive and living in California. I'm here to look for her."

Gillian leaned forward and slapped a hand down on the table. "Shut *up!*"

Cara nodded and stared out at the orange and salmon sky above the sea.

Gillian looked at Kevin, who also nodded. "I'm going with her."

"Wow," was all his sister could utter. "That's some intense shit."

"Yeah, and as if that wasn't enough, I voluntarily turned my whole life upside down before coming here. I packed up everything I own, put it in storage, rented out my house, and moved in with a sister. Then I negotiated a long sabbatical from my job and flew out here. I think all the stress finally caught up with me last night when I had a meltdown in front of poor Kevin at the Blue Dolphin."

"Oh honey," Gillian cooed, reaching over and laying a hand overtop Cara's. "You had a meltdown?"

"I'm okay, now. Really. I've had the best day ever."

"Would you like me to work on you?"

Cara stared at her. "You mean…"

"A massage! I think it just might be the thing you need right now, before setting out on this Magical Mystery Tour. Stress is just a bunch of toxins stored in your muscles, and you don't need that."

Cara tried to disguise her reluctance. "Gosh, I would hate for you to go to any trouble—"

"No trouble at all, sweetie. Consider it my Welcome to California gift." Gillian gave Cara's hand a pat. "I've got a portable table in the car, and I would love to help. Just say the word."

To Cara's surprise, Kevin piped up, "That's a really good idea, Gillian. Thank you so much for offering."

Cara felt her entire body soften, humbled at the outpouring of care and concern from someone she barely knew.

"When's the last time you had a massage?" Gillian asked, sitting back again.

Cara focused on the sky again, trying to remember. Just before the split with Greg, she and Frannie had taken an afternoon off to get treatments at a day spa that had just opened in Blue Ash. Had it been that long?

"Well, never mind that, what do you say? Want me to go set up the table?"

Cara simply nodded and smiled. Kevin leaned over to put an arm around her. "You'll feel like a new woman, Cara. She's awesome."

"Okay, then." Gillian jumped up and attempted to step over the bench, but one of her feet caught and sent her toppling in slow motion to the deck. Her skirt flipped up just enough to let them know that she hadn't been kidding about going commando.

"Whoa! Geez!" Kevin cried, averting his eyes. "Not the mental image a brother wants to get stuck with!"

"Are you okay?" Cara asked, making a move to help.

"I'm good!" Gillian insisted, scrambling to sit up. Her chime necklace tinkled frantically. It was then that she caught sight of her skirt and blushed. "Oh. Oops."

Cara buried her face in Kevin's shoulder, shaking with laughter as Gillian got up with a groan and more tinkles.

"Well, that was graceful," Gillian laughed, rolling her eyes and smoothing her hair.

Cara raised her head again. “Are you sure you’re okay?”

“Of course I’m okay. I’m as tough as boiled owl.”

When Gillian had disappeared around the side of the house, Cara burst out in cackles once more and asked Kevin, “Boiled owl?”

“Our dad used to say that,” he chuckled, then shook his head. “Don’t ask me what it means. He was just as whacked as Gillian. The apple didn’t fall far from the tree there.”

Cara let the last of her giggles out, took a deep breath and stared at the sunset. “You know, as pissed off as you were, I’m really glad she showed up.”

Kevin gathered their plates and glasses into a stack and put a dramatic hand over his heart. “Cara, as much as it pains me to admit it…so am I.”

* * *

Perhaps it was the hypnotic CD Gillian played—a slow, rhythmical drum beat and didgeridoo behind a tribal flute. Or maybe it was the rose, jasmine, and sandalwood-scented oil that she used, but Cara went completely out during her massage. All the nagging thoughts, worries, and plans that had been chattering in the background of her mind were silenced. All the muscles that had been complaining since the plane ride were eased. Her breathing slowed to the speed of the music and her consciousness drifted out into the cosmos. Gillian performed therapeutic massage as though it were a dance, moving all over the place in a continual rhythm. She was so effective that the next morning, Cara couldn’t even remember getting off the table afterward and slipping right into bed.

Chapter 25

"Hey, Sleeping Beauty."

Cara's face eased into a drowsy smile as she opened her eyes and saw Kevin staring down at her from the edge of the bed. He grinned and lifted a mug of steaming coffee in the air, indicating that he'd brought it for her, then set it on the night stand beside the bed.

"What time is it?" she croaked.

"Nine-thirty," he replied, his grin widening. "Man, Gillian really knocked you out!"

Cara closed her eyes again with a long sigh. "I can't even remember the last time I've felt this relaxed. That was so wonderful of her."

"Yeah, as much as I bitch about her, she's a good egg," Kevin admitted. "Before she left, she told me to tell you goodbye and good luck with your mission."

"I need to call her and thank her."

He gave her arm a light caressing. "How are you feeling? Are you ready to get on the road today or do you need more time?"

She cleared her throat and rubbed her eyes. "No, I don't need more time. I'd like to get going, if that's okay with you."

"It's *absolutely* okay. Just enjoy your coffee, take your time getting up, and I'll start packing some food to take with us."

Cara put a hand over his. "Thank you so much, Kevin."

"You bet." He stood up with a jostle of the bed and turned to go.

Cara stared at the ceiling, a mixture of eager anticipation and dread churning in her gut. In the next few days, she would probably see all kinds of beautiful scenery and meet many interesting people. There was also a chance that she might walk into a winery and see Arianna, back from the dead. Then what?

* * *

"Damn it! I tried to get us here before the rush hour, but the rush hour keeps getting earlier and earlier."

Kevin downshifted as he eased into a sea of brake lights that stretched into the distance as far as the eye could see. They had reached the San Francisco city limits just as traffic was beginning to thicken with late-afternoon commuters.

"It's totally okay," she assured him, ignoring the traffic and peering instead at the many hillsides sprinkled with homes and buildings up ahead. "At least it's finally starting to look like San Francisco, now!"

"Yeah, but we're still a ways from downtown and Mike's neighborhood."

Cara turned to look at Kevin. "This is so nice of your friend to put us up for the night."

"Brother," he corrected.

"Mike's your *brother?*"

"Yeah, I mentioned that last night at dinner. Did Gillian's massage wipe out your memory, too?"

She laughed with him. "Apparently so."

"Between Mike's thriving law practice and his partner's fortune—made during the dot-com boom—they were actually able to *buy* a Victorian up in Pacific Heights, the lucky bastards."

Cara lifted an eyebrow. "Pacific Heights? Isn't that a high-end neighborhood?"

"*Shyeeah!* And we're staying there."

"How lucky is that?"

"Pretty damn lucky."

"Did I know your brother was gay?"

"Probably not. I hardly ever talked about my family during our phone conversations."

"You sort of mentioned them collectively when you talked about growing up in Monterey."

"Ah yes, a town that I would very much like to show you on the way back."

Cara felt her purse vibrating through the noise of the wind and traffic. It was the first call she'd received since arriving in California. She retrieved her cell phone and checked the screen. "It's a text from Seth!"

"Really? How is *smokin' hot*, anyway?"

"He's already asking me where I've been. I've only been gone from the boards two and a half days!"

"Seth knows all," Kevin said with exaggerated solemnity. "He's got his finger on the pulse of the EC at all times."

Cara clutched her phone, returning the message as best she could in the car's stop-and-start lurches. "I'm telling him that I took a little road trip and will be back soon."

"Ask him if he's gotten any messages from saffire."

She looked over at Kevin. "Good idea."

In a few minutes, Seth's reply came back: *Nada. Why? Did you ever get her IP address? Does this road trip have anything to do with saffire, by any chance?*

Cara snapped her phone closed after reading it aloud to Kevin. "I'm not sure I want to answer those questions. Not now."

He looked over at her, one eyebrow raised above his Ray Bans. "Still not a word from Saffire…ever since the night you PMd her. Unbelievable."

"And that is exactly why we need to stay under the radar."

As they progressed into the city, Cara studied the terraced houses and picturesque hillside streets. She braced herself against the dashboard as Kevin dodged a few erratically moving cabs, wove through tricky intersections and headed up a cobbled street embedded with trolley tracks. He reached into his shirt pocket for his cell phone, which was set on vibrate.

"Hello?"

Cara watched him closely, always wondering how people talked on a cell and drove a stick shift at the same time.

"Hey! Mike! We're minutes away, buddy."

He lets go of the wheel, that's what he does! Oh my fucking gawd! Cara's eyes widened as the car cruised down a side street and Kevin let go of the wheel with his right hand each time he shifted. *Where was his hands-free set?*

"Sure, we could do that. It's perfect, in fact, because I wanted to take her sightseeing anyway."

The car never once veered off center, so she began to relax and enjoy the views, which were getting lovelier by the minute.

"Okay, then. We'll talk later." Kevin pressed the end-call button and tucked his phone away. "Mike and Drew have to attend a benefit downtown this evening, but they want to meet up with us later tonight when we all get home."

"Excellent. I can't wait to meet yet *another* Tierney."

"Yeah, and don't worry. This one's *much* tamer than the last."

With both hands on the wheel again, he climbed a few more steeply pitched streets until they reached the intersection of Divisadero and Broadway—one of the highest hills overlooking both city and bay. They pulled up in front of a pale, dusty-rose Queen Anne Victorian perched on the corner. Trellises of red roses adorned the walkway leading up to its steps. Above, a large patio-like balcony surrounded a second-story doorway, enclosed by a white balustrade.

"Oh, no way! They *own* this?" Cara stared up at its turret, mouth agape. "I hate them already! First you and your ocean view, now these guys with their Victorian. You all suck!"

Her unusual display of raw derision fell on deaf ears as he studied the street with a frown. "I forgot to ask Mike about parking. Parking's an absolute bitch in this town."

"Not for us!" She pointed ahead to a large SUV pulling out of a generous space just around the corner.

Kevin threw the MG into gear, turned left and slipped neatly into it. Then the two spilled out of the tiny car, relishing the feel of movement and space.

"My butt's numb," Cara remarked, giving it a brief rub.

"I could massage it if you like," he told her with a wink, unlocking the trunk and grabbing both their bags. When she tried to take hers from him, he turned and held it just out of reach. "I got it."

Cara breathed a long sigh. "Kevin, seriously…thank you. For your chivalry, for driving us up here, and for *this.*" She gestured up at the grand home. "Here I was prepared to stay in some dinky Mom and Pop motel outside Napa, and instead I get a castle! I cannot wait to see the view from the top floor."

"Which is exactly where the guest room is."

Kevin set the bags down on the porch, did a quick glance around the block to see if anyone was watching, then reached under a small urn where a key lay hidden. When he let her inside, Cara felt like she'd stepped into a home-remodeling show on cable. Their hosts' impeccable décor included shiny hardwood floors, creative paint schemes, carved vintage moldings, and carefully placed artwork. The only thing missing was the hunky carpenter. Cara sniffed a few times. "Mm, what is that wonderful smell?"

Kevin took a sniff, looked around and pointed to a glass bottle on the mantle of the fireplace with little wooden sticks sprouting from its top. "I think it's coming from those."

"Is that some kind of air freshener?" she asked, walking over to it and sniffing again.

"Yeah, the scented oil soaks up through the wood and evaporates into the air. Pretty cool, huh?"

"Redwood Forest," Cara read on its label. "No wonder!"

"Didn't these guys do a great job with this place? I'm so jealous of all the space they had to work with."

"It really is beautiful," Cara agreed, studying a framed photograph sitting on the mantle. "I guess this is Mike and Drew?"

Kevin walked up beside her. "Yep, that would be them."

She pointed to the man on the right. "Is that one your brother? He's got brown eyes and less hair, but I see a definite resemblance."

"Yeah, that's Mike. He's about eight years older than me."

"Man, Drew's really handsome," Cara said with a slight blush. "He looks a little like Dermot Mulroney, the actor."

Kevin leaned closer to the photo. "I see what you mean, now that you mention it."

"They're not as handsome as you, though. Just so you know." She flipped her hair and marched off toward the staircase, leaving him smiling after her. "Come on, lead me to that breathtaking view."

Together they climbed up two flights of steps to the third floor guest room, which was a remodeled attic complete with antique four-post bed and armoire.

"This looks like something straight out of Dickens," Cara said, hopping onto the bed butt first and bouncing a few times. "Don't you love these high old beds?"

"Yeah, they're fun…and surprisingly cozy, too." Kevin pushed back filmy curtains to open the window facing the city. Then he crossed the room and opened the one facing the bay. A cool breeze filled the room, lifting strands of Cara's hair. She jumped from the bed, rushed over, and put her hands on the windowsill.

"Oh, check it out!"

"Yeah, huh?"

The Golden Gate stretched across the bay, its reddish hue contrasting with the blue-green hills behind it, and the sky had just begun to fill with the misty glow of evening.

"This is postcard perfect," she told him with a smile.

He took her hand and led her to the other window where he pointed out the pyramidal tip of the Transamerica Building, the Bay Bridge, and other famous landmarks.

Cara leaned against the window frame and sighed. "I just love this city with its hills and trolleys and architecture and…bright, glowing *uniqueness*."

"Yeah, it's one of a kind, for sure. I really loved living here back in my college days."

"That's right! You went to art school here." She turned to look at him, her eyes skipping all around his face. "I'm trying to imagine what a twenty-something Kevin looked like then, rushing around to all his classes."

He squeezed his eyes closed and shook his head as though shaking off a bitter taste in his mouth. "Naw, don't try that. I was a geek back then. You wouldn't have looked twice at me."

"Oh, I don't know…I happen to think some geeks are pretty hot."

Kevin's gaze went far away for a moment. "I was so happy to have *finally* found my niche when I first started at the academy. I walked around with this stupid grin on my face most days. And the school is spread out all over the city, so you weren't kidding when you said 'rushing around to all his classes.'"

Cara listened, folding her arms in a more attentive stance.

"The people I hung with back then were some of the greatest friends I've had in my entire life. We were always running out to see live music at various little hole-in-the-wall clubs…or kickin' around the Haight until the wee hours."

"And this was the eighties, right? You probably got to see really cool bands when they were still obscure, like the English Beat, the Violent Femmes…"

"…the Smiths, XTC…oh, *hell* yes."

"I've always liked your taste in music, Tierney."

"And I like yours as well, Shannon."

They stared at each another with playful grins, and for the first time Cara noticed telltale lines of age around Kevin's eyes and mouth—exposed by certain light angles through the window. The lines contrasted sharply with the youthful glow that old memories had brought to the rest of his face. Her gaze rested on his deliciously shaped mouth.

"I would so love to kiss you right now."

"Go right ahead."

Cara leaned in and softly touched her lips to his. She felt a warm arm slip around her back and pull her closer. Their mouths moved in graceful motion this way and that, pressure alternating with whispery lightness. Then he pulled away, trailing fingers through a handful of her hair. When she opened her eyes, he was flashing his sunny smile.

"Wow," was all she could whisper.

Kevin turned to stare out the window again, and Cara gently leaned her head against his. As they watched the bustling city in a shared silence, she knew it was one of those timeless moments that she'd remember in vivid detail years later—the bay breeze rustling the curtains, the scent of their warm, sun-baked skin, and the growing closeness between them as they looked down on San Francisco from a lovely Victorian in Pacific Heights.

Chapter 26

"Tell me about Arianna. What was she like?"

Cara swallowed an icy sip of dirty martini, set it down on a bar napkin that read *Visions of Joanna*, and stared thoughtfully at Kevin. It was hard to even picture her niece anymore. Arianna was forever frozen in everyone's memory as an obscure twenty-something-year-old who had become worldly and elusive. "You know, toward the end, she'd changed so radically that I couldn't honestly tell you what she was like. Once she moved to England we hardly saw her or spoke with her."

"Start from the beginning, then."

Cara's eyes went far away, gradually melting into a warm glow. "She came into my life when I was in nursery school. Can you believe that? I was a four year-old aunt."

"Wow." Kevin lifted his pint of Guinness for a contemplative drink.

"Yeah, so we were playmates throughout our childhood. It worked out rather well; she had the Fisher Price family village, I had the Barbie penthouse. She had the Close-n-Play, I had Jenn's old forty-five records. Of course we fought like cats and dogs and were insanely jealous of each other at times, but for the most part…she was the little sister I never had and I absolutely adored her."

Kevin's eyes softened as his mouth formed a faint smile.

"She was *such* a beautiful child with her big brown eyes and fiery red hair. People were always stopping to admire her when my sister had her out in public. Melanie found it hard to deal with when she was in a hurry, and women kept peeking into the stroller with oohs and ahs."

They both smiled at this as Cara paused for another drink. When she set the glass down, her eyes darkened.

"It was when Arianna reached her teens that things started to change. Drastically. Being fourteen is tough enough on anyone, but that was also when Melanie filed for divorce. Arianna's world was turned upside down as they moved to another house and Mel began dating someone right away. My niece then became the quintessential unsmiling, difficult, and sullen teen. She dyed her hair black, pierced everything, and hung out with a questionable crowd. Worst of all, she showed every sign of severe clinical depression.

"At the same time, though, she was unbelievably brainy and intelligent. She could quote great literary figures at the drop of a hat and carry on lengthy discussions with professors that her father worked with at Miami

University. In college, she studied abroad and had been to South America and much of Europe by the time she was twenty-one years old!"

Kevin leaned intently on the table. "Wow, what a life! How did she ever have time to be depressed?"

Cara pointed a finger and shook it. "That's what a person who's never experienced the disease always thinks, but we soon learned what an ominous and debilitating creature it can be."

Kevin sat back in his chair and admitted, "I do have experience, actually. One of my best friends had to check himself into an institution a few years ago. It was a bad scene."

"And it's tricky because it comes and goes. When Arianna seemed happy, the family would get a false sense of security and stop worrying. Then she'd go missing for a few days."

"How old was she then?"

"Early twenties."

"Where did she go?"

Cara sighed. "The first time it happened, she was still living at home. Melanie filed a missing persons report, but it turned out she'd gone to a friend's up in Dayton. The next time was when she was rooming with some girls in college. I don't know where she went that time, but it freaked them out. And whenever Arianna was away in Europe, Melanie always feared she wouldn't come back. Watch what you fear, huh?" This last statement weighed heavily on Cara's heart, forcing her to lift her glass and drain the high-end martini without really tasting it.

Kevin made eye contact with their waitress who stood at the bar and asked Cara, "One more?"

"Please."

Kevin held up two fingers, then pointed to their glasses. He took the last few swallows of his ale and leaned one arm on the table again. "How did she end up married in London? I remember you telling me it might've been a green card marriage?"

Cara stared at a spot on the floor and shook her head. "That was crazy. Just crazy. She met him while she was working for some translations department in Washington D.C. A British guy named Colin who was visiting her office on business. He sounded like a big player to me, hitting on all the women while he was there. I don't know what he did or what he said to my niece…or how desperate she was for a boyfriend back then, but the next thing we knew she was moving back to London with him. After only knowing him a month."

"Wow, that *is* nuts. Did she have a formal wedding before she left?"

Cara's eyes widened. "She barely said *goodbye* before she left. Just sold all her stuff, gave her notice, and poof."

“Just like that.”

“We never even *met* Colin. Arianna’s dad thought she may have done it so she could work in London. Tom said she’d always expressed an interest to live there but didn’t want to mess with work visas and citizenship and whatnot.”

“Hmm.”

The waitress brought their beverages and set them neatly on two new napkins. Cara thanked her, then gave her olive-laden skewer a couple of swirls. “My mother begged me to talk to Arianna. ‘She listens to you,’ she told me. ‘Tell her marriage is not to be made a mockery of, and that it’s a sacred institution!’” Cara rolled her eyes. “That was her staunch Catholicism kicking in.”

“Of course.” Kevin grinned and took the first sip of his new drink.

“So I told Mom that Arianna was on her own path and that it wasn’t my style to meddle or interfere. I figured if it was a mistake, she’d know it and come back. But I sincerely hoped that she would finally be happy…*wildly* happy in the arms of her new man.” Cara’s voice broke as the last words left her mouth.

A strained look of empathy from Kevin made her look away.

“I mean, *Christ*…it had been such a long time since Arianna was ever truly *happy*. It’s all we ever wanted for her, but it wasn’t ours to give. She had to get it for herself, you know?”

He gave a solemn nod.

Cara blinked away tears and tried to keep Kevin’s face in focus. “When she was over in England, I felt more helpless than ever. All I could do was email every so often, but she hardly ever wrote back. She stopped talking to Melanie and Tom, too. We knew something was wrong. We just knew.”

Kevin gave her a moment to process, then delicately asked, “When was the last time you saw her?”

Cara took her bar napkin and dabbed at her eyes. “The Christmas before she died, about seven years ago. It was only three months into her marriage, yet Arianna came back alone. She gave us a lame excuse for Colin, like he couldn’t be absent for the holidays or it would traumatize some godmother or great-aunt who was visiting from Yorkshire. Gimme a *break*.”

They both laughed irreverently at this, then Cara’s face shone as if someone had lit a candle inside of her.

“Arianna was extraordinarily lighthearted during that visit. Very smiley—which was rare—and constantly cracking jokes and laughing. I’ll never forget the afternoon she made the mistake of unpacking her espresso pot.”

"Why was it a mistake?"

"Because that poor girl ended up making espresso all frickin' day! She'd no sooner sit down, then someone else would walk in and go, 'Hey, is that espresso? Got any more?' And she would just roll her eyes, haul herself up out of her comfy chair and good-naturedly make another batch. It was refreshingly different."

"How so?"

"Well, Arianna was typically moody and a little aloof at times. But that visit was so…so *heartwarming*. She actually let me wrap a blanket around her when she came down with a cold, and give her a big hug." Cara's smile was wistful as she floated her gaze back to Kevin. "I'm grateful to have those happy memories as my final ones."

With another smile of empathy, he nodded and reached for his drink. Cara took a drink from her martini. After the brief silence, he bowed his head and cleared his throat. "If you don't mind talking about it…how did it happen?"

Cara set her glass down and stared into the vodka, steeling herself. "The summer after her last visit, Melanie gets this call from Colin. He said they'd found Arianna by the lake house of a friend who was living out of country. The cause of death was an overdose of sleeping pills. She'd been missing for a couple of weeks, so her remains were barely recognizable."

Kevin winced and put a hand over his mouth.

She looked up at him with a slow shake of the head. "My sister just came undone. Her husband almost checked her into an institution, it was so bad."

His eyes began to glisten. "I should say so. Her *only child*. Shit."

"Yeah," Cara said through an exhale. "We grieved bitterly. It was such a complete and utter waste! Only twenty-six years old with so much living left to do. But it seemed like no matter what she did, happiness would forever elude Arianna. Even with the help of anti-depressants. There was a peace that this world just could not give her."

Kevin took a deep breath and swallowed hard. "That's just incredibly sad."

Cara turned her martini glass around and around on the table by its stem, watching the clear, cold liquid slosh back and forth. "It *was* sad. Suicide is what happens in other people's families, not your own. And trying to come to terms with the death of someone I loved, when there was no body to mourn over, was even more difficult."

"No body?"

"Arianna's husband had her remains cremated, and then her father brought the ashes back to the States where we could give her a proper funeral."

"Oh *geez,* are you kidding me? Her husband didn't even have a funeral for his own wife? He didn't keep any part of her ashes for himself?"

"I'm telling you, it was a weird, weird situation."

"Did they suspect foul play?"

Cara nodded. "There was a full investigation to rule it out. Her husband had an alibi and there was no evidence found at the lake house to suggest anything other than a quiet suicide. But when Tom went over to England, he had a sit-down with Mr. Huxby...I think he had to look that guy in the eyes and hear everything for himself before he could rest easy."

"Yeah, I would've done the same thing," Kevin agreed, shifting his weight and scowling.

Cara paused for a hearty drink, and then gave the table a firm pat. "Anyway, all of this ambiguity is what makes the idea of a living Arianna totally plausible. If, for some reason, she just wanted to leave it all behind and disappear...they probably could've used a little ingenuity and done it."

"But how?"

"Arianna could've traded identities with someone who died, planted a different body...who knows? My sister might try to contact British authorities and ask questions about the autopsy while I'm out here searching."

A lull fell in the conversation as a jazz saxophone played seductively on the café's XM sound system. Cara lifted the skewer from her glass and bit off one of the olives.

Kevin leaned back in his chair and stared at the city lights outside the bar's front window. "You know, I feel really fortunate. I've never lost anyone close to me through death. I can't even imagine what that would feel like."

Cara stared out the window with him. "At first, you don't feel anything because it just doesn't seem real. Then when you realize the person is never *ever* coming back again, the grief hits like a Mack truck. Suicide, of course, dredges up all kinds of nagging questions...was there anything we could've said or done to prevent it? What made her hurt so badly? Why did she opt to check out rather than conquer her demons? Finally, you end up taking a good hard look at your own life. Your own mortality."

Kevin turned back and locked eyes with Cara, transfixed.

"I think Arianna's death had that effect on everyone in the family. My sister Jenn left her job as a CPA and went to school to be a hairstylist. She told me she needed something far more creative in her life than the soulless, left-brained environment of her company. Something that put her in direct contact with the public all day, rather than in a stifling cube farm.

"Then my cousin suddenly wanted to have children. She and her husband had decided not to when they got married, but she was getting closer to forty and realizing that her time was running out, biologically. She wanted to leave a human legacy after all. They now have a six-year-old son."

"Interesting," Kevin replied. "All this, because of Arianna?"

"I'm telling you, there's nothing like sudden death to make you realize that life is short…and it might be high time to start breaking with convention."

Kevin lowered his head and regarded her quizzically. "What about you? Did it change the tide of your life?"

Cara, about to raise her glass to her lips, stopped in mid air. She considered his question for quite awhile before answering, "I was in a long-term relationship at the time, but I knew he wasn't the one. I was tired of wasting my life on a moody and emotionally draining man. I wanted to use that precious time to try and find the *right* person, so I broke up with him."

"Wow."

"Yeah." The martini continued its path to her mouth. After setting it down again, she folded her arms thoughtfully. "You know, relationships aside, I also began to think more earnestly about life goals. Back then my job as an editor was new and fresh, so it was still fulfilling in many ways. I was also writing a lot of short stories and essays and even a novel about my grandparents coming to America. I'd always hoped to make some sort of documentary or mini-series about their adventures."

"Really."

"Yeah, they weren't your typical Irish immigrants…but that's another story for another night."

"I'd love to hear it!"

Cara smiled. "I told myself that I would work toward leaving some kind of legacy in this world—be it a child or a published book or whatever—and that I would live life to the fullest. Make every second count."

Kevin raised his glass. "Right on."

"See, this is why I was getting restless back in Ohio," she explained, twirling the stem of her glass again. "The job wasn't going anywhere, Mr. Right kept eluding me, and I wasn't about to waste away in Unmarried Home-owning Suburbia."

His eyes twinkled at the phrase.

"I mean it," she insisted, flashing him a look of conviction. "After my mission here, Arianna or no Arianna, I hope to gain clarity about which direction to go."

Kevin gave a nod of affirmation. "I wish you all the best with that."

Cara suddenly rubbed her temples and closed her eyes. "Oh lord, I've done it again."

"What's wrong?"

"I gotta remember that I'm a one martini girl these days. I tend to get a little swimmy after my second."

"No worries, my dear. You've got a designated driver."

"Yes, but can he carry me if I can't even stand up?"

"Of course he can. He'd be honored."

Cara smiled and looked away. "Well, it's not as bad as all that. I just have the nicest little buzz…"

Kevin finished his Guinness and checked his watch. "What do you say we get back to the house and meet up with the guys?"

She swallowed the last of her drink and set her glass down with a worried thunk. "Kevin, do Mike and Drew know about what's going on? Why we're up here?"

He shut his eyes and shook his head. "All I told them is that we were going up to Napa for some wine tasting."

Cara's shoulders went slack and she breathed a sigh of relief. "Thank you."

He stood and offered her a hand as she rose unsteadily from the table. "I'd say a good night's sleep is in order, after we say hello to the guys. You'll need to have your game on tomorrow when you meet and greet the winery owners."

Feeling no pain, Cara let Kevin bundle her safely into the MG, take her back to the house, and navigate her gracefully through the meeting of their hosts. Later still, she slid into his warm and protective arms in the four-post bed on the third story of the stately Victorian.

Between the sedative effects of alcohol and affectionate spooning, Cara was able to avoid what could have been a sleepless night of gut-twisting panic over her pending mission the next day.

Chapter 27

"It makes perfect sense that Arianna would want to live here," Cara said loudly over the wind.

Kevin glanced over at her as they sped along Route 29 into the heart of Napa Valley. "Why's that?"

She made a sweeping gesture to the right of the car. "This whole area reminds me of the Monte Baldo Valley near Lago di Garda…the flanking mountain ranges, the rolling hills, the vineyards and even the golden light. It was one of Arianna's favorite spots when she went to Italy in the early nineties."

He nodded. "People compare Napa to Italy all the time."

Cara stared across the sprawling rows of grapevines—as straight as if they'd been aligned with a ruler—and saw that they were all in green, leafy bloom. She fell into a tranquil silence until Kevin slowed down and took their first turnoff to the right. "Are we there already?"

"Yeah, the sign back there said Casa Miranda Next Right."

Prickles of nervous energy shot through her gut as they followed a winding dirt road to the family-run winery with a quaint little tasting room tucked away behind a grove of trees. Miranda herself, recognizable from the website photo, was sweeping a stone patio as they arrived. She greeted them with a bright smile and a handshake. "We're not quite open yet, but I'd be happy to answer any questions you might have since you've come all the way down the drive."

"Oh, gosh, I'm sorry we showed up outside of your business hours," Cara said ruefully. "I wasn't sure when they were. We do have a question for you, actually."

Miranda waited in polite expectation.

Cara retrieved Arianna's photo from her purse and held it out for the woman to look at. "This girl helped us choose some excellent wines last time we were in Napa. We'd really love to work with her again, but we forgot where this photo was taken. We think it might have been this winery."

Miranda took the photo and studied it. Her brow gathered into a slight crease. "You know, this gal never worked at my place, but it seems to me there was quite an infamous redhead over at Chateau Brielle."

Cara's heart skipped a beat. "Infamous?"

Miranda grinned and handed the picture back to her. "Yeah, she was really good for business. Did all kinds of outrageous things like tell dirty jokes, lead sing-alongs and do Irish step dancing. Not your typical fu-fu wine snob stuff, right?"

"Is she still there?" Cara asked without hesitation.

Miranda shrugged. "You know, I'm not sure. The last time I heard a visitor in our tasting room mention her, it was last autumn during harvest."

Cara shot a wide-eyed look at Kevin, who gave his brows an upward twitch.

"Chateau Brielle," Cara repeated, digging out her winery map.

Miranda was more than happy to provide quick directions.

Kevin gave a gracious nod when they were ready to go. "Thanks so much, Miranda. Beautiful place you have here."

"Stop back again when you've got time," Miranda invited, reaching for her broom. "We don't have any outrageous redheads, but we've got some excellent wine."

Cara laughed. "Will do. Thanks so much."

As they walked to the car, she clutched Kevin's arm. "Arianna took step dancing when she was little."

"Did she?"

"We all did. It was a Shannon family tradition. I'm just sayin'..."

Driving away from Casa Miranda, Kevin noted Cara's silence and grinned. "Your heart is going about one hundred beats per minute right now, isn't it?"

She put a hand over her chest. "You can probably hear it from where you are."

"Do you have a speech prepared, just in case it's her?"

"I did, but I've forgotten it now." Cara let out a shaky breath and gave him an intense stare. "There are a million redheads in the world, Kevin. I'm trying not to get my hopes up."

Chateau Brielle had all the usual characteristics of an established winery, except for the bizarre Picasso-like artwork and comical dancing-animal sculptures that graced the patio. From the décor down to the behavior of the staff, the winery's air of playfulness made it stand out from all the rest.

"Ow!" Kevin cried as they walked along the pathway to the tasting room.

Cara realized that she'd been squeezing his hand increasingly harder as they neared the front entrance and eased up. "Sorry, Kev."

A couple of staff members scurried by, preparing the patio tables for the first wave of guests. When asked, one of them directed Kevin and Cara to the manager who had just stepped outside.

"Trey Ramsey," the man said, looking from one to the other and giving them both a hearty handshake. "How can I help you?"

"Mr. Ramsey," Cara said in her most engaging and businesslike voice. "Last summer we went on an extensive wine tour in this area and connected with a sommelier who was extremely helpful. We wanted to find her again, but forgot which winery she represented."

Trey Ramsey folded his arms and nodded.

"Miranda, from Casa Miranda told us about a redhead who works here, who sort of matches the description." Cara held out the photo of Arianna so he could see. "And we're wondering if your redhead is our redhead."

The man peered at the photo, then shook his head. "No. If Miranda was referring to Fiona, then this definitely isn't her."

"Did I hear my name?" asked a sultry voice from the shadows inside the tasting room. A shapely woman stepped outdoors into the sunlight, swinging a mane of strawberry-blonde hair over her shoulder. She wore a sage peasant blouse with the buttons open just enough to reveal ample, freckled cleavage. Her mischievous green eyes flashed as she smiled at Kevin, then Cara.

"This is our redhead," laughed Trey, throwing an arm around the woman's shoulders. "Fiona Farley, all the way from County Clare, Ireland."

In a faded Irish accent, Fiona joked, "I realize we Irish are better known for our beers and ales than fine wines, but I do know a thing or two about Pinots and Cabernets."

Cara glanced over at Kevin, whose eyes lingered a little too long on Fiona's breasts. When he finally met Cara's gaze, they widened in guilt above a sheepish grin that immediately vanished when he saw the crestfallen look on her face. Stepping up for her, he cleared his throat and offered a diplomatic smile.

"I don't doubt it, Ms. Farley. We'd stay for some tasting if we could, but we've got to keep moving if we're going to find the person we're looking for sometime today."

"Good luck to you," Trey told them. "If there's anything we can help you with at Chateau Brielle, please let us know."

Cara managed a polite smile. "Thank you." She took Kevin's hand again as they walked away and let out a long breath. "I tried not to get my hopes up, Kevin…but I couldn't help it."

Kevin gave her hand a squeeze. "I know. That was a close one. But chin up, Cara mia. We'll just move on down your list and keep going."

They climbed back into the MG and traveled down one dusty road after another, passing vineyards and Tuscanesque estates. Kevin and Cara talked to several winery owners, managers and pourers, presenting their questions with Arianna's picture. None of them turned up even the tiniest shred of hope.

After leaving the last winery on her Napa/Sonoma list, Kevin put his hands on Cara's slumped, shoulders and peered into her weary eyes. "Let's go to that cute little café we saw back on Route 29. You need to get some food in you before you pass out. Then we can regroup and decide what to do next." Cara nodded and focused on a distant plane leaving a white, billowy jet stream in the bluest of skies.

"You okay?"

"Yeah," she said, turning and shuffling toward the parking lot. "I'm just starting to feel a little foolish about this whole thing again."

"Why?"

"Well, what if saffire just totally made everything up? What if she *had* no job at a winery? Maybe she just works at a Safeway in St. Helena."

"Well, let's drive back through St. Helena and check all the supermarkets, then."

Cara tried to hold back a grin. "I'm serious. This could be a total wild goose chase. All this time and trouble dragging you up here…"

"Hey, *do not* worry about me, okay? I'm here because I want to be, whether we find Arianna or not." They reached the MG and he held her door open for her. "But you know what I've been thinking? Maybe the turnover at these places is such that the people we're asking may not have even worked with Arianna. I mean, she could've left for another winery before they started, you know?"

"Right, or gotten out of the business completely," she added dismally. "Astrea said she was expressing the desire to leave a more commercial winery for a smaller, family-run place…but what if she never found one?"

"Well remember, she could've also moved down to a Central Coast winery. Let's not forget that possibility. How many places are on your list from that region?"

"Oh man, there are so many all over this frickin' state. It'll be a needle in a haystack."

When they were both buckled in, Kevin started the engine. "All we can do is try, right? We could head back down the coast to Astrea's and get a few more people on our search team. Especially the guy with winery connections!"

Cara slid her sunglasses on and leaned her head back against the seat. "Yeah, that's just about all there is left to do, huh?"

"I think so. But the first order of business is lunch. And a couple of glasses of wine."

Cara turned toward him with a sudden smile. "Yeah, right? Spending all this time up in Napa and not drinking any wine? That would be a travesty!"

"We will *not* be guilty of that sin on my watch."

Kevin threw the MG into gear and they went peeling out of the drive like two teenagers on the last day of school.

* * *

From: cali4nyapix
Subject: Need Your Help
Sent: Jun 25 - 11:30PM, PST

Dear Mr. Gold,

I've been a long time listener and supporter of the Eclectic Café for three years. In that time, I've gotten to know several users personally, and have made many new and wonderful friends. One of those friends is in a very difficult situation right now, and I am wondering if you can help.

Cara Shannon (Moonflower on the boards) has great reason to believe that the user saffire_21 is a relative who was thought to be dead, but might actually still be alive. Cara is here in California searching for her, and I am helping her check wineries all over the state (we have reason to believe, from talking with her, that saffire might work in the tasting room of a small winery). We are not having much success, and given that the list of wineries in California is endless, it would be extremely helpful if we could narrow our search.

I realize it's not customary for you to give out such information, but I am asking you most humbly and sincerely, for Cara's sake (who is currently crashed out from exhaustion and anxiousness), to give us the IP address of saffire_21 so we can know exactly where to look. Time is of essence. We are currently up in San Francisco but leaving the area late tomorrow morning, so your timely response would be greatly appreciated.

Sincerely,
Kevin S. Tierney

From: Vincent_Gold
Subject: Re: Need Your Help
Sent: Jun 26 - 10:20AM, PST

Hey there Kevin,

Wow, what a situation! Given the circumstances, I can definitely make an exception for you guys and I trust it will stay between the two of you.

saffire_21's IP address is in Paso Robles, California. Sounds like wine country to me. Good luck, best regards to Cara, and let me know how things turn out.

~Vincent Gold

Chapter 28

"I figured this would be the perfect place to take an aspiring novelist," Kevin said as he pulled out a chair for Cara at a white umbrella table. "A café right on Cannery Row, in the stomping grounds of Steinbeck himself."

Cara beamed at him as she took her seat in the bistro outside the Monterey Plaza Hotel, then turned to stare at the bay. "Oh, *look* at this view! What a super-cool place to grow up."

He sat down across from her and stared across the expanse of blue water to the edge of the peninsula. "It was, Cara, it absolutely was. I have so many great childhood memories of Pacific Grove and running around Monterey as a teenager. This town is full of interesting places and history…" he stopped when he discovered her staring at him. "What?"

Through a widening smile, Cara said, "Oh, nothing. You're just my hero today."

He caught her contagious grin. "Why's that?"

She sat back and shook her hair so that the ocean breeze would blow it out of her face instead of across it. "Because you made everything better today. I was ready to give up, and then you just worked your magic and got Vincent Gold to help us. You are so….so *capable*."

"Sometimes a little bit of truth goes a long way."

"Amen to that."

Kevin pushed his sunglasses on top his head. "Are you down with eating outside? I know it's a little windy…"

"Outside is perfect! It's a beautiful day and we should soak up every ounce of it."

"I couldn't agree more."

The server arrived with two glasses of ice water, then took their order for two sourdough bread bowls of clam chowder, Monterey Bay calamari, crab spring rolls, and a bottle of Chardonnay from a local winery.

Kevin settled back in his chair with a sigh. "It's nice being able to *talk* to you again, without shouting over the convertible wind."

"It is," she agreed before taking a healthy sip of water.

For a moment, the two sat smiling at each other with nothing to say. Then Cara set her glass down and asked out of the blue, "So Kevin, what's a California Peter Pan?"

He scrunched up his brow. "A what?"

Cara hoped she wouldn't regret unearthing a subject that had seemingly annoyed him before. "Remember when Gillian said you were in the

California Peter Pan Club? I've been wondering what that meant ever since."

He rolled his eyes. "Oh, *that*. According to Gillian, it's a term commonly used by females for a certain class of California men."

"What, do they all wear green tights and hang out on pirate ships?" Cara asked with a wink.

Kevin didn't smile. "Apparently, California Peter Pans refuse to 'grow up'. They're older guys who keep themselves looking young and buff in order to chase hot, twenty-something women. They're incapable of embracing true *intimacy* and the *responsibility* of settling down." The last words were uttered with an eloquent sarcasm that Cara had never before observed in him.

"So your own sister is accusing you of being one," she said, mulling it over. Then she looked him square in the eyes. "*Are* you?"

His gaze was unwavering. "I don't think I am, but I can see why others might. I'm almost forty-seven years old, I've never married, and I *have* dated a lot of younger women…but in all fairness, I've also dated some older ones, too. I don't pick women based solely on their looks or age. I just go with what I feel for them overall."

She nodded. "That's what I do with men, too."

Kevin flapped a hand. "A lot of my friends ask me if I have issues with commitment, and I don't know how to answer them. The way I see it, *forever* is a pretty big promise. I'm not going to make it hastily just because of timetables or age or because I'm afraid to grow old alone."

Cara stared intently at him, resonating with every word.

"If I have any deep-seated issues about commitment, I'm sure as hell not aware of them. Gillian thinks I should do some therapy, to make sure."

"Why is she so focused on *your* issues all the time?"

"She's concerned that I've been scarred for life by a relationship I had in my twenties."

"Oh, yeah…Maura or Mira or something? Gillian told me to ask you about her. Not that it's any of my business, really. So don't feel like you have to tell me."

Kevin's face melted from its stony defensiveness to mild amusement. "You're so *appropriate*, Cara. You probably never engage in catty girl-gossip either, do you?"

"Oh, I have my days," Cara confessed, holding up her hands. "But I try not to."

"Her name was Maya." Kevin took the lemon wedge from the rim of his glass and stared down at it with a slight smile. Then he squeezed it into his water. "It was the longest monogamous relationship I've been in, to date. Four years."

Well, he's got me beat, Cara thought drably to herself, slipping on sunglasses.

"I met her in art school. After I graduated, she transferred to UCSB for her final year, so we went down there together."

"So it was a woman that brought you to Santa Barbara!"

"For the most part, yeah."

"Bet you were glad to be out of the cold and fog too, huh?"

"Yes. A good deal all around."

Before he had a chance to go on, the server returned with the clam chowders and Chardonnay. Kevin picked up his glass and raised it to Cara's.

"To the loves in our life...old and new," Cara proposed, clinking her glass to his.

After his initial sip, Kevin set the glass down. "Long story short, we moved into a crampy little one-bedroom apartment together and found out real quick how incompatible we were at playing house. After a year, she asked me to move out."

"Wow, that was extreme."

"Yeah, it wasn't a breakup or anything, just a temporary need for our own space. But living apart led to me meeting other women. Santa Barbara was and still is a virtual buffet of available young beauties. So rather than be tempted to cheat on Maya, I asked if we could take a little break."

Cara looked up from her soup. "Uh-oh. If we learned anything from Ross and Rachel, it's that no good can ever come from taking *breaks*."

"Ross and who?" Kevin squinted, poking around his bread bowl with a spoon.

"You never watched *Friends?*" she asked, incredulous, then suddenly remembered their age difference.

"Oh, *hell* no. Are you kidding?"

"Sorry, never mind." She brushed her hand dismissively in the air. "Go on."

"So my request for a break happened just as she was graduating and thinking that our next step would be marriage. You can imagine how well *that* went over."

Cara squeezed her eyes shut and gave her head a slow shake.

"She knew, Cara." Kevin stared at her, conviction darkening his blue eyes. "She knew I was a lost cause. Her time was valuable and she didn't want to sit around waiting on a 'maybe.' So there was no break. There was a definite break *up,* though."

Cara nodded, his words painfully familiar to her as she remembered all the *maybes* of her past.

"At the time, I took her decision in stride and thought it was probably for the best. With hindsight, though, I wish someone would've smacked me over the head and told me to hang onto a good thing when I had it."

"You wouldn't have listened."

He rolled his eyes. "You're right. In my late twenties, I always had this nagging fear that an even *better* woman might be out there. Settling too quickly would keep me from finding her. Or if I did find her, I'd already be stuck with the wrong person. It was a foolish notion and an expensive lesson, because Maya was the best."

"Wow, really?" Cara swallowed and dabbed at her mouth with a napkin. "You never met *anyone* better? And that was, what, almost two decades ago?"

"Yeah, about that long." He paused to take a bite of soup.

She took off her sunglasses and leaned forward with a pointed look. "Come on, Kevin, there had to have been something about her that, deep down, you *knew* wasn't right for you. Because if she were truly the best, and the one you wanted to share your life with, then nothing would've stopped you. You wouldn't have felt any doubts, any inkling to date other women, or the need for a break. This is what my friend Seth finally got me to understand about men. Or women, for that matter."

Kevin considered this with a quiet, "Hm."

"You know what I'm saying?" Cara continued to drive her point home. "Looking back, were there any red flags? Anything that made you think, 'Oh man, this might cause huge problems down the road.'"

He stared distantly across the bay. Then, after a moment, he zeroed in on her face and said with reluctance, "She *was* kind of high maintenance."

They both laughed.

"Well, so then what happened? How did life after Maya pan out?"

"I dated my share of those Barbie Dolls, as you call them, until I got bored with their cookie cutter personalities. Then I started throwing all my energy into my career. I built up my portfolio and private web design clientele—back when websites were a brand new thing. I photographed all sorts of people, places, and events. I even had a regular political cartoon in the News Press until it got canceled. Then I started the Adult Ed gig. All of that kept me pretty busy."

"Too busy for relationships?"

"I don't know if I stayed busy to avoid them or was so busy that I kept missing out on them. I dated every so often, but there just didn't seem to be anyone I could get close to."

"Wow."

He shot her a maniacal grin. "Aren't you glad you met me? I'm a real promising guy, aren't I?

Cara just shook her head and laughed.

"For awhile, I used to blame the selection of women in town, but then I decided maybe it was *me*. Maybe I was afraid of letting some wonderful woman invest all her time and love in me, because I'd only hurt her and drive her away when I didn't want to settle down."

She sat back in her chair, draping an arm over the armrest. "That's an awful damn long time to play the *what if* game, Kevin."

"Well, and as time wore on, a fierce sense of independence set in. It was harder to share space with someone, physically and emotionally. I need *lots* of space. After hitting the late thirties and early forties, one starts getting set in one's ways."

"You sound just like my friend Frannie," Cara chuckled. She joked, but the red flags waved furiously in her face. *He won't share space...he's a loner getting set in his ways...and he's a non-committal workaholic. Listen to what he's telling you. Do NOT look at him as a long term guy!* She dismissed the inner warnings, leaned forward again and picked up her fork. "So when you're not working or helping online friends hunt people down, what do you do for a social life?"

Kevin pondered the question as he finished a large bite of his bread. "I have a few different circles I hang with—my outdoorsy hiking and surfing friends, my wining and dining friends, and my artist friends. They're all a mixture of married and single, male and female, and varying ages."

"When's the last time you dated someone?"

Again, he had to stop and think. "I had a very brief relationship about a year and a half ago."

Before she knew what was happening, Cara blurted out, "My friend Frannie is a firm believer in fuckbuddies...for those in between days. Have you ever had one of those?" *Oh, holy shit. I did NOT just ask him that. Damn that Chardonnay! And damn that Astrea for making me suspicious!*

Kevin blushed and stared at her with an incredulous grin. "Well now, that's kind of personal, isn't it Ms. Shannon?"

Her hands flew to her mouth. "I know! I can't believe I actually—"

He stopped her with a wave of absolution. "I'd be lying if I said I never had a friend with benefits. It never works out for very long, though. Feelings always get in the way. Only college girls can do that with any regularity...but I'm so old now, I'd feel like a perv hooking up with them."

Cara let a nervous giggle slip out, still embarrassed over her brazen inquiry.

"It was pretty sad waking up one day and realizing that all the 'hot twenty-two year-olds' don't even know who John Lennon is. And every time you blink, they have their noses buried in their stupid text messages." He made a goofy face and pantomimed working his thumbs furiously while clutching a cell.

She laughed harder, holding a napkin up to her mouth.

Kevin's eyes twinkled at his appreciative audience, then he pointed an inquisitive spoon in her direction and lowered his voice. "What about you? Have you had any…*fuckbuddies,* as you so delicately call them?"

Cara took a huge drink of wine, stalling for time. A drop lingered on her upper lip, so she licked it suggestively, lowered her eyelids and asked him, "What do you think?"

"I think that I want you to answer the question."

"But I really want to know. Do you see me in that role?"

Kevin eyed her closely. "At first guess, I'd say no. But if I'd known you longer, I might throw in a maybe."

Cara grinned, one eyebrow rising. "Never had one."

"Ever?"

She shook her head slowly.

"Not even a little slippage with an ex-boyfriend?"

"That doesn't count."

"Ah-ha!" he pointed again, chewing his next bite with a smirk.

"No, it doesn't *count*, I tell you! An ex isn't a…" Cara glanced around at the people next to them and mouthed, "…fuckbuddy."

Kevin maintained his smugness through another bite and a sip of wine.

"An f-buddy is someone who you've never had a relationship with, other than for casual sex."

"Whatever."

"Kevin!"

He finally broke out laughing. "I'm just messing with you, Cara."

She rolled her eyes, shook her head, and tried to will the red out of her cheeks as she scraped the last of her chowder from the bread bowl's doughy bottom. Then she stared at him again, feeling compelled to spill even more guts on the table. "I am fully aware that holding out for relationships is like cutting off my nose to spite my face—especially in those long and horny dry spells—but it's just how I roll. I've *fantasized* about behaving differently…even been on the brink of tempting situations…but when it comes down to it, I just can't deliver the goods unless I really, *really* feel something for the person."

Kevin poured more wine in both their glasses. "I'm guessing there are lots of women—*and* men—who feel the same as you. That's not a bad thing."

"Well, my friend Frannie gives me crap about it all the time. She won't ever let me complain about the dry spells, because she feels there's always something I can do about it."

He nodded his understanding. "I've come around to your way of thinking over the years. After awhile, you come to appreciate how much better it can be when it's meaningful."

The server returned with the remainder of their order.

"You gotta try the calamari," Kevin insisted. "It's from here in the bay, and not like anything you've had in other restaurants." He watched as Cara dipped a piece in the creamy mustard sauce, then sampled it. Her eyes widened in delight. "See? Am I right?"

She nodded, still savoring her mouthful.

Conversation gave way to hunger, and the two of them devoured the spring rolls and calamari in a matter of minutes. As he finished up, Kevin put his fork down and said with obvious disappointment, "Mom and Dad are in the San Juans this week, or I'd take you to see them. But I can still show you around town when we're done."

"I'd love that."

Kevin slid his chair back and excused himself for a trip to the men's room. No sooner had he left then Cara's cell phone went off. Digging it out from her purse, she saw that it was her sister.

"Jenn!"

"Well?" her sister demanded. "You haven't called me since you left! It's been four days!"

Cara laughed and lowered her voice so as not to be an obnoxious restaurant-cell- phone-talker. "I'm sorry, it's the stupid time zones. I haven't had much time to talk until evenings, and by that time it's past midnight for you."

"So how are things going?"

"Well, there's good news and bad news. The bad news is that there was no trace of Arianna up in Napa. We looked all day long yesterday, and it was pretty exhausting. Lovely scenery, though."

"I'll bet! And delicious wine, too. So what's the good news?"

"We found out that saffire's IP address is in the Central Coast, so we're going down there to look, with the help of one of our online friends who lives in the area."

"Good deal! Where are you now?"

"Monterey. We're having lunch right on the bay…it's such a pretty seaside town! Kevin grew up here back in the day."

Jenn's tone dropped and she asked suggestively, "So…who *is* Kevin, anyway? Sisterly intuition—along with the tone of your voice—tells me he's more than just some online chum. I want all the details!"

Cara saw Kevin making his way back across the patio. "Well, he's coming back to the table. Guys are always so damn fast in the restroom!"

"Give me the *Readers Digest* version, and talk quickly."

"He's wonderful, Jenn. Really handsome and interesting and funny…does all kinds of creative work for his job and takes fantastic photographs! He's treated me like a freakin' princess the whole time I've been with him. We kind of have this thing for each other, but I'm not sure where it's going. We're just sort of staying in the moment with it, for now."

"I thought so!" her sister cried in jubilation. "How lucky that you have someone like him, helping you out. Who else is with you?"

Cara hung her head. "Actually, Jenn, I told a white lie. He's the only one I'm with. At least until we get to Astrea's house."

"You crazy girl."

"Yeah, I am," Cara admitted with a blush. "But I'm pretty much loving it, too."

Kevin sat down and smiled across the table at her. She winked at him.

"How's Sophie, Jenn? I miss her like crazy!"

"As long as we keep her dish full, she's a happy cat. She doesn't even think about you anymore. I asked her yesterday and she said, 'Cara? Cara who?'"

"Oh, ha *ha!*"

Jenn snickered on the other end of the line.

"Well, I should go. I'll call you later when I can talk longer… after we look around the wineries."

"Good luck, Cara. I am on pins and needles with our little secret back here."

"I'll call you tomorrow."

"Okay, babe. Be safe. Love you."

"You too. Bye."

"That was your sister, right?" Kevin asked. "Did you tell her our good news?"

"I did. And I also told her what a beautiful town this is."

"Well let's go see it!" he invited, digging out his wallet and reaching for the bill.

Cara attempted to throw a twenty dollar bill on the table, but he ordered, "Put that away."

As they left their table with a view, Cara studied the back of Kevin's khaki shorts, black tank top and white linen over shirt. Sometimes it was hard to stay in the moment. She wanted so badly to make a definitive call on their situation. Would he only amount to a summer fling or could he very well be the One?

His discourse about meaningful relationships had left Cara with such a feeling of lightness that she was almost giddy. Perhaps her suspicions about him and Astrea being casual lovers were completely off base. Soon, she would meet the woman. Then she'd know for sure.

Chapter 29

"Oh, *look* at you! What a beauty!"

Astrea clasped hands with Cara and stared warmly into her eyes. She wore a wrap-around skirt made of fringed batik fabric, and her long, Rapunzel-like hair—which accentuated her willowy stature—was still a deep shade of red burgundy. In a waft of patchouli and sandalwood, she reached out and gave Cara a full-body hug, squeezing hard and cooing in her ear. "It's so good to finally see you, Moonflower!"

Cara closed her eyes and received the hug, which felt exactly like being wrapped in a thermal blanket. Her skin tingled when Astrea pulled away again. *Wow, what the hell was that?* While Cara stood there glassy-eyed, the hostess turned to Kevin and gave him a full-lipped kiss. He embraced her warmly, not letting go for a good twenty seconds or so. Once again, Cara had that uneasy feeling about the two of them, but tried to ignore it as best she could.

"Welcome to my little commune!" Astrea laughed, gesturing for them to come inside the rustic wooden chalet that sat in a meadow of wildflowers and sage.

After spending most of the day in Monterey, Kevin and Cara reached Cambria just as the sun was sinking in the west. Cara had been enchanted by Moonstone Beach and the quaint summer cottages perched on hillsides overlooking the sea. Astrea's place was just outside town in a more remote, woodsy area.

"Does one of your roommates own this house, or are you all renting?" Cara asked, looking up at a stone fireplace in the great room. "This is fantastic!"

Astrea smiled. "We rent, but the landlord is thinking of selling and giving us the option to buy it. I don't know…four people's names on a mortgage could get very complicated. But we do like it here."

"I *covet* this house!" Kevin cried, shooting Cara a wide-eyed glance. "If I could afford to buy it, Astrea's room would be my studio. It's the most perfect little loft in the whole place with a view of the ocean."

Cara's heart sunk. *Hmm…he's been in her room. Why the hell would Kevin have ever seen Astrea's room if they weren't…*

"Would you two like anything to drink? We've got every kind of herbal tea under the sun and some freshly made chai."

Kevin smacked his lips. "Mm, StarAngels's homemade chai latte! Feel like going to that much trouble?"

"What, boiling water then mixing in tea and milk?" Astrea winked behind a radiant smile. "Oh, that's *so* much trouble, Kevin. Come into the kitchen, you two."

Laughing at both himself and the smartass remark, Kevin took Cara's hand and followed Astrea into a cozy yellow kitchen with all-modern cabinets, appliances, and a cooking island. She had them sit in the breakfast nook while she put a kettle on the stove and chose three mugs from a rack.

"How was your journey down through Big Sur?" she asked, spooning the chai from a hand-crafted clay canister into each mug.

"We didn't actually go there yet," Kevin replied, sharing a secret look with Cara. "We saved time and came down the 101, because we got a very lucky tip-off as to saffire's whereabouts."

Astrea turned from the counter. "Oh yeah?"

"He talked Vincent Gold into giving us her IP address," Cara told her, "and it's in Paso Robles."

"*Paso?*" Astrea put one hand on her hip then dropped her head sharply toward the floor in disbelief. "That little wench! She was living *so close* to me all this time and never said one word! We could've met up somewhere…easily. She is on one weird trip, that girl."

"Well, you know saffire." Kevin gave Cara another secret stare. "Ever the mysterious one."

Astrea's face brightened. "At least we'll be able to find her in no time at all."

"Hopefully," Kevin said with a trace of doubt in his voice. "Her IP address might be from Paso, but there's no telling where she works. She could've quit and moved on, like she said she wanted to."

For a brief moment, they all stood watching one another in silence. Cara couldn't help but notice that with her tall, supple figure and captivating eyes, Astrea looked like a rendering of a Celtic goddess in a mythology book. If Kevin ever had been her lover, Cara couldn't blame him one bit.

"Well," Astrea said finally, "there are a handful of places I know we *won't* find her, because I've already checked. Other than that, do you have some kind of search method?"

"Yes." Cara folded her arms tightly against her chest, still chilled from their drive toward the coast—where the fog had engulfed Kevin's convertible like the Mists of Avalon. Perhaps it was both the cold and road-weariness that made her brain go lax and blurt, "There are quite a few wineries in this area that never responded to my emails about Arianna. They're the ones I need to visit."

Astrea broke into a curious smile. "Arianna? Is that saffire's name? Did Vincent Gold give that up too?"

Cara looked at Kevin, who stared back in alarm. Then she let out a long breath, turned back to Astrea and said, "I guess it's time I told you the whole story about who I'm looking for."

For the next ten minutes, she revealed to her intrigued friend everything from Princess Hineybutt to the hummingbird earrings. She admitted to there being no logical explanation for how a young American living in England could've faked her own suicide, but that no one in the family had ever really seen a body. She concluded with the fact that saffire had disappeared ever since being confronted.

"Kevin and I keep checking the boards whenever we have access to the Internet," Cara said, over the shrill of the teakettle's whistle.

Astrea snapped out of her fascination trance and turned to lift the kettle off the stove. After pouring the steaming water into each mug of chai, she set the kettle down lightly and turned back to her guests. "You're right, she *hasn't* been on in a long, long time."

"Her last post was the one she'd written just before Cara asked if she was Arianna," Kevin said.

Astrea added cream to the chai and brought two of the mugs over to the table She gave them each a stirring spoon, before taking her own mug over to the computer in the living room. "Now you've got me curious."

Astrea sat down, logged into the Eclectic Café, and did a search on saffire_21's profile. Cara and Kevin stood behind, peering over her shoulder into the illuminated screen.

"Cara's been keeping her presence in California off the boards, in case saffire is lurking," Kevin added. "Cara doesn't want her know she's being hunted down, just in case she decides to run."

"Wow, this is *incredible*," Astrea said in an exclamatory whisper. "It sounds like the storyline of a major motion picture or something."

Cara let out a sigh of exasperation. "That's why I feel crazy every day that I wake up and think about what I'm doing. And as Kevin pointed out, once…what if she doesn't want to be found? Will she be angry at me for looking? Would she swear me to secrecy?"

"Yeah, no kidding," Astrea said, backing out of saffire's profile and clicking into Planet Indigo.

"Hm, last post was by Caroline an hour ago…the forum is dead tonight."

Cara checked the clock on the computer. "Well, and the East Coasters are all asleep now."

"Have we missed anything good?" Kevin asked, glancing over the posts of previous members that day.

"Mm, no." Astrea shook her head. "It was a pretty quiet day. Just the usual *hey, what's ups*. I wasn't around much myself; it was a long day of harvesting the lemongrass." She rose from her chair and turned on more lights. "Let's sit in here where we can all be comfortable."

The great room was warm and inviting with a huge Turkish rug under the chairs, couches and coffee table. Angel sculptures made of smooth acacia wood graced each corner, and beautiful landscape paintings lined the walls. Exotic plants added an earthy finish to it all, springing from various mosaic-tiled pots and planters by the patio door. The place definitely seemed to shout: *Artists live here! Deal with it!*

Astrea lit a candle on the coffee table and sank carefully onto a huge satin throw pillow, trying not to spill her chai. Kevin set his mug on an end table and plopped down next to Cara on one of the loveseats. He glanced around and cocked an ear toward the upstairs. "Where are your roomies, girl?"

"Oh, let's see…" Astrea's eyes narrowed from the effort of recollection, "…one is chairing an AA meeting, one is teaching a sculpting class, and our chef is working late at his café. Now Jason, who works at a winery on Route 46, is the one we need to speak with when he gets in. I don't know where he is…he left with his girlfriend before dinnertime."

Cara watched the familiarity between Kevin and Astrea, still wondering about the extent of their relationship. Although Astrea was very seductive in the fluid way she moved and the breezy way she talked, it didn't seem to be directed at anyone in particular. Cara wondered if there was a boyfriend in the picture, getting to capitalize on this goddess of a woman. Trying to sound matter-of-fact, she asked, "Astrea, did you and Kevin first meet on the boards or in person?"

Astrea's crystalline eyes lit up as she looked at Kevin. "I'd been in the Café a few months when he first joined. He was checking everyone out back then, sending private messages and asking all about them. I got one with the subject line of, 'Hiya, neighbor!'"

A blush rose in Kevin's cheeks. "I had never met people online, before setting foot in the EC. For the longest time I just listened to the music. Then one day I wandered onto the boards and people were so incredibly cool I could never get enough of them."

"I think that's how we *all* started out," Astrea admitted, sipping her chai. "We lurk for awhile, then we dive in head first."

Cara nodded. "That's *exactly* how I did it. Planet Indigo felt like a big, warm Cyber-*Cheers,* where everybody knew my name!"

They all laughed at this, then Kevin raised his mug toward Astrea. "I was just excited that there was an EC listener close enough to actually meet. And we found we had a lot in common, growing up in the same area."

"Well, I was from Santa Cruz, but that's close enough," Astrea told Cara. "Anyway, after we started PM-ing and talking on the phone, I told him that I sometimes made deliveries for the herb farm down his way. So he invited me for a margarita at Lobo's."

Cara stared at Kevin with a devilish grin. "Well of *course* he did. Lobo's, after all, is the center of the universe…isn't it, Kev?"

Kevin tipped his head toward Cara. "She makes fun of how I keep raving about their margaritas."

"Well, they *are* pretty good. Have you taken her up there, yet?" Astrea asked, looking from one to the other.

"No, he *hasn't!*" Cara said, throwing a sidelong scowl Kevin's way and pretending to be miffed.

Kevin leaned toward her. "*Hello?* Gillian?"

"Oh no!" gasped Astrea, putting a hand to her mouth.

"See?" Kevin turned a palm toward Cara. "Gillian's reputation spans three counties!"

Cara giggled, nearly spilling her chai down the front of her, then immediately turned solemn. "She gave a damn good massage, though."

Astrea's eyes sparkled warmly. "She gave Cara a massage? That sweetie."

"Cara needed it. She was a little stressed."

Cara set her mug on the end table nearby and relaxed deeper into the love seat, throwing her head back with a loud vocal sigh. "I am so done with stressing, you guys. I've been perched on the fence and worrying about things for the last three months! Whether or not my niece is still alive. Whether or not I should sell my house. Whether or not I should find a new job. But being here in California has helped me let it all go. Right now, I'm just happy to be far away from my office, bills, phone calls, and home owning responsibilities."

Astrea slapped her knee. "No way! You own your own home? They must be pretty affordable in the Midwest, I'm thinking."

Kevin nodded in commiseration. "I'm sure we could find a way to do it, given the right loans and locale, but it just seems so futile in Santa Barbara. And probably here, too, I'm guessing?"

With half-closed lids, Astrea gave a slow nod. "If I had a mortgage payment, I'd have to do more than just work at an herb farm. Kelly says I can always come back to Santa Cruz if I want. Who knows, maybe I will one day. I just had to prove that I could stand on my own two feet. Life was getting pretty stagnant."

"Oh my *God* can I relate to that!" Cara told her, sitting up straight. "That is exactly why this trip was so perfectly timed. I really needed to step outside my life awhile, possibly find a new direction. Or at least gain some new perspective from a distance."

"Right on." Astrea nodded again. "I hope you find whatever it is you're looking for. Lord knows, this land is inspirational with its mountains and ocean and sun. How long are you going to stay?"

Cara once again exchanged glances with Kevin. "Well, I'm not exactly sure. I guess it all depends what I find up here in wine country. If the search for saffire is a total bust, then I might just hang out for another week. Maybe rent a car and travel around, if Kevin gets sick of playing host."

Kevin laid a hand on her knee. "You can stay as long as you like, m'dear. I'm growing quite fond of the company."

Cara smiled at him warmly, then looked across the table in time to see a glint of awareness in Astrea's eyes.

Astrea lifted a long, slender finger and gave it a couple of jabs in their direction. "So. You two. Anything happening there?"

Cara felt the heat rise in her cheeks. She hadn't the heart to see Kevin's reaction, so she stared at the couch cushion between them. Before she could stop herself, she heard herself say, "I was going to ask the same about you two."

There was a brief silence, then Astrea let out a snicker. Kevin followed with a loud laugh. Then the two of them broke into such a ruckus of cackling that Cara grew uneasy.

"*What?*"

Kevin pointed at Astrea. "You tell her."

"I can't believe you haven't already! What the hell, Kevin?"

"Hey, it never came up!"

"Tell me what?" Cara demanded.

"I play for the All-Girls team, dear."

Cara's face felt feverish. "Really?"

"Really. Gosh, I thought everyone knew."

Kevin continued to laugh under his breath.

"Well I knew about Bellybutton, but..." Cara's hand drifted to her chin as she studied Astrea with new eyes.

"Kelly, the woman I mentioned in Santa Cruz? She was my main squeeze for years. But like I was saying, I woke up one day with a burning desire to go off on an adventure of my own. She was so confident I'd come back to her, she sent me away with her blessing and told me to take all the time I needed. Bless her heart."

Cara looked from one to the other, still dumbfounded. "Yeah...what a woman."

"So, no. Kevin and I are great friends but definitely not an item."

Kevin stifled a new bout of laughter, which got Astrea going again, and together they reduced Cara to giggles of embarrassment. More than anything, she was giddy with relief that she would never *ever* have to wonder about the two being lovers again. At the same time, the path to becoming Kevin's lover *herself* was wide open.

Chapter 30

After the housemates—who had come home and livened up the conversation with their witty and eccentric personalities—retired to their rooms for the night, Astrea turned to her guests and asked a second time, "Seriously, now, are you two together?"

Kevin and Cara glanced at each other and grinned, but neither admitted anything.

"I'm not trying to be a nosey-butt, you guys. I just need to know because it has everything to do with sleeping arrangements. If you aren't together, we can break out an extra air mattress. If you are…" she pointed to the couch behind her, "…there's a hide-a-bed in here."

Kevin seized the initiative. "We'll take it!"

"Sold!" she cried, pounding a fake fist gavel on her palm. "You two can pull it out while I go round up some sheets, okay?"

"You bet," Kevin said, heaving himself off the loveseat and onto his feet. "Thanks, love, for putting us up."

"You are so very welcome," Astrea assured them. Halfway to the stairs, she stopped and turned around. "Oh, and if you'd like to use the hot tub, go right ahead."

Cara looked at Kevin with the face of a pre-teen who'd just been promised her own cell phone for Christmas. "Hot tub?"

"Yeah, you wanna?"

"I definitely wanna!" She stood and helped Kevin move the necessary pieces of furniture and cushions out of the way. Then, on the count of three, they both gave the couch handle a yank and dragged the bed into full extension.

"You two don't waste any time!" Astrea said, returning with an armful of sheets and blankets. She pointed out the nearest bathroom, then gave them each a hug and a kiss goodnight.

"Sleep well, my lovelies. We have a long day of wine and debauchery tomorrow."

Kevin and Cara bid their hostess goodnight, and set about making the bed. Afterward, Kevin pulled off his shirt and began to unbutton his shorts. Seeing Cara's hesitation, he told her, "I wasn't going to bother with a swimsuit…I hope that's okay."

"Oh, absolutely not!" she teased, shaking a finger. "Under no circumstances will I share such close proximity with your naked, Apollo-like body!"

He laughed as he slipped out of his boxers, then watched as Cara did a slow strip tease with her sundress, bra and panties. Imitating the high-pitched voice of the singer for electronica group Goldfrapp, she sang the chorus to their song "Strict Machine" and undulated to its beat.

"The pole dancing song!"

"You remembered!" she said, clapping her hands. Whenever the song had played on the Eclectic Café, Cara almost always made a post in Planet Indigo saying that it would make a good pole dancing song in a strip club. When her last article of clothing dropped to the floor, Cara hurriedly reached for one of the two towels that Astrea had brought them.

"No, wait," Kevin stopped her. "Let me just look at you for a moment."

Cara froze, standing naked in an unfamiliar living room and feeling completely awkward.

"I have never seen such a well-proportioned form on a woman in my life," he told her, hands on hips, eyes moving all around her body. "I've sat in several drawing classes with several nude models, but they either had it all up top or down below." Walking closer to her, he added, "And other women I've known had fantastic bodies, but none as evenly built as you."

Cara had no idea how to respond to such a flattering statement. He obviously didn't care about broad shoulders, flat butts, or gravity starting to have its way with her boobs. She silently commended herself for all the Pilates classes and the ten pounds lost over springtime.

"Anyway, thanks for indulging me." He gestured toward the door. "After you."

Cara had politely avoided staring at him, but since they were being so open about things, she blushed and said, "You know, I was thinking those same things about you. I've always loved a tall, sturdy-looking guy." She moved closer, evermore brazen, and gazed down. He was slightly longer than average, but not *too* long…with a girth that promised a pleasant fullness, should it be called upon to perform its duties. She looked back up into his eyes and winked. "*Very* nice."

Kevin stood a little taller as he opened the patio door for her. "Why thank you, Cara mia."

The hot tub was set at the perfect temperature—not scalding, but not like a warm bath either. Just hot enough for tired bodies that had been traveling all day. The two of them leaned back into the soothing jet bubbles, eyes glued to the starry sky, and enjoyed the occasional and sensual brush of skin against skin. For a long and wordless while, Cara nearly forgot why she was in California. Then, suddenly, the jets shut off and left a quietude of chirping crickets and peaceful night noises.

"California has its own night smell," Cara told him, eyes closed. "I suppose it's the smell of the sea mixed with eucalyptus."

"All I smell is the redwood that this deck is made from," Kevin told her, sniffing. "I suppose I'm desensitized to the smell of California."

Cara smiled and opened her eyes. "I noticed you don't have any fireflies, either. Or do they hatch at a different time of year?"

"No, no fireflies. But I sure did love them when I was in Georgia."

"They're magical when you're little," she told him. "Arianna and I would stay out all night, catching them and saving them in a jar. But the rule was that we had to let them go after we'd enjoyed our nature-lanterns for awhile."

In the dim light through the patio door, Kevin listened with a fond but sleepy expression. "I love your little kid stories."

Cara was silent for a while, then said in her softest voice, "It blows my mind to think that I might actually see Arianna tomorrow. Or in the next couple of days."

"It freaks *me* out a little, too, knowing I might be witness to such an event."

They were both quiet again, their feet hooked together under the water, until a yawn took Kevin by surprise. "Well…you about ready for bed?"

In reply, she echoed his contagious yawn and made a motion to stand up.

"Wait."

Kevin took her hands, pulled her close, and circled his arms around her. Cara rubbed noses with him and gave a breathy little laugh. She tried to ignore all the tingles erupting throughout her body in response to the sensation of being pressed up against him. He gave her a quick kiss, then a longer and more succulent one.

"This has been one hell of a great day," he said, looking into her eyes as best he could in the dimness. "I really enjoyed showing you my hometown."

"And I enjoyed seeing it."

Ten minutes later they were turning out the lights and snuggling into their hide-a-bed together. Cara heard Kevin sniff a couple of times. "These sheets smell good."

"Nag Champa," Cara said softly. "Astrea must burn incense near the linen closet. Or maybe she's got Nag Champa-scented Tide."

He laughed and sniffed again. "I like it."

"Me too."

Cara laid there with the obvious and burning question on her mind. *Are we going to get sexual?* Their first night had been innocent and cautious. Their second night, she'd gone comatose after her massage. The night before, she'd conked out from two martinis at Visions of Joanna. But now, seconds after their naked escapade in the hot tub—which was more than enough to send them over the edge—it seemed only natural that they would want to. True, they were both overtaken by weariness and nearly lulled to sleep by the soothing water, but one never knew.

Kevin finally reached for her and gathered her in his warm arms. She nestled against his chest, the faint smell of chlorine lingering there, and listened to his heartbeat mingling with her thoughts. *Oh* God *how I love this. I couldn't feel more peaceful than I do right now. If this is how the night ends, it's more than enough.*

Just as they were both about to drift off, a bump broke the silence. Kevin and Cara both reflexively raised their heads toward the noise. It came from outside on the patio, followed by a loud, "Shhh!"

"That must be Jason and his girlfriend," Kevin whispered. "He's the only one who didn't come home."

The hushed voices of the young couple drifted in through one of the screened windows.

"Jason is a hoot. Wait till you meet him tomorrow."

Cara yawned and lay her head back down. Kevin echoed the yawn and relaxed once again into his pillow. Just as they were about to drift off again, there was a moan. Cara thought it was her imagination at first, until it was followed by a few gasps and an even louder moan. Her eyes flew open.

"Climb on, babe. You know you like that best."

"No *way*," Kevin said.

They both sat up, shameless in their voyeurism, and stared out the patio doors. With the three-quarter moon fully risen in the night sky, the figures outside were highly-defined silhouettes. Jason was sitting back on bent legs with his girlfriend astride him, moving up and down in rhythmic fury. The moans became more frequent along with some other choice phrases straight out of a porn flick.

Cara felt her pulse quicken. "Wow…this is really hot. And they're not even being quiet about it, either. Do you think everyone upstairs can hear them too?"

"I was wondering that myself," Kevin snickered under his breath.

The girlfriend climaxed with a few short and squeaky cries, then after holding each other for a minute, they stood up and moved toward a patio chair slightly out of view. Both Cara and Kevin leaned to their left and craned their necks. The girlfriend bent over and braced herself on the back of the chair, while Jason grabbed her hips and went at her from behind, moving even more furiously than she had.

"*Fuck,* yeah," they heard him grunt.

"Go, baby, go," she coaxed.

Cara put a stifling hand over her mouth.

"Oh…oh, YEAH!"

There were more moans from the woman, then they both went slack.

Kevin sat back and declared, "Now *that* was better than the Playboy Channel."

"And *Cinemax After Dark,*" Cara added.

"Oh, snap!" Kevin tensed and turned to her dramatically. "They don't know we're in here! How awkward will *that* be, when they walk in and find that they've got an audience on their foldout couch."

"They're going to be even more surprised when they find the doors locked."

"What?"

"I locked them when we came back inside." She stared at the patio doors, horrified. "I'm going to have to let them in, aren't I?"

Before they could decide what to do, there was a jingle of keys at the front door. Kevin and Cara hurriedly ducked back down and held their breath as the sexually replete couple made their way inside and stumbled up the steps to Jason's room.

Cara lay in an awkward silence, unable to relax. Thanks to Jason and his little late-night quickie, she was all hot and bothered again. Her inner voice of common sense, who'd been warning her all week not to have a full-on affair with Kevin, was strangely quiet. The only voice she could hear was that of her libido, crying out to attack Kevin with everything she had. She wanted to feel tongues connecting, limbs intertwined, skin sliding over skin…and from the sound of his breathing, Cara sensed he was right there with her. She reached over and touched his face with her hand. It was all he needed.

A warm hand was on her back, pulling her closer. Lips melded with hers, soft and moist. Cara's breasts pressed deliciously against his chest through the slippery satin of her nightie, and he writhed around a little, enjoying the shared sensation. Another warm hand moved underneath the gown and caressed, leaving little tingles in its wake, until not one curve was left untouched.

"Mmmm," Cara hummed, utterly relaxed. "You have *such* a nice touch."

"It's because you're so soft and silky," he breathed in her ear, then lingered over her blue satin bikinis. "And these are nice too… you've got really sexy lingerie, girl. I hope to see more of your collection."

"Okay, but you're not trying any on."

"Aw, why not?" he played along, seductively sliding a hand beneath them and squeezing.

Cara let out a tiny squeal.

"I've wanted to do that all damn day."

"Oh, really? And what else?"

Kevin released Cara slowly onto her back, and sat up in a beam of moonlight. He took the hem of her nightie in both hands and began to lift, then paused halfway up her midriff. "Something like this, maybe?"

"Oh, yes...*please* proceed," she told him, breathless.

He floated the garment up over her arms and head, let it fall to mattress, and hovered motionless above her.

Cara tried to read the expression on his face. "Why did you stop?"

"I just want to enjoy this lovely image for awhile."

Cara stared up at him in wonder. Had any other man taken that pause before? Just to admire the *sight* of her for the second time in one night? If anyone had, she couldn't remember.

"You look so beautiful in the moonlight, Cara. A true Moonflower *indeed*."

Unable to find her voice, Cara simply smiled her gratitude.

"I've been watching you for the last few days...the graceful way you carry yourself, your Botticellian curves, that sexy bellybutton peeking out from under your tank top...and I kept imagining what it would be like to..." Kevin put a hand over his heart. "Anyway, that's why I'm savoring every second."

Cara watched his eyes closely, trying to determine whether this was just player-speak or if he really meant it. She decided on the latter. They locked gazes intensely until he lowered himself down to begin his feast.

The man was a master at reminding a woman's breasts why it was such a wonderful thing to be breasts. Straying from the predictable moves, he thought outside the box...invented new flavors of his own...traveled over, under, and all around the places that made her squirm with delight. There wasn't one spot that felt left out or underappreciated.

In the midst of her blissful trance, Cara noticed that there was something unique about Kevin's kisses. A quality that surpassed all the other lovers in her life...but what was it? *Lightness*? Yes, the lightness of a kitten...yet operating with the ferocity of a hungry lion.

When Kevin paused for a breath, Cara took advantage and began a tactile exploration of her own. Her hands studied every recess and swell of his muscles. She squeezed the toned biceps, wanting very much to reach up and take a bite of one. She ran her fingers across the baby-fine, barely-there hair on his chest.

Liking this new turn of events, he rolled over and closed his eyes with an appreciative sigh. "Here…I'm all yours."

With a tiny growl, Cara leaned over him. She started with his neck, leaving a trail of kisses down to the tender hollow just inside the collarbone. Then, slowly, she let the rest of him become a playground for her tongue. When she got dangerously close to the borderline of foreplay and oral delight, Kevin sat up quickly.

"What? Was that not okay?" she asked with alarm.

"Oh, no, are you kidding?" He ran his hands through her hair, stroking and smiling at her. "That is *most* generous of you…it's just…I want to keep going. I want you to be first."

Cara's eyes widened in delight as he pulled her back down, and together they continued the sensual romp with a thrilling sense of naughtiness and daring. Fooling around in someone else's living room was fraught with constant, electric awareness that they could be heard or walked in on at any moment. Cara giggled softly to herself.

Kevin stopped kissing her long enough to ask, "What's so funny?"

"I'm making out with cali4nyapix…in StarAngel's living room!"

"And I'm devouring Moonflower under the full moon," he murmured, burying his face in her neck and flicking his tongue around her ear.

Cara noticed the hardness inside his boxers increasing by the minute, and it excited her. She threw her arms overhead and rested them on the pillow. "This is what I love about men. You help us remember how to be women. We spend all day working and making our way in the world, but then we come home to the safety of your bed at night and just lie back…and feel your *strength*."

He paused again. "Wow, Cara, that's really turning me on."

"I mean it. I feel so safe with you."

"I know. I love that."

Kevin rose up in the yogic cobra position and stared down with longing; the pivotal moment. How would they proceed? They'd never discussed the proper precautions. They'd never really planned for this to happen at all. Though they were both lying there on fire, maybe it wasn't too late to slow down. *Oh, but I want to feel him inside me. I want to be that close to him. It's not a fling if I care for him, is it? I can love him without falling in love, right? For the first time in my life, I could just be in the moment with sex—really, I could!*

Kevin's eyes searched hers, humbly asking for some sort of green light. Seeing confirmation, he tenderly freed her from her satin panties. Then he leaned on one elbow and held eye contact with her as he placed a warm hand on her belly. She shuddered with pleasure under his touch.

Further down, his fingers moved with the finesse of an artist. Every noise of delight she made brought a smile of accomplishment and satisfaction from him.

"Cara?" he whispered in her ear, without stopping.

"Yes?" she gasped.

"You're not going to say 'meow' are you?"

She let out a whispery laugh. "Not if you don't want me to."

"Good."

It wasn't long before Kevin produced a sweet, slippery waterfall that fueled his desire even more. He pressed her close and continued with intensity. Cara closed her eyes and surrendered to this plan. *All right, as much as I'd love to feel the real you, this will be just fine...for now...oh yes...*all thinking abruptly ceased as she left her head and existed fully in her body. She began to rock and lurch in time with the movement of his hand, gasping so hard she felt she would hyperventilate.

Sensing the rising wave of arousal in her body, Kevin covered Cara's mouth with his to muffle her cries. Her entire body shuddered. One of her legs reflexively wrapped around his hip and squeezed hard. He held her close as she buried her face in his shoulder and caught her breath. When she opened her eyes, he grinned at her again. "I loved watching your face as you came."

Cara blinked a few times and laughed weakly.

He swept a strand of her hair back. "I only wish we didn't have to be so quiet, because I have a feeling you can make some pretty exciting noise. I *love* it when women are vocal."

She nodded, closed her eyes and let both her breath and heart settle into normal rhythms again.

Kevin gave her forehead a tender kiss. "Thank you for letting me do that for you."

"You're thanking *me?*" she exclaimed, opening her eyes and cradling his cheek in her hand. She wriggled up to a sitting position and stared at him like a cheetah staring at a lone gazelle in the middle of the grasslands. "I do believe it's *your* turn, now." Before he could respond, her hands were on the waistband of his shorts, lifting carefully over his erection and tugging down his legs. When they caught at his ankles, Kevin kicked them off.

Cara paused, considering all of her best moves. Then, with renewed fire in her eyes, she pinned his legs down with her upper body and slipped her hands between him and the mattress. "Kevin Tierney, you have the best forty-six year-old ass I've ever seen."

"Aw, Cara mia, you're too kind!" he beamed.

She gave a little squeeze. "Seriously, this is like *Calvin Klein* ass."

He laughed, and it was one of the sweetest sounds she'd ever heard him make.

Moving with tantalizing slowness, Cara lowered her head and breathed over him. He squirmed a little beneath her hands. *Oh yes, I've got my own fabulous tricks as well, Casanova.* With just the right amount of wetness, she began her Fellatious Symphony in C Major. She closed her eyes and thought of a super-sized cherry Blow-Pop—an appropriately named lollipop if she ever saw one—and marveled over the rose-petal-softness of this most sensitive area on a man.

Kevin, who'd been making low purring noises, let out a long, ragged breath. "Oh God, Cara, that's so nice…"

Feeling victorious, Cara proceeded to let loose with everything she loved to do, bringing rapid results.

Afterward, she stared down at his tranquil face. People *do* look beautiful at their point of release, she mused. When he'd caught his breath, she slunk down next to him and lay her head on his shoulder. She felt his heart beating below her chin and his rapid breath in her hair.

Kevin kissed her forehead once again. "You're amazing, Cara."

She traced a finger around his navel. "Oh, what I could've done with more time…and no one around to hear us."

"That was *plenty* good, thankyouverymuch."

"Oddly, I'm left with a lot of yearning, still."

"How so?" he asked, turning his face toward her.

"It would've been so good to feel you inside of me."

He put a hand over hers. "I know. I was thinking the same thing."

"What made you…why…?" she floundered for the right words, trying to be delicate.

"I don't know," he said, shaking his head. "Something told me we should wait. I'm not sure why. Maybe there will be a better time and place, when we're more prepared…"

Cara sighed. "Yeah."

He gave her another squeeze. "Don't get me wrong…it's not that you're not desirable. I pretty much wanted to fuck your brains out."

Cara shrank at such blatant language, then felt a thrill of flattery deep inside her. "Yeah, me too."

"I'm sorry, Cara…something just told me…"

"Shh, it's okay. It's like you said before, I'm just savoring every second of lying here with you and being in the moment."

"That's good."

A satiated silence fell over them, along with a cool breeze from the open window. Kevin pulled the borrowed duvet over them and continued to hold her until he drifted off. Amazing, Cara thought, how sexual release was like mental Novocaine. She would have to continue the seemingly hopeless search for her departed niece the next day, but it didn't matter. Nothing mattered. In that moment, all was right with the world.

Chapter 31

"Okay, lovebirds, rise and shine."

Cara's eyes fluttered open. She was lying on her side, spooned up against Kevin who stirred slightly at the sound of Astrea's voice. Raising her head, she saw the Celtic beauty padding into the kitchen bleary-eyed, wearing nothing but her bath towel.

"Or at least put some clothes on. The house is waking up and will soon be upon you."

Kevin turned to face Cara, blinking away the heavy fog of sleep. Gradually, a secret twinkle filled his pool-blue eyes. "Good morning, you goddess, you."

Cara's mouth turned upward and her cheeks immediately warmed.

After rustling around in cupboards and drawers, Astrea started the morning coffee then sauntered over to where they lay naked beneath the covers. "Did we sleep good?"

"Like a log," Kevin croaked, stretching.

"I feel so Bohemian, lying naked in the middle of an artists' commune," Cara confessed, pulling the covers up to her neck.

Everyone laughed and Astrea reached down to ruffle Cara's hair. "So! I'm going upstairs to throw on some clothes. Breakfast will be served on the deck in half an hour, and Jason will bring you all his winery maps and brochures."

Kevin smiled up at her. "Thank you, Star."

When she'd gone, Cara sat up and looked around for her nightie. It lay draped over the opposite arm of the couch, so she reached across Kevin to retrieve it. He lifted his head up and kissed her naked breast. "Hey!" she cried, arching upward. He grabbed her and pulled her back down, growling and pretending to maul her like a tiger. She heard primal laughter erupt from deep within her that she hadn't heard in years.

With great reluctance, Cara and Kevin crawled from their love nest and stared at each other with matching grins of shyness.

"It's nice to see you in the daylight," she told him, nightie dangling from her hand.

"I was going to say the same thing about you."

Hearing loud footfalls upstairs, they leapt into action grabbing up their belongings and making a mad dash for the bathroom.

* * *

The western portion of California State Route 46 was a scenic stretch of golden hills, vineyards, and roadside boulders connecting the Pacific Coast Highway to the 101. From its coastal vistas one could see the signature rock of Morrow Bay in the distance, rising up out of the sea just off shore. Further inland were several small wineries with original names such as Midnight Cellars, Grey Wolf, and Peachy Canyon. Some had gravel drives leading up to rustic country homes, while others had fancy signs and parking lots. Cara tried to appreciate the beauty of it all as best she could with her stomach in knots and her throat so tense she could hardly breathe.

After their first few stops, which turned up nothing, Cara's trepidation began to lessen. She quit bracing herself for the sight of Arianna every time she walked into a tasting room. The friends quickly learned that many of the wine stewards were the owners themselves, with no outside employees save for family members—and not one of them a redhead.

"Buck up, little Moonflower," Astrea said to Cara's disappointed face in her rear view mirror as they reached the end of 46 West. "There's a lot more wineries across the interstate, and Jason seemed to think we'd have more luck over there."

Cara looked up and grinned. "I'm fine. Really. What's a few more miles on this Insanity Tour, right?"

"That's the spirit!" Astrea cried as she veered onto the 101 and headed for 46 East.

The more commercial wineries, whose names Cara recognized from grocery store shelves, lay scattered across the drier, flatter region east of Paso Robles. With the afternoon growing hotter and Cara's nerves wearing thinner, the decision was made to start sampling as they searched. Astrea, being their designated driver, was careful to use the spit bucket.

* * *

"I think I'm finally getting the hang of this," Cara told her friends as they got back on the road for the what felt like the hundredth time. "I can now taste a difference between the Syrahs, Cabernets, Pinots, and Chardonnays of each vineyard. I can tell how much finer the earlier years are…and I actually understand terms like *angular, floral,* and *woody*."

"Psh!" said Astrea. "Not *me*. It's either dry and tart, or fruity and sweet."

Kevin laughed at them both from the back seat and gave Cara's shoulder a gentle squeeze. He'd been touching her a lot more that day…little shoulder caresses, hand holding, or an arm around her as they walked. He even gathered up her hair and blew on the back of her neck when temperatures crept into the hundreds. Things had definitely changed between the two of them.

"It is fucking *hot* out, today!" Astrea cried, letting go of the wheel and steering with her knees while she quickly gathered her long hair into a clip.

"Man, no shit," Kevin agreed. "Is your A-C broken?"

Astrea stared sheepishly into her rear view mirror. "Yeah, sorry. I'm saving up to get it fixed."

"Hey, see that place?" Cara said, pointing to a sign for Sorella Luna Cellars. "Let's stop there. It says on Jason's map that they have a deli for creating your own picnic, and I for one could use a little nourishment before I start seeing double! I mean, it's probably a good idea to be coherent and sober before meeting up with a dead niece, don't you think?"

Kevin and Astrea both stared across the car at Cara.

She shrugged. "I'm just sayin'…"

After a brief pause, they all exploded into laughter.

"Was that incredibly dark or what?" Kevin asked.

"Sometimes dark is necessary," Astrea pointed out.

Cara nodded. "Word."

Three miles later, the travelers were revived from their withered state by the shady and exotic Sorella Luna Cellars.

"Whoa, this one's *really* nice," Kevin said.

"It's gorgeous," Cara effused, admiring the ivy-covered building as they pulled into the drive. Just outside the tasting room was a stone veranda lined with green umbrella tables. An Italian marble fountain stood in its center with sunlight glistening off its top spout, and purple petunias cascaded from flowerboxes. She glanced at Kevin, then Astrea, completely charmed. "This could easily be a café in Tuscany, Verona…or Florence."

"And *definitely* where I'd be working, if I were saffire," Astrea added.

The inside of the winery was as lovely as the outside, but proved to be another dead end in the search. So the weary friends assembled a picnic from the deli, bought a bottle of Zinfandel, and took the moveable feast back to a table by the fountain.

"How many wineries left to go?" Kevin asked Cara, removing his sunglasses and mopping at his damp forehead with a napkin.

Cara leaned on the table and rested her chin on one hand. "About twenty, between here and the Edna Valley."

Astrea's jaw dropped. "Wow! For real?"

"The list got longer after I saw Jason's map, because a lot of the wineries on it never turned up in my Internet searches."

"Well," Astrea put a hand on Cara's shoulder, "you don't have to do them all today. You're perfectly welcome to take your time and stay as long as you need to."

Cara sighed, patted Astrea's hand, and smiled her gratitude.

After Kevin poured the wine, the three proceeded to eat slowly, relishing the cool shade and mist from the fountain. Toward the end of their meal, he flipped open his cell phone and checked the time. “Let’s hit one more place before heading back to Cambria. Then we can spend the rest of the day at the beach.”

“Telvin Barnes,” Astrea said, leaning over and pointing to a name on Cara’s map. “Jason said that was a pretty popular winery, with a staff of about five or six people. It’s just down the road a few miles.”

“Sounds good to me,” Cara said, draining her last glass of Sorella Luna wine. “This heat is beginning to wear me out.”

“I’m so glad we had Jason to help us,” Astrea told them, sitting back in her chair. “He’s really on top of things.”

“Well…except for last night,” Kevin said under his breath.

It took Cara all of ten seconds to make the connection, then she nearly spewed Zinfandel everywhere.

Astrea looked over at her. “What?”

Cara waved her hand and swallowed hard. “Never mind…you don’t want to know.”

Chapter 32

"Oh, *Telvin Barnes!*" Kevin cried with sudden recognition as they pulled into the dirt parking lot of the winery. "I totally forgot…they're an old client of mine. I did their logo a few years back before they changed their name."

Cara pointed up at the bright yellow sunburst on their sign. "You designed *that?*"

"Eee-yup."

They climbed out of the car and Astrea looked up at the sign, shielding her eyes from the sun. "Huh. Nice job, Kevin."

"I can't believe it!" Cara marveled. "How cool that something you made is now on wine bottles everywhere!"

"Well, not *every*where. Just certain groceries in California. But thank you…both of you."

They walked from the bright sunlight into a large, open room that resembled an old saloon from the Wild West. The mahogany bar was high, sturdy and heavily shellacked so that it glistened in the spotlights shining down from the ceiling. Behind it, an altar-like display of Telvin Barnes' various wines were spread out over yellow draping and surrounded by blue chalices bearing their sunburst logo. A long wall mirror showed a perfect reflection of both the display and their flushed, weary faces as they bellied up for a new tasting session.

The wine pourer was Amanda, the owners' niece, who they learned had been working at Telvin Barnes throughout her years at Cal-Poly State in San Luis Obispo. She was knowledgeable and easy to talk to, which prompted Cara to start the inquiry during the round of "creamy" and "tropical" dessert Zinfandel.

"Amanda, we were on a wine tour up here last summer, and there was a young woman who was very helpful when we picked out our wine. We're pretty sure we met her here at Telvin Barnes, but it also could've been Sorella Luna."

"Hm," Amanda said, looking up from her bottle without spilling a drop.

"She had unforgettable, flaming-red hair," Kevin spoke up, after swishing the Zin around in his mouth, "and a sassy personality."

"Sassy, but sometimes prone to mood swings," Cara added. In the next second, she realized her mistake and averted her eyes. All that wine had made her careless.

Predictably, Amanda's demeanor changed like an iron door slamming shut. Her eyes remained friendly, but her voice was cool as she told Cara, "You seem to know an awful lot about this person."

"Yeah, we all became e-pals for awhile," Astrea piped up, attempting to salvage the story's authenticity, "then we lost contact with her. We'd love to say hi, if she still works here."

Cara threw her friend a grateful look, then pulled the worn, dog-eared picture from her purse and laid it on the bar. "This is a picture we took of her."

Amanda put the bottle down and studied the photo carefully. Then she slowly shook her head. "No, there were only about two girls that age who used to work here, and your friend isn't one of them." Her face relaxed again and she looked up with an apologetic smile. "Have you been to Sorella Luna yet?"

"No," Cara lied, putting the photo back in her purse. "But we'll try them next."

"Good luck," Amanda told her, gathering up their empty glasses. "I think it's cool that you remembered her all this time. We get so many people through here and no one ever comes back to say hello to *me*." With a pretend pout, she pulled three more glasses from the rack and set them down on the bar. "Okay, next we have last year's Sauvignon Blanc…"

They dutifully resumed their wine tasting until the last round was poured, then thanked Amanda for all her help. Cara purchased a bottle of the dessert Zinfandel for good measure.

On their way out, Astrea found a table of cowboy hats in the souvenir area. She picked up a hot pink one and put it on her head, then placed another one on Cara's. "Yee-haw! Come on, Cara, embrace your inner cowgirl!"

Cara adjusted the hat at a fashionable angle, then threw her head back. "Woohoo!"

"Photo-op!" Kevin cried, hurriedly digging his camera out of its case. "Astrea, put your arm around Cara."

Astrea threw an arm around Cara, encircling her in a waft of patchouli, and leaned in as close as her hat would allow.

Kevin snapped a picture, then another, then one more from a different angle.

Cara and Astrea turned this way and that like Supermodels, giggling and yee-hawing a few more times while curious patrons stared.

After they returned the hats to the shelf, Cara peeled the backing off a Telvin Barnes logo patch she'd received from Amanda and stuck it on her forehead.

"Hey! Good idea!" Astrea cried, peeling her own sticker.

They stuck a third one on Kevin's forehead and made him pose for a picture. He reluctantly agreed, trying to grin and bear it. Then the three of them spilled out the door of Telvin Barnes in a dust cloud of laughter, frivolity and drunkenness. They stood in the shade to catch their breath and regroup.

Kevin checked his cell phone again. "It's four o'clock. Do we still want to go to the beach?"

"I would love to go to the beach," Cara said, leaning tipsily on a wooden post. "I'm pretty much toast for the day."

"All right, *vamos!*" Astrea slipped on her sunglasses and dug a ring of keys out of her large macramé purse.

"Are you okay to drive?" Kevin asked, giving her a scrutinizing stare. "I don't recall seeing you use the spit bucket in there."

Astrea waved a hand at him. "I'm fine. I'm just naturally silly."

Just then, a surfer-looking young man of about sixteen or seventeen walked through the doorway with an old, tired sheepdog following faithfully behind him. They'd noticed him earlier, quietly shooting the breeze with one of the attendants in the gift shop. As he approached, they quickly peeled the ridiculous stickers from their foreheads.

"Hey," he greeted them. "My name's Rod. My mom and dad own the place."

"Hi," all three responded. Kevin shook his hand.

Rod gestured for them to move down the sidewalk and away from the door. They followed him, exchanging curious looks with one another.

In a sincere and measured voice, Rod told them, "I overheard what you guys were telling Amanda about that girl you're looking for, and it sounded a lot like Giselle."

Cara stepped closer to him, her hazy eyes morphing into full on alert.

"Giselle worked here until a couple of months ago. She was kind of sassy, like you were saying, and funny as hell…but also kind of moody."

"Oh, wow," Cara breathed. *She left about the same time saffire disappeared from the boards!*

Rod held a hand high over his head. "She was up here when things were going good…" the hand plummeted toward the ground "…but crashed hard when they weren't. I think she was bipolar or something."

"How old was she?" Cara asked.

Rod thought for a few seconds, crinkling up his eyes. "Oh, maybe twenty-five or twenty-six."

"Did she ever talk about online—"

Kevin took Cara's hand and squeezed it to assuage her eagerness, lest she seem too obsessive. "So she doesn't live around here anymore?"

Rod shook his head, then stared solemnly at the sidewalk. "She, uh…she got sick. Too sick to work anymore. She went to live at the Dhyana Peace Center."

Astrea took a turn in the questioning. "You mean that retreat place in Big Sur?"

"Yeah," Rod replied, looking up at her and squinting against the late afternoon sun. "She knows someone there who's letting her stay for free."

Cara handed Kevin her bottle of wine so she could retrieve the photo of Arianna from her purse. Her hand shook as she held it up for Rod to see. "So, is this Giselle?"

Rod glanced at it and shook his head again. "Naw, that's not her, although Giselle's hair *was* that shade of red. She kept changing it from red to black to *that* color." He pointed to Astrea's hair. "But we still called her the 'feisty redhead' no matter what shade it was, because that was her nickname."

Kevin, Cara and Astrea all stared at one another, wide-eyed.

"You're *sure* this isn't Giselle?" Cara gave the photo a little shake as if it would jog Rod's memory into a higher realm of accuracy.

"No, Giselle's a short little thing with green eyes. Not brown."

Cara's arm dropped to her side and she lowered her eyes, unable to speak.

Rod shifted awkwardly from one foot to the other.

Kevin's face snapped into a cordial smile and he extended a hand quickly. "Rod, thanks so much. I appreciate you coming out here to tell us all that."

Rod shook hands again, looking each one of them in the eye. "Well, sorry for the false alarm. Good luck finding your friend."

Astrea smiled. "Thanks, Rod. We really enjoyed the wine."

He raised his hand in a slight wave. "You guys take care. Come back again and join our wine club."

After he turned and went back inside, they all ambled toward the car in silence. Kevin and Astrea walked on either side of Cara, watching her head droop even lower. When they got to the car, she leaned against it and folder her arms in agitation.

"I feel so incredibly stupid, right now. My niece is *dead*. She didn't fake a fucking suicide! Why the hell did I ever think she would do such a thing? Was I that bored with life that I needed to create this ridiculous drama and drag you people into it with me? You and my poor sister! I'm really sorry, you guys…" her voice cut out as a bout of sobs shook her entire body.

"Cara, no," Kevin told her, laying a hand on her shoulder. "You are *not* stupid. And we weren't 'dragged' into this. We're here because we care about you and we wanted to help."

Cara sniffed and looked up at them through her tears. "That girl he described…it's probably saffire. But it's *not* Arianna."

Kevin pulled Cara close and wrapped his arms around her, rocking back and forth as she cried.

"I really wanted it to be her, Kevin," she mumbled into his shoulder.

"I know. You have every reason to be disappointed."

"It's like grieving her death all over again, but this time I did it to myself."

"Shhh…it's okay. There was a lot of convincing evidence."

When Cara's tears subsided, Astrea unlocked her trunk and opened a red and white cooler. She dug out an icy bottle of water and handed it to Cara. Then she got one for herself and Kevin. "I think Cara's right. I think we actually might have found saffire. And I, for one, would like to go see if it's really her."

Cara took a drink from her bottle, wiped her eyes and cheeks with the back of her hand, then said to Astrea, "You know, so do I. I want to find out why there were so many freaky similarities between her and my niece. I know I'll feel a lot better once I do."

Kevin leaned against the car next to her. "If we're even *allowed* to visit her. I'm wondering just how sick she is. What kind of a place is this Dhyana Center? Is it like Hospice?"

"No," Astrea replied. "It's a spiritual retreat center that people visit from all over the world. But perhaps she has some kind of arrangement to convalesce there. How wonderful for her. Gosh, I hope she's not that bad off…."

They all stood in silence for a minute, the wheels of their minds spinning and humming. A warm wind blew across the dry landscape, whipping Cara's and Astrea's hair in all directions.

"Well," Kevin told them, pushing off from the car, "it's been a long day, ladies. Why don't we let go of all this for a while and just chill. We can hit the beach, maybe throw something on the grill tonight?" He posed the last sentence as a question to Astrea.

"We can *absolutely* do that," she assured him, shaking her keychain. "Lord knows Cara could use the calm and centering energy of the ocean about now." She reached out to smooth back strands of Cara's hair from her face. "You doin' okay, girl?"

Cara offered a rueful smile. "Yeah. Thanks for standing by while I had my meltdown. Everything's always more dramatic with alcohol, I think. Especially wine." She raised her bottle. "And thanks for the water."

"Think nothing of it." Astrea gave her shoulder one last squeeze, then turned to climb into the driver's seat.

Kevin held the passenger door open for Cara until she was safely inside and buckled in. Then he fell into the back, bumped his head on the way, and laughed at himself. "You know, I think this is the most wine I've ever drunk in one day. I'm going to need a complete blood transfusion."

Astrea laughed and said over her shoulder, "Just jump in the ocean. That sea salt will draw all the toxins right out of your body."

Cara laid her head back, let out a long breath, and wondered if the sea could also draw out old and painful memories once and for all.

Chapter 33

"Are you family members?" the man at the reception desk asked in a sleepy voice, looking them over one by one through his John Lennon wire-rim glasses. He wore a white linen shirt and sported the facial hair of Jerry Garcia.

"We're good friends." Cara's bouquet of bluish-purple flowers crackled in its cellophane as she shifted it from one arm to the other. "We heard she was sick and wanted to bring her these."

He picked up a portable phone from its cradle without taking his eyes off them. "I'll let her know you're here. Who should I say is visiting?"

Cara looked at Kevin. If they told the truth, would "saffire" refuse to see them? And if Giselle wasn't saffire, would it freak the poor girl out?

Kevin thought fast and cleared his throat. "We're old friends from the winery."

The man waited a few seconds before he clicked the phone off. "She's not picking up. Let me make one more call…" he pushed a speed dial button, sniffed, and waited again. Then his face lit with a warm smile. "Good afternoon, it's Anthony. I was wondering if you could help me locate Giselle McCreary. She's not in her room." His eyes focused somewhere across the atrium of the center as he listened to the person's response, then nodded. "Excellent. So, then, I'm guessing she's well enough for some visitors?"

Needing a little strength in a moment of uncertainty, Cara reached out and looped her arm through Kevin's.

With a smile in his eyes, Anthony said calmly, "They're her friends from the winery, and they've come bearing gifts."

Cara noticed Astrea focusing a warm gaze on Anthony—working her usual good-energy charm—and smiled to herself.

"Should I just send them out there?" he asked, locking eyes with them once again. He gave a deep nod. "Very good. I'll see you later today. All right, goodbye." After hanging up the phone, the man adjusted his glasses and smiled up at them. "Giselle is out in the garden by the labyrinth. Have you been to the Peace Center before?"

"I have," Astrea told him. "But it's been awhile."

Anthony rose to his feet and came out from behind his station. "I'll just point you in the right direction, then."

"Thank you so much," Cara told him, putting a hand on his arm. "This means the world to us."

He took her hand warmly in both of his and squeezed. "It'll probably mean the world to her, too."

Cara looked at Kevin with a mixture of fear and ardor, her shoulders melting in relief. Astrea gave her a victory pat on the back as they followed Anthony down a corridor to a back entrance. White French doors opened onto a stone terrace, where a huge statue of Buddha smiled serenely at them from its far end. Beyond the terrace was a sprawling lawn overlooking the sea, bordered by flowering shrubs and a long wooden fence.

Anthony stopped, faced them, and gestured like ground personnel flagging an airplane to the gate. "Walk out across that lawn until you see a labyrinth off to your right. Then go toward the labyrinth until you see a small flower garden on your left. Giselle should be sitting on one of the wooden benches there."

Cara, Kevin, and Astrea thanked the man one more time before setting out across the lawn, where a steady ocean breeze offered refreshing contrast to the hot afternoon sun.

"This place is unbelievably gorgeous," Kevin said, studying the view in all directions. To their right was a cascading stone fountain around which people drifted through graceful motions of Tai Chi. To their left, another group stood painting in a cluster of easels on the cliff's edge.

"I once came here for a week-long yoga retreat and felt like I'd spent a week in heaven," Astrea told them. "There's a clothing-optional beach at the bottom of the cliff, a meditation house with stained glass windows that face the evening sun, natural hot spring pools, outdoor massages…and the food! Oh my *God* the food! It's all vegetarian, but it's the best sort of vegetarian food you'd ever want to eat! They must import chefs down from San Francisco."

Cara walked in an intense silence, her eyes glued to the spot where Giselle would be. As they drew closer, the labyrinth came into view. Two women circled around and around its path in serene meditation. Just before it, as promised, was the flower garden where a young, red-headed woman sat facing away from them on a bench. Cara stopped and motioned for the others to do the same. "There she is."

They all stared for a moment, unsure of how to proceed. As if sensing them, the woman turned and looked over her shoulder. Her brow furrowed in concentration as she tried to make out who they were.

Cara began walking toward her again with slow and tentative steps. Gradually, the redhead's expression changed to one of realization and her eyes filled with alarm.

"Giselle?" Cara asked.

She continued to stare, but said nothing.

At last, the three came to a stop in front of the bench. The woman's green eyes were piercing in the bright sunlight, their hue intensified by a dark green sweater wrapped snugly around her. The fiery bobbed hair, along with her turned up nose and petite features, were reminiscent of fairy illustrations from Cara's childhood storybooks.

"Giselle, do you know who we are?"

Although her gaunt face had the telltale pallor and weariness of long-term illness, her eyes came to life with a faint twinkle. She pointed to Cara's bouquet. "Would your *indigo* flowers be a little bit of a clue there?"

Cara grinned and looked down at her bouquet. "You totally got it."

"If you all hadn't posted pictures of yourselves on the boards, I would've been clueless. Let's see now…" Giselle leaned back and looked at each of them closely with the scrutinizing eyes of Judi Dench-as-Queen Elizabeth. "Cali4nyapix, also known as my good friend Kevin?"

Kevin bowed a humble head and looked as though he might burst into tears. "I can't believe it, saffire, here you finally *are*. I mean Giselle. Oh hell, you've always been saffire to me…I'd rather just call you that."

"Go right ahead," she insisted. "I was never fond of Giselle anyway." Then she fixed her gaze on Astrea, softening a little. "*StarAngel.* Sweet StarAngel. You lived so close to me all this time and I was too chickenshit to face you in person. Don't ask why, I couldn't tell you. I'm just a fucked up, crazy chick."

"No you're not." Astrea shook her head, tilted it to the side with affection, then rushed forward to stoop and embrace her. Giselle was too weak to protest, so she relaxed into the hug and smiled as Astrea pulled back again.

The last to be addressed, Cara stood staring at the woman who had unintentionally been the catalyst for some of the most radical changes in her life. For the longest time, saffire_21 had worn the face of Arianna in Cara's imagination. While this fragile young stranger was every bit as sassy as Ari, it was hard to accept her as the *real* saffire.

"And you must be Moonflower." Giselle put a hand to her mouth in time to shield a couple of violent coughs.

As words failed her, Cara simply let out a long breath and nodded.

"Who probably has a million questions for me, I'm sure."

"You bet I do."

Giselle sighed, staring off across the lawn. "Fair enough."

Kevin turned and checked the empty bench sitting cattycorner to Giselle's. "Mind if we sit down?"

"Oh, geez, yeah…don't mind my horrible lack of manners." She held an outstretched arm toward the bench.

Kevin and Astrea sat down together, leaving Cara the spot beside Giselle. Cara lowered herself to the bench and laid the flowers in between them.

"So they told us at Telvin Barnes that you got really sick this past winter," Astrea said. "Is it serious?"

Giselle rolled her eyes and tossed her head. "I can't believe you all went *looking* for me! That's pretty fucking obsessive, man. How many wineries did you go to before you found the right one? Geez!"

Astrea stared, her kind expression diminishing.

Giselle shook her head and buried her face in one hand. "I'm sorry. That was really rude." She looked up again, rueful. "I have cancer. It started in my guts, then worked its way into my lymphatic system. Last month they discovered a huge mass in my lungs. My oncologist recommended immediate termination of chemo, so it'll probably be just a matter of a few weeks, now."

Cara, Kevin and Astrea sat with horrified stares. Cara wondered how in the world Giselle was able to deliver that kind of news in such a cool and detached manner.

Astrea wrung her hands, her eyes beginning to shimmer. "Oh, man, that is *not* cool."

"That definitely sucks beyond words," Kevin muttered grimly.

Cara reached over and put a hand on Giselle's shoulder. "I am so sorry, Giselle."

Giselle shrugged. "Yeah, well…what are you gonna do? To paraphrase the Foo Fighters…it's a shame we have to die, but nobody gets out alive." She sat up tall and defiant. "And don't worry, I'm well past the Denial stage. I'm even past Anger, if you can believe it. I've been feeling so fucking lousy for so long, going in and out of chemo, that I'm just ready for it to be over." A corner of her mouth turned up impishly. "Guess I'm drifting happily along in the Acceptance phase, now, and it feels pretty damn good. I'm incredibly tired at times, and have this nagging hack, but other than that, I'm fine. I mean, look at this…" she made a sweeping motion across the lawn and ocean vista.

"It certainly is a beautiful place to complete one's life." Astrea took a quick swipe at her eye. "How did you land such a sweet deal?"

"Believe it or not, my great-aunt was one of center's founders. Because of that connection, I stay here free. I get gourmet cooking, lovely views, a comfy bed…and a DNR order that won't let anyone drag my ass to a hospital when I code. Nope, I get to die right here by the sea."

Astrea kept trying to wipe away the tears running in a steady stream down her face, but they came too quickly for her to keep up. Kevin cleared his throat and swallowed hard, his face turning flush.

"When did you first find out you were sick?" Cara asked.

"That's the weirdest part," she told them with an acerbic laugh. "I was fine last Christmas. Finer than fine. I ran two miles every morning, did yoga twice a week, and worked a full schedule. Then, somewhere in the middle of January, I started getting abnormally fatigued all the time. My boss thought it was mono or something. I told him, 'Yeah, *right*. Like I've even scored so much as a kiss in the last year.'"

Cara folded her arms tightly in her lap and breathed out laughter, secretly admiring the woman's extreme moxy while staring death in the face. Feisty redhead indeed.

"I didn't want to go to the doctor, but everyone at Telvin made me. One appointment and a couple of tests later…I was officially diagnosed."

"What about your family, saph?" Kevin asked. "Do they live close by?"

The question shut Giselle down. Her face went blank and she was quiet for a good while before replying, "I know this is going to sound really awful, but…they don't even know I'm sick."

She was met with looks of astonishment from all three visitors.

"In order to understand, you'd have to know the relationship I had with them all my life. I was the stereotypical middle child, always lost in the shuffle. Number four in a family of six. Dad's a drunk and Mom might as well have been a ghost, for all her involvement and leadership. Some of my sibs are married with kids, now, and the youngest is in high school…and not a *one* of them ever calls or emails. Out of sight, out of mind. I don't know what I ever did to piss them off, but if that's the way they want it…fuck 'em all. They can just get the phone call one day. They aren't even getting my ashes, because I'm having my friend Janette scatter them in the Pacific."

The mention of ashes triggered a memory for Cara…an image of her sister placing Arianna's wooden urn into a hole they dug in the garden. "I'm sorry, Ari," Melanie had said in the smallest, most sorrowful voice Cara had ever heard. Everyone's tears mingled with rain on their faces as the heavens opened up on their private funeral. It was one of the saddest days of Cara's entire life.

"Your family's crazy," she said to Giselle. "I would've given anything to be with my niece before she died. At least we tried. We tried like crazy to reach out to her, but she wouldn't have it."

"I know! I could never understand why someone who actually *had* a nice, loving family like she did would choose to distance herself from them. I was so envious of her, sometimes."

Cara turned and stared at Giselle. Then she slowly nodded. "You knew Arianna, didn't you?"

Chapter 34

"I gotta hand it to you, Cara," Giselle said with a shake of her head. "You're *much* more polite than I would've been, asking all about me and my sickness instead of plowing ahead with the obvious questions about your niece."

Cara stared, unable to conceal the pain in her eyes.

"I met Arianna in a rehab center in London, a few months before she died. We were both being treated for our chronic depression, which had flared up in some rather ugly ways for both of us. I was going to school over there at the time, and she was working at some international firm."

"Cheswick and Mann," said Cara.

"That's it, that's the one. So needless to say, we spent a good deal of time together, exchanging stories about our childhood and our families. People thought we were sisters because of our identical shade of red hair. We even found that our birthdays were just five days apart."

Cara felt the light bulb go on over her head. "So *that's* what the twenty-one in your username is! Your *birthday*."

Giselle touched a finger to the tip of her nose in affirmation. Then she took a deep breath and continued her story with darkening eyes. "Believe me, though, we weren't just all about the birthdays and fluffy love. Arianna and I were in some rigorous group therapy together, so I learned a lot of extremely intimate things about her. It tends to create a rather unique bond between people, going through shit like that."

Cara's eyes darted all over the grass by her feet, adding things up one by one. "So is that how you knew about Princess Hineybutt?"

"I *loved* that nickname." Giselle gave a faint giggle. "She actually called me that one morning when I refused to get up for a yoga class. Then, of course, I made her tell me the origin of it."

Cara felt the sting of tears in her eyes and a bittersweet smile forming on her lips. This girl was the lucky one who Ari let in, who Ari trusted more than her own family, who got to be with Ari in those final months…and Cara was downright envious. "What about the Snuffleupagus? Was that just something you had in common?"

"Yeah, we compared notes on Sesame Street and Mr. McAfee…and realized we were both Snuffy fans. I loved her imitation of him when he used to sigh, '*Oh, bird'* to Big bird."

Cara wiped a tear away and managed to utter around the lump in her throat, "And I'll bet she taught you about brewing with the moka pot."

"She bought me one after we got outta the 'joint' as we started calling it, and insisted that I brew coffee no other way."

Cara laughed and nodded. "Yep. Sounds like something she'd do." Then, after thinking a moment, she asked, "What about nummies? How did you find out about that?"

"Nummies!" Astrea piped up, clapping her hands together. "I always love it when you come in with your customized nummies for everyone!"

"Oh man, I always thought *nummies* was a saffire signature!" Kevin said, disappointed.

"Nope, I stole that too." Giselle stared at her lap with a sigh. "Like it's not totally *obvious,* already…Arianna was a huge influence on me. She was like the big sister I wish I would've had. Whenever I told her that, she'd always say, 'Well you're the *little* sister I wish I would've had, damn it.'" She paused to look over at Cara. "After rehab, we met for coffee at least once a week to check up on each other and make sure we were both doing okay."

"Well what the hell *happened?*" Cara cried, turning toward Giselle. "She looked so happy and so at peace when she came home for Christmas…none of us ever suspected that she would go and off herself!"

Giselle looked into Cara's imploring eyes and mirrored the look of anguish. "I wish I knew, Cara. The month before she died, she never returned any of my calls. I thought maybe she'd actually gone and moved to California like she always wanted to…until I found out from one of our counselors that she'd overdosed."

Cara flinched, reliving the moment when she'd gotten the news herself.

"I wanted to believe it was an accident. Sometimes when you have all these meds to take, like we did, you can accidentally take too much or mix it with something else and land yourself in the hospital. But it wasn't an accident."

"No, something got to her…something that made her feel incredibly isolated and alone…" Cara stopped and scowled. "And where the hell was that so-called husband of hers, through all this? Did you ever meet him? We sure as hell didn't."

"Oh geez, what a loser that guy was." Giselle's eyes narrowed to slits. "I met him once, and he just seemed like a big slacker who didn't give a shit about anyone but himself. And she wasn't very happy in that marriage, either. She wanted to leave him."

"Oh, God." Cara clutched Giselle's arm, shaking her head. "I was so afraid of that. Do you think she felt stuck? Like she was too embarrassed to come home and admit that she'd made a mistake?"

"Could be," Giselle said, her face growing morose once again.

Cara's lips curled into a seething snarl. "*Colin Huxby*. I'd love to catch the next flight to London, find that little fucker and kick his limey ass!"

This brought a spark to Giselle's eyes as she turned and gawked. "*Wow,* girl...I'm seeing a side of you I've never seen before!"

"Well damn it, I know suicide victims are the only ones responsible for their deaths, but Colin had a hand in her misery! She was doing okay before she left her home and family for that creep."

"But she always had choices."

"*That* is what kills me," Cara said, smacking a hand on her leg. "It was hard to come to terms with the fact that life had gotten *so bad* for her that she felt she had no other options. I used to repeat the mantra over and over, 'It's her journey, it's her path, it's her lesson' until I was finally able to let go and know that somehow, somewhere, she was at peace."

"Well…I certainly hope so." Giselle reached over and took her hand.

Cara's heart grew even heavier when she felt how cold and frail the grip was.

"Arianna told me she'd always loved the California climate and pictured herself working in some winery next to rows and rows of sunny vineyards. So when she died, I decided I would carry on that dream for her. My family was out here anyway, up in Sacramento, and I was failing most of my classes because of all the rehab, so it just seemed like the right thing to do."

Cara sat back and expelled a long, heavyhearted breath. It was then that she became aware of the empty bench next to them and glanced around. "Where are Kevin and Astrea? I didn't even see them go."

"Me either," Giselle replied, looking over her shoulder toward the main building with a smirk. "Guess they felt a little left out."

Cara laughed at this and looked over at Giselle, whose face went instantly somber again.

"If there's one thing I learned, after all that went down with Arianna, it's that life is for the living. And even though my time's getting short, I'm still trying to focus on that. Really making the most of every second, you know?"

Cara's reply came out a whisper. "Yeah."

For a long while the two sat in silence, hands clasped, united by the loss of a loved one. They watched a couple of Tai Chi people stroll by, heading for the labyrinth. Cara was the first to speak again, with brutal honesty.

"Giselle, why didn't you just tell me who you were when I asked you in that PM? Why did you let me go on wondering if my niece was still alive? That was kind of shitty, you have to admit."

"It was." Giselle let go of her hand and looked her in the eye. "And I'm sorry. It's like I told Astrea—and I know it's a lame excuse—but I can be an impossibly unruly chickenshit, sometimes. I was seriously freaked out that you were a relative of Ari's. Right there in the EC. I mean, she used to talk about her 'Aunt Cara in Ohio,' but I never imagined running into you online. It kind of dredged up a chapter of my life that I'd just as soon forget. I didn't want to have to explain it all."

Cara turned her gaze toward the calming sea. *How can I stay angry with her? Sure, her honesty could've saved me loads of trouble and heartache, but what's done is done.* She drew in a breath, absorbing the empowering energy of the waves, and then faced Giselle. "Apology accepted. I'm a firm believer that everything happens for a reason. This whole ordeal enabled me to step outside my rut for awhile, come out here to this *beautiful* land, and…"

Giselle eyed her closely, waiting for more.

"…and, well, it gave me a chance to really get to know Kevin."

A sly grin spread across Giselle's face. "Did you two hook up?"

Cara felt flushed all the way to her toes as she gave a shrug. "I guess we did. We're sort of in this undefined space."

"Sounds like par for the course when you're dealing with California Peter Pans."

Cara's mouth fell open. "You mean *you've* heard that term too?"

"Oh, yeah. San Luis Obispo and Paso Robles…not good places to meet men. Either they're older, confirmed bachelors who will never settle down…or a bunch of young college dudes."

"Wow," Cara said, folding her arms again and staring out at a boat making its way through the choppy water. "And here I thought the older guys in *my* area were lost causes. They might not be very desirable, but at least they'll *commit*."

They both laughed at this.

"Cali4nyapix and Moonflower." Giselle put a hand to her chin, thinking. "I can totally see you two together. Who knows if he's a Peter Pan or not. Maybe he just hasn't found the right person, yet."

"Lord knows, I sure haven't."

"So you're both in the same boat."

"That's exactly what I told him, but really, relationships are the least of my problems these days. I'm far more concerned about my career and the direction of my life. It's time to move on. To what, I'm not certain, but I know that it will involve writing and publication. I'd love to finish a project and use my connections to push it through the door."

"Well then, keep focused on it. If that's what you truly want, then I'm sure you'll find a way to make doors open for you."

"I hope so."

After another pause in conversation, Cara realized with a twinge of guilt that discussion of future dreams might not be the most appropriate topic. She twisted and knotted the strap of her purse, struggling with what to say next.

"What's up, Cara? Your energy just changed big time."

Cara's hands stopped moving. "Well…I suddenly became painfully aware that life goals are a moot point for you. And now I feel bad for even going there."

"No, no, no…don't do that," Giselle told her sternly. "As I said before, life is for the living and right now I still have a heartbeat. Right now, I am totally enjoying meeting Arianna's favorite aunt and finding out what makes her tick."

Cara stared at her lap, feeling both flattered and humble. Then, in her most sensitive tone, she asked, "What makes *you* tick, Giselle? Did you have any dreams on the horizon when you moved out here?"

Giselle held her head up with a prim smile. "I wanted to start my own winery. Hire some people to do the agricultural part, and run the business end of it. And, like most women, I eventually wanted to get married and have a kid."

Cara nodded, then fixed her eyes on the ocean again. The gravity of listening to a dying woman reveal all the things she'd wanted to do in life was almost too much for her. She couldn't help but think how Giselle was the same youthful age as Arianna at the time of her death, but unlike her niece, Giselle wasn't going have a choice. She swallowed the lump in her throat and asked, "What were you thinking of naming your winery?"

"Well *Saffire,* of course!"

Cara clapped her hands together. "Perfect."

Another silence fell over them. Cara rifled through her brain trying to think if there was anything else she needed to address with Giselle. Eventually, a final burning question surfaced. "Giselle, did you give up the EC because of me?"

Giselle looked over. "Oh, that was partially it, but it was also because I came to live here. Normally, there's no Internet available to the guests at Dhyana, but I donated my computer to their office under the condition that I'd get to come use it whenever I wanted."

"That's a good deal."

"Yeah, but I hardly ever use it. I've been spending a lot of time sleeping and going outside and doing other things with my precious time.

Besides, it would make me too sad to have to go in there and explain things. I'd feel like such a drama queen."

"Drama queen?" Cara cried. "Are you kidding, Giselle? Explaining your situation has nothing to do with drama! Those people in the EC are all so *fond* of you. I think they would definitely want to know what's going on, so they can say their goodbyes."

Giselle leaned forward, elbows on knees, her face in a quizzical scrunch. "You know, I could never figure out what the big deal was…why they all flock around when I come in and make a few posts. What did I ever do to be in demand like that?"

"Well, I haven't been there as long as you," Cara said, "but from what I've seen, you're snarky and you make people laugh. You use quirky terminology and playful imagery to help them connect with their inner whacked selves. Many have connected with you personally, and forged special friendships. Isn't that more than enough?"

Giselle shrugged. "I guess so. I'm just not one who enjoys a lot of spotlight, you know? That's why I never stay in there long. Hell, I don't know why I ever started talking on the boards in the first place. What a complete and total time-suck, when there are so many things to be done in the real world."

Cara gave a laugh and a nod. "But you know, Giselle, maybe you were getting needs met by EC friends that your family was unable to meet. I mean, they're this clan of brotherly and sisterly people who are *always* there when you need them, who value your presence, and who genuinely care about what's going on in your life. Sometimes they're more available than family and friends right in my own city!"

Giselle considered this silently for a moment. Then, unexpectedly, her tough exterior crumbled. She bowed her head and tried to hide a grimace as her rounded shoulders shook with heavy sobs. Instinctively, Cara threw an arm around her and felt the lump returning to her throat.

"It's all right…I'm okay…you don't have to…" Giselle wriggled away a little and tried to compose herself.

"Oh, just let it out," Cara urged. "I know you're a strong person, but Jesus…I think you deserve a little meltdown, considering what you've been through…and some comfort from someone who cares."

This unleashed more tears, and Giselle slowly collapsed against Cara's shoulder as she cried. Looking up, Cara spotted Kevin and Astrea lurking in the shadows of a nearby sugar pine. She motioned for them to come back to the benches, which they immediately did. Kevin stood behind and put his hands on Giselle's shoulders. Astrea sat on the other side of her, wrapped a comforting arm around her and whispered, "We love you, saffire."

They silently soothed Giselle until her tears began to subside. Astrea pulled a clean tissue from her purse and offered it.

Cara told them, "I was just telling Giselle that she's dearly missed in Planet Indigo, and that everyone would probably appreciate a chance to say some final words and farewells. How often do we get a chance to hear such things from people while we're still alive?"

Astrea admitted, "Well, it *would* be good to have you back, Saff…but I also want you to be comfortable in doing it."

"Yeah," Kevin agreed. "I wouldn't want it to open up a whole new can of pain."

Giselle snuffled and used the last half inch of sodden tissue to wipe at her nose. "Let me think about it. As much as I squirm with the idea of explaining everything, I also hate the idea of just fading away without warning…right, Cara?"

Catching the allusion to Arianna, Cara gave a dismal nod. "Right."

Giselle raised her head to look them all in the eye one by one. "Thanks so much for coming, you guys. I know I play the tough-girl all the time—vulnerability has never been one of my things—but deep down I'm just as sensitive as the next person. And I want you to know how much this visit meant to me."

They all moved in for another group squeeze, after which Giselle told them wearily, "I should probably go back to my room, now. You wouldn't believe how insanely *tired* cancer makes you. Even when you're just parking your ass on a bench."

The three friends helped her to her feet and stood around her as she took a few laborious steps through the grass.

"Wait," Kevin said, stopping them. "Will you let me carry you, Giselle?"

She looked up at him with a gleam in her eye. "Will I let a tall, gorgeous man carry me through the Dhyana Peace Center? Hell *yes* I will! That would absolutely, positively, fucking *rock*."

Bittersweet laughter erupted from everyone as Kevin bent and scooped Giselle up in his strong, careful arms. As Cara followed behind with Astrea, she was moved by the image before them. Kevin was quickly becoming one of the most admirable men she'd ever met in her life. They continued inside and down a private hallway to a room that had become Giselle's final home on earth.

Once there, Giselle opened a box on her bedside table and sifted through a tangled mess of rings, necklaces, bracelets and other trinkets. After a moment, she found what she was looking for and turned to Cara. "Give me your hands."

Hesitantly, Cara held out her palms.

Giselle pressed two delicate hummingbird earrings into them. “Arianna gave these to me just before she died. They were her favorite earrings and she wore them a lot, so I guess I should’ve seen that as a warning sign…oh well, never mind that now. I want you to have them, Cara.”

Cara closed her fingers around the earrings and drew them to her heart, then looked up at Giselle with shimmering eyes. “I gave those to her.”

Giselle managed a tired smile. “I know.”

“Thank you, Giselle.”

Giselle squeezed Cara’s arm, coughed a few times and asked, “How long are you staying in California?”

Cara’s eyes met briefly with Kevin’s. “I’m not sure yet.”

“Well, I want you to have a fucking *blast* while you’re here. Put all this crap behind you, now, and just…do some quality living. Promise me you’ll do that.”

Cara smiled at her. “I will, believe me.”

Giselle pointed a finger at Kevin. “Make sure she does.”

He smiled, but his eyes were sad. “I’m all over it.”

Giselle put a hand on Astrea’s arm. “I’m sorry I never called you sooner. I completely robbed myself of a kickass friendship by dropping that ball. But you’re welcome to come visit anytime you want…for as long as I’m here.”

Astrea nodded, unable to speak.

The three of them gave Giselle one last hug goodbye, helped her into bed, then walked back to the car in total silence. After a day like they’d experienced, there was simply nothing left to say.

Chapter 35

Click.

Cara turned away from the breathtaking scenery to see a camera pointed at her.

Click-click.

"Kevin, that's the hundredth picture you've taken of me since I got to California. Are you afraid you'll forget what I look like?"

"You photograph well."

"With my hair blowing all over the damn place?" she laughed, trying in vain to push some of it behind her ears. "I feel like these winds are going to blow me right over the edge!"

"Don't get too close, then." He snapped a few more shots of the frothing waves far below them. "I don't want to have to climb down after your ass."

Cara gave him a loud, juicy raspberry before turning and crunching through the gravel on their roadside precipice. "This is just…" she swept her free arm toward the view, at a loss for words, "…this is *stunning*."

Kevin grinned behind his sunglasses and gave his gum a few chomps. "I couldn't wait to get you up here. I knew you'd love it."

"I *absolutely* love it! All the photographs I've ever seen of this place are wonderful, but they're just a fraction of what you experience when you're standing here in front of the real thing."

"That's so true." Kevin sidled up beside her to share the view in silent awe.

The two of them had stayed on at Big Sur and Cara was finally taking her long-awaited tour of Highway 1. The views were all splendid variations of the same scene: Land angling downward toward a cerulean sea—sometimes covered in dark green chaparral, sometimes rippling with golden-brown grasses—then ending in jagged rocks upon which the waves crashed relentlessly and dramatically. Layer upon layer of cliffs stretched as far as the eye could see in either direction, with a meandering ribbon of roadway making a serpentine path in and out of them.

They'd driven up to the famous Bixby Bridge south of Carmel, then worked their way back down again, stopping at every vista and lookout. The photo opportunities were some of the most glorious Cara had ever shot in her life.

With hair whipping around in the wind, she remarked, "Just when I think it can't get any more gorgeous, some newly spectacular view is right around the bend!"

Snap. Kevin captured yet another image of her.

"Your hair was standing straight up in that one, just like a troll doll. I couldn't resist."

"Gee thanks, Kevin. I've always wanted a picture of me looking like a troll."

"Hey, I know, let's get one of us both!"

With no fellow travelers or tourists in sight, Kevin balanced his camera on a boulder nearby and set it up for a timed shot. Kicking into art director mode, he positioned Cara to get the best lighting on her face and capture as much scenic background as possible. Then he finally pushed the button and ran to her side. She felt a warm arm slip around her and smelled his sun-baked skin as he leaned in close. The orange warning light flickered and flashed. He gave her a squeeze. "There it is."

Cara kissed his cheek and squeezed back. In a trigger response, Kevin turned his face to hers and planted a tender kiss full on the lips. Their sunglasses clicked together, so he took his off, threw an arm around her and went in for a more passionate one. It went on and on, his other hand finding its way into the windblown tresses of her hair and pressing her head even closer. When he pulled back ever so gently, Cara stood swaying and gasping for air.

"My God, Kevin! I think I just swooned."

"I've always wanted to ravage a woman on this cliff," he told her, standing proud and giving a little sniff.

"You mean in all of your Casanova history, you *haven't?*"

"Oh, come on…" he waved, rolling his eyes.

"Seriously? You haven't?"

Kevin raised his eyebrows, shook his head and stared into her eyes.

It was Cara's turn to stand tall. "Wow, I feel *uber*-special, now."

"As well you should," he murmured in her ear, nuzzling her cheek. "You're the first woman whose passion for this place equals my own. I can see it in your eyes and in the way your whole body pays homage to its sacred beauty as you stand here."

Cara breathed, "That was downright *poetic*."

"I meant every word."

After holding each other and savoring the moment for a bit longer, Kevin pulled away to pack up his camera. "I have *so* many places left to show you today. We should be able to check into our room, now, too."

"*Vamos!*" she said, shoving her own camera into its case and hopping back into the MG. Kevin jumped in beside her and shifted the idling car into gear.

Cara raised devil-horns fingers in the air and yelled, "Rock on, Mollie!"

"You remembered my car's name!" he cried over the wind.

"Well of *course* I—" she cut off with a yelp of delight as he pealed out, causing her to fly backward against the seat and grab on for dear life.

Kevin laughed, stuck a mix CD into the player, and turned up the volume. The rhythmic, hypnotic notes of Delerium's "Just a Dream" began to play.

"What a perfect song for this landscape!" Cara exclaimed, leaning back with glee. "I love the way this song starts out sampling Erik Satie's 'Gymnopedie #1'."

"Yeah, me too!" Kevin said over the wind. "You know, if it weren't for the EC, I never would've *heard* of Delerium. Now I own just about every CD they've ever made."

"Long live independent Internet radio stations!" Cara shouted, raising a fist in the air.

Chapter 36

"How are you doing?"

Cara opened her eyes and smiled at Kevin through the steam rising off the bubbling water. "My dear man, I am better than I've been in *months*."

Under the water, his toes brushed against her ankles. "Good to hear, Cara. I'm sure it's a major relief to have things resolved."

"Yes." She sunk deeper into the tub and sighed. "Time to just relax and have fun."

"Amen."

For a full minute, there was only the faint hum of the jet motor filling the silence between them. Then Cara spoke. "This little inn is *so* peaceful, all nestled away in the woods."

"I thought you might like it here. It's one of my favorite getaway spots."

She gave a slow shake of the head. "I'm absolutely reeling from all the beauty I've taken in today."

"What did you like best?"

"Well…" Cara thought for a blissful moment. "I don't think I can pick just one place! Pfeiffer Beach was gorgeous. I've never seen pinkish-purple sand before…and I love how the water went rushing through those arched, stone caves."

Kevin locked his feet with hers. "Um-hm."

"Oh, but the redwood forest at the state park was surreal and fairylike. And that swimming hole in the Big Sur River really hit the spot after a hot day in the sun!"

"Yeah, that was awesome."

"The martini in that old bar with a view…what was that place called?"

"Nepenthe."

"Yes! That was a decadent and delicious stop." She lifted a dripping hand out of the water to point an emphatic finger. "But the Henry Miller Library, that had to have been the most *unique* place. Hands down."

"Another good place for a budding author to visit, to soak up the spirit of his Muses."

"A *budding author*. I like the sound of that. You've always believed in me, Kevin. And the library was indeed…inspirational."

Kevin jostled her feet. "Might you be referring to Anais Nin's erotica books?"

Although it was dark, Cara sensed a wicked grin on his face.

"Hell, she and Henry were *all about* the erotica! After reading a few pages, I had to put it down before I lost control and dragged you off into the bushes."

"Oh, *really?*" Kevin said, the grin most likely widening.

Out of the stillness a night breeze, carrying the scent of pine, washed over their heads and rustled the leaves just above their private balcony. Cara took a deep breath of it while simultaneously catching the first glimmers of something rising over the tree line. Her arm came out of the water again with a slight splash as she pointed. "Kevin, the moon!"

Kevin turned and looked. "Man, that thing is huge! Probably the brightest full moon I've ever seen."

Cara stared up at it, relishing every second of every sensation she'd experienced in a charmed day that kept getting better by the minute.

Without taking his eyes off the sky, Kevin slid around the tub for a better view until he was next to her. He threw a warm, wet arm around her shoulders while she draped one leg over his, and together they cuddled and stared at the moon until it was standing solo in the sky, shining down on them with full force.

"*I see a bad moon risin'…*" sang Kevin in a nasally falsetto.

Cara chuckled. "I was thinking more along the lines of Sting." She sung the lines from "Sister Moon" about howling all night and going out of one's mind for the celestial body.

"Ooh, good one. Or how about some classic Dino?" In his best Dean Martin voice, Kevin crooned the musical simile of the moon and a pizza pie in the opening lines of "That's Amore."

Cara echoed, "*…that's amore!*"

There was a brief pause as the two of them went through their mental rolodex of moon songs.

Kevin did a perfect Van Morrison, singing about how marvelous the night was for moon dances.

Cara countered with the opening line of "Blue Moon," in a mellow, 1940s torch singer voice.

"Nice," Kevin nodded. He cleared his throat for his best Neil Young impersonation and sung about wanting to see his love dance again under a harvest moon.

Cara smiled dreamily, then her eyes sparked. "Hey, speaking of Neils…"

"Yes?"

She gazed upward at the moon and sang slow, sultry lines about standing wild and naked under moonlight…and feeling no shame, but rather one's spirit awakening.

"Neil Finn."

"Yes! Oh, you actually know that one! You are a god, now."

"Hey, you're talking to a guy who's been a die hard Split Enz and Crowded House fan his entire life."

Cara's eyes glowed. "I especially love the line where he says that the closest he gets to contentment is when all his barriers are taken down. That really speaks volumes to me."

"How so?" he turned and Cara felt his breath on her cheek, sending a shower of tingles down her spine.

"Well, there comes a time in your life when you stop letting old inhibitions keep you from the things you really want to do."

"What kind of inhibitions?"

"Social mores, other people's expectations of what's real or practical, but mostly deep and personal fears. To just shed them once and for all, step outside that comfort zone and find the contentment of your authentic self…that's what those lyrics mean to me."

"Have you found that, Cara?"

"I think I'm on the threshold. The awareness and realizations about how to spend the rest of my life are slowly coming together. That's what this big hiatus was all about, I think…not just finding saffire."

She turned to see Kevin's reaction. Bathed in pale, silvery light, his penetrating gaze spoke for him. Then his lips were on hers, full and delectable. Without breaking contact, he pulled her onto his lap and they both luxuriated in sensual friction under the water. His hand made a seductive circuit around all of her curves, applying the necessary pressure to keep her from floating away. Their feast of moonlight kisses was suddenly interrupted by Kevin's arousal, announcing itself just to the right of her navel. Cara reached down and held him lightly in one hand, forcing a gasp of pleasure from his mouth.

Letting out a slow exhale, Cara was hit with a profound awareness. It wasn't just about physical yearning anymore. This was no longer a fling or a casual distraction from life in Ohio. A slide show of her history with Kevin flashed rapidly through her mind. The phone calls and getting to know each other, their first kiss at the airport, his charming home, his creativity, his perception of beauty, his sense of humor, the way he interacted with people… his love of nature and music, all his words of encouragement…and his loving attentiveness. It all added up to one stark realization: Kevin Tierney had proven himself, and she hungered for a deeper connection with him. She walked the fine line between affection and love, while her brain kept insisting *you haven't known him long enough to love him.*

"I don't care," she said to the voice in her head.

"What?" he asked, opening his eyes.

"Kevin," she said, laying a hand over his. "Let's make it all or nothing this time."

"I think," he said, covering her neck with more succulent kisses, "that would be beyond wonderful."

Cara pulled away and cradled his face in both her hands. They stared at each other, unable to wipe the silly smiles from their faces. For a brief second, she wasn't sure who was going to drive, or where it would happen. Then, suddenly inspired, she dropped her hands to his shoulders and asked, "Permission to come aboard, Captain?"

He laid his head back on the edge of the tub and closed his eyes in gleeful anticipation. "Permission *granted.*"

Cara's eyes widened as she moved toward him, like a child nearing the edge of the diving board for the first time. She wriggled into an awkward straddle, fighting the tricky buoyancy of the water by hugging her knees against his hips to anchor herself. Then, slowly, she lowered herself onto him. They both closed their eyes and breathed out a murmur of pleasure and awe, savoring that full and electrifying sensation of the first plunge, the first joining of a new lover.

Cara had an affinity for the lap position she'd chosen. With full control over rhythm and depth, she was able to achieve ten times the sensation of other positions and look directly into her partner's eyes. Kevin watched her with the spellbound look of one watching a musician perform an intricate solo on stage. He's so *beautiful,* Cara thought through her sexual haze. She moved slowly at first, then picked up speed and vocal expression. At fever pitch, she saw him close his eyes, set his jaw, and move his hips opposite hers, helping to enhance her experience. When she snapped up, suddenly, from the brushfire ignition of climax, Kevin seemed to feel it too and urged her on. "*That's* it, babe...."

Several bursts of color exploded like fireworks behind her eyelids, and Cara felt as if she were on the rollercoaster ride of her life. Eventually, her rocking slowed and diminished into violent shivers every few seconds. She sunk down in the water and threw her arms around him tightly. He held her until she drifted back down to earth, then looked into her eyes with an adoring smile.

"I feel dizzy," she told him with a breathless laugh.

"I'll bet you do." He brushed a strand of her wet hair out of her eyes. "Man, Cara, those noises you make...they *really* turn me on."

"Was I very loud?"

"Who cares? It was awesome."

A trace of concern darkened her eyes. "Kevin, did you—?"

"We have all night," he assured her with a wink, "and I was having *plenty* of fun just feeling and watching you." He ran both hands through her hair and bent to kiss one breast. "You are so incredibly beautiful, Cara. Especially in this woods…under the moon."

Cara caught the lunar reflection in the twinkle of his blue eyes and felt as if she might cry. She was so profoundly happy, in that moment, that she couldn't speak. Instead, she raised a hand to his cheek and pinched it.

"Ow! What the hell?"

"Just making sure you're real."

"Oh, I'm real, baby," he teased in a Barry White voice, brushing up against her to let her know that he was still going strong. "Every last inch of me."

With a laugh and another shiver, Cara nodded. "Yes…yes you are."

"Come on," Kevin said, standing up and pulling her with him. "There's a nice, comfy king size bed inside with our names on it." He helped her out of the tub and she followed him on wobbly legs to their room that smelled faintly of cool night air and pine.

For the first time since leaving Santa Barbara, Kevin and Cara were afforded the luxury of stretching out, taking their time, and rolling around with limbs intertwined. They left the bedside light on so they could enjoy the visual feast of each other's bodies as they continued to explore, titillate, and bring innovative measures of delight to the other.

At one point, Cara broke away from a kiss to catch her breath. "Where in the world did you get such staying power, Kevin Tierney? You've set a million bonfires all over my body. I've lost count of how many times I've….and you just keep…"

He laughed softly in her ear. "It excites me to be able to turn you on all night." Then, as an afterthought, "And yoga. Lots of tantric yoga helps."

Cara smiled and slid her hands around his waist, touching her nose to his. "You never told me you took yoga!"

"I don't. I lied."

She giggled and gave him a big squeeze. *You love him. Quit pretending you don't.* The words were right there on her lips, longing to be spoken. *But not now. Now is definitely not the time to tell him. Just show him.* Cara rolled over until she was lying on top of him. "All right, Kevin, it's *your* turn."

"My turn?"

"Yes. Here's the plan. First, things are going to get very *wet*."

One eyebrow shot up. "Go on."

"Then there's going to be lots of writhing and gasping for breath."

"I'm liking this more and more."

"And then…the screams of ecstasy. Are you down with that?"

Kevin frowned. "Well, I don't know, Cara. The people in the room next to us might not like it. They might think you're murdering me and call 911…" he waited for the giggle then gave her a little shake "…hell *yes* I'm down with that!"

Fueled by all the affection, gratitude, and admiration that had been slowly building since she'd gotten to California, Cara dove in and felt things pouring out of her from places within that she never even knew existed. She delighted in every little sigh, moan and sharp inhalation. She loved the way he moved when he was on top of her, fluid and graceful like ocean. When his movement began to quicken, so did his breath.

"There you go," she whispered, excited by the fervent upsurge of energy between them. She began to feel her own body igniting once again and instinctively wrapped her legs tightly around his hips.

Kevin's ragged breath was in her ear, tickling. "Oh my God, this feels *too* good."

A swell of pride washed over Cara, and she felt another smile bloom.

He raised his head and locked eyes with her in an intense stare, as if searching for something deep in the recesses of her mind. This only added to the intensity of her climax that happened right in time with his, in harmonious wails. After a few more staggered cries, they fell into weak laughter.

"Oh, Cara *Marie*," he sighed, sinking down and covering her with his warm, glistening body. "The things you do to me."

Cara held him for a long while, every muscle in her body humming loudly. When she was able to speak again, she asked, "How did you know my middle name was Marie?"

"I didn't, I just made it up. You mean it really is Marie?"

"Yes!"

They laughed together for the umpteenth time.

When he was no longer inside her, Kevin planted a tender kiss on her cheek and carefully rolled to one side, taking her with him. She felt one of his hands in her hair, smoothing and stroking each strand.

Lying against his chest, she listened to the driving beat of his heart until it slowed to normal. "I do believe," she told him drowsily, "that a man's heartbeat is one of the most soothing lullabies in the world."

He let out a long and contented sigh. "You're wonderful, Cara."

Cara snuggled closer into his chest and kissed it. "So are you."

Then a huge yawn erupted from his mouth and triggered one from her.

"We ought to sleep like babies after that marathon session," he laughed in her hair.

"Oh, it'll be so nice to just *sleep in* tomorrow morning."

"With nowhere to go and no place to be…"

"Mmmm."

Cara let go of him long enough to reach over and turn out the bedside light, then pulled the covers over them and nestled back in.

The next period of silence seemed timeless. Cara eventually heard Kevin's breathing change, falling into a slower, more drawn out rhythm.

"Kevin?" she whispered, before he slipped away.

"Hm?"

"Have you reached that place of contentment too? The one we talked about?"

There was no response for a good long while, then he gave her back a light stroke and replied, "I don't know."

If Cara hadn't been utterly exhausted, she would've been tempted to lie awake wondering if she and Kevin had a future together. If two people—who lived on opposite sides of the country in completely different cultures, landscapes, and climates—could somehow find common ground on which to settle. There were a million questions to ask, but her brain wisely chose sleep instead. A sleep more deep and peaceful than she'd known in months.

Chapter 37

"You know, Cara, deep down I knew it wasn't going to be her."

Forgetting about the time difference, Jenn had awakened her sister at five-thirty in the morning, wanting to know how the search was going. Watching dawn's lovely colors spread across the eastern sky, Cara had huddled in her terrycloth robe out on Kevin's deck and told her sister the long story of how they found Giselle.

"So, are you thinking I'm pretty much the biggest fool on earth?"

"Not at all. You had a lot of credible reasons to investigate."

Cara's eyes tracked a seagull as it soared past the house. "Actually, it was kind of nice to meet someone who'd known Arianna so intimately, you know? I was almost envious of her, getting to be that close to our niece at a time when she was so reclusive with us."

"Yeah, no kidding."

Cara relayed everything Giselle told her about Arianna, and ended with a heavy sigh. "Sorry I didn't tell you right away. I haven't really had a private moment to call until now, and besides that, I needed a day to just process everything. You wouldn't believe the stuff it brought up, Jenn. It was like reliving Ari's death all over again."

"I can only imagine," came Jenn's sympathetic voice. "Good thing it was a false alarm, so that we didn't have to bring it all up again for Melanie, too."

"How is she doing?" Cara asked.

"She's doing okay…her usual, workaholic self."

"How's Mom?"

"Same old, same old…hanging out with her friends at the senior center and playing bridge and doing crossword puzzles."

"And Sophie? *Man* I miss her."

"She's getting a little needy and yowling a lot, but otherwise doing fine."

"Aw, poor baby. That's how Kevin's cats were when we came back from being gone for a few days. How's the weather there?"

"It's been gorgeous in the last few weeks. We got a big whompus thunder boomer the day after you left…and it brought in the most beautiful sunny and dry weather."

"That's what it's like here *every day,*" Cara told her sister, shifting in her chair so the rising sun wouldn't hit her straight in the eyes. "Kevin said their cloudy and foggy period that usually happens in June happened earlier last month, so I've been lucky. But you know what? There are no lightning bugs here at night. Weird!"

"Really?"

"Nope. No lightning bugs, and no warm summer nights. It always gets cool after the sun goes down, because of the coastal winds."

There was a pause, then the question Cara had been expecting all along.

"So, have things progressed with you and Kevin?"

Cara felt her whole face light up. Through a wide smile, she lowered her voice and said, "Yeah, pretty much."

"Woohoo!" her sister cried, causing Cara to pull the phone away from her ear drum to keep it from shattering. "You know, I was thinking after our last phone call…it just *figures* that you finally meet a good man and he's two thousand miles away."

"I know. I'm not quite sure what's going to happen, Jenn."

"There's no sugar-coating it; long distance relationships are tough. Eventually, someone has to move or it fizzles."

"I know."

"What's the thing you like best about him? What sets him apart from all the others?"

Cara didn't know where to start. There were so many things about Kevin that she adored. "He's not a fixer-upper, Jenn, I like him exactly the way he is. He's successful in his work, he's self-confident, and he enjoys life. At a time when I was starting to slip severely out of my usual positivity, his came and lifted me back up. Aside from all that, we seem to be passionate about all the same things…music, nature, traveling…"

"And I'm guessing the chemistry is good?"

"Oh my *God*." Cara shivered, still feeling the sensation of him inside her from the night before. "It's electrifying, sometimes."

"I should look you two up in my astrology relationship book. When's his birthday?"

"October twenty-sixth."

"Ooh, a *Scorpio*. Libras and Scorpios are usually a pretty sizzling match, Cara! I'll let you know what I find out." She paused and Cara heard traffic noise in the background.

"Are you driving, Jenn?"

"Yeah, I'm on my way to work…so how much longer do you think you'll be out there?"

"I'm not sure. I told my supervisor that I might be out for at least a month or so, but I can only afford to stay one more week. It'll be nice to enjoy a little more of Santa Barbara before I leave."

"Keep me posted on your flight times when you finally make them."

"Will do, Jenn."

"Okay, well… sorry to get you up so early. I'll try to remember the time zones next time."

Cara laughed. "Don't worry about it."

"Take care of yourself, Cara, and have fun!"

"I will."

After hanging up, Cara laid her cell phone on the tiny wooden table nearby and stared out at the ocean. The connection to home had triggered a feeling of uneasiness. Eventually, her time in paradise would end and she would have to go back. Back to humidity and Cincinnati traffic and urban sprawl. Back to her sterile office and endless deadlines. With the mission of finding saffire complete, all that remained were those sticky things in her life that were unresolved. She was finally getting an inkling of what changes to make, but unsure of how to proceed. So many variables at play…

A movement on the surface of the water caught her eye, suddenly. She thought it was her imagination at first, or the shadow of a wave, until the triangular black form rose up a little higher. *A dolphin!* In a microsecond, she was out of the chair and straining over the railing, trying to stay focused on it. Another fin broke the water, lolled lazily, then went under again just as a third one came up behind it. Soon there were four of them, swimming along and occasionally arcing all the way out of the water and leaping together.

A warm hand touched her shoulder, startling her. "Aren't they beautiful?"

Cara turned and saw Kevin standing in his flannel lounge pants. His bedhead was extra wild that morning and his groggy eyes squinted against the morning light.

"I just scared you, didn't I? I'm sorry."

"It's okay. They *are* beautiful and I was so focused on them I didn't hear you." She turned to see if the dolphins were still swimming past. "I could watch them all day."

He reached around from behind her and folded his arms over hers, resting his chin on her shoulder. "Now you know why my work desk faces *away* from the window."

Cara laughed, and they stood watching the frolicking fins until they moved way up shore and out of view.

"Was that your sister on the phone?"

"Yeah, I tried not to wake you."

"No worries, I usually wake up early anyway. So did you tell her about Giselle?"

"The whole long and complicated story."

"What did she think?"

"She was pretty relieved."

"I'll bet."

"When we got back here into better cell reception, I realized there were all kinds of voicemails on my phone," she laughed. "Seth Kane left a couple; one about this new girl, Kïrsten, who he met through MySpace. And one saying he's figured out that I'm in California with you, because you haven't been on the boards either. He said to tell you hi."

Kevin just shook his head and laughed. "Man, ya gotta love that guy."

Cara turned to face him. "So, you're going back to work today, right? I'll try to stay out of your way as much as possible. I'll go for a long walk on the beach or maybe downtown again. It's close enough to ride a bike, isn't it?"

"It is," he affirmed, then stared into space thoughtfully. "We don't have much food in the house, so I'll have to make a grocery run later today."

Suddenly, the rich aroma of French Roast coffee came wafting out of an open window. Her eyes lit up. "Oh, Kevin, you started the coffee! My hero!"

Impersonating Barry White again, he said in a low voice, "Aw, baby…I know what you like."

She lowered her eyelids into a come-hither stare. "You do *indeed*. In more ways than coffee."

"Mmm," he purred, burying his face in her hair and then whispering, "You tasted *so* yummy."

Cara's cheeks went hot.

He pulled back and looked at her with devilish eyes. "Ooh, look at those red, red cheeks."

"Shut up," she laughed, looking away.

"Redder than a fire engine."

"Well, whose fault is that?" she teased, giving him a shove.

He tugged at the belt of her robe, causing it to fall open.

"Kevin!" she scolded through gritted teeth, glancing over at the Winters' windows. Thankfully, their blinds were drawn.

"I could take you right here and now, against the railing. It would be so *9 1/2 Weeks!*"

"Oh, don't tempt me," she said, rolling her head slowly to the side in resistance. "I've always had a penchant for the outdoors."

"*Really!*" he cried, stroking an imaginary beard. "Well, my dear, I know some places…"

Her eyes widened. "Yeah? Like on the beach? I've never had sex on a beach and I've always wanted to. And how about the woods, or on a mountaintop? I've always wanted to have a Rob Roy picnic!"

"A what?" he laughed.

"Did you see the movie *Rob Roy?*"

"Yeah," Kevin replied, then realization struck. "*Oh.*"

"You remember that scene?"

"In the meadow, with his kilt on, and her sitting on top of him?"

"That would be the one."

"That was pretty hot."

"And that's what I call a Rob Roy picnic. *Meow.*"

Kevin shook his head and chuckled. "You crack me up with your little terms!"

She shrugged. "What can I say, I'm a writer."

The words had no sooner left her mouth when the black cloud of doubt hovered over her once again. She often felt like an imposter when she called herself that, because a writer was what she *wanted* to be. The canyon between what she wanted and what she currently did seemed impossible to cross. Kevin noticed the abrupt change in her darkening eyes.

"Whoa, Cara, where did you go all of a sudden?"

She stood back, pulled her robe around her again and leaned on the railing. "I've still got this dilemma of what to do with my life. I was thinking about it a few minutes ago, after hanging up with Jenn."

Kevin took her hands in his and shook them. "Hey, remember what you said up in Big Sur the other night? About that Neil Finn song, and finding your authentic self?"

"Yeah, but talking about it and making it so are two different things."

"Well, let's go talk about it over coffee," he invited. "I can help you sort it all out on paper, if you like."

She stared at him with another surge of admiration as they walked inside. In all of her relationships with men, she couldn't remember a one of them ever being so willing to get involved with *her* life and *her* issues. Often, it was all about theirs. And Kevin had only known her for a short time. *I'm telling you,* said the pesky inner voice again, *he's a gem in the rough*. The voice of reason countered, *but does he want to be claimed and kept?*

Kevin poured two mugs of coffee with cream and sugar. Carrying one in each hand, he beckoned for her to follow him into the bedroom. Once they were settled side by side, he reached into his night table and took out a notebook and pen. Cara watched as he drew a line down the center of the paper. At the top of the left column he wrote *Current Job*. On the right, he wrote *Ideal Job*. Then he set the notebook in her lap with the pen. "Write down what all the plusses are in your editing job on the left."

Cara thought awhile, then wrote in list form: benefits, a steady paycheck, the people, connections to the publishing world, and development of writing skills. She looked over at him to see his reaction.

Kevin took a sip of his coffee. "Okay, now on the right I want you to think about other things that you'd like to do for a living. Skill sets you have that could be profitable, and what their plusses are."

Cara had to think much longer for that one. Eventually, the words began to trickle forth one by one: freelance writing or editing (no office politics and more control over income), traveling (could acquire clients all over the country), working for self (can deduct lots of things on taxes, including part of the rent). The list stopped short and Cara threw down the pen in frustration. "I don't know how I'd make the transition, Kevin. It takes a lot of time and marketing to build a lucrative clientele…so I couldn't just quit my job right away. But if I kept working at my company, when would I have time to build a business?"

"Yeah, that's a tough one," he agreed. "What about small business loans, to get you on your feet? Perhaps you could make your business something even larger than freelance work, like your own literary agency to represent other writers! Or do writing for people's websites…good lord you wouldn't believe the copy people send me. I wonder if they've even passed the sixth grade, the grammar is so bad. There are all kinds of self-employment opportunities for writers, Cara."

Kevin helped her brainstorm until their first cups of coffee were empty. When he returned from filling them, she cast him a doleful stare. "There's still the issue of living arrangements. My house is being rented out now, so when I go back I either live with my mom, with my sister, or in an apartment. But honestly…I'm tired of Cincinnati. The river valley gets so miserably damp and sticky in the summer that it gives me mold allergies. I want to live in the mountains, or somewhere a little drier."

Again, Kevin had her make a list of possible places she would like to live. The list only frustrated Cara, but she couldn't figure out why. "Kevin, what about you? I know you said you're not planning that far ahead, and that you'd like to keep all options open…but is there anywhere else in the country that appeals to you besides Santa Barbara?"

Kevin sat back and thought. "I'm pretty happy here, although it would definitely be cheaper to move inland or to another state where I could buy a home. Some of my friends moved to Wyoming and down to Arizona for that reason. Every so often I think about the possibilities of leaving, but it never amounts to anything." He glanced over at her. "I do know that I could probably do my work from anywhere I wanted, since I work for myself. That's always a plus, so I can see why you want to do it too."

Cara let out a long, disappointed sigh as the reason for her frustration became apparent. Not once did he so much as allude to the possibility of them sharing any kind of life together. Was it there on the tip of his tongue, and he just couldn't figure out how to broach the subject? Was he waiting for *her* to bring it up? Or was he only seeing their relationship as a beautiful and memorable hookup? For that matter, did Cara know *herself* what she wanted out of the relationship?

"Is any of this helping?" Kevin asked, sensing her despair.

"A little," she said, patting his leg. "Thanks for doing this with me, Kevin. At least it's given me lots to think about. Maybe I'll do that on a long beach walk later today."

"That sounds like a good idea." He glanced out the window. "Hey, who took the sun?"

Cara looked up from the list and noticed the overcast sky. "Wow, this is a first since I've been here. That's okay, though, I like cloudy days. Good for walking and pondering one's life."

Kevin gave her a little squeeze around the shoulders before springing from the bed and disappearing into the bathroom. Then he backed up into the doorway with a fluffy wine-colored towel in his hands and a gleam in his eyes. "Want to join me in a shower?"

He didn't have to ask twice. Cara was off the bed in a second, letting her robe slide to the floor as she went.

"Woohoo!" he cried, smacking her behind as she slunk past him.

Wrapped in towels, they crept outside and down the short path to the shower. As luck would have it, Mr. Winters was out in the driveway watering a flowerbed. He simply grinned and raised a hand.

Kevin gave a nod, wearing a smug look. "I'm going to have to introduce you to them later."

"Oh, geez...*that's* gonna be awkward. Especially now!"

He laughed and swung her into the shower with him, turning her in a pirouette as she moved past him. "Don't you love how much room we've got?" He draped their towels over the side and turned on the water, adjusting it to a comfortable hot. Immediately, steam rose up around them.

Cara stepped into Kevin's arms. They let the soothing water form in pools between them like a human fountain, then splash down in a torrent when they separated. When he tried to kiss her, water ricocheted off their shoulders into their eyes, forcing them to squint against the spray and give up in laughter. Playful at first, their tryst became more ardent as they shifted to groping and caressing. Before Cara knew it, Kevin was backing her up against the side of the shower wall with a protective hand behind her.

"Here's to the great outdoors," he whispered in her ear.

She squirmed, ticklish whenever he so much as *breathed* near her ears, and tried to balance herself as best she could. Years ago, an old boyfriend had tried this and it hadn't gone very well. Kevin seemed like a much better fit.

"You can do it," he coaxed. "You've got long, strong, beautiful legs to help you."

Cara smiled and wriggled around until Kevin gained perfect access. Fighting back noises of pleasure, she buried her face in his neck and moved with him while her imagination took off. *This is like something out of one of those soft-core porn scenes in a French film. And there would also be long shots from the perspective of Mr. Winters seeing our feet together under the shower wall and snickering at us!*

Kevin was a wild man that morning, his eyes squeezed closed in carnal abandon. It was raw, unadulterated, *animal* sex. She loved the way he communicated with his eyes just before climax…that secret look of power, as if to say, *I hold the key to you, now…you're all* mine.

Later, as they tittered and stumbled back inside, Kevin insisted, "This is all Henry Miller's fault, you know. Henry and his damn library with those DAMN erotic *banned-in-America-until-the-sixties* books!"

Cara stopped giggling and looked him in the eye. "Kevin, I think you are the most sexually compatible man I've ever been with."

"Really?" he cried, brightening. "Wow, I rule!"

She didn't have the heart to tell him that she could still count the sum of her lovers on one hand. Somehow, it might diminish the compliment.

Kevin poured them both a glass of water. "Yeah, we seem to be right in synch with just about everything."

Cara leaned on the bar, feeling dangerously bold. "It helps when you're really fond of someone. When that person is perhaps one of the finest men you've ever met."

Kevin tilted his head slightly, his face melting. "Cara mia…*thank* you." He reached out and folded her up in a warm embrace.

She pressed her cheek against his. *Oh please say something in return. I really want to know how you're feeling about me these days…*

With a kiss on the forehead, Kevin released her and announced, "I'm going to throw some clothes on and get started on those jobs. Feel free to do whatever you like…mi casa, su casa."

Cara maintained a pasted-on smile, but the light in her eyes faded. "Thanks."

Chapter 38

"You're awfully quiet over there," Kevin said, taking a break from the digital animation he'd pored over for nearly an hour. He stretched in his chair and looked across the room to where Cara hovered intently over a laptop she'd borrowed from him. The tiny computer's cooling fan protested loudly from over-exertion.

After a few clicks and a smack on the Enter key, she peeled her eyes from the screen, looked over at him and blinked. "What?"

"I said you're awfully quiet. I never knew sizing photos could be that captivating."

A faint smile formed on her face. "I'm sort of reliving all our memories as I go through them," she explained, "and it's making me think about stuff. So I'm moodling."

"Moodling?"

"It's writers' slang for tossing story ideas around in one's head for later use. Like doodling, only with words."

"So you're finally writing? How cool is that? I knew the Muses would get you if you stayed here long enough."

"It's just a little idea."

Kevin padded across the floor to her nest of throw pillows, plopped down beside her and gave her a loud smooch on the neck. He peered at the screen and pointed to a colorful sun dog over Monterey Bay. "Wow, who took that one?"

"You did."

"I did?"

"And I couldn't help but notice how many of these Big Sur shots are the exact same views as the ones in your touched-up photos."

"Heh. Yeah. My experimental photos that just sit around the studio gathering dust."

"Do you ever do illustration or cartoons anymore?" she asked, reaching over to pet a sleeping Rennie who was curled up beside her.

"Every now and then. Why?"

Cara studied the screen again. "I was just thinking about what you told me in one of our phone conversations. How you were going to quit your Adult Ed job and focus more on illustrating."

"Yeah, that *is* the plan, although I haven't been pursuing it very diligently."

Cara closed the laptop with a click and looked over at him. "I think I'm going to continue this moodling on a nice long beach walk."

"Sounds like an excellent plan."

"Too busy to join me?"

He smiled with regret. "I really am."

She leaned over and kissed his cheek. "Okay, then. See you after a while."

On her way out the door and across the deck, Cara was secretly glad that Kevin couldn't come with her. There were things she needed to think seriously about, uninterrupted.

* * *

The low tide left ample beach for Cara to wander down at her leisure. Rock formations that she hadn't seen before jutted out of the receded water, with starfish and anemones clinging to their undersides. For the longest while she lost herself in exploration of the tidal pools, observing various shells and scalloped patterns in the sand. Then she began to notice everything in her Impressionistic sunlit scene; the yellow, pink and red wildflowers dotting the cliff side just above the beach…the gentle tumbling of waves mingled with the voices of beach-goers, filling the fresh salt air…and little children with sandy-bottomed swimsuits, squealing as the cold water lapped at their toes.

The further Cara walked, the more scant people became, leaving her alone with her thoughts…which spouted like a big stream-of-conscious geyser that couldn't be shut off. *So what would you like to see happen with Kevin? Are you in love with him? Have you known each other long enough to warrant taking it to the next level? And what is the next level, living so far apart? Could you leave everything behind in Ohio and try California? Would you cohabitate right away? Because after everything he's told you about sharing space, he may not want to give up his bachelor pad. So could you afford a place of your own in this expensive town? What would you do for work?*

What it all came down to was what Kevin wanted. If she could just speak openly with him about everything then she'd know for sure, but the thought of doing so terrified her. She couldn't shake the black cloud of dread that her feelings for him were not mutual. That he was viewing their time together as meaningful, but temporary.

The sun, which had burned through its morning veil of clouds, beat heavily on her bare shoulders as she walked along. She slid the spaghetti straps of her brown tank top off her shoulders to avoid a tan line and wished she'd remembered to sunscreen before leaving. A red tail hawk shrieked high overhead, looking for lunch along the dry and rocky cliff tops where the ground squirrels burrowed. Cara stopped and watched it for a long while, then looked back at the sea with deep remorse. *I shouldn't have gotten romantically involved with Kevin. I should've insisted on separate beds and no messing around. I can never get physical like this without developing feelings and attachment. What the hell was I thinking?*

The hopeless romantic in her rose up, suddenly, and chimed in. *But what about all the things he's ever told you about how much he admires you? Those were pretty involved. And what about the scads of photographs he's always taking of you? How can a man hold and touch a woman like he has, without some degree of love? Would he seriously be able to let you walk out of his life after all this?* Then, once again, the voice of reason countered: *And if he did, would you really want someone like that?*

"Aaaghhh!" Cara screamed at the ocean, putting hands to her head and clutching at her hair. "What the fuck, Universe? WHAT THE FUCK?!"

With heart pounding, she quickly looked around to see if anyone was watching or listening. Thankfully, there were only sandpipers eyeing her nervously as they skittered along in formation, racing the waves and digging for food. With another deep sigh, she said to the birds, "I'm going to have to talk with him. That's all there is to it."

* * *

"Hey," Kevin said cheerfully over his shoulder as he peered at his computer screen and clicked away on his mouse. Cara walked up next to him and saw that he was putting the finishing touches on a web page advertising a beach volleyball tournament. There was a balanced collage of volleyball players in mid-jump against a beach background and other eye-catching graphics that let you know *this* event was the place to be in mid-August. "The deadline is tomorrow," he laughed nervously. "So I thought I'd get it out of the way first."

"It's great," she told him, resting a hand on his shoulder and giving an affectionate squeeze. "And it's fun to see you doing your design thing…in those sexy professor glasses!"

Kevin leaned back in his chair and looked up at her with a bleary-eyed grin. "As soon as I finish up here, we can run over to Albertson's and get some food. Do you feel like starting a list for us?"

"Sure," she replied, "and after everything you've done for me, I would love to cook for you this week, if that's all right with you."

"Oh, that would be more than all right. That would be fan-freakin-tastic!" He grabbed a notepad from his desk, tore off a sheet, and handed it to her. "There's a pencil on the kitchen bar. Thanks, Cara."

As Cara set about peeking in cupboards, checking the refrigerator, and alternately writing items on the grocery list, Kevin continued his work and took a few phone calls from his clients. She smiled to herself as she listened to his "professional" voice and design lingo. This was a side of him she hadn't seen before, and she liked it.

How lucky, she thought, to be able to sit in the comfort of home while you work! No sterile office, no annoying coworkers, no boss breathing down your neck…then again, there would be no over-the-cubicle banter with someone like Frannie. She tried to imagine what a home office would be like, doing editing and writing for her very own clients. It would take time and ingenuity, but she was up for the challenge.

"Hey Cara, come here," Kevin called to her, laughter in his voice.

Cara put down her list and stepped over to the computer again, where he'd pulled up a small guest chair next to his. "Lots going on in Planet Indigo this morning."

Together they peeked in.

Not_Morrissey: *No way, man! You can't have "go-go" in the name, because there's already a Whiskey a Go-Go in L.A.*

BloominElle: *Yeah, it has to be something as catchy as all the other classic New York venues, like Studio 54, the Limelight … or the more recent Webster Hall.*

smk02: *Hey, whose club is this? MINE, that's who! It's MY f*cking club! So I'll call it whatever the hell I WANT!*

20thCenturyFox: *Easy there, smokin' hot…how 'bout I just start the designs while you think on it a little longer. Oh, and were you thinking maybe an upstairs lounge with leather and velvet couches? Where people can look down on the dance floor?*

"Seth is pipe dreaming about opening a nightclub in New York City," Kevin told her, "And 20thCenturyFox is going to design it for him."

Cara smiled, reading over the posts. "We should say something."

Kevin glanced over at her. "Are you ready to out yourself and your whereabouts?"

Cara gave him a conspiratorial stare. "I can say I'm just out here on a little California getaway."

His face darkened. "Do we mention that we found saffire?"

"That's up to Giselle, don't you think?"

"Yes, wholeheartedly." He turned to the keyboard and started typing.

Cali4nyapix: *Hiya peeps! You'll never guess who's sitting next to me right now.*

NoShite: *StarAngel?*

GreatScott: *Scarlett Johansson? You dog!*

BloominElle: *Your imaginary twelve-foot rabbit friend named Harvey?*

Cali4nyapix: *Nope, nope, and nope…guess again. She's not imaginary, she's WAY cuter than Scarlett, and she's not a celebrity. At least not yet. She may be a famous author one day, though.*

Cara read his post and melted inside. "Wow, Kevin…*thanks*."

StarAngel: *It's not me . I'm sitting in my living room getting ready to go to work. Hi you two! Glad you made it back safely.* 

Eire_Forever: *All right, we give!*

Not_Morrissey: *Like we really give a flying f*ck who you're sitting with! Geez, Kevin, get over yourself! It's not always about YOU, okay?*

Both Cara and Kevin burst into laughter.

Cali4nyapix: *Oh, I think you WILL give a flying fuck, NM! It's someone you know and like!*

smk02: *I know who it is!! I guessed it a few days ago! Moonflower, you suck (and not in the good way)! You didn't even tell anyone! I hope you're having fun on the beach while the rest of us slave away in our offices…holy crap, I need a vacation. SO jealous.*

GreatScott: *WHAT? What the hell is she doing all the way out there?*

BloominElle: *Hey, Cara! We've missed you.*

20thCenturyFox: *What's all this, then? Cara's in California? I step away to get some Fritos and miss all the good stuff!*

TheRub: Hey! *I'm headed that way myself in a few months. Got a bodywork seminar in Laguna Beach.*

Kevin slid aside so Cara could open a separate Internet window and log in.

Moonflower: *Hey everyone! Just having a little getaway. Kevin and Astrea have been such wonderful hosts.*

StarAngel: *Ah, sweetie, you were a wonderful and charming guest. Come back any time!*

Cara saw the bold red print announce: **1 New Private Message**. She opened it and saw that it was from 20thCenturyFox, wanting to know if there was a budding romance with her and Kevin. "Oh check this out!" Cara pointed. "I knew that's what people would immediately start asking."

Kevin read the message and gave her a wink. "We're going to be the topic of a lot of curious PMs flying back and forth right now, I'm thinking."

Cara answered questions about how long she planned to stay and where they'd been, and of course there were demands for pictures.

Kevin got back on and told their cyber-friends that he and Cara would post a journal entry with pictures later that day. Then the two of them said their goodbyes to Planet Indigo and got up from the computer. Kevin raised his arms high over his head with a huge stretch and a yawn.

Cara continued to stare at the monitor with a far away look in her eye.

"Penny for your thoughts."

She looked up at him. "This is the twenty-first century, dude, it's going to cost you more than just a penny."

"Okay, twenty bucks for your thoughts. And dinner at Lobo's."

Cara smiled at the mention of Kevin's favorite haunt yet again, and rose from the chair. "I was just thinking that, five months ago, all you were to me was an online guy from California. Posting from your little oceanside cottage. Just words on a screen."

Kevin grabbed his jingling keychain from the kitchen bar and took her hand as they walked outside. "Five months? Wow. It seems like I've known you for a year."

Cara watched his face closely. *A whole year. And why is that, Mr. Tierney? Could it be you've made a deeper connection with me than you realized?*

Noting her thoughtful stare, Kevin asked, "*Now* what are you thinking?"

Cara opened the door of the MG, which was looking a little gritty from their road trip, and hesitated. She didn't relish the idea of launching into the talk she needed to have with Kevin on their way to the grocery, shouting over the wind. And anything she said right then would certainly lead to that talk.

"It can wait until later."

He eyed her suspiciously as they slid down into the seats. "Are you sure?"

"Yeah, no worries." Cara waved her hand. "Let's shop."

Chapter 39

Their plan was to meet up somewhere in the middle of the store. Cara had taken a hand basket, to quickly round up all the alcohol they needed for martinis, margaritas, and other mouthwatering beverages. Kevin had taken a cart for everything else.

In the booze aisle, Cara was trying to decide between Absolut and Grey Goose, when the opening notes to U2's *It's a Beautiful Day* came on the store's music track. Reflexively, her foot started tapping in time to the music, then something moved in the corner of her eye. Turning her head, she saw Kevin round the corner of her aisle, doing a perfect mimic of Bono. He slunk toward her with sunglasses on, lip-synching along with the first verse.

Cara glanced behind her, making sure no one was watching the spectacle, then looked back with a shake of her head. "You goof!"

Kevin bent his arm at a dramatic angle, holding an air-microphone to his mouth, and kept going until he got to the passionate chorus. Then he leaned in close, putting his face right up to hers, imitating one of Bono's extreme close-ups into the video camera.

Cara, laughing out of control, almost dropped her bottle of vodka.

With the aisle still free of other shoppers, Cara formed her own air microphone and joined Kevin in actually *singing* the second verse and chorus. When they belted out the *TOUCH me* part, he reached out and put a hand on her breast, making her shriek with laughter. Naturally, that was when an elderly woman shuffled around the corner with her cart. Cara laughed harder, imagining the thoughts entering the poor woman's head. But then again, it *was* California.

Kevin put his arms around Cara and gave her a squeeze of affection. "Cara Shannon, you rock the Kasbah. No other woman in my life would've ever been whacked enough to do that. Not a one!"

The woman stared at them in amused astonishment as they sauntered past.

"How ya doin'?" Kevin called out to her.

Around the corner and out of earshot, they both exploded into laughter and then tried to stifle residual giggles all the way through checkout—where Cara hijacked Kevin's cart and insisted on paying for everything.

* * *

When Kevin turned up Highway 154 toward the mountains instead of heading for home, Cara looked over at him. "Where are we headed?"

"It's a surprise."

"Will it take very long, with our spoilable groceries in the car? It's pretty warm out."

"That all depends."

She opened her mouth in a wide smile. "What's going on?"

He shook his head. "Damn it, woman, it's a surprise! Stop asking questions."

Cara felt a slight thrill in her stomach, sensing that it might be naughty in nature.

The mountain road wound up and up and up until the breathtaking view of the entire city and bay lay behind them. As they rounded the crest of the pass, a new view lay ahead...layer upon layer of expansive mountain ranges as far as the eye could see.

"This is the Santa Ynez Valley," Kevin announced, looking over and watching her wide-eyed reaction with a pleased look.

"I've been wondering what was on the other side of these mountains," she told him, "and what a pleasant surprise!"

"That's not *the* surprise, though."

"Oh no?"

They turned right down a narrow, bumpy road that snaked along the very top of the ridge. Once in a steady gear, he nonchalantly laid a warm hand on her knee.

Cara looked down and watched it slide tantalizingly upward under the hem of her short crepe skirt. His fingertips made little swirls and circles, then he checked her face for signs of progress. She met his gaze with a gleam in her eye and leaned back in her seat to let her leg fall toward him until it was touching the gear shift. She was now certain what his surprise was, but sketchy on the details.

Just ahead, a huge formation of boulders jutted out of a grassy knoll alongside the road. It was there that Kevin pulled over. He trotted around to open her door, take her hand and pull her up out of the car. Without a word, he led her behind the rocks onto a grassy patch of land that looked out over the valley. The sun shone down as the breeze rustled the chaparral, sage, and wildflowers around them.

"My dear, welcome to your Rob Roy picnic."

Cara looked over at him as if he were a triple-decker slice of chocolate cake, lowered her eyelids and whispered, "*Meow.*"

* * *

With only a week left in the Golden State, Cara made every day count. When Kevin worked, she would either do some writing or explore more of the town. In the afternoons he would take a break and they'd walk on the beach, roller skate down Cabrillo Boulevard, or visit a new hiking trail in the mountains. Cara got to climb boulders, soak in hot springs, swim in more waterfall pools and stand atop several beautiful vistas. They even pioneered some new and memorable lovemaking spots along the way.

Evenings were usually spent stargazing from the deck, enjoying a good bottle of wine, or logging on to the Eclectic Café to talk with their cyber-friends—who proclaimed both appreciation for and jealousy over the photos from their coastal drive that Cara had posted.

Cara got to meet more of Kevin's local friends when they were invited to a Fourth of July cookout on the Mesa. She could tell, from the looks on their faces, that they were glad to see Kevin with a girlfriend again. A couple of days later, the friends invited them to shoot pool at Dargan's Irish Pub, and then go dancing at Soho—one of the live music venues downtown—where their favorite funk band, Area 51, was playing.

In that final week, Kevin and Cara got to experience what everyday life together might be like. She relished every second of being with him, and also felt herself growing more attached to Santa Barbara by the day.

"Come on, let's get outta here and walk up State Street," Kevin had yelled in the noisy and bustling Palace Grill restaurant, where they'd just enjoyed a delicious dinner on their "fancy" evening out. "There's nothing like it on a Saturday night in summertime."

Kevin's words rang true as they made their way through the throngs of people pouring out of movie theatres, laughing over drinks in sidewalk cafes, and hanging out on street corners. Music played everywhere they went, whether it was the homeless saxophonist on the bench by the art museum, the pulsating rock band through the open doors of a disco, or the flamenco guitarist who walked around the top level of a parking garage, playing just to enjoy the structure's resounding acoustics.

At one point during their walk, Cara pulled Kevin close and whispered in his ear, "Don't be jealous, but I think I'm in love with Santa Barbara."

He just winked at her. "You and thousands of others."

* * *

Cara sipped her icy martini while turning the breaded chicken breasts a final time. Sautéed green beans and almonds were ready in the pan next to the skillet. Looking up from the stove, she saw early evening sunbeams angling through the windows, casting glowing stripes across Kevin's floor. The door stood open, letting in a cool ocean breeze, and music from the Eclectic Café played softly in the background. I could definitely call this place home, she thought to herself with a contented smile. And at that moment, she felt very much like a wife, cooking dinner as her husband finished up work for the day.

"You know, Kevin, I gotta say…I'm usually not so…"

Kevin looked up from his computer where he was working on a brochure for a small winery. "So—?"

"So out of control with the sex."

"What?"

"Well, we've only been together for what, a couple of weeks? And we are seriously going at it like rabbits, twenty-four seven."

"And you're apologizing because…?"

She set down the tongs spoon and walked over to him, a tad unsteady from the vodka on an empty stomach. "I want you to know that I don't just hop in the sack with anyone. I definitely have strong feelings for you or it wouldn't be happening." She made herself look him in the eye. "In other words, this is not a fling. You're not some booty call to quench my long and horny dry spell, okay? I just wanted you to know that."

"Oh, Cara," he said, rolling his chair out from the computer and looking at her with concern. "I hope you don't think for *one minute* that's what I thought about you."

Cara lowered her eyes to her half-empty glass.

Kevin removed his glasses, stood up and put firm hands on her shoulders. "And I hope you've realized, by now, the high regard in which I hold you."

"Yeah, but I guess I'm a little scared."

He cocked his head to one side. "Why?"

"I'm afraid we might be using each other like a recreational drug, feelings or no feelings. We didn't get the appropriate warm-up time that people usually get when they live in the same town and start casually dating…before moving on to the deeper stuff. I'm afraid it's only destined to be a temporary fix."

"Fix for what?"

Cara's head felt woozy and she wasn't quite sure what would come out of her mouth next. "For loneliness?"

Kevin sighed and dropped his hands to his side. "The way I see it, we are two adults who have chosen, in these last few days together, to share ourselves completely. And that choice was based on mutual affection and desire. Was I lonely before I met you? Yeah, maybe. But in no way does that detract from the quality of feelings I have for you." He searched the floor as if the words he was struggling to piece together were lying there. "I am very much drawn to your energy and beauty, Cara, and the chemistry we share is amazing! Getting to know you has been one of the highpoints of my entire year so far, and I've felt especially close to you since you've been in California."

Cara stopped breathing for a second. The conviction in Kevin's eyes was so strong that she dared not look away.

His voice softened. "Since you've been here, I've had no idea if we would have just a few days or a couple of weeks, or if I'd even *see* you again once you left. So...I have been savoring you like a crème brulee, because I can't pretend to know what the future holds for the two of us. I am making every moment count. And I hope that's okay...I mean, the last time I checked, you seemed to be enjoying the hell out of yourself. And that makes me happy."

Cara nodded, grateful for his honesty. "I *am* enjoying myself. Completely." She raised her eyes to meet his once again. "So far, this trip has been one of the best times of my entire life."

"*Excellent*." He leaned toward her and kissed her tenderly on the lips. "So we're cool?"

Suddenly, Cara sniffed the air and her face morphed into alarm and panic. "Shit!"

Hurrying to the stove, she whipped the pan of chicken off the burner and turned it off. "Whew! Just in time. You definitely don't want these Cajun style."

Kevin laughed and came over to lean on the bar. "So is it dinnertime?"

"Yes, pour the wine," Cara ordered, forcing a smile. But things were *not* cool. There was so much more she needed to say to him, and had no idea where to begin.

Chapter 40

"There went another one!"

"What? *Where?*"

Kevin pointed to the left half of the star-filled sky above them.

"Damn it, I keep missing them!"

"Keep watching…it's a meteor shower. It's going to go all night."

She snuggled closer to Kevin on the deck chair that he'd pushed up against his, and pulled their shared blanket up around her shoulders. Then she turned her head at the sound of a motor in the drive.

"Brian and Vanessa are home," Kevin said, speaking of his landlords, the Winters.

"It was so cool meeting them yesterday."

"Yeah, they told me it was nice to finally meet 'the Mystery Woman'."

Cara laughed and watched the old couple make their way to the front door in the driveway's motion-activated spotlight. Her eyes zeroed in on the couples' hands, clasped lovingly together. Kevin noticed it too.

"Look, see what I mean about them holding hands?" he whispered. "Don't you love it?"

"It's very sweet," Cara replied, "and inspirational. They're what, seventy-something years old? You can tell they've been best friends the entire time they've known each other."

"Yeah, Brian even told me once, 'Ours was a friendship that caught fire one day.' Isn't that cool?"

"It really is."

After the Winters had gone inside, Cara hugged her arms around herself and shivered. "It's getting a bit nippish, all of a sudden."

"Well, follow me," Kevin told her, throwing back the blanket and pulling her to her feet. "I've got just the thing."

Inside, he flipped a switch by the tiny fireplace. Gas jets whoofed and orange flames leapt into action behind the small glass doors. Cara kicked off her sandals and padded over to help him arrange throw pillows into a comfy nest before the hearth. They lay quietly together, watching shadows on the ceiling and listening to a down-tempo guitar and violin piece playing on the Eclectic Cafe. Outside the open windows, the gentle break of ocean waves provided accompaniment. It was another timeless moment of tranquil beauty that Cara knew she'd always remember, and one that should've probably been left to the silence. But talk of the Winters churned up all her concerns again, and she felt the time just might be ripe to talk about their future.

No, said one inner voice. *Not tonight! Don't ruin this!*

Now, said another. *The time is ripe, I tell you!*

Cara cleared her throat. "Kevin, in the time we've known each other, has the possibility of a future ever crossed your mind?"

He paused for an uncomfortably long time. She was beginning to wish she hadn't asked when he finally replied, "Actually, it *has* crossed my mind. Several times."

When he offered no more, she turned her head to look at him. "Really?"

His eyes darted all over the ceiling and she could almost hear the vibration of his mind thinking. "Well yeah, but it keeps coming back to the complications of distance and our two different worlds…"

"I know."

He finally turned to meet her gaze. "Like we talked about earlier, I've chosen to stay in the moment. I didn't want to start worrying about the details of that issue, because I didn't want to detract from the wonderful time we've been having and miss what's happening right now."

"Oh." Cara stared back up at the ceiling again. This time, there wasn't any burning chicken parmesan to save her. This time, she'd have to tell him everything in her heart.

"Is this what you were leading up to earlier today?" he prompted. "Just before dinner?"

Cara sighed. "Yes."

"Ah ha. All that booty call stuff makes more sense now."

Another long silence ensued, then they both started talking at once…and promptly stopped to laugh.

"You go first," Kevin invited.

"Well," Cara began, "I kept telling myself to be rational about things. After the way my last relationship ended, I was a big, jaded ball of caution. I thought, 'Cara, you hardly know this guy. Just enjoy being friends with him.' But when I came out here and spent time with you, you just…you stole my heart. And I'm sure you didn't even mean to."

Kevin let out a faint laugh.

"I can tell you're uneasy, Kevin, so let's just talk about it. Let's lay all our cards on the table. Aside from living far apart, what are your reservations?"

"My reservations." He put a hand over his eyes for a second, gathering his thoughts. "My reservations are what I've done in the past. Time after time, relationship after relationship, I've let lust and infatuation get the best of me early on. I rushed into commitments without thinking, like a romantic fool, without really getting to know the person. Then, later, she'd leave in disappointment because she thought we were the *ones* for each other, and all I saw were the incompatibilities that I overlooked at first. I don't want to false-advertise again. It's just not fair."

Cara felt a knot forming in her stomach. "Were you honest when you told me all those things you admired about me? And how close you were feeling?"

"Absolutely," he said, sounding slightly annoyed at the allusion to him lying.

"Then this isn't just lust and infatuation getting the best of you, right? This is far more?"

"It's so much more. We have a great connection."

"So logically, when you share that kind of connection with someone, you want to keep them in your life, right? When there is such great potential for a successful relationship?"

"Yes, but when you throw the issue of geography into the mix, it's a little complicated. Long distance relationships have never worked for me. There's no time to get to know someone on a day-to-day basis for an extended period of time. There's no one you can go out with, because you're being monogamous with someone who lives miles away, and who you only see once every few months...it just...it doesn't work for me."

"Me either," Cara agreed. "But if there's potential, there's always the option of someone making the move to be with the other person and seeing where it goes."

"Well, I'm sorry to be so brutally honest, but I wouldn't want to leave Santa Barbara anytime soon. I have a huge client base here and it wouldn't be the best thing, financially. Also, I'm pretty attached to this climate. I'm not a winter person and the older I get, the colder I get. I guess I'm a real wimp!"

Kevin turned his head again to see if his comment added the necessary lightheartedness to what was becoming a difficult and intense topic. Cara wasn't smiling. She was thinking hard.

"What if I moved *here?* Just temporarily, to see how things go? I've already rented out my house and I could probably find a job in publication somewhere in town."

"We'd need a bigger place."

"With two people sharing rent, I think that would be manageable. Or, I could even get my own place if you're not ready to be live-ins."

Kevin reached for her hand and held it for a while without speaking. Finally, he told her softly. "It's a lot to think about, Cara. Lots of changes for both of us. I've been a damn bachelor for so long, now, I'm not sure I'd be such a good housemate."

Cara's heart sank. Maybe Gillian was right. Maybe Kevin *was* a California Peter Pan. She let go of his hand, rolled onto her side and gave him a pointed look.

"Okay, my turn to be brutally honest. At forty-six, do you look at your life and have any desire at all to start thinking about who you want to grow old with? Or do you *still* need to shop around?"

"It's not that. My wandering days started winding down ages ago..." he stared up at the ceiling again. "It's just that, no matter what the age, I believe in taking it slow. And living in the places we do, we don't seem to have that luxury. This big step you want to take of moving out here...it's huge, Cara. It's quitting your job, leaving your family and friends whom you dearly love, and moving to a completely new and expensive place. It's essentially dropping your life to be with me, and that's not taking it slow."

"But see, it doesn't feel like *dropping my life,* to me. I've given it way more thought than you realize, since before even coming out here. And I really *love* Santa Barbara. Do you think I'd make such a decision if I weren't absolutely sure I was ready? I would do this willingly and happily."

"Okay, so you're ready to do it. Ultimately, there is a fifty-fifty chance of our relationship succeeding. If things don't work out, I will feel *so bad* that you went to all that trouble of moving and changing your life to come here."

Although frustration welled up inside her, Cara kept her voice calm as she replied, "We'll never know if we don't try, will we? You're not responsible for my happiness, Kevin. I'm a big girl, and I can take care of myself. If it doesn't work, it doesn't work and I will move on to something that does. But I see great potential here, and I think you do too. Sometimes it actually *scares* people to know they're so close to the real thing."

Cara paused to watch for a reaction to this, but he didn't look her in the eye.

"If you can stay in the moment with this visit, can't you also stay in the moment with a bona fide relationship? All I'm asking is for you to consider giving it a chance."

"I know, but—"

"Kevin, I love you."

He reached for her hand again, still unable to look at her.

Cara continued, "My life is at a point that's ripe for trying something completely new. At our age, why mess around? Why wait? You're worth it to me."

He closed his eyes and swallowed hard. "I guess that's a little overwhelming to me, Cara. I mean, why should you be the one to give everything up? I feel selfish that I'm not willing to do the same for you."

With a voice on the verge of trembling, she dared to ask, "Is it about not wanting to leave your part of the country, or about me not being the right person for you?"

Kevin finally had the courage to look her in the eye. "I'm afraid."

"Fear is normal. Especially when you've been a bachelor most of your adult life. But fear can be worked through, if a person is really right for you. What I need to know is if you feel the same about me."

"Cara," he told her softly, his eyes beginning to shimmer with tears. "I do love you. Very much."

Cara's heart nearly stopped. She was never quite sure of his true feelings, even when he looked so deeply into her eyes during lovemaking that she swore he could see right through her soul. Even in the way he was always doing things for her, laughing with her, and lending his encouragement at every turn. She needed to hear the words, sometimes, and here they were at last. Finding her voice, she choked, "Well, then?"

Kevin held his gaze on her, and she saw his eyes go through an entire kaleidoscope of emotions…from the awe of revelation to tender affection to steely fear and finally excruciating sadness. He didn't even have to speak the words for her to know what came next. She'd been there before, so many times that she had the script memorized.

Frannie's words suddenly came back to Cara, like an angelic whisper of affirmation. *A man is either into you, or he's not. From now on, if he's not moving toward you with both arms open wide, I'm sure you'll be less likely to stick around as long as you did with Greg.* Once again, she felt the iron doors of protection close around her heart. Her voice grew steely as she said, "You know what? Never mind."

"No, Cara, wait—"

"When a wonderful woman is willing to overcome obstacles to be with the man who loves her, a natural response from the man would be, 'Oh my God! I can't believe how *into* me she is! How lucky is that?' That's what the normal and healthy response would be. And perhaps, 'Hell yeah, come on out and let's give it a try.' But the fact that you're not saying these things is proof that you don't want me in your life on a permanent basis."

"Oh Cara…"

"No, it's okay. Timing is everything, you know? We must be in two different places with it. Even though there are so many amazing…compatibilities." She broke off when the lump in her throat grew too large to speak. *You did it again, you silly girl. You fell for a wishy-washy, non-committal man. And I warned you. This time, you have no one to blame but yourself.*

Kevin reached for her tentatively, tears sliding down his cheeks. "Can

I please hold you?"

With a nod, Cara leaned into him and let him wrap his warm, safe arms around her. At this point, she just wanted to savor every last drop of him left in the bottle. His sobs triggered sobs from her, and they sat crying together for what seemed like a long and tragic eternity. When they'd recovered somewhat, with swollen eyes and snotty noses, Kevin reached for a box of tissues on the coffee table.

They sat up to mop off their faces, and then Kevin held her even more tightly. He breathed into her ear, "I'm so sorry, Cara. I didn't mean to hurt you."

Feeling a little whacked and sarcastic, Cara opened her mouth and completed a play on the musical phrase by John Lennon. "You're sorry that… you made me cry?"

Kevin shook his head. "Don't do that."

"I couldn't help it," she told him, a wry smile on her face. "Sometimes things are so unbelievably sad that I have to laugh at them."

With nothing more to say, the two of them went to bed. They held each other in a desperate, koala bear embrace until sleep showed its mercy and delivered them from grueling unease. But it was a dreamless sleep of the emotionally exhausted.

Chapter 41

"Well?" Kevin asked, eyeing her eagerly.

Cara took one more sip of the margarita, just to be sure. She smacked her lips, nodded and told him, "You're right. These *are* the best. Hands-down."

Manuel, the co-owner of Lobo's, gave Kevin a wink and a nod. "Uh huh. See? Everyone thinks so. Are you ready to order now?"

Kevin chose the platter of combination fajitas for the two of them to share. When Manuel had gone, he leaned on the checked plastic tablecloth and studied Cara's face. "Are you okay?"

"Yeah."

"Are you sure?"

Cara lowered her eyes, managed a smile, and said, "I couldn't leave Santa Barbara without seeing this damn place, now, could I? After all that fuss?"

Kevin took a huge swallow of his margarita, still watching her with concern.

"Besides," she told him, brightening. "I think it's only appropriate that our last night be a celebratory one, don't you? We've shared some wonderful adventures this summer. Touring the California coast, hunting down dead people and finding mystery users from the Eclectic Café! This is the stuff that mystery novels are made of."

"Is that what you've been writing about?" he asked, suddenly curious.

Cara's smile faded. "No. But speaking of our mystery girl, has she made a journal entry yet?"

"Not as of this afternoon," Kevin replied with a sigh. "I sure wish she would."

"I know. It's hard to just sit back and keep this secret when it could be told, and she could be benefiting from all the love and support of the EC peeps."

"Yeah, no shit."

Cara sat back and looked around the place, which was half-full of hungry Santa Barbarians. It was certainly nothing fancy—just an old rustic tavern with wooden floors and dark wooden walls. A collection of sombreros, Mexican dolls, old license plates, and antique metal signs hung on the walls, most of which were in Spanish.

"So how do you like Lobo's? Isn't it classic?"

"Way cool," Cara agreed, her eyes lingering on a ceramic, Aztec-looking sun face she hadn't yet noticed. Then her gaze rested on the vintage jukebox that Kevin had raved about, sitting against the back wall. "You know what? I think it's time for some music."

Kevin got up with her and they made their way across the café to the old pile of chrome, glass, and colored lights. "No way!" she cried, taking a closer look inside of it. "Real records? Where did they find these?"

"I told you it was a *vintage* jukebox. Some of these forty-fives have never left the machine, and I'm sure they found others on eBay." Kevin smiled at the antique wonder. "This thing's been here since the place was a little country bar back in the day."

"Wow," Cara murmured, turning the knob and flipping through the eclectic blend of old songs.

"Here, let me see," Kevin said, digging a quarter out of his pocket and stepping up to look. Memorizing the numbers, he quickly dialed them in and Cara watched a Cuban number begin to spin, from the Buena Vista Social Club.

"Know how to salsa dance?" he asked, taking both her hands in his.

"I took an introductory ten-minute lesson once, at a singles mixer back in Cincy."

"Well, come on out here, chica," he commanded, swinging her around onto the tiny dance floor. "Just step back on your right foot while my left follows, and we'll mirror each other."

After a few rocky starts, he had Cara in the basic one-two-three, four-five-six salsa steps.

"Now watch my eyes and just feel what I'm doing with our hands."

Cara followed and the next thing she knew, she wasn't even thinking about her feet anymore. That's when Kevin decided to throw in a few spins and cross-body turns. He was such an expert leader that it was easy for her to follow right along with him and sense what move he was about to do next.

"I love this!" she cried, breaking into an ecstatic smile. "This is a dance that lets you *become* the music!"

Kevin gave a nod and his eyes twinkled at her elation.

When the song ended, he grabbed her and lowered her into a dramatic dip. Cara shrieked, holding on for dear life, then laughed at herself. "What fun, Kevin. Thank you."

He gave her a chivalrous bow before walking her back to their table. Manuel yelled something in Spanish from the kitchen that sounded congratulatory, and a few people who'd been casually watching them clapped. Two of them got up and ambled over to the jukebox to make some musical selections of their own.

Kevin and Cara sat down to their margaritas and a basket of fresh tortilla chips.

"So did your mom start to wonder why your 'business trip' was taking so long?"

Cara nearly snorted margarita out her nose. She covered her mouth, swallowed hard and told him, "Jenn refused to lie any longer. She finally told Mom I was visiting Internet friends, and Mom was all, '*Internet* friends!? For heaven's sake!'"

"Our parents just don't get it," he said, shaking his head.

"Parents, and certain spouses of our cyber-friends," Cara added. "Remember how EireForever's husband used to resent all the time she was spending online with *strangers?* Until he finally met NoShite and some of the other UK members?"

"Really? They had a meetup in the UK?"

The fajitas arrived just then, furiously spitting and sizzling.

"You know the drill," Manuel told them dryly as he set the platter down. "Mucho caliente. Be careful. Common sense."

Cara and Kevin thanked him with a laugh, then set to work assembling the beef, chicken, shrimp, and veggies into tiny tortillas complete with mouthwatering guacamole and sour cream. As they feasted, discussion turned to the other members of their online community and what people had been up to lately. Seth got a promotion at his job and was steadily dating his MySpace woman. 20thCenturyFox was working too hard, as usual, and WhiteHeronMagic had taken her sons on an Alaskan cruise, which explained her absence from the boards of late.

A couple of meetups were underway all over the country; Not_Morrissey and his family visited Bellybutton during a trip to Austin, and BloominElle went out west with her husband to join GreatScott and family at Yellowstone. The_Rub, who was getting ready to come out to California, had been disappointed to learn that Cara was just leaving. He'd expressed interest in meeting her and Kevin at the Santa Monica Pier.

After awhile, Kevin pointed to Cara's plate. "You're not eating nearly as many fajitas as me. Are you sure you're—"

She held up a hand to silence him. "My appetite was bound to be a little funky today. Let's just keep having a good time and not worry about it. I really, really don't want to be bummed out on our last night together. So no more asking how I am, okay? Promise?"

He reached for his margarita, raised it to her, and replied, "Promise."

Much later, when their plates were cleared and the check was paid, Kevin took a deep breath and asked, "Ready to hit the road?"

Before Cara had a chance to reply, the Rolling Stones' *Wild Horses* came on the jukebox. She turned her head and stared dreamily across the room. "Oh, wow…I *love* this song. It's one of my very favorite Stones ballads."

"Yeah, it's a good one."

Cara looked back at him. "Let's dance, Kevin. One last time."

He stared at her, a blend of delight and desolation in his eyes. "I'd be honored."

Slowly they rose to their feet and found a spot in the middle of the floor. Cara looped her arms around Kevin's neck and locked her hands lightly behind it. His rested his gently around her waist.

As they swayed, barely covering any ground at all, Cara tried to empty her mind and just enjoy the moment. But too many of the song's lyrics resonated with what they were both going through, especially the ones about sweeping exits not causing bitterness or unkindness. They awakened her inner voices and teemed with conflicting thoughts directed at Kevin. Thoughts of deep gratitude for all that he'd done for her, and thoughts about wanting to smack him upside the head for letting such a great opportunity slip away.

From the steady thump of his own heart and his long, drawn-out breaths, Cara sensed that there were things Kevin wanted to say too. But neither said a word. Instead, they let the chords and the longing in Mick Jagger's voice speak for them.

* * *

"What are you doing?" Cara asked, turning from her open suitcase in time to see Kevin grab one of his pillows and slip quietly out of the bedroom.

"I'm gonna crash, now. Go ahead and finish packing...I'll see you in the morning."

She stood up and stalked into the main room where Kevin was about to lie down on a nest of throw pillows. "Why are you in *here?*"

"Come on, Cara…do you have to ask?"

"It's our last night together!" she cried.

Kevin stood speechless, pillow dangling from his hand.

Cara moved closer, her eyes flashing. "Get back in there and don't be stupid."

He bristled. "Don't call me stupid. I'm just trying to be respectful of—"

"Don't do this, Kevin," She grabbed the pillow from him with one hand and clutched his arm with the other. "Don't become a stranger on our last night together."

He shrugged out of her grip angrily, so she grabbed his other arm. He pulled away again and for a brief moment, they were nearly engaged in a slapping match. Then Kevin froze, his hands locked onto Cara's shoulders, and stared at her in disbelief. "What the hell are we doing?"

"I don't know."

They both stared at each other, breathing heavily from the adrenaline rush. In the next second, they were locked in a kiss and pulling off articles of clothing as they stumbled toward the bedroom.

Their final lovemaking was more of a spiritual experience than anything else. Every movement and touch was done with fervor and intent. They poured their hearts into each other, their bodies conveying what they could not express in words...carefully creating memories that would get them through the pain and uncertainty of separation. Cara wondered, with more than a little unease, if the quality of the memories could ever be outdone by another.

Chapter 42

"I don't feel I have the right to say those three words to you, anymore."

Cara studied Kevin's eyes that seemed to have dulled from their usual swimming pool blue. She shook her head slowly. "That's ridiculous, Kevin. Of course you do."

"Well, what I *can* say is...I wish you clarity and inspiration in finding your new direction. You deserve to hit the goldmine, for once in your life."

She mustered a smile. "Thank you. I will accept all the wishes and good vibes anyone has to give me right now. I'm going to need them."

Kevin tried to mirror her smile, but failed. "I've loved our time together, Cara."

"Me, too."

The crackle of the intercom in the tiny Santa Barbara airport broke in. "Attention passengers, United Express Flight 6227 with service to Denver will begin boarding at Gate Seven in just a few minutes."

Kevin folded her in his arms one last time. "Goodbye, Cara mia."

Cara closed her eyes and savored the feeling of their last moment, trying her best to keep the resentment and heartbreak at bay until she was in the air. "So long, Kevin."

They held each other for a long while, oblivious of the other passengers slinking past them. Gradually, Cara slid out of his arms and grabbed the pull handle of her bag. He kissed her goodbye and waved as she entered the doorway leading to security.

Walking across the tarmac, she squeezed her eyes shut in frustration knowing that the rest of her summer would be another long and arduous road of getting over someone. A man who had been the best and most admirable in all her life.

By the time she fell into her seat on the tiny commuter, her mind was made up. In the ten-hour day of flying ahead, there would be no crying on the plane or drowning her sorrow in airport bars. No wallowing in the past or replaying of memories like a worn-out DVD. This time, there was no room for drama. She would arrive safely in Ohio with her head held high and her eyes on the future.

Chapter 43

"Wait, go back!"

Cara looked up from her laptop at Jenn, who was hovering over and watching a slide show of the digital photos from California. "Which one?"

"The picture taken through the wooden structure on the cliff top. That was absolutely gorgeous! Hell, they've *all* been gorgeous. But I wanted to see it just a little longer than five seconds."

With a couple of clicks, the photo filled the screen once more.

"Where is that?"

"Um," Cara tapped her fingers, thinking, "it's this neat little resort along the Pacific Coast Highway on the way to Big Sur…and I can't think of its name." She reached into a drawer for her travel journal, in which she had carefully recorded every detail of her road trip with Kevin.

"The blue-green of that ocean is almost surreal," Jenn remarked, "and those cliffs!"

Cara's voice dropped to a low shade of wistful. "Yeah, that place was pretty amazing." As she flipped through the journal's pages, a small scrap of paper fluttered out onto the floor. Ignoring it, she put her finger on a particular passage and said, "Ragged Point. The place is called Ragged Point. We had lunch there on the way home."

Jenn bent to retrieve the piece of paper that had fallen. Her mouth twisted into an amused grin. "What's this?"

Cara glanced at the piece of paper, took it from her sister and breathed out a faint laugh. "Oh man, I forgot all about that."

On the scrap of paper was a cartoon Kevin drew for Cara when they'd returned to Santa Barbara. He'd left it on her laptop while she was taking a break from sizing photos. In the picture was a rough pencil sketch of a man and woman driving in a convertible. The man wore an artsy beret and the woman had crazy spring-like curls flying up from beneath a headband. Big Sur cliffs lay behind them in the background. The title above it read: *Kevin and Cara Do the PCH*. The caption below added: *Eat your heart out, Henry Miller.*

"Cute!" Jenn said, staring at it. "He's good!"

"Yeah, he is," Cara agreed. "He's a mega-talented guy all right."

"You guys make good cartoon characters. Except your hair's not really that curly."

"And he never wore a beret, either. He took artistic license."

"What does the Henry Miller thing mean?" her sister asked, glancing over. "Should I ask?"

Cara sighed. On the morning after their night in Big Sur, Kevin had boasted, while buttoning his jeans, "Henry Miller's got nothin' on us *now*." She shoved the memory away before it made her heart lurch, and shook her head. "It's nothing, really."

But there was no hiding anything from her ever-perceptive big sister. Jenn laid a hand on Cara's shoulder and said, "I don't have to see the photos right now. I can look at them later, on my own."

Cara put her own hand over her sister's. "Whatever…I'm okay."

Remembering Cara's new mantra, Jenn said, "Focus on the next chapter of life, right?"

"Right."

"Any book ideas yet?"

"A few," Cara replied, then studied the wrinkled little cartoon thoughtfully. "But new and better ones are coming every day."

"Are you doing okay at work?"

"Yeah. Funny how nothing's really changed there since I've been gone. New projects, same crap. I know it sounds pessimistic, but it's true. Just ask Frannie."

"Are you going to stay?"

"I think I should, for now. At least until I have a few more of my own clients."

"Sounds good, Cara. Just take it one month at a time." Jenn cocked her ear at the sound of a motor humming in the drive. "Hey, Liam is home. Are you hungry? He's got filets for the grill."

"Thanks, Jenn, but I already promised Mom I'd cook dinner for her." Cara got up from the computer and stretched. "And after that, I think I'll go to the coffeehouse and be a writing recluse tonight. I'm suddenly feeling lots of Muses around me." She tucked Kevin's cartoon into her purse. "I think I'm onto something big."

* * *

In her dream, Cara was sitting in The Coffee Cat on Anacapa Street in Santa Barbara. Bells were ringing in the courthouse tower across the street and palm fronds flapped in the cool breeze outside the window. Just as she was about to take a sip of her latte, Arianna blew in the door with her gorgeous red hair spilling all around her shoulders, and a glowing look on her face.

"I thought I might find you here," she said as if her being alive was nothing unusual and they ran into each other on a regular basis. She made her way over to Cara's table and plopped down with a grin and a wink. "I heard you were looking for me."

All Cara could do was smile in awe. The feeling of sitting across the table from her living-and-breathing niece filled her with such profound joy that words simply weren't necessary.

"Didn't I tell you California was the best?"

Cara found her voice. "I love it here."

"There's a reason you came to Santa Barbara. You know that, right? Everything happens for a reason."

"I know."

"So have you started it yet?"

"Um…"

"The book. Don't be afraid to start it. Believe in it. I think it'll be a huge success."

"You do?"

"Oh hell yes…it'll be the cat's meow!"

Both women burst into raucous laughter that rang out loudly above the other voices and espresso machines and jazz playing in the café. People turned and stared.

"I miss you, Ari."

"I miss you too. But I gotta run."

Cara's smile faded. "There was so much I wanted to talk about…"

"Everything's gonna be all right," her niece assured her, with a gleam in her eye. "Better than you ever imagined. That's all you need to know."

"But—"

Arianna was already on her feet. She leaned over and gave Cara a quick hug before clunking off in her Doc Martin boots. Before walking out the door she turned and pointed a finger at her aunt.

"I wanna be in the credits. Put me in the credits or I'll kick your ass."

Chapter 44

"What's this?" Frannie asked, stopping to poke her head inside Cara's cubicle. "This doesn't look like work, it looks *fun*."

Without raising her head from the pages spread across her desk, Cara replied softly, "Oh, just a little experiment I've been working on during our slow period."

Frannie walked in for a closer look. "Are those the pages to a dummybook?"

"Um-hm."

Cara rolled back in her chair to give her friend a full view of the layout she'd just finished. On the left was a photo of one of the more stunning cliffside views at Big Sur. On the right was a rough pencil sketch of the same view, with Kevin's cartoon of the man and woman in the convertible pasted into the scene. The text beneath the sketch read:

Sid and Sierra are tempted to fly at breakneck speed around the delicious curves of the Pacific Coast Highway (cool people call it the PCH) with the wind in their hair. However, it's best to go slow because they'll need plenty of time to take in the stunning views...or quickly veer off into one of the many roadside pull-outs for a photo-op.

"Well this is fun *and* adorable. Is this work, or a little side project you got goin' on?"

Cara swiveled toward her and lowered her voice. "It's mine. I've had little ideas about it formulating and coming together for the past few weeks."

"So it's the actual photo on the left, and an illustration of it on the right?"

"Well, more like quirky and hip little cartoon characters on the right, who educate people about beauty spots and tourist attractions all up and down the Pacific Coast Highway. I even have them making a detour into wine country along Route 46."

"And this is for adults?" Frannie asked, shooting Cara a curious smile.

"Yeah, definitely for adults, because they even tell people where some remote areas for...well, outdoor *nookie* can be found. So it's a highly unique and humorous travel book with gorgeous eye-candy photos and whacked cartoons. If it does well, perhaps Sid and Sierra can become a series and go all over the country. Possibly the world."

"Wow! Brilliant, Cara!" Frannie raised her hand in a flash of bright red fingernail polish for a high-five. "That means you get paid vacations everywhere!"

Cara smacked the hand lightly, a trace of uncertainty in her face. "Well, we'll see. I think it's a pretty original idea, so there's a fighting chance that one of the major publishing houses will like it."

"Who took the photo?"

"Kevin did. He took most of them."

"And who's going to do your illus—" Frannie stopped and turned her head slowly toward Cara, eyes full of dread. "Oh, don't tell me…"

"I haven't asked him yet, but that was the general idea. The characters I envisioned were taken from one of his sketches."

"Is this wise, dear?" Frannie put a hand on her hip. "I mean, you're finally starting to seem yourself again after walking around here like a zombie for two months. That guy really did a number on you, I can tell. The fact that you wouldn't even talk about the trip speaks volumes about how much you wanted to forget all about him."

Cara's eyes flashed. "Let the record show, that he didn't do *anything* to me. That's victim talk, Frannie, and I'm not having it. He didn't want the same things I did, so I came home and resumed my life."

Frannie raised a dubious eyebrow.

"Besides, it's not like we aren't talking to each other anymore. We still exchange friendly emails, although not near as many as before."

"Cara." Frannie's eyes burned with her *don't bullshit me* look. "A project like this will keep you attached to each other. Way more than just a few friendly emails."

"I *have* thought about that," Cara said, tapping a pen on her desk blotter, "and what I keep asking myself is, how bad could a book deal and thousands of dollars be if this idea takes off? At least I would've gained *something* from our union, you know?"

"True," Frannie admitted, folding her arms. "But come on, you couldn't do this with some other photographer and cartoonist? Hell, we got all kinds of talented people down in the art department."

"Yeah, I know." Cara looked up, her face aglow with conviction. "Frannie, this just *feels* right. I can't explain it in any rational way. I've been waiting and waiting for some sort of inspiration to show up in my life, and this is what knocked on the door. I even had an affirming dream about it the other night, in which Arianna told me to go for it."

"Well," Frannie said, giving the cumbersome packet of manuscript pages in her arms a boost, "when it's all done and you're ready to pitch it, let me know. I still have my New York connections."

"Oh, Fran!" Cara cried, springing from her chair. "You'd do that for me?"

Frannie made a fist and knocked on her head as she sauntered out of the cubicle. "*Hello*. BFF?"

Cara turned back to her dummybook and looked down at it as if it were her own newborn wriggling in a crib. For the first time since leaving California, she actually felt something that resembled excitement. There was finally a new mission in her life that was already receiving accolades and support from well wishers. As her eyes rested once again on the sketch of Sid and Sierra, her smile slowly faded. Maybe Frannie was right. Maybe it wasn't a good idea to collaborate. She could let the publishers decide on a cartoonist, as they always insisted on doing, and let this be her own singular project. But the graphic style of Sid and Sierra were unmistakably Kevin's, and therefore caused a bit of a dilemma.

Cara swiveled toward her computer and brought up the Internet screen, which was parked on the home page of the Eclectic Café. She'd been trying to stay away from the boards as much as possible, to avoid awkward moments when Kevin was there at the same time.

Kevin had been more faithful about keeping in touch than Cara, sending an email every few days or a "How are you doing?" private message. She would always respond to him, but never instigated anything herself because it would break the communication etiquette of someone he'd more or less rejected.

In a nanosecond of eerie coincidence, a private message appeared from Kevin when she peeked into the forums.

Hello Cara ,

I just wanted to let you know that I went up to visit Giselle yesterday, because she doesn't have much longer. It was a very moving and eye-opening experience for me. Can I call you tonight and tell you about it?

Love, Kevin

Cara sighed and leaned her head against her hand. It made her sad that he was now asking permission to call her, when calling used to be an everyday thing with them. She hadn't *wanted* to shut him out these last couple of months, but she had to. The feelings she'd developed for Kevin far surpassed those of boyfriends past. Being with him had been so easy and playful and sensuous and wonderful. Their matching creative minds, which inspired her *On the Road With Sid and Sierra* idea, seemed a once in a lifetime find. So getting over him was extra challenging, and the less contact they had, the easier it was to move on.

Some, Cara knew, would argue that *no* contact was even better.

"Our relationship reminds me of a stillborn baby," she'd told Jenn in her darkest hour, after returning from California. "All those months of excitement and anticipation for something that's growing and about to take on new life…and then it dies without a chance to take its first breath."

Jenn had been understanding about things until she heard that Kevin was still in contact. That was when she kindly but firmly administered a dose of tough love to her sister. "You're grieving a death, Cara, but it's kind of hard to acknowledge it when the corpse keeps talking."

Cara couldn't disagree, but try as she might, and in spite of Jenn's advice, she hadn't been able to completely cut ties with Kevin. Now, with news of Giselle, all of her compassion for everyone and everything was bubbling to the surface and dragging with it buried feelings for him that were still alive and kicking. She hit reply and positioned her fingers over the keyboard.

Dear Kevin,

She stopped, backspaced, and typed again:

Kevin,

This is very sad news. I'll be home after seven this evening, so go ahead and call then (on my cell). Take care for now.

~Cara

After hitting SEND, Cara sat there remembering the haunting image of Giselle wrapped in her blanket, bent with weariness. She sincerely hoped the poor girl wasn't suffering too much. The fact that Kevin had called his visit "eye-opening" piqued her curiosity, and as much as she hated to admit it, she very much looked forward to his call.

Chapter 45

"Oh, bloody *hell,*" Cara griped on her way out of the office building.

The day that had dawned bright and clear as she left home that morning had somehow degenerated into a mess of rain, dampness, and overcast skies. For the first time that September, the air had turned uncomfortably cold. Cara ran her after-work errands in a hurry, squinting against the pelting droplets as she hurried in and out of buildings and across parking lots. Her last stop was the gym, where she jumped onto the elliptical machine to work off the nervous tension building in her body.

Halfway through her thirty minutes, U2's *It's a Beautiful Day* came on her iPod. The lyrics hit her like they never had before, as if Bono was singing directly to her about her life in the last few months. Feeling stuck in the same old town, finding a new friend to deliver her from it all...and definitely the part about hearts blooming from the stony ground. She had finally learned to love again, to trust again...and it had indeed been a beautiful day—every single one that she spent in California with Kevin. But unable to heed the song's advice, he let it get away.

Her eyes became glazed and far away as she remembered Kevin singing in the aisle of the grocery store. The song's effusive chorus filled her head with a slide show of images from her Santa Barbara experience. One line in particular stood out and seemed to make a plea to her...a plea not to give up on Kevin because he was not a hopeless case.

With a frown, Cara reached down and clicked to the next tune. *Damn writer's imagination. As much as you would like to think it is, Cara Shannon, life is NOT one big fucking rock video.*

* * *

When seven o'clock came, Cara was tucked safely away in her room at Jenn's with Sophie sleeping next to her. After a grounding, post-workout soak in the hot tub and a cup of herbal tea, she was very much renewed and ready for the big phone call.

At 7:05, her cell phone rang. Cara let it ring three times before clicking it on. "Hello, Kevin."

A short pause. "Cara?"

"Hi," she greeted once more.

"Hey, how are you?"

"Doing okay, thanks."

"Did you have a good day?"

"Pretty good. And you?"

"Well, it was okay. I was still processing a lot of what happened yesterday, so I didn't get much work done." There was a long sigh.

"Well, go ahead and tell me," Cara said in a calm and inviting tone.

"Okay."

She heard him take a deep breath.

"Astrea called two nights ago and told me that Giselle's condition had worsened, so I decided I'd better get up there. When I got to the Dhyana Center the next day, they sent me to her room where a Hospice nurse was taking her vitals. After he left, Giselle told me to sit down and listen to her. Her actual words were, 'listen to me good, Bachelor Boy.'"

Cara let out a hollow laugh, but her eyes were solemn. "How did she look?"

"Oh God, Cara, even more pale and thin than before. It was really difficult to watch her labor over her words and keep running out of breath, and often she'd just talk with her eyes closed because she was so tired."

"Wow." Cara sank back in the cushions on her bed. She set her mug of tea on the night table. "Did her parents ever come see her? Or any members of the family?"

"They actually did. I was so glad to hear she finally broke down and called them. They drove down to see her, and she got to talk and make her peace…which is a good thing when you're about to make a final exit."

"Yeah, no kidding."

"Anyway…" she heard him take another deep breath, "…Giselle had questions. About me and you."

Cara felt a small knot twist in her stomach.

"She asked whatever became of us once you left, because she could tell, from just the one visit, that we were good together. 'Standing next to you two was like standing next to a fucking power station,' she told me."

Cara chuckled. "Spoken as only saffire_21 could."

"Yeah, right? So then she admitted that she'd been discussing it with Astrea during a phone call or two, and that they both were sorely disappointed with me."

Cara didn't want to say it out loud. *That makes three of us.*

"Giselle said, 'Kevin, you're forty-six fucking years old. Do you like the idea of being alone when you're a gray old dude with protruding nose hair and false teeth? When are you ever gonna give this commitment thing a whirl?' And then she said…"

Kevin cut off, and Cara thought the call had dropped. Or that he was tending to a nearby cat. When he resumed speaking, his voice was increasingly shaky and she realized he'd been overcome.

"...she said that she would've given anything to have met someone that close and that wonderful who was willing to move across the country for her..." there was a longer pause, with muffled throat-clearings, "...and she really drove home how life passes like the wind, and that it's wise to seize opportunities when they present themselves. Especially ones that might be regretted later, when the window of opportunity closes and it's too late."

"Amen to that," Cara told him without emotion. Her iron wall would not be taken down easily this time.

"Cara," he said, almost in a pleading tone. "I miss you."

Cara closed her eyes and let out a long breath.

"I miss you so much my heart literally aches. I realize, now, that I made a huge mistake."

Her hand went slack and the phone nearly dropped out of it.

"Giselle said sometimes things don't come in neat, tidy packages. She said real love can be so life-changing that we can't even imagine it, and therefore we ruin it for ourselves by denying it. I'm pretty sure this is what I've been doing."

Cara nodded to herself, but said nothing.

"Commitment has always been frightening for me. I've failed at it too many times, for one reason or another. You know that song that they play on the EC by Nada Surf called 'Inside of Love?' That's me, man. Me and a lot of other people that I know. I was freaked out by how many of my buddies who I stood up for are now unhappily divorced. I guess I've always put this pressure on myself to do things *right*. Both in my work and my relationships. You, of all people, deserve to have it done absolutely right. You deserve to be wildly happy. So I kept thinking that if I was to screw up again, I didn't want it to be with you."

"Kevin," Cara said, putting a hand to her forehead. "I've told you again and again...you are not responsible for my happiness. I can be wildly happy on my own."

"I know that, now."

"You were the icing on the cake. I was one hundred *ten* percent, with you beside me. That's the beauty of the power of two."

"I know. Oh *lord,* do I know."

There was a long silence. Cara could hear Kevin breathing hard.

"I realize it might very well be too late, but...I want you to know that I'm willing. I'm willing to work on a plan for us to be together."

As he uttered his last few words, Cara could tell that he was crying.

"I'm so sorry I put you through all that pain. I can't even believe what a dumbass I was! It's almost like I was standing outside my own skin, *watching* it happen."

Cara expected the sting of tears in her eyes at any moment, but they never came. Perhaps it was the emotional wall of protection doing its thing again, or perhaps she'd become stronger, wiser, and more realistic. Or maybe it was just too soon. She would definitely need a little more time for him to prove his sincerity.

"I, uh..." she floundered, "I accept your apology, Kevin." There. It was a good start.

"Thank you," he whispered, then snuffled loudly.

"And everything you've just told me...I really need to sit with it awhile and let it sink in. I've spent the last couple of months behind a cast-iron shield, trying to convince myself that I'm okay and that this whole thing wasn't as bad as all that. I had to act as if I didn't care about you. I simply focused on my own future, and envisioned moving on."

Kevin fell silent for a long time. Cara wasn't sure whether to add anything or wait or what, so she reached over and absently petted Sophie, who jumped up from a deep sleep, yawned, and licked one of her paws.

"I can't say I blame you for that," he told her, finally.

"Yeah, so...as much as I'd love to just say 'okay, let's work on that plan,' I have to first work on not being numb anymore. Right now, I'm having trouble conjuring what it felt like to lay beside you or kiss you or...or even be intimate with you. I blocked it all out, somehow...it's weird, Kevin."

"I am so sorry for that."

"Well, it's done. No need to keep apologizing. But I really do appreciate you being honest like this. I'm glad you had a breakthrough."

"Me too. Now you know what I meant by eye-opening." He sighed heavily. "I just really hope it's not too late. But if it is, I'll understand that it was my own damn fault for missing the boat when it was leaving."

This brought a wry smile to Cara's face. With slight hesitation, she sat forward and told him, "Well hey, Kevin, I've got something to share with you too."

"You do?"

"Yeah, I found that clarity you've been wishing for me. It's kind of crazy, but bear with me."

"Okay."

Cara proceeded to tell Kevin all about the Sid and Sierra book plan. She described the pages she'd completed thus far and her ideas about a future series. "I don't think anyone's ever tried this before, so I think we have a really good chance of success."

He listened quietly to her entire pitch and waited until she was done talking before offering a response. "I like it, Cara. I think it sounds very promising!" He gave a little laugh. "Where did you get Sid and Sierra?"

"Those were the names that came to mind when I saw your cartoon...when I imagined a trendy yet slightly bad-ass couple who weren't afraid of living on the edge. Some of it I envision as being very raw, you see—like the two of them pointing out the best places to have outdoor sex in various spots along the PCH."

"Whoa!" he cried, laughing harder. "I'm *really* liking the sound of it now!"

Tension melted from Cara's neck and shoulders. He was down with her idea, and it made her day. "This is the inspiration I was longing for, Kevin. I know I could easily find any cartoonist to do this with, but these characters..."

"Cara, I would be *so* honored if we could work on this together."

Cara leaned back again with a shaky exhale. "Well, good. Good. Me too. Great minds, you know."

"Yes, great minds. So, can you send me a page or two? Is the entire manu done yet?"

Before she could stop them, Cara heard the words leave her mouth. "What do you think about coming to Cincinnati to review what I've got so far? Autumn is here, and they've predicted a really gorgeous and colorful season. It's the best time to visit the Midwest."

Cara thought Kevin might weep again as he immediately replied, "Yes. *Yes!* I'd love to come to Cincinnati. And the thought of seeing you again makes me unbelievably happy."

She nodded to herself. This felt safe. They would call it a business meeting, and she'd show him around the Queen City. Other than that, she dared not have any expectations.

"All right, then. Plan on coming around the second weekend in October. They're having Tall Stacks this year, and you'll want to see that."

"Absolutely!" was Kevin's trigger response. "Um...what exactly *is* Tall Stacks?"

"It's a weekend festival of riverboats that they hold every couple of years," she replied, gazing down at a Tall Stacks flyer that she'd stolen from the bulletin board at work. "A lot of the bigger and more famous boats, like the Delta Queen, sail into Cincinnati and people can ride on them. They have all kinds of vending booths and three days of live music with really big names. Lots of Eclectic Café artists, in fact."

"Oh, excellent, Cara! You're right—what a perfect time to visit."

Cara smiled and fixed her gaze on the diminishing sunset outside the window. She was alarmingly aware of that old familiar glow creeping into her...the one she used to feel when Kevin first started calling her. In the silence that followed, her thoughts drifted slowly back to Giselle. "Kevin, how much longer does Giselle have? Did the doctors say?"

"Yeah, uh..." he sucked regretful air through his teeth. "...just a couple of days, if that. Things in her body are shutting down one by one."

"Oh." Cara's face fell as sorrow for the dying friend returned. "I guess there's no way she can do a journal, now."

"At this point, I think she'd be too weak."

"Maybe she could dictate one. Are you going back again, or is Astrea?"

"I think Astrea has been going every day."

"Then maybe we can have her persuade Giselle to do it. After all, the EC is her online family. I think it would be beneficial for everyone."

"Yeah, me too, Cara. I'll give Astrea a call and see what we can do."

There was a short silence as they both wondered how to end the call.

"Kevin, I had the craziest little vision of Giselle when she enters the Great Beyond."

"Let's hear it."

"I imagine her finally meeting up with the *real* Arianna at a little martini bar in heaven, and both of them laughing their *asses* off at me."

Chapter 46

A Farewell From saffire_21
Posted by StarAngel - Sep 16 - 7:47pm PST

Dear Friends of the EC,

I'm sorry I've been away so long and that it's taken me months to write these sad and difficult words to you. In my usual style, I will just be forthright and blunt. I am dying. I've been battling cancer for the last few months, and have been fortunate enough to convalesce at a retreat center in Big Sur until my final exit. The name of the center is Dhyana, which means "meditation with intense love" in the Buddhist culture. I've been spending a lot of time doing just that, as well as enjoying the sights, sounds and feel of nature. I've also visited with my biological family and made peace with them — something I never thought would happen in this lifetime. The only thing left for me to do was visit my online family one last time. Thanks to the dictation of one golden-hearted StarAngel, I am able to do this.

More than anything, I want you to know that through my communication with you all, I have found a real place of belonging that I never found anywhere else. I've enjoyed your quirky posts, your raunchy jokes and your ability to take what I could dish out to you, while holding your own!

Long story short, thank you.

If there is one message I would really like to leave with you, it's this: Live! Live life to its absolute fullest. Take no one or nothing for granted. Do whatever is necessary to find contentment—even if it means breaking "the rules." If you're in a career that sucks, pursue what you love to do. Give your spouse a hug the minute you get home. Tell your kids how proud you are of them on a weekly basis. If there is someone you're romantically interested in, tell them! You've got nothing to lose, really, because every "no" brings you closer to a "yes." Take the time to do things you've always wanted to do and quit putting it off for another day. Because you never know if you'll HAVE another day, and if time might suddenly be at a minimum.

I'll be "lurking" in a big way, now, so you better listen! (And yes—I even dictated which emoticons to use.)

I love you all and wish you full and wonderful lives.

saffire_21

Comments:

Moonflower: *Thank you for everything you were to me this year, sweet saffire. Had it not been for you, my life would be completely different. Say hello to Arianna for me, and Happy Birthday to you both. I wish you much peace on your continuing journey.*

Epilogue

"This is unseasonably warm weather for October." Cara shrugged off her hoodie and let the sun beat down on her welcoming skin. "It happens every few years."

"Yeah, well, it just so happens that I ordered this weather especially for your birthday," Kevin said, smiling over at her. They both leaned on the railing of the blue suspension bridge, nicknamed the "Singing Bridge," that spanned the Ohio River from Cincinnati to Covington, Kentucky. Massive riverboats sailed under them, their decks decorated with colorful banners and their paddlewheels happily churning. Somewhere in the throng of festivities on the Ohio side, a steam calliope played its cheery melody.

"Oh did you, now?" Cara smiled back.

"This is a great festival, Cara, I'm so glad I could be here to see it. I never grew up with huge rivers like this, so it's all very novel."

Cara watched as he snapped photograph after photograph of each steamboat that passed, the Cincinnati skyline, and the many bridges that stretched across the Ohio. She found herself once again admiring Kevin's strong biceps that peeked out from his black t-shirt, and his sturdy long legs that looked so yummy beneath his jeans. Since he'd arrived, a few days before Tall Stacks, she was relieved to feel herself slowly warming up to the idea of being with him again. He made it so easy. Everyone makes mistakes, she'd told herself. Everyone has to figure things out for themselves and be sure of what it is they want in life. And if anyone deserved a second chance, it was the man who loved her.

"Do you think Sid and Sierra would have a lot to say about riverboats?" she asked him, in the middle of his photo safari.

He turned to her and removed his sunglasses so he could look in her eyes. "I think they could report on riverboats, on the trails and mountains of Appalachia, the shores of New England, the Rockies and even the Southwestern deserts. Sid and Sierra could visit *lots* of places together."

"Don't forget New York City," Cara added, with a wink. "We'll need to meet with our publisher, occasionally."

They stood staring into each other's eyes for a few moments as people passed them in a steady stream across the bridge.

"I'm not sure where our home base will be," he told her, "but I know I want to have one."

"Me, too." She pivoted lightly from side to side, her eyes filling with warmth. "And you know what? Energy follows intention. That's how the universe works."

"Does it?" Kevin's signature smile lit up his entire face. He raised a dramatic arm to the heavens and did a quick *Matrix* beckoning gesture with his fingers. "Bring it."

Cara laughed and grabbed him around the waist in a sudden bear-hug.

Kevin closed his arms around her and they rocked back and forth a couple of times.

A child of about five or six, walking past with a red balloon tied to her wrist, let go of her mother's hand and lagged behind to gawk at them. "Look, Mommy. Those people are in love."

"Shh!" the mother chided, taking the girl's hand again and attempting to hurry past.

Cara and Kevin turned to the child, who continued to stare as she was pulled away. Kevin gave her a thumbs-up, nodded at her, and then kissed Cara's cheek.

The little girl smiled smugly and looked up at her mother. "See, Mom! I *told* ya!"

Printed in the United States
150027LV00003B/83/P

9 781598 588842